ALL THAT'S LEFT TO SAY

Also by Emery Lord

Open Road Summer
The Start of Me and You
When We Collided
The Names They Gave Us
The Map from Here to There

THAT'S
LEFT
TO
SAY

EMERY LORD

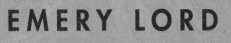

BLOOMSBURY
NEW YORK   LONDON   OXFORD   NEW DELHI   SYDNEY

BLOOMSBURY YA
Bloomsbury Publishing Inc., part of Bloomsbury Publishing Plc
1385 Broadway, New York, NY 10018

BLOOMSBURY and the Diana logo are trademarks of Bloomsbury Publishing Plc

First published in the United States of America in July 2023 by Bloomsbury YA

Bloomsbury books may be purchased for business or promotional use. For information on
bulk purchases please contact Macmillan Corporate and Premium Sales Department at
specialmarkets@macmillan.com

Library of Congress Cataloging-in-Publication Data
available upon request
ISBN 978-1-68119-941-2 (hardcover) • ISBN 978-1-68119-942-9 (e-book)

Book design by Jeanette Levy
Typeset by Westchester Publishing Services
Printed and bound in the U.S.A.
2 4 6 8 10 9 7 5 3 1

To find out more about our authors and books visit
www.bloomsbury.com and sign up for our newsletters.

Senior Year

This is my third time in the Head of School's office. Once, for a parent meeting before I officially enrolled. The essay incident—a misunderstanding, of course. And now, awaiting my fate on senior prom night.

I sit facing the desk, centered at a large window and framed by plaid curtains. The office doesn't have a globe, but it looks like the type that would. From somewhere I cannot see, an analog clock ticks away. I pace an inhale for four beats and hold it for the same count. My lungs ache or maybe my heart does—it's hard to tell anymore.

Somewhere, the Head of School is probably behind the wheel of her car, closing the distance between the Fairchild Hotel and her office. Cursing me, maybe, though I don't know her well enough to guess. Her first name is Elizabeth; she wears a wedding band. Does she live in a sleek apartment or a big old house? Does she host wine nights and do plucky group fitness classes with friends? Has anything ever rearranged her entire life and sense of self, the way this year has for me?

The door opens behind me, but it's only the freshman chem teacher tasked with ferrying me from the prom to the school for my sentencing. She hands me a school-issued gym towel, coarse and white. "Shouldn't be much longer. You need the restroom or anything?"

"No, thank you." I dab my hair, which has dried stringy by now. My gown sticks to every part of me, though the black fabric hides it well.

"I tried your mom's cell phone . . ." the teacher says tentatively.

"Yeah, she's at a show." Another would-be special memory that I've ruined tonight. "I'm sure she'll call back soon. Sorry in advance about that."

"Okay, then." What else can this teacher say? Not "I'm sorry"—this was my fault. Not "It'll be okay"—it might not. So she smiles wanly, and then I'm alone again.

The sweaty, shivery feeling of dread shoots through me. I haven't had enough time to process the events of tonight, to study my game board for moves. How much will I reveal to the Head of School?

I imagine my classmates, outside of this place, like dots on a scatter graph. Going home to shed their formalwear, maybe off to house parties. Some will come here to the school for After Prom. Everywhere, I'll be the central gossip. Did anyone film the fight or did it happen too quickly? Closing my eyes, I can see my own view of it.

The entire senior class was huddled in the hotel parking lot, ears still ringing from the fire alarm. We'd evacuated into a misty rain, tux jackets held over smooth blowouts and careful curls.

The whisper that I had pulled the alarm spread through the crowd—anger and confusion and, finally, my resigned expression. "Why would you *do* that?" Zoe had shrilled at me, looking so betrayed that it physically hurt to withstand. "Why would you ruin this? Are you honestly that jealous?" Steeling myself, I'd locked eyes with Gabi, and I said, "Yep. That's it. Guess I'm just that green with envy." Surprise fell like a shadow on Gabi's face, but I didn't blink. "You really want to do this right here?" she muttered. Her stare was hard, but so was mine. She took a big breath. *Here we go*, I thought.

"She's Sophie's cousin," Gabi said, projecting her voice now. "She's been hiding that from all of you this year, like an absolute freak, and I let it happen because—hey! Grief does weird things to people! But you need *help*, Hannah."

Every last student and chaperone turned to stare at me, as I stood there in my silence—no denials, no defense. The teachers recovered after that moment, moving to separate us and disperse the crowd. Catherine wrapped an arm around Gabi, looking over at me as she turned away. I saw Christian weaving through the crowd, and I gave him my best "stay away from me" face. My date was somewhere out of view, which I preferred. The sight of him would have hurt.

The door opens behind me again, and this time, it's Dr. Ryan, our Head of School. She's wearing a rose tweed dress with a matching coat, demure as afternoon tea. Anger makes her face harsher—mouth drawn, eyes blazing. "Well, Hannah.

3

In my career, I have certainly seen promising students make foolish decisions. But never have I been quite so baffled by one."

I look to my lap, trying to hold off tears. "I know. And I'm very sorry."

It's the truth. I really do wish I could have done this another way, but I had about two minutes to make a choice.

"I confess—I don't even know where to start. The yelling match? The deception of your classmates?" She settles into her desk chair, and I wonder how many people have trembled here. It feels like facing an elder queen, well-installed on her throne. She flips through some paperwork, obscured from me, and I can feel her deconstructing my motive. Am I a foolish, grieving girl who got herself into a pickle? Am I a misguided kid, angry at the world? Or something more nefarious than that? "Actually, let's start with the crime you committed tonight, as you may well need a lawyer. The hotel manager is considering pressing charges. And I can't say I blame him."

Even through layers of makeup, I'm surely blushing with shame. I twitch my nose, which is throbbing the way it does when I'm about to cry. "Me either."

"You've jeopardized so much for *what*?" she asks. Every word is perfectly contained, the rage boxed up neatly between the letters. "Pulling a fire alarm could be a class D felony. Was this a dare? Some kind of senior prank or hazing?"

A teardrop slips free, tracing a quick, straight line to my chin. I flex the muscles in my jaw. "Nothing like that."

"Give me *something* to communicate to the hotel manager, Hannah. I told him that you're Sophie Abbott's cousin, and that at least gave him pause."

God—of course. I wish Sophie could be remembered for

her sneaky insistence on being herself, for her earnest environmental work, for her good and golden heart. Instead, her name is synonymous with dying by overdose. Opioids. She's the Ingleside Country Day School poster girl for *We just can't believe it. We had no idea.*

I press my teeth into my lower lip. "Soph would have been prom queen, you know. It's not just me who thinks that—everyone does."

Dr. Ryan looks briefly sad for me and then closes her eyes for a good ten seconds, watching the puzzle pieces zap together. "Tell me you didn't pull the fire alarm to keep Gabi Reyes from being crowned."

"There's more to it than that."

"Did Gabi say something to you at prom?" she demands.

"No."

Nothing bad, anyway. She said, "Thank you" after I told her, "Nice suit." It was, too—smoky silver and tailored within an inch of its expensive life. With round, acid-green gemstones in her ears, she looked like the olive and the martini and the ice-cold glass.

For just a flash, the Head of School hesitates. "Is this . . . the fallout of a breakup?"

She means a romantic breakup—Gabi's been out for years, and Ingleside is the kind of place that prides itself on being progressive in a kind of watery way. "A friend breakup."

Dr. Ryan stares in a way that feels like she's circling me, studying all the angles. "When you applied to this school, Gabi Reyes provided you with a glowing peer recommendation."

True. I stare down at my balled-up hands.

"I want to be very clear, Ms. MacLaren. Hotel aside, the

school board may suspend or expel you," Dr. Ryan says. I knew it coming in, but that doesn't make it easier to hear. If it comes to that, I will tell the truth of why I pulled the alarm. I'd just rather not. "So, if there's a story here, then I suggest you tell me. Do you blame Gabi for what happened with Sophie?"

I look off to the corner as if a holographic Gabi flickers there awaiting my reply, nearly as present as I am in this room. I miss sitting together in her room, both of us barely surviving the irreparable, Sophie-shaped gash through our lives. Truthfully, I wish she could hear me now. "No. Gabi could have made different choices and changed something—or nothing at all. But that's true for me, too. For her mom, for her sister. All of us."

The Head of School's eyebrows give her away, the tiniest flinch of sadness.

"It's not like I hate Gabi or anything," I add. That's why the lie hurt so badly. But I've left even my anger behind. We wound up here, and that's all there is. "It's hard to explain."

Dr. Ryan's patience is worn thin, a fabric about to split. "Try."

Junior Year

The whole thing began with two white dresses. The first was tucked away in the trunk of Sophie's car on a late July afternoon.

A few hours into my solo study date at the art museum, someone plopped down at my makeshift workstation. I grimaced, eyes locked on my debate position research in the hopes that the person wouldn't make conversation.

"Well, this is a new low," a familiar voice said, cheerfully. Sophie gestured at the laptop, two open notebooks, and three well-employed stacks of Post-Its. "Homework, by choice, on the last week of summer."

"I've got that debate camp thing." I stacked my notebooks protectively, shielding them from criticism. "The director sent the topic yesterday."

"The debate camp thing," she repeated. "As in, you do a

quick showcase for middle schoolers? You could do that in your sleep."

Yes. But the director's email also revealed that she'd invited my rival to act as opposition. I'd always been competitive, but especially against him. "You could have texted. I'd have met you outside."

"Eh, I was early," Sophie said, gesturing around the museum. I studied here occasionally as a treat, wandering the galleries when I needed a break. "I wanted to see what the fuss is about."

I lifted my eyebrows. "Curious enough to make an appearance in the polo?"

"I am a proud representative of the Parks department," she said, chin lifted regally. As if she hadn't complained about the shapeless, poly-blend uniform top for the first half of summer. "Be nice to me. I brought you lunch, despite your disgusting taste in sandwiches."

"Tuna melt from Charlie's?" I asked hopefully.

"Ding, ding. It's in the car, smelling up everything."

"You're an angel."

Sophie swept her strawberry blond waves back. "I try."

She'd certainly landed the more cherubic genes in our family tree—a rounder, friendlier face and curvier body. I got the complexion and body type of a Popsicle stick, with light brown hair fit only for my too-long ponytail.

Sophie waved one hand at a nearby portrait while I finished packing up. "Like, what am I supposed to get from this? I have no idea who this person is, so I don't even know if the painting looks like her. How would I know if it's good?"

My interest in art started when I was a little kid desperate to connect with my dad. He'd lived in California my whole life, while I lived in Maryland with my mom. During our video chats, he always lit up about painting, so I kept asking questions. Eventually, we went on virtual museum tours, and his contagious interest pulled me in. Any time we could scrounge up money for a visit, art museums were first on the to-do list.

"Well, realism isn't necessarily relevant," I said. "Does it make you feel anything?"

Sophie squinted. "Yes. Annoyed that I don't get it."

"Does she seem coy? Reticent? Proud? What is she asserting in the pose, the gown? Those are the kind of questions I think about. Then you can read the placard for some context."

"Don't you use your debate voice with me," Sophie said, with a laugh. "So, you like it? The painting?"

"Not particularly. I was just making a point."

"You?" she replied, sarcastic.

We traipsed out to the car, sharing the day's annoyances and small triumphs. My mom once joked that the first thing I would do about a minor headache was text Sophie, then take some aspirin. But that was how it had always been: the two of us swapping every moment of mundanity, every childhood phase.

The late summer humidity had weight to it, a soft push from every direction. I grimaced, tugging at my white tee. "It's disgusting out here."

"I know," Sophie said. "But guess how many volunteers showed up this morning."

Her internship, which she'd imagined as gritty, robust environmental work, had mostly been making social media content for an office full of millennials. "Twenty."

"Twenty-*nine*," she said proudly. "And I doubled my 'under 21' turnout. More data points for my CV!"

Between the two of us, I'd always been the one obsessed with college—the grades, test scores, and debate numbers that would get me out of Maryland. But Sophie's competitive private school had gotten to her in recent months. She was smarter than half those kids, but she was a nervous test-taker and daydreamy in classes outside her interests.

My lunch was waiting on the passenger seat, beside a pastry bag from the bakery near Sophie's house. I peeked inside to find my favorite, which always came with an agenda. Heart-shaped sugar cookies were for cheering me up. But pistachio muffins? And Sophie going out of her way for a tuna melt?

I rolled the rim of the bag back down. "Okay. What's the favor?"

Sophie smiled over beatifically, turning the engine. "You're my favorite cousin. Have I ever told you that? And you've been such a big help with my fundraiser speech. But you know what would help even more?"

"Being there when you give it." In other words: putting on a dress to trot around the country club. I tipped my head up to the car ceiling and groaned. "The speech is great. You'll nail it."

"I need moral support!"

I'd been to the country club only once before—Sophie's surprise eleventh birthday, in a room with parquet floors. All the other girls wore near-identical dresses, as if they'd planned it. Never before had I felt like the outlier in Sophie's life. Usually, it felt like the two of us, and then everyone else, orbiting outside our little world. "So, I'd have to dress up *and* go to the club . . ."

"Yes, but—"

"I won't know anyone but you."

"My parents will be there . . ."

I gave her a look, which I knew she could sense despite keeping her eyes on the road. "And you know Gabi!"

Not really. Sure, I'd been around Sophie's school best friend before. We tiptoed politely, both clearly certain of our role as Sophie's most important person. The jealousy was hypocritical; I had Lincoln, after all.

Sophie threw me a tentative smile. "Maybe your mom could come with you?"

That suggestion would have sent my mom into her loud, musical laugh, which sounded easily at rich people things. My aunt Ginny was a rich person, but my mom considered having some money to be an annoying hobby her older sister married into, as opposed to an identity.

I snorted. "When I went to that thing for your dad's campaign, my mom suggested I wear a neon-yellow beach cover-up just to see your mom's face."

Sophie turned in delight. "*Please* do that."

When Sophie turned onto Larkspur, my own school best friend was outside, cradling a lacrosse stick. His corner lot yard was the only one big enough to throw a ball around. Since the day I moved in, Lincoln had lived thirteen houses down on our long, jam-packed street. Sophie slowed the car, pulling over to a stop.

"What are you doing?" I demanded.

"Hey, Lincoln!" Sophie yelled, leaning over me. "Come here a sec!"

"Oh my God," I muttered.

Lincoln trotted over, his shaggy blond hair bouncing. "What's up?"

"Ignore her," I warned.

"What are you doing next weekend?" Sophie asked. "I'm hosting an event with free food, and some Ingleside lacrosse guys will be there."

Lincoln considered it for only a moment. "Sold."

I shook my head, disappointed. "And here I was trying to spare you . . ."

"From free food and seeing the guys from lax camp?"

"You have to dress up."

He shrugged. "I look good in a blazer."

"Perfect." Sophie smiled smugly, talking right past me. "How's marathon training going?"

"Great," Lincoln said, looking to me for a nod of confirmation. We'd worked up to a 10K in the spring, and then committed to a fall half. Lincoln was in it for speed on the lacrosse field; I was in it for the rush of freedom I felt, going and going until I finally wore down.

"Well, see you next weekend!" Sophie called to him. Then, pulling back into the street, she added smugly, "There. One problem solved."

"Bulldozer," I muttered.

"*Mehhh,*" she said, in a low, bleating voice. "*Mehhhhh!*"

I laughed despite myself. She always made that noise to signify a ram—my zodiac representative and apt stand-in for my stubbornness.

Sophie parked in my driveway and snapped her fingers. "I almost forgot. I brought that horrible gown for you to look at."

I followed her to the trunk, where she unzipped the garment bag for the big reveal. My aunt—whose priorities seemed to be how her daughters looked, how her daughters behaved, and how many people saw Sophie and Maddie looking nice and behaving well—signed Sophie up for a ball in September. Ginny claimed it wasn't a coming out event, and yet she insisted on a white dress. Sophie bartered by saying she'd only wear something secondhand, figuring Ginny would fold. Instead, she took Sophie to an upscale consignment shop, where the choices were outdated wedding gowns.

"It's not that bad," I said, weakly. "The fabric is really nice, actually."

"Hannah." Sophie gave me a dull look.

I examined the back. "I can fix it. Take the sleeves off, for sure, and change the neckline. We can pin it before my mom gets home."

Though she would have agreed that cotillion is archaic and silly, my mom would not have agreed with blatant deception against Ginny.

Sophie tucked the bag under her arm, satisfied. "Expect another muffin in three to five business days."

I retrieved my food from the front seat and walked up the little sidewalk to my porch.

"Hey," I said, glancing to Sophie as I unlocked the front door. "I was always gonna go to your fundraiser."

She smiled over at me. "Yeah, I know."

Senior Year

I touch down on the last day of July, in the clear heat of late afternoon. As I exit the airport, I can almost see the specter of my two-months-ago self, walking in the other direction toward Departures. Nervous and tentative and so incredibly sad.

In the almost-year since Sophie died, grief has eaten through a part of me that won't regrow, and that's fine—it has to be. But this summer, new leaves began to sprout. Now, I'm a girl who has traveled out of the country, met new people, spent real time with her dad. I got to watch him at work, lighting a movie; I got to shadow the on-set tailor. I learned to love hiking; I changed my hair.

When I spot my mom in the pick-up line, I break into a run, suitcase wheels thudding behind me. She jumps out of the car, and we meet in a colliding kind of hug. After she visited Vancouver in late June, I missed her even more.

"Oh, honey." She's crying a little, and I am too, inhaling the scent of her homemade lavender soap. Someone honks for us to hurry up, and I feel my mom's hand leave my back. I know without looking that she's giving them the finger. My laugh rattles both our bodies.

"Look at you," she says, holding me out for examination. My haircut and dye job aren't new to her, but they're still startling— sometimes even to me. Since that first week in Canada, I've been a blond, with bangs and a bob that hits just above my shoulders. "You bloomed, kiddo. You look like a flower that finally got water and sun."

We haul my suitcase into the trunk, laughing at the weight. I'd already sent home a box of local thrift finds and wardrobe department castoffs. My mom accused me of overrunning our home and helped herself to a vintage raffia purse as a tax on my goods. It suits her.

"How are you feeling?" she asks. "Hungry? Wiped?"

I clicked the passenger seat back a few degrees. "Extremely both."

My mom paused to check her blind spot. "So hypothetically, if there's a small welcome home celebration awaiting you, that would be . . . unwelcome?"

I swallowed down a groan. My fantasy arrival at home involved total sloth, pretending that the first day of school wasn't a week away. "No, that's great. Just the guys?"

"Just the guys. George and Elliott wanted one last grill-out before moving Lincoln in."

Lincoln and I left things fine, in the end, but my stomach still clenches up. We've been apart for months with minimal contact, and soon he'll be off to a college three hours away. "Perfect."

"You want to drive through campus to see the house?" my mom asks brightly.

I keep my gaze out the window, the highway rushing by. "No thanks."

"Okay! Well, it won't hurt my feelings if you close your eyes," my mom says, reaching to pat my leg. "Rejuvenate before you ease back in."

I read once that every time you revisit a memory, you warp it a little. That first remembrance—not the original event—becomes what you recall the next time, and so on. Before this summer, I'd rarely been far enough away from home to have to remember Larkspur Street. Sometimes, trying to fall asleep in my dad's apartment, I saw my house like an illustration in a storybook.

The summer I turned ten, my mom landed an administrative job at Yardley and signed the lease on a tiny, ramshackle Victorian with crooked doorways and nicked wood floors. It was the first house either of us had ever lived in, after years of apartments. She hung tapestries and plants and, in a creative interpretation of the rental agreement, removable wallpaper. In my top-floor bedroom, the ceiling tapered down, so my bed felt nestled in the corner like a fort. I loved it so much that I fought my attachment, certain we'd be gone by August.

Once Mom had steady hours, I went to an elderly neighbor's house after school, where I heated up dinners and learned how to sew.

I kept a pathetically hopeful lookout for potential neighborhood friends. At the corner house, I'd only ever seen two men coming and going, but there was a kid-sized bike in the driveway. Of all the houses on our street, that one seemed the most likely to have the good candy bars on Halloween.

My first real memories of them were from our living room window. I watched while my mom sipped coffee on the porch and Elliott jogged in place, chatting. I remember George coming over to point at areas of the yard and talk gardening. Finally, a boy around my age, white and wiry with moppy yellow hair, strolled up our driveway one Sunday morning. I was on the porch step, with sidewalk chalk on my palms and an art book from the library open beside me.

I could tell he was nervous, which made me less nervous. "My dad is making pancakes. I'm supposed to invite you guys over."

He meant George, but that was before I inherently knew which dad he meant.

"I'll go tell my mom," I said, though I knew she'd be game.

That day, I found out Lincoln was one grade older and went to the neighborhood school a few streets over; he had just started playing lacrosse. He loved movies and a video game called *Stargazers* that I'd seen kids play at the library. He showed me the basics while our parents sipped coffee.

I unpacked my boxes.

My heart surges at the first sight of our house, with its mossy green exterior and the AC window unit surely wheezing away in my room.

"Garden looks good," I tell my mom.

"The tomatoes turned out gorgeous," she agrees.

Inside, I do a quick walk-through, soaking in the rightness of everything in its place—all but the Orioles cap on the kitchen table beside the mail stack. In trying to reassure me before I left her for months, my mom joked that she'd have six boyfriends by summer's end. She did wind up with one—Mitch, who sounds like a creation from Father's Day cards. He's really into sports and smoking meats, and I don't have to meet him until I'm ready. That's been the rule since I was twelve, after my mom's breakup with a man who wasn't quite as divorced as he'd suggested.

My mom grabs a salad she made earlier, and we trek down to the guys' house, following the side path to their deck.

I have no idea how Lincoln spent his summer, really. I texted at first, and I sent him a picture when I changed my hair, captioned *I asked for Atomic Blond.* He sent a photo from the shave ice truck and said: *Strawberry-rama misses her biggest fan.* Our friendship, proximal since day one, didn't easily translate to texting.

That's what I told myself, anyway. But maybe I needed to detach from every part of my life at home—let go of who I was and could never be again. And soon, Lincoln will be moving into a dorm room. No longer a two-minute walk from my front door.

But here he is—my friend, rising from a patio chair. His hair is considerably shorter, but he's wearing his same old West Grove lacrosse shirt, the color of dandelions.

"Hey," he says, smiling hesitantly.

My throat aches, same as it did when I set eyes on my mom at the airport. "Hey."

With a sheepish look, Lincoln holds out his arms, like *Are we gonna do this as a hug type of thing or what?* Yes, we are—I step forward and squeeze his torso so hard that he laughs.

Any weirdness between us fades like landscapes on my flight home—a blur of a place passed over. When we pull away, I say, "So! Haircut."

"You're one to talk!"

"I know," I say, ruffling my bangs. "Is it weird?"

"Nah. I mean, it kind of looks like a wig. But a wig that suits you."

I might be offended if I hadn't had the same thought. I bend toward Dorothea, the beagle mutt busily sniffing my feet. "Missed you too, Thea."

Elliott emerges from the sliding door, balancing a tray of corn on the cob. "Well, well. Who is this sophisticate?"

George, filing out behind Elliott, leans to kiss my cheek while also reaching out a glass of white wine to my mom. "Look at you, Hannah Lou. A beauty."

"She was always a beauty," Elliott says.

"Of course." George checks my expression for any hint of offense. "She knows what I mean. You look contented."

"Thank you," I say, and I ease into my usual seat.

In Vancouver, I *was* something resembling contented. The on-set tailor kept me hustling between garment bags and hemlines. My dad worked a lot, but we had plenty of time for cheap restaurants, local galleries, and hiking. Running didn't feel as vital anymore. I'd already run all the way to Canada.

I used my alone time to explore or to toil over my college applications. It felt easier, three time zones away from my previous life, to imagine a future where I'd moved on, even a little, from grief.

A few kids my age lived in the apartment complex, and we hung out every now and then. One of them became a summer fling, as simple at the end as it was at the start. We talked or we didn't, and it felt good to be with someone who had only ever known me on the other side of Sophie's death.

I'm quiet through dinner, which tastes familiar and right. I gulp George's iced tea like I can consume the feeling of knowing and being known.

"I'll do dishes tonight," my mom announces grandly. "You two should catch up."

Normally, Lincoln and I are on dish patrol while the adults polish off the wine. George and Elliott follow my mom to the kitchen, balancing plates, and I turn to Lincoln.

"So. You wanna tell me who you were texting with that shit-eating grin on your face?" I noticed earlier his hands hidden under the table but clearly typing fast.

"Shit-eating?" he says, but the smile sneaks back up. "Parker."

"Oh my *God*." I tip my head back, my triumph lifted to the sky. She's a junior lacrosse player, and Lincoln has been denying his blatant crush for ages. "I *knew* it."

"It felt weird to tell you over text," Lincoln says. "But . . . yeah, for about a month officially."

"Officially!"

"Not great timing, with me off to school," he adds. "But we're gonna try to keep it going. You'll like her."

"I know I will."

In the silence that follows, my imaginings of this year project out like movie screen. I'm not sure when I'll be around Parker again. The usual scene—West Grove's overcrowded hallways, permanently smelling of chicken sandwich breading—won't include me.

Lincoln must be thinking the same thing, because he says, "You're really going through with it?"

For years, I'd scoffed at Andrew and Ginny's attempts to win me over to Ingleside Country Day School. I was already besting the academic game; why use a cheat code? But something changed last year. Well. A lot of things changed.

"I am. Yeah." From Vancouver, I'd ordered a stash of uniform pieces to mix-and-match, wincing as I clicked the purchase button. I have less than a week to tailor them for the ways my body has changed with less running and more hiking. "Nothing to lose, really."

Lincoln nods, with a smile he has to pry up at the sides. At his graduation, he had plenty of other friends to pose with. I've never fit in with West Grove's ecosystem of giant, overlapping friend groups. But neither of us wants to drudge that argument back up. "If you say so."

"Maybe I can hang with Parker when you're home for fall break," I say, and Lincoln looks pleasantly surprised. He's gone out with girls before, and I had a boyfriend most of my sophomore year, but we always did our own thing. "You feeling ready for school?"

"Yeah. It helps to know the lacrosse guys a little."

I'm about to ask if we should pick school-themed movies for the last movie night before school starts. But I catch on something—will he still want to, after last year? Before I can decide how to bring it up, Lincoln adds, "I've got a couple more weeks until I leave. So, if you need a wingman for early Ingleside parties . . ."

I love him for this, though I hate that I'm still the girl whose mom always coached her to go say hi. "I met people this summer, you know."

"I know," he says quickly. "Just saying. You don't have to do everything alone."

Well. I sipped the last dregs of my iced tea. Some things, I do.

AUGUST

- - - - - - - -

Junior Year

For Sophie's fundraiser, I wore a white sundress, cotton and simple. I'd found it on a thrifting expedition, and my mom claimed, in a mocking British accent, that the dress was "perfectly suitable for such an event."

Since I learned to sew years before, I'd loved clothing—the history, the construction, the craft. Hemming skirts for a busy, local tailor certainly beat a customer service job. But, in my own modest closet, I always wore black and white, from everyday T-shirts to my running clothes to my Debate Club suit. If fashion was performance, I worked on stage crew.

But despite alterations to my exact measurements, the dress still felt like I'd borrowed it from someone else's closet.

I stepped off the porch, to where Lincoln was climbing out of his car.

"Hey," he said, gesturing at his outfit. "Is this okay for the thing?"

"Yeah. You look nice. Great jacket."

"Rude of you to sound surprised." He shrugged off the blazer, navy with a windowpane plaid. "But thank you. It was my dad's in college."

I turned, showcasing a different angle. "Is there something weird about this dress?"

"Looks fine," Lincoln said. "Just . . . quit standing like that."

"How am I standing?"

"Like you're a dog being forced to wear little shoes."

"Linc!" I whined, though I did feel that way—like I'd forgotten how to hold my body.

"Look at you two!" my mom cooed, emerging from the side of the house in her floppy, truly embarrassing gardening hat. "I need a picture."

"Mom."

"You look so cute! The braid brings me back to your *Frozen* days."

Lincoln laughed as he joined me on the porch, and I frowned at them both. Throughout elementary school, I'd always played contemplative Elsa, while Sophie was spunky Anna. We'd dressed poor toddler Maddie in an Olaf costume more times than I could count.

After the photo was taken, my mom squeezed my cheeks. "You're a very good cousin, Bug, and you look beautiful."

"Mmph," I said, my lips squished together. "Send the least awkward one to Dad."

"Sure thing." She released me. "Tell Gin I'm making Nonny's

blackberry pie tonight in case she wants to pop by this week. If she's currently eating carbs, that is."

I shot her a be nice look, which she answered with an angelic smile. "Have fun!"

"Know where you're going?" I asked Lincoln. He'd inherited this sedan when he turned sixteen. His dad Elliott's cologne still lingered on the upholstery, balancing lacrosse bag smog from the trunk.

"I've got it in my phone," he said. "Trying to avoid move-in weekend traffic."

Our town—West Grove—framed the left side of Yardley College, a prestigious, mid-sized school older than the US Constitution. The route took us through Hathaway—the northern suburb with a Target and a lot of 1950s ranches—and into Eastmoore, where Sophie lived. On a green-light streak, it took nine minutes to get from my house to hers. There, the lots widened around big white houses, full of beautiful, impervious children. Even the sounds changed. The roar of the highway faded into the *whick-whick* of built-in sprinkler systems.

Almost there, I texted Sophie.

Thank God, she wrote back immediately. *My mom is being very My Mom.*

Ginny hovered and nagged, but I'd never worked up the nerve to tell Sophie that I wished my own mom could be just two percent more like hers. For as long as I could remember, the refrain in my house was, "It's your life, Bug." I wanted to quit piano when I wasn't good after three lessons? No problem. Decide what I watch, even if it gave me nightmares? Well, that's how you define your boundaries. Sometimes, however pathetic, I wanted to whine: *I'm just a kid. Tell me what to do here.*

My mom and Ginny grew up a couple hours outside of LA, in a motel their grandmother ran. When I was little, I imagined it like a sitcom—cozy and quirky, with a rotating cast of surprising guests. The older I got, the more I understood that their stability was held together with packing tape and a prayer. They spoke of their Nonny like she was a mythical figure—the gray-haired mage shepherding them out of danger. If they spoke of their parents at all, it was with shadowy undertones.

After Nonny died, my mom moved to be with her pregnant older sister—in Maryland, where Ginny had moved for journalism school. A few weeks later, I showed up in the form of two distinct pink lines. My parents had broken up amicably in California, but my mom saw an opportunity to raise me alongside Ginny and the baby who would be my cousin. Though my dad supported the idea, neither of my parents wanted him to leave LA. He'd landed an apprenticeship in TV lighting after years of painting pet portraits, and he was four months into recovery from alcohol use disorder.

Sometimes I stared at my mom and aunt, wondering how two such different people could be from the same upbringing. My mom often rolled her eyes at Ginny's controlled, manicured life. But if anyone else criticized Virginia Farris Abbott, my mom would yowl like a wildcat, haunches back to pounce. Ginny, I think, would stay quiet if someone spoke ill of my mother, then plot a silent, thorough revenge.

The Eastmoore Country Club waited at the end of a long, tree-lined drive, tucked away from the mortal world. The main building spanned wide and white as a sheet cake, with two-story columns lifting upward.

Lincoln slowed the car, leaning forward to get the full view.

"They use this place as an exterior shot for movies, right? This is totally where the Rich Guy lives."

Inside, we stood at the wide doorframe, staring into an elegant room. The top showed a crowd that seemed to be almost entirely white people. Women in flamingo pink and palm green mingled; men in seersucker blue clapped one another's backs. The bottom third became—abruptly, almost solidly—beige. Spray-tanned legs, khaki pants, taupe heels, pine wood floors. The scene looked like a framed watercolor that had been dipped in beige paint.

These people weren't yacht-sailing, Fortune 500 rich. Anyone with that kind of money would live nearer to DC. But they were wealthy enough for the airs and the plumage.

I allowed myself a quiet groan.

"Speak for yourself," Lincoln said. "Check out that appetizer lineup."

As we walked in, a few girls glanced over, clearly assessing Lincoln and I as a couple. Our friendship was befuddling to some people, and they often landed on "Oh, you're like siblings." No. Like best friends.

Almost immediately, a voice called out Lincoln's last name—a lacrosse bro summoning him. I waved at him to go, already on my path toward Sophie. She was huddled near the beverage station, taking a long drink of ice water. With her powder skin and peachy hair, Sophie always looked fit for a Rococo painting, but especially in her sky-blue dress. My eyes traced down to her platform sandals as she gave a relieved sigh. "You're here."

"Is your ankle okay in those?"

"Oh my God, *Mom*. Yes," she said, with an affectionate eye roll. "Can you please run interference with my actual mother?

She keeps hovering, and it's throwing me off. Gabi was trying to help, but—"

"On it."

"Thank you." Sophie nodded, businesslike. "Okay, back to mingling."

Ginny was in the thick of the crowd, talking to a man around her age. I hung back, ready to engage if she headed toward Sophie.

The motivation for this event ran deep. Sophie could fundraise for local parks and acquire some event experience. My uncle Andrew could play supportive dad while glad-handing potential campaign donors. Virginia Abbott, meanwhile, could thrive as proud mother and wife.

Since my uncle announced his campaign, Ginny had all but created a future state senator's wife character, who nodded solemnly and held hands in prayer pose. Ginny was a newscaster before staying at home with Sophie and Maddie. The hair remained—a teased blond, perfectly smooth and resting on the shoulders of her linen dress. She may have been a rural California girl, but Ginny looked as East Coast as hydrangeas.

I was slow-sipping a sweet tea when she spotted me. Her waving hand said "Come over here," but her intent eye contact said "or else."

"Hannah, you look lovely!" Ginny braced her hands on my shoulders. "And thank you so much for helping Sophie with her speech."

"Yeah, of course."

She gestured to the man she'd been talking to. "Marty, meet my niece, Hannah. She's a nationally ranked debater."

"Wonderful!" he boomed, low-ball glass shifting in his hand. "Ingleside or St. Anne's?"

"West Grove High, actually." I lifted my chin a little, as if to say *That's right, Marty. Public school.* Ginny's grip tightened.

"Hannah's top of her class there, though I'm sure the Head of School would love to steal her away," Ginny continued. "She's planning on law school."

"Is that right!" Marty said it like he might clap my shoulder. "I'm a Yardley Law grad myself, so let me know if you have any questions. I can connect you with the alumni association folks."

I almost laughed. I'd been here—what—five minutes? And lo, the network appears like the sheer lines of a sticky web. "That's very kind. But I'm hoping to relocate to a bigger city. LA, ideally."

Marty laughed again, for some reason. "Wonderful! Great to get the adventures in when you're young."

My aunt offered to show me my seat, which seemed impossible to refuse. I stalled, but she wriggled out of the conversation in several deft maneuvers. I'd settled in at the table, aimlessly scrolling my phone, when a voice said, "Ginny evaded you too?"

I looked up at Gabi Reyes in a lavender jumpsuit, with two straps running parallel down her shoulders. Gabi had always been a study in symmetry, from the center part of her dark-brown hair to the faint chin dimple.

"She did," I admitted.

Gabi took her seat on Sophie's other side, leaning back. "Good summer?"

"Yeah, okay," I said. Even the scar on her forehead—a short line across light-brown skin—was centered. "How about you?"

"Good. Busy."

We traded thin, trying-our-best smiles. In the early middle school days, I knew her as "Gabi from soccer" in Sophie's stories, but they quickly became a duo off the field, too. Sophie used to invite me along, but the three-person dynamic didn't work. Does it ever?

Inevitably, I'd witness how easily she and Sophie wove between conversations and inside jokes. My competitive drive would kick up, and I'd vow, once again, not to be impressed by Gabi.

But Gabi Reyes is an impressive person. You can like her or loathe her, and it's still going to be true.

"The speech is really good, by the way," Gabi said.

I relaxed a little on our safe, common ground: Sophie. "Thanks. She practiced it for you?"

"About a dozen times. And, oh my gosh." Gabi snapped her fingers as if just remembering. "The edits you made to Mr. Abbott's stump speech? A big improvement."

"Oh, thanks," I said, less enthusiastically this time.

Gabi squinted briefly, noticing my dip in interest. This was what got me about her: the perceptiveness. "Not psyched about his foray into politics?"

"No, it's fine." *Don't*, I told myself. "He's well-meaning and competent, which is more than a lot of candidates can say."

"Well-meaning and competent," Gabi repeated, nodding. She propped her elbow on the back of Sophie's chair, really settling in. "What traits would you prefer?"

"I'm just cynical about politics." That should have been enough, but I felt like I was losing an argument—failure to provide evidence. I dropped my voice. "He hasn't experienced, like, anything that the average person does. He's always had a safe home and food and health insurance. So, he can talk about policy change, but will he really push?"

Gabi ruffled one hand through her hair, though it settled perfectly back into place. "Doubt it."

I blinked at her. "Aren't you volunteering for the campaign?"

"I helped Soph a few times." Gabi was already a head delegate in Model UN and had lots of causes, many of which overlapped with Sophie's. "I've mostly been shadowing the mayor's chief of staff for the past few weeks, so I'm more focused on that."

The jealousy stung like sunburn. I'd spent my summer monogramming initials onto custom baby outfits, squirreling away money for college. "That's cool. Did you just, like, reach out about that?"

"Pretty much. My dad's the advisor for Yardley's Latine grad student group. Martina came to speak about local government." Then, with a quick eyeroll, Gabi added, "And my mom thought I could use a Chicana mentor that I 'actually listen to.'"

My shoulders eased a little. Huh. Gabi—who always seemed so sure of herself—had a mom who accused her of not listening. "Does your mom want you to stay close to home?"

"Yeah, but I want to anyway—stay near my grandma, explore DC. What about you? I know law school, but any particular type of law?"

"Haven't decided." I knew from Sophie, who spent a lot of time at the Reyes house, that Gabi's dad was a labor law professor. Her mom was a software engineer. I added, wryly, "One that gets me a benefits package?"

Gabi gave me a bewildered look. "That's the priority?"

"Uh, kind of." My tone had turned against my will, edging toward defensive. How would I ever pay off law school loans without a good job out of the gate?

"Okay." She lifted one shoulder in a shrug. "You just strike me as someone who'd enjoy putting a few dents in the system."

My jaw clenched. Sure, that would be great, except I'd spent most of my life watching my mom juggle multiple jobs to keep from being crushed by said system. I'd like to do deeply meaningful work as much as the next person. But until then, I wanted basic stability without owing anyone. "Just trying to be realistic."

I scanned the crowd again, as if a subject change would appear like a vision. When I glanced back, Gabi wore a small, amused smile. "You hate all this."

"No," I said, a bit hotly. There it was: Gabi's laser-bright perceptiveness. I wanted to seem like the supportive cousin who felt perfectly comfortable breathing rarified air. "I'm just not good at, like . . ."

"Faking it?" Gabi guessed.

My cheeks burned. Was she criticizing me? Or calling out the phony niceness of a crowd known for judgment and gossip?

"It's not really my scene," I conceded.

"Mm," Gabi said, with a nod. But what was she affirming? That I don't belong here? That it's not her scene either?

"Hey." Lincoln pulled up his chair. "Sounds like they're about to start."

Thank God. I directed my attention toward the podium, where Sophie stood with clasped hands. She wobbled a little in her introduction, but she recovered when outlining the pro-climate initiatives she'd worked on this summer. Andrew and Ginny kept glancing around, smiling as the world took in their daughter's shine.

"I'd also like to thank my dad, Andrew Abbott, candidate for State Senate," Sophie said. Hold for applause. "As we all

31

know, individual action can be a meaningful pursuit, and consumer behavior can be a tool. But there's no path to a healthy planet for my generation without significant government investment in green energy."

I tucked my mouth under my hand, willing down a smile. She really did it—said the lines we'd left off the Ginny-approved written speech. Andrew's position on climate was okay, but not nearly good enough. Amid the uncomfortable, delicate applause, a few enthusiastic claps rang out and, from somewhere, a wolf whistle.

Afterward, the official event bled into an average country club evening. Lincoln went outside to throw the ball around, and I wandered a bit, studying portraits of waxy-faced old men and fireplace paintings of the hunt. The whole place breathed smoke—cigars and hunting rifles and champagne vapor curled from the bottle's mouth.

When the dress began to itch, I returned to find Lincoln and say our goodbyes.

"MacLaren?"

I froze at the entryway. Of course I'd expected Sophie's classmates to be here, but not Christian Dailey. When I turned, he was heading my direction, wearing what seemed to be the uniform here: navy blazer, khakis, simple tie—off-center, in his case. In recent years, he'd worn his hair long enough to push back in an act of preening vanity. I could never decide if he was attractive or simply so convinced of his own attractiveness that bystanders were lured into the illusion.

"Oh my God, of course you're a member here," I muttered.

He leaned in, one finger to his ear. "What was that?"

I put on a false smile. "Hello, Dailey."

He only had a few inches of height on me, and I wished I'd worn heels to close the gap. His skin, always with an olive undertone, held a tan well into late-season debates. While he'd never explicitly mentioned having a boat to take out all summer, I wouldn't be surprised.

"Hannah MacLaren," Dailey murmured. "At a country club. Wearing a dress."

"Nice to see they keep you sharp in the off-season."

We'd always been the youngest people on our respective debate teams—natural rivals and, this year, the only juniors on varsity.

"Who are you even here with?" he asked, marveling. Of course, he'd want to know about my connections. This was the thing with Christian Dailey and his boat-shoed cronies.

"Counterargument," I said sweetly. "How is that your business?"

"Guess I should have seen that one coming." He slid his hands into his pockets. "So. How was your summer?"

I recognized this question for what it was: an entryway for him to regale me with internship stories. Pass.

"Amazing—spent most of it at the Vineyard." I brought one hand back to sweep my ponytail. "It wasn't all fun and games, of course! Mother stuck me with an SAT tutor, but I endured honorably."

"Sarcasm! Thrilling." Dailey shifted his weight, which was never a good thing. It meant he was finding his angle, a boxer about to deliver his blow. "Did you see I'm doing the debate showcase with you?"

"Oh, yeah," I said, as if I'd forgotten. Dailey had only gone to debate camp for one summer, so I resented his inclusion.

I usually spent the last Friday of summer hyping kids up for debate. This year, I'd have to share space with the demon prince. "Should be fun."

He smiled crookedly. "Always is."

"And by 'fun,'" I said, turning away, "I of course mean 'unbearably tedious.'"

I walked off before he could get the last word. My eyes darted through the crowds, looking for anyone familiar to harbor me. When I spotted Soph, she was already looking my way, conspiratorial by a fireplace with Gabi like evil stepsisters at the ball. I slowed my beeline to them only when the stamp of my shoes drew disapproving glances.

"Um, hello?" I huffed, more to Sophie than Gabi. "You couldn't have bailed me out of that conversation?"

Gabi spoke around the tiny cocktail straw in her drink. "We were enjoying the show."

"It was like Animal Planet," Sophie said, "when the lions circle each other."

I touched two fingers to my temple, where the tap of my pulse was becoming a thump. "Sounds right. Male lions posturing while female lions do all the work."

"No," Sophie said, pushing down a smile. "We think you two are gonna bone."

Gabi laughed over the rim of her ginger ale.

"Oh, you're gross." I pointed to one, then the other, but they were snickering away at their little joke. "Both of you. *Gross.*"

"*Bone,*" Sophie mouthed.

"Do you not remember what he did? I hate him."

Sophie looked briefly chastened but then waved me off. "That was a hundred years ago."

"What did he do?" Gabi asked.

"Nothing," I snapped.

Sophie gave Gabi an apologetic look that she did not need. It wasn't her business, and I probably would have said so if Lincoln hadn't appeared at that moment. He had his blazer slung over one arm, shirt rolled at the sleeves. "Hey. You ready?"

"No, stay!" Sophie pled. She gripped my arm and looked to Lincoln like maybe he could make me. "We're about to ride out to the ninth hole and hang for a while."

"Won't your mom be mad if you bail?" I asked.

"She's already cold-shouldering me over my little 'stunt.'" Sophie gave me the lower lip, her last stand.

"You were amazing," I said. "But I need to be in stretchy clothes within the half hour."

"Fine, go." She sighed, pretending to shoo us away. Then, smiling, "Thank you both for coming."

"Nice to see you, Gabi," I said.

"Yeah, you too."

Sophie texted me before Lincoln and I even got to his car: *Thank you for coming, even though it meant a dress and the club* ❤

I'd do much worse for her, of course—same as she would for me. *Real love. (Of you and the pistachio muffins.)*

Once in the car, I slipped off my shoes and slumped back in the passenger seat. Lincoln plugged in his phone while I stared out the windshield. The wide, nectarine sun had almost dropped below the tree line and, around the side of the club, I could make out Sophie's and Gabi's silhouettes in waiting.

A golf cart pulled up in front of them, and a tall guy with red, swoopy hair—Warner, Sophie's friend and neighbor—climbed out of the driver's seat. He had a wine bottle hanging from one hand, and Sophie, presumably the only non-drinker in the bunch, took his place at the wheel. Gabi climbed onto the back with two others, completing what was clearly a well-honed routine.

Lincoln backed out of the parking spot as music rose up all around us. The golf cart became a dot in the distance.

Senior Year

I get to Sophie's grave before anyone else. The rectangle of sod in front of her headstone is no longer greener than its surroundings. She's been gone a whole year.

Someone has left a small vase of black-eyed Susans, only just beginning to droop. I'd bet my meager savings account that my aunt will bring a huge bouquet of white flowers to our small memorial later. But I like the yellow blooms, humble and bright.

"Hey," I whisper.

I lay down on my side, grass tickling as I rest my head on my elbow. This is how Sophie and I fell asleep during childhood slumber parties, turned into each other and whisper-laughing. What did we have to talk about until after midnight? I wish I could remember. Nothing. Everything.

Last time I sat here, I made a promise. The time before, I sobbed till I was almost sick. The time before that, I wasn't alone.

Many things are different now.

The promise still stands.

Junior Year

I stood outside my local library for a moment, bracing for memories of the story I wouldn't let Sophie tell: how Christian Dailey and I met.

The summer after sixth grade, I biked to the library when my mom was working and Sophie was busy. I holed up in the teen corner with a stack of plastic-covered books or attended free activities in the meeting room. *The Basics of Debating for Middle School (6th–8th)* flyer featured gavel clip art and the promise that I'd "learn how to argue to win." Debate Camp was every Friday afternoon, taught by a local professor, and I loved it.

After camp, I pressed my history teacher to start a middle school debate club. My mom was openly surprised that I'd choose a public speaking hobby, but I liked researching my arguments. I liked having a set amount of time to talk about a prescribed topic. And, above all, debate is for good listeners.

My third and final debate camp—the summer after eighth grade—I was paired up with a boy my age, new to the program. He had overgrown hair and a bright-eyed look to him, like his parents hadn't forced him to be here. When we introduced ourselves, he said he lived in Hathaway, the town between Sophie's and mine.

Christian was a natural. His mom had finished law school a few years before, and he wanted to follow in her footsteps. In a room full of boisterous kids, he could disappear into his mind and return with an answer. He watched as I filled my notebook—neat towers of outlined notes, shocks of yellow highlighter—and asked about my system.

He asked about everything.

When I told him about my family—a mom I lived with, a dad who lived in California and always had—he didn't flinch. He lived with his parents, an older brother about to start college, and a new rescue puppy named Dodger. By the third session, we flew through our rhetorical exercises like a seasoned team.

Sometimes, Christian stopped by the library on other days, and it felt like he was showing up to see if I was there. My crush ballooned into a heady feeling, like spinning.

On the last day, we won our final debates, and he made up some excuse to exchange numbers. I biked home feeling like I could lift off from the chipped sidewalk like Elliott in *E.T.* Even if Christian didn't have a crush on me, I'd still made a new friend—never so easy for me.

When I finally worked up the nerve to text, he didn't respond.

I told myself it was a misunderstanding. The boy I'd spent half the summer with wasn't callous. I allowed myself one sniffling cry and hoped I'd get the full story in mid-October, when my school debated Hathaway.

But, in late September, I spotted him across the room at the Ingleside match, of all places. He was wearing the uniform blazer and plaid tie, not quite aligned with his shirt buttons.

"Christian! Hey!" My heart leapt as I hurried toward him. I wanted to ask him about high school so far and how his puppy was doing and if he missed his older brother yet. "I had no idea you went here."

"Just started." He smiled in a pressed-down, awkward line and glanced at his teammates.

I opened my mouth to tell him that my cousin was at Ingleside too. But the stares from his teammates stopped me. In matching uniforms, they looked like a family of expensive dolls, sold as a box set. And there I was, a nobody in a secondhand suit. The JV captain—a cute, mean-faced sophomore—looked at me like I could be crushed beneath his loafer.

"Okay, well," I stammered, giving Christian one last look. "Good luck."

He smiled uncomfortably. Guiltily? "You too."

I turned away, cheeks stinging, and the captain muttered something ugly. A common insult toward West Grove students, nothing new. But still, I waited to hear Christian's familiar voice calling him out.

I heard nothing. *Great*, I thought. *Got it.*

Private school Christian was too good for me, apparently. As freshmen recruits, we didn't even participate, we only watched our older counterparts do battle. The debate turned to warbling in my ears as I sat with my arms folded.

That winter, Christian and I went head-to-head in, ironically, a friendly debate between our schools. I'd funneled all my hurt into my preparations. *Mr. Dailey has, tellingly, omitted a fundamental case study from last year, which . . . A clever argument from my opponent, but ignorant of several key facts, as follow . . .*

I wanted Dailey to regret his little friendship bait-and-switch. Instead, he looked bewildered and pissed off, in turn.

Season by season, match by match, we cranked the dial higher. Where I was prepared with a well-crafted argument, Dailey was naturally quick and believably passionate. In other words, I had the goods, and he had smoke and mirrors.

And now, I had to spend the last Friday of my summer with the human incarnation of "let's just say, for argument's sake . . ." In the same library meeting room where we met.

The camp director had two seats waiting for us.

"Cute braid," Dailey said under his breath.

I scowled, running my hand along the intricate braid Sophie had done that morning, warming up for her role as soccer bus hair stylist. "Cute personality."

The camp director introduced us, cutting off our snide exchange. As I argued my side, Dailey bobbed his head the tiniest bit, like he was listening to music in his mind instead of hearing my argument.

In the end, I guessed all of his counterpoints, though he took one of them a slightly unexpected way. A judging panel could have reasonably named either of us the winner, which was usually how it went.

We exited quickly to allow the campers time for discussion. I draped my jacket over one arm and, waving to the library staff, left out the back door. Sophie would be picking me up any minute.

"Sophie Abbott is your cousin," a voice said.

Christian Dailey leaned against his car door, where he was—God—waiting to antagonize me?

After the country club, I figured he'd ask around. The August heat felt unbearable, even worse than being stuck inside with him. "Bravo, Nancy Drew."

I glanced at the parking lot entrance, willing Sophie's car to appear. If he hadn't pieced it together, he would have realized imminently anyway.

Dailey moved closer. "How did I not know this? Seems like Sophie would have mentioned it."

According to Soph, they'd always been chitchat friendly in shared classes and soccer activities. Sophie swore herself to secrecy after Dailey blew me off. She'd never give him the satisfaction of glimpsing how much it hurt me.

"I'm sure she has no idea our schools debate each other," I said, though of course she knew. She came to watch debates from time to time, but never against Ingleside. I got too nervous—another fact that I would lie about to Dailey's smug face.

"Well!" he said. "Guess it's not all Ingleside kids you hate."

"Nope," I said, chipper.

"I'm just special, then?"

"*Very.*"

His tie was crooked, as always. Maybe tugging at the knot was a tic or maybe an affectation to make him look charmingly disheveled. That was Dailey: too full of bravado to fuss with the details. It served him well enough onstage. Nobody liked a disaffected rich kid, and he came in hot with almost every issue we'd ever debated.

I was ready to step farther away when Dailey announced, "You were good today."

"Gee, thanks."

"This is the part where you could say, 'You were good too, Christian.'"

"Could I?" I glanced up at the true-blue sky. "Hmm."

He held his hands up in surrender. "Just trying to be nice here, MacLaren."

Stepping closer, I cocked my head. "Are you, though? Because, if I accept your unsolicited feedback, I accept you as an authority on what is good."

"I *am* an authority on what's good," he said. I opened my mouth with a rebuttal, but he added, "And so are you. I know when you're on your game; you know when I'm on mine."

True enough. It tethered us, in an infuriating way. "I know when you're leaning so hard on pathos it could break under your weight . . ."

He grinned like he carried a toothpick in his back teeth, with the undeserved swagger of a small-town sheriff. "While you cling to logos like a life raft?"

I matched his smile, stepping forward. "We can do this all day, Dailey, but you're not gonna rattle me."

"Is that my goal?"

"Of course." I took another step, on offense now. "You're not sure if you would have won today, so now you'll try to mess with me, which I guess you count as a win in a different way."

"Flattered you pay such close attention," Dailey said. But now—was I imagining it?—he looked thrown off. I felt it like a zing of power, my arms tingling.

"It's simple," I said, "when you're so obvious."

I reached out to tug his tie back to center. I meant the correction to be patronizing, the fixing up of an obnoxious child. But he inhaled sharply, and I froze too, realizing I'd crossed the line in what had always been a war of words. I meant to stomp a puddle, and I fell into the sea. But too late now—I'd committed. I slid the strip of fabric between two fingers, straightening its fall. My knuckles skidded against each button. He swallowed, his Adam's apple shifting.

I stepped back abruptly. "That's been annoying me for years."

"Of course it has," he said, eyes flicking heavenward. "Even one little thing out of place . . ."

Finally, our gazes met. He looked like a freshman again for a split-second, younger and less certain. *You win*, I thought bitterly. *I'm rattled.*

"Look, I didn't—" I began, right as Dailey started with, "MacLaren, I—"

The pulse of a summer pop anthem interrupted us. Sophie pulled to a stop with the windows down, sunglasses on. I bolted toward the car, the tips of my ears gone hot.

"Hey, Soph," Dailey called. I resisted shooting him a bratty look, like: *Don't talk to my cousin, and especially don't use a nickname.*

"Hey," she replied. "Hannah give you a hard time today?"

"Always," he said cheerfully.

I climbed into the car and called, in a voice that I hoped sounded menacing, "See you at quarterlies!"

Dailey only waved. "Better be ready for me!"

Of course, I would see him much sooner than that, and I wasn't ready at all.

Sophie pulled on the main drag, her lips pressed together thoughtfully. She had her wet hair tied up, the strands gone copper from the pool. "He's nice to me, you know."

"Everyone's nice to you." Before she could huff in denial, I added, "Yeah, yeah. Not Allison Granger, I know. She's on my lifetime grudge list."

I'd never met the girl who was mean to Sophie in middle school before moving away. But cousin loyalty is petty and eternal.

Sophie nodded approvingly. "I know Dailey was an asshole to you freshman year, but people do change."

"Do they, though? You think Allison Granger has?"

"Humph," she said. "Such an Aries. I wonder if Dailey's a fire sign, too. Or Mars-ruled, maybe."

"Which sign is the smuggest jerk?"

Sophie sighed, like I was personally burdening her with my lack of knowledge. "Well, if you'd listen to that astrology podcast I sent to you . . ."

"I did!"

"Like *one* episode." She rolled her eyes, repeating the words in a mutter to herself, "Such an Aries."

———————

The day after, I brooded over Christian Dailey during every step of my morning run with Lincoln. I'd spent plenty of time wondering why Dailey rankled me with such ease. Yes, he hurt my feelings, but that was years ago. Why couldn't I let it go?

Because I could easily imagine Dailey strolling into a courtroom someday. When I visualized myself as a lawyer, carrying my briefcase, it was like watching myself costumed, in a play. I blamed the difference in money and access—of course he could see himself filling the shoes set out and shined for him.

Sophie FaceTimed as I was leaving for movie night at

Lincoln's house. She was sitting at her vanity, mascara wand in hand. "Hey. Is this cute or tryhard?"

She stood up, backing away so I could take in her shorts and a daisy print shirt, skimming her stomach.

"Cute," I decided. "Ginny's not letting you out of the house in that."

"She's at a campaign event," Sophie said, turning to the side. "Does this look say, like: 'I'm an independent woman, but please do flirt if you're interested?' Stop laughing! This is important."

I forced my expression into something resembling serious. "You look confident and approachable. This is for Warner's back-to-school thing?"

"Yep."

Last year, Sophie's first serious boyfriend moved away the week before school started, and they decided to end things. Sophie made it half an hour into Warner's annual party before showing up at my house for a wallow session and sleepover. Then, in the late fall, she turned her ankle badly in a soccer game. All in all, it had been a very down winter in Sophieland. But she fought through it—both the physical therapy and the blue mood that stretched into spring. "Your triumphant return."

She fluffed her hair. "I like to think so. You heading to Lincoln's?"

"Yep."

"'Kay," she said. "Text you later."

There was no prickle of suspicion, no hint from the universe—just Sophie, singsonging goodbye as the call beeped out.

I'd go back over this moment later—how I should have told her that I loved and admired her. I should have told her that I'd come get her from anywhere on the planet—from a bad party, from a dark path, from the ends of a postapocalyptic Earth. I'd pull her out with every last reserve of my strength. Same as she would for me.

But she knew, right? She had to know.

After that, I passed a deeply average Saturday night at Lincoln's house. George ordered pizza; Elliott talked to me about the merits of custom insoles. They left for a wine bar date while Lincoln and I settled in on the couch. After playing video games for most of the evening, we switched to the first five minutes of a B horror movie.

"Okay," Lincoln said, hitting pause. "Name your player."

"Old lady neighbor."

"Gutsy. I choose the young guy with too much product in his hair."

I closed my eyes, pretending to make snoring noises. Our system doled out points for many things: whose chosen character lived longest, who could guess which animal would be shown in a spooky, establishing shot. I jotted down the other guesses on my phone: method of first murder, the two characters I believed would hook up, and which would get murdered shortly after.

Halfway in—with me in the lead and gloating—my phone lit up on the ottoman. Lincoln reached to grab it for me, and it buzzed again. Again.

"Since when do you text with Claire Hilson?" Lincoln asked.

"I don't." We'd exchanged numbers for a science project last year. Claire was in the upper echelon of West Grove popularity, with a boyfriend at Ingleside. I only knew this because Sophie and I ran into her once while grabbing takeout near campus.

Hey, I was at Warner's and the party broke up.

There are sirens, and someone said the ambulance is for Sophie.
But she seemed totally fine when I saw her earlier!

My spine stiffened, bolting me upright. That made no sense. Sophie didn't drink, so it's not like she'd be puking or passing out. An ambulance for what? Did she blow out her ankle again?

"What's wrong?" Lincoln asked.

It's probably nothing, Claire added. *But wanted to text you in case.*

"Probably nothing," I repeated. "Rumor mill. The party Sophie's at."

Call me right now, I typed to Sophie.

My nerves flickered. I expected my phone to light up right away—Sophie's name between the shooting star emojis she chose the day I got my phone—with a text that said *omg chill.* When neither happened, I dialed, turning away from Lincoln. Maybe I was muttering *Pick up, pick up, pick up* or maybe only chanting in my mind. *Hi, you've reached Sophie,* the voice mail said. *I'm ignoring your call because it should be a text.* She'd recorded that to annoy her mother, the only person who left voice mails anyway.

"Soph," I said. "Call me back, okay? Claire Hilson sent me this weird text that—well, whatever. Just call me."

Then I held my phone out to Lincoln, wordless, and let him read the texts from Claire.

"Weird," he decided. "Maybe the cops broke up the party and everyone scattered. Sophie's probably hiding in a neighbor's swing set or something until the cops leave."

"Probably." I clung to the thought so hard that my hands went clammy. Something felt irreversibly wrong, but no—I had spoken to her hours before. My hand traced down the braid she'd woven with her own two hands yesterday. She was fine. Of course she was.

"Do you have Gabi's number?" Lincoln asked.

I didn't. But I did check her social media, as if—what? She'd be live-streaming a busted party? I sent her a message there, knowing full well I'd be embarrassed by it in about ten minutes when Sophie got back to me.

"You can unpause it," I told Lincoln, nodding at the screen. Maybe pretending I wasn't panicked would make me less panicked. But I couldn't even hear the dialogue. I stared at my phone as another few minutes passed—every second another bean on the scale, tipping further toward fear.

In my mind, time played like a sustained violin note, stretched out and wavering.

Lincoln paused the movie again. "Do you have any idea where the party is?"

Warner lived a few streets away from Sophie—they carpooled to school sometimes. "I know the general area."

Clapping his hands on his knees, Lincoln stood decisively. "Let's go. She'll probably text you back, and we can give her a ride."

We were almost out the door when I said, in a voice that sounded too loud, "I'm sure she's fine. She'll give me so much shit for worrying."

"Oh, definitely." Lincoln turned to meet my eyes, one hand braced on the doorframe, and nodded.

We made it halfway to Eastmoore before my mom called, frantic, telling me to go straight to the hospital.

What else is there to say? The ambulance was for Sophie.

Senior Year

Through my windshield, I stare up at Ingleside Country Day School. My monster, my mountain. The gray stone buildings and old beech trees rise from pristine lawns, and I do see its beauty—a place that makes you pull your shoulders back to face a formal challenge.

At 7:02 a.m., the last Ingleside uniforms are swishing through the doors. For the first day, everyone wears blazers, and I decided on the classic plaid skirt. The tartan looks forest green from afar but, up close, thin lines of yellow and red run vertical against blue squares.

Flipping down the visor mirror, I consider my handiwork. The makeup isn't a lot, though it's more than I used to wear. I do miss my long hair and the ease of ponytails. But every time I saw my reflection last year, I expected to see Sophie's grinning face near it, like every childhood photo. At least this way, I'm someone else entirely.

The Upper School's interior is all high-shine mahogany, with the faint smell of citrus and old books. I had Friday afternoon orientation to acquaint myself with this place and pretend any of it seems normal. I attended alone; every freshman was flanked by parents in dress shoes. Dr. Ryan herself guided me to my counselor's office. They welcomed me and spoke kindly about Sophie.

Today, there will be a school-wide moment of silence. The Head of School offered to let me say a few words in Sophie's honor, but I politely declined by saying I don't want my Ingleside experience to be defined by grief. As if it could be anything else.

Somewhere, my cousin Maddie is starting her first day of high school at St. Anne's. I send a thought into the universe—an envelope with wings, wishing her a new start. If only one of us can have it, I'd ask that it be her.

Seven minutes of first period are dedicated to the school's closed-circuit morning news. On the screen, two student anchors welcome freshmen and transfers. A tradition of scholarship and community, et cetera.

"As many of you know," one anchor begins. She has a steeled look on her face, determined to remain professional. "Yesterday marked one year since the loss of our friend and classmate, Sophie Abbott—a bright light in our graduating class, missed by so many. Please join us in a silent moment of remembrance."

I grit my teeth, trying not to scan the room too obviously. To my right, Noma Al-Ahmad moves her hand, discreetly clearing away a tear—Sophie liked her. They'd bonded at parties, taking pics that they called the Sober Squad Selfie Series. In front of her, Liam Kendall is shaking his head a little. Sophie thought he was a jerk, and I wonder what she'd make of him wrestling with her absence. Ben Ashby, beside me, runs a thumbnail between his front teeth. I'll mark that down as "troubled." When Ben Ashby transferred to Ingleside sophomore year, Sophie thought he was cute. He's tall and white, with a kind of sullen resting face. Something sculptural about it, to Sophie's credit.

"Thank you," the anchor says. "And now, a statement about Friday's pep rally from—"

It's a hard moment, but not the hardest.

I knew I'd see Gabi in second period AP Enviro, and I thought I'd prepared for it. But our eyes meet in the hallway, coming from opposite directions. It's visceral, our history mashed with the present.

Just get through this part.

The floor between us rattles with the weight of these past months. It's not the type of thing you can prepare for: everything Gabi reminds me of, everything I've lost. The way I still— *still*—expect Sophie to appear by her side.

We stop outside the classroom door, several inches left between us.

"Hey." Gabi searches my face, taking in a summer of changes. She's cut her hair to just past her ears, though the middle part is the same.

"Hey," I manage. Then, attempting a smile, I nod to the open door. "Go 'head."

We stand there for another second, mouths full of words we won't say. But she does go ahead, leaving me with the slightest nod. I've learned to live with the discomfort, like everything else.

In my early classes, a few people glance at me, but no one

goes out of their way to say hello. My presence is a small novelty, but not an oddity. Ingleside has a core group of since-Pre-K lifers like Sophie, but plenty of kids move in and out as parents get new jobs. Seniors already have their friend groups and one foot out the door.

For fourth period, I'd weaseled into Advanced Drawing and Painting with my sewing portfolio and an effusive essay about several Maryland-based painters. The teacher shares my admiration for Amy Sherald and Derrick Adams.

"We have two new students," she begins. "Mr. Mason is a longtime Ingleside scholar, but new to our art cohort. Peter, we'd love to hear more about your goals in this semester."

Hands tucked in his pockets, he explains his digital animation. "A college counselor said that adding another medium would be more 'dynamic' for admissions committees. So, go easy— especially you, Chaudry."

The class laughs. I smile through the first of the inside jokes, which will fly over my head like so many squawking birds.

The professor turns to me. "Next, we have senior transfer Hannah MacLaren. Welcome, Hannah. Could you share how you came to join us?"

I smooth the hem of my skirt as I stand. "Hi, everyone. I'm Hannah. My primary medium has always been textiles—fashion sketching, design, construction. I'm a beginner in almost every other area, as I'm sure you'll witness soon. But I've always loved paintings as a viewer, so I'm excited for this class."

The professor tips a pen to her mouth. "And you interned in costuming this summer, yes?"

"I did. On a movie set in Vancouver."

"Interesting stuff. We'll look forward to hearing more about that." She slips from the corner of the desk. "All right, everyone. Time for a still life to shake off the dust."

The classroom is outfitted with benches, and I move quickly toward the one I want. Other students chatter as I hold my pencil up, eyeing the proportions. The trick to a good sketch is erasing. Redoing, reconsidering. Luckily, I'm patient. *And stubborn.*

On my way out of class, I smile at a girl packing up her things. She has fair skin and thick brown hair like an old movie star's, brushed a hundred times on each side. Her sketchpad is still open, with a pear so round and dimensional I could almost grasp it. "Wow. That turned out incredible."

"Thanks." She has very pale blue eyes, making for an intense gaze. When I move toward the door, she's in step with me. "Hannah, right? Zoe. I have to know: What movie did you work on?"

"The working title is *Barton Valley*, but it's not out till—"

"With Gemma Wong?" Zoe whips her head to me, hair flying. "Did you do fittings for her?"

"Helped with a few, yeah."

"No way. That is so freaking cool. How do you even get a gig like that?"

"My dad," I say, trying to sound sheepish. This is the shorthand of connections, spoken fluently at Ingleside. I'll shower off the grime of it once I'm home.

We turn a corner, moving from a tributary hallway to the main, bustling river. Zoe speaks a bit louder over the din. "So, what do you think of Ingleside so far?"

"It's really nice." It's the glossy, red veneer shielding a poisoned center. But . . . nice. "Have you always gone here?"

"Pretty much. Cannot *wait* to skip town." She smiles over. "Is this your lunch period? We should sit together."

That easy? I think. In the lunch line, Zoe chatters about the sleep-away art camp she attended in Vermont, while the Ingleside staff offers me a grilled chicken sandwich with—I'm sorry—*aioli?* Tomato that is bright and firm instead of watery pink?

"This food looks, like, surprisingly great."

Zoe glances down at her own tray. "Yeah. Some of the stuff they do is pretty good. So, what are your extracurriculars?"

"School paper," I say. "What about you?"

"I'm a swimmer, which is mostly summer and winter," Zoe says. "And I'm also class president—a stressful gig, but worth it. And I can promise our reunions will be cool someday."

"Maybe at an art gallery?"

She flashes me a smile. "Exactly."

I trail behind to her table, feeling suspended in slow motion. Scanning the room quickly, I spot Christian Dailey on the far side of the room, deep in conversation. He doesn't notice me or, at least, he can't tell it's me from a distance. He'll know when he hears my name in our shared class, but that's a problem for next period.

"Everyone," Zoe announces, "this is Hannah."

"I'm the new girl." I wrinkle my nose, attempting be cute about it. "As a senior."

"Oh, poor thing!" one girl says, patting the seat beside her. "Sit!"

"She just moved from Vancouver," Zoe adds, "where she got to work on a Gemma Wong movie set."

There's a flurry of questions—*Is Gemma nice in real life? Who else did you meet?* But my answers aren't salacious enough to hold attention. The conversation rolls along to first day gossip.

Just after the bell, two guys slide into the last remaining

seats. They're talking about dropping a class with an intimidating syllabus, and I stop chewing mid-bite. One of them sets his eyes on me. He has pale white skin and bright red hair, charming and rumpled as an English storybook character. "Hey. I don't know you."

I swallow my bite of food, buying myself a moment for composure. "I'm new this year."

"Welcome aboard," he says. "I'm Warner."

Yes, I think, fighting a thick knot of emotions in my throat. *You are.*

The other guy is prep school pretty—a brunette white guy primed to be cast on *The Bachelor* someday, with the kind of square head that those guys always seem to have.

"Brooks," he says, raising one hand.

"Hi," I say. "I'm Hannah."

———————

After lunch, I straighten my blazer and put on my game face. I would have expected Dailey in an AP Government class, even without online class rosters.

Midway through the roster, our teacher reaches, "Hannah MacLaren."

A few people glance with mild interest. Only one head swivels back. Christian Dailey stares at me with flagrant shock. His lips form the word slowly: "*What the . . . ?*"

I write the date at the top of my notes, enjoying the pen stroke on fresh paper. Enjoying—I admit—the confusion ricocheting around Dailey's mind.

From here, I've always known my move. He'll approach me, and I want him to—I need to get this part out of the way. But

I also need to limit who sees us together. Knowing Dailey, the intensity will be all over his face, and I don't need my social life at Ingleside to begin with some weird Dailey entanglement. After class, I'll ask the teacher a question that requires only a brief answer, leaving enough time for our classmates to file out, but not so much that Dailey can't corner me before next period.

"Excuse me, Mrs. Bauer," I say, dodging through the downstream of people after the bell rings. In my peripheral vision, I see Dailey moving toward me, but I'm quicker. "I did have one syllabus question . . ."

Sure enough, he's waiting outside the door a minute later.

"Almost didn't recognize you with that hair," he says, pushing off a locker. He's had almost an hour to prepare, and he's better at extemporaneous speaking than I am. But beneath a casual front, his shock glints in the light. "Gotta say, MacLaren. This is a weird curveball. I heard you left for the summer."

I clutch my textbook tighter to my chest. "I was with my dad for a bit."

Dailey looks different, in a way I can't place. If he's taller, it's not by much. "So . . . I don't get it. Suddenly you're a blond and an Ingleside kid?"

"Evolution in order to survive," I say lightly. To my surprise, tears leap forth. I turn away, horrified to be weak in his presence.

"Whoa, hey." Dailey touches my arm but thinks better of it. He's not talking to the spitfire he once knew, but a mourner, broken open. "I didn't mean—I'm not—"

"I'm, like, finally the tiniest bit better." In these words, I'm not telling a single lie. The crack in my voice is real. "And I just wanted a fresh start."

"No, I get that." Dailey holds his hands up, palms facing me. For anyone else, the sheer emotion would stall them out. But Dailey's brain funnels everything through logic, which I know because mine does too. "But doesn't this place drudge up worse feelings?"

I glance off at the ridiculous, wainscoted walls. I want to scuff them with my new shoes. "Probably. But I need a scholarship in order to have options next year, and Ingleside gives me better odds."

"Makes sense." His expression has gone soft, but he's still watching closely. "It's just . . . why the school where people will bring up Sophie to you constantly?"

I press my front teeth into the side of my lower lip. "Actually, no one has realized that I'm her cousin so far. Which is weird, but . . . really nice, it turns out. I get to be the new girl, doing her own thing."

His eyes narrow.

"I'm so sick of people feeling sorry for me," I add. "You have no idea."

"I do, actually," he says. "But what about Gabi?"

Well, she's a liar, I almost say. "We don't really talk anymore. But she gets the fresh start thing."

Dailey is temporarily quiet, and I use his brief silence to add, "I'm not going out for debate team, so don't worry about me trespassing into your territory. I just want to keep being an anonymous new girl. Please, Dailey."

"That it?" he asks. I nod once, bracing for his cross examination. "Okay, my turn. What are you *talking* about, not doing debate? I can obviously handle an on-team competitor. Of course you're doing it. We can—"

"Not this year. Don't have it in me."

"Tell you what. Come to my meeting." God, of course it's *his* meeting. Captain Dailey, one leg proudly perched on the rowboat's bow. "And—"

"I'm focusing on journalism. School paper."

The first bell sounds, warning us.

"MacLaren . . ." His expression has fallen into sadness, which I do not want from him. "Are you okay? For real."

"Yeah," I say, with a nod. "I'm okay. Thanks."

I'm not, of course. But I will be once I figure out what happened to Sophie at this miserable, monstrous school.

AUGUST

- - - - - - -

Junior Year

The first grief was crystalline—bright and piercing. Even as I mourned for Sophie, a lifetime of muscle memory made me reach for my phone, nearly texting her a hundred times. I wept until I wore my body out, and then waking up felt like a crashing down. The howls woke my mother.

Sure, I had considered that my parents would die someday or sooner. But when that fear kicked in, I imagined moving in with Sophie. I never once imagined losing her—never once imagined being an adult without her.

No. I'd live in a small apartment in a big city. After work, I'd change into lounge clothes and stir pasta sauce at the stove, with Sophie's voice in my earbud telling stories from her day. Maybe I'd have a breakup or a work crisis, and Sophie would take the red eye, show up at my building, and make me oatmeal while I blubbered. Just like I would for her.

Except I wouldn't. I couldn't.

I don't remember where I was when I found out Sophie's cause of death was opioid overdose—at the hospital? At home? I remember sobbing and clawing, as my mom tried to contain me in her arms. I remember Lincoln *Mm-hmm*ing at my frenzied theories: *She wouldn't have taken pills, Linc. Maybe someone drugged her.*

I called my dad on one of the first nights, in a pitch-black hour of insomnia. His hello reached my ears, but all that came out of my mouth was a wail. "Dad."

That's the only word I got out for some time. I wanted to tell him that Sophie knew how I felt about substance use disorder. Why hadn't she come to me? He sat on the other end of the line with his quiet voice over my gasping sobs. "I'm so sorry, kiddo. I know."

"But how?" I gasped out. "Dad, how? It doesn't make sense."

I wanted explanations, and he'd witnessed the spectrum of pain and healing at a thousand AA meetings.

"I don't think . . ." he began, slow. "I don't think I can give you the answer you want. Much as I'd like to."

Deep down, I knew he'd say that. After we hung up, he texted me to call again any time, even just to sob while he listened. *Don't bottle it up*, he said.

Between Sophie's death and the funeral, I didn't leave the house, though my mom shuttled between Ginny and me often. One morning, I woke up and Elliott was reading at our kitchen table. He made me an egg sandwich, which I ate to be polite, and he didn't try to get me to talk.

My clearest memory came from mid-week, sobbing as my mom finally, gently, took the braid out of my hair. I stood in the shower for a while, letting the hot water pelt me. I felt detached from my body. My hands tied my robe; my feet carried me down the hall.

I startled to find my mom standing at my bedroom closet. On the back of the door, she'd hung a garment bag, halfway unzipped to reveal that white gown meant for Sophie. The sleeves were still pinned and waiting.

When my mom turned to me, her face blazed with anger. She said, in a too-quiet voice, "Ginny tore her house apart looking for this dress. I *told* you that. You said nothing. What were you *thinking*, Hannah?"

I hardened, arms closing like a barricade. "Sophie *hated* that dress."

"Well, my love," she said, in the shrillest tone possible before outright yelling. "You don't get to take burial decisions from a grieving mother. Are you *trying* to hurt her?"

"Of course not!" Through the blur of hot tears, I couldn't make out my mom's expression. I gestured at the black streak of garment bag. "The girl in that awful, prudish dress only existed in Aunt Ginny's imagination. And zipping Soph's body into it for all time is cruel, Mom. It's ghoulish!"

I could hear the rebuttal I would write: *Soph is gone, Hannah. She doesn't care about the dress. The outfit choice is a way for Ginny to mourn, so just let her.* But no. I would not allow Sophie to look like an obedient little doll.

My mom lowered herself onto my bed and pinched the bridge of her nose. I stayed in the doorway, my damp hair soaking through flannel. "Bug, listen to me. You loved Sophie in a way no one else did, and I respect that. Okay?"

No one else, *no one else*. I didn't realize, until that moment, how much I needed someone to acknowledge it. "Okay."

"But Ginny lost her child, Hannah. She loved Sophie in a

way you can't understand, either. She may show it by giving her daughters the things we didn't have as girls, but it's the best way she knows to protect them."

I felt doused in shame. I knew this about Ginny—at least, as much as my mom would allude to. But, somewhere beneath it, I also believed I was right. Hadn't my mom always said money could protect from the bad but also poison the good?

"Hannah," my mom said, in this pained way. "I need you to hear me on this one."

I held myself tighter. "I hear you."

"If we're going to get through this . . ." She paused, maybe realizing what she'd implied. *If* we get through this. "We can't hide from each other. No squirreling away dresses or anger or any of it."

Meanwhile, she had not disclosed even one personal feeling to me about her niece's death. She'd comforted me, rubbing my back and whispering *I'm here*. She had not—and would not— meet me in the pain of it.

"I'm going to go deal with this," she said, standing to zip the bag. "I'll apologize on your behalf and suggest another outfit."

The most logical move was to agree—to get out of the way and let the bleak mechanics of funeral planning roll on. But my loyalty to Sophie blazed, even without her beside me. "The dress she got when they were in Charleston. Please, Mom. I *have* to do this for her. I have to do this one last—"

I couldn't say it, only sniffle.

"Okay," she said, gathering me up. "Okay."

Everyone who knew me should have realized: Sophie hadn't dropped my hand once in her whole lifetime. I certainly wouldn't drop hers now.

— — — — — — —

She was laid to rest in her favorite dress, pale blue with tiny white flowers.

At the visitation, Maddie and I were excused from the receiving line, deemed too young to weather the crashing waves of sympathy.

All my life, I'd watched my aunt hold up polite facades, like sleight of hand. Sophie and I once found a DVD of Ginny's news anchor clips and marveled at the bad lipstick and familiar tonal shifts. Young Virginia Farris could go from brightly bantering with her coanchor to solemnly reporting a neighborhood tragedy. It sounded like Ginny turning away from a cheerful conversation with a friend to nag Sophie for slouching.

But now, Ginny's face remained slack as people gave their condolences. Occasionally, Andrew put an arm around her, and I couldn't stand to look at them. It was like staring at a black hole—an absence that swallowed every light in its path.

I stood with Maddie until her friends began to arrive, surrounding her in a big circle. It looked safe, like she couldn't collapse in any direction without someone there to catch her. For me, Lincoln was a perfect sentry—quiet and always close enough to lean on. No one approached me anyway. I didn't know these people, and they didn't know me.

The room filled up fast, and we wandered through explosions of lilies, wide as my shoulders. Ingleside sent an enormous, standing wreath with a silver lion figurine resting in the curve. How ridiculous—thousands of dollars spent on plants that would wither in days. And yet, the room was otherwise anonymous, with pastoral, vaguely Christian paintings that had witnessed a thousand grievers. At least these flowers made the room for Sophie.

Most of the faces in line were blurred ovals to me, but I did register Christian Dailey, standing with a girl I didn't recognize.

He raised one hand from across the room, and I raised mine back, then fled to the kitchenette for a cup of pitiful coffee.

"You okay?" Lincoln asked, once I returned. This had been our little two-step: *You okay? Yep.* We both knew I wasn't. It was just quicker than him saying *I see you going somewhere in your mind that seems particularly painful,* and quicker than me replying, *Correct, but I'll let you know if I need you to pull me back.*

This time, though, I whispered, "Do you think anyone here knew about the pills?"

"Um, I dunno," Lincoln said, in a tone that made it clear he would love to not discuss it at a crowded visitation.

The thought had occurred to me before. But I could barely accept that Sophie was gone, let alone that it had really been an overdose. Some of these people were certainly at the party with her. Did one of them know how those pills got into her hands? Was this a known network at their school? An average weekend?

The room began to spin, a carousel of faces that Sophie might have seen before her eyes closed a final time.

I turned, trying to focus on individuals. Did anyone appear guilty? Impossible to tell with the stricken looks on strangers' faces. One of you, I thought. One of you.

Warner Evans was slumped in a chair, sallow-faced and staring into nothing as a girl talked to him intently. Maybe I should feel terrible for him—this poor, unsuspecting kid who Sophie had always liked. All he did was host a party. Or maybe he knew damn well what was happening under his roof. Christian Dailey could have been at the party, too. Who else?

Take a breath. Not here.

I knew from my mom, who knew from my aunt, that Gabi had no idea about the pills. The word "gutted" was used. I hadn't seen Gabi yet, and I had no idea what to expect. She didn't seem like the histrionics type. Would friends and classmates fuss all around her? Would she weep theatrically?

I also knew from my mom that Gabi had agreed to speak at the funeral. My aunt asked me first, but I declined. I imagined opening my mouth to speak at the podium, and, instead, I'd let out a whale song from great depths. Besides, a lifetime of memories belonged to Sophie and me, and now they were only mine. I wouldn't dole them out to strangers so they could feel touched. But even as I dreaded the speech about Gabi's perfect friendship with Sophie, I envied her wherewithal.

This is what I was thinking about as one of my mom's work friends cornered me on my way back from the bathroom. Weeping, she told me how sorry she was and that, as a mother, she just couldn't imagine.

But she could. That's precisely why she was crying.

I withstood it, my jaw locked, until a hand clasped my wrist gently. "Excuse me. So sorry. I need to borrow Hannah for a moment. Thanks so much."

If I'd expected anyone, it would have been my mom or Lincoln, returning to bail me out. But it was Gabi, ushering me away with a confident stride.

I followed on autopilot, too surprised to protest. She pushed open a door in the hallway, which revealed a small, private sitting room. A stained-glass window cast primary colors onto the floor.

Gabi locked the door and turned to me. "God. Those people are so fucking obtuse."

Yes, I meant to say, but nothing came out of my mouth.

In a charcoal suit and oxford buttoned to her throat, Gabi

looked as understated as I'd ever seen her. Her wire-framed glasses didn't quite mask the caked-on under-eye concealer.

"Anyway." She crossed her arms, maybe unsure what she intended to do after rescuing me from someone else's sloppy emotions. "Hi."

That's when it hit me: Gabi actually understood. I was looking at the tear-puffed face of the only other person here who had just lost her best friend.

"Hey," I said, my lips dry. "How are you holding up?"

She glanced at me for just a beat, and her hands flew to her face, covering the tears. And there, stepping into a square of blue light, I wrapped my arms around Gabi as quickly as I would have if it were Sophie herself. She cried on my shoulder like a little kid, not even fighting it. And, finally, I sobbed in the soggy, full-body way I'd been fighting for hours.

In that tiny room, no one was thinking about how Sophie's death affected the community, about their own kids, about a greater epidemic outside these walls. It was only us, destroyed with longing for our person.

"How can it be real?" Gabi croaked out, minutes in. I shook my head, crying too hard to speak. Still, the relief moored me to earth—someone else couldn't accept it either.

I'd always been so jealous that Sophie had another best friend. But now that she'd left us—*how could it be real?*—she'd also left us each other. It was the least alone I'd felt in a week. The least alone I'd feel for weeks to come.

———————

After we collected ourselves, Gabi asked me to edit the eulogy she'd written. The draft was earnest and huge-hearted, if too long and desperate for structure. Late that night, I trimmed, shored up some of the central ideas, and emailed it back to her.

Gabi delivered a near-perfect speech. In a way, it was reassuring to know I could still feel a bolt of envy toward her. She mentioned some of Sophie's accomplishments, but also noted how special Soph would have been even without those things. Sophie was unparalleled at pep talks, picking restaurants, guessing rising signs. The list went on. Gabi spoke about their plans to change the world—to do the climate activism that they both believed in. "I'd especially like to offer my condolences to Sophie's parents, her sister Maddie, and her cousin Hannah," Gabi said. "She loved you so much." I cleared away a tear, grateful to be acknowledged in a sea of strangers.

Before we left the graveside, Gabi tugged away from the mourners who swarmed to compliment her tribute.

"That was beautiful," I told her. "Really."

"Thanks." She spun back, glancing at the crowds all around us, before meeting my eyes. "Hey. You didn't know anything about Sophie and the pills, right?"

I shook my head, resenting my own ignorance. "Did you?"

"No." Her voice had a bitter edge. "Can I put my number in your phone? Maybe we could talk when things calm down a little?"

I didn't expect the open door—or the relief that washed over me. Was I pitiable to her? Or just as lost as she was? "Yeah. That sounds good."

Senior Year

In the first weeks at Ingleside, my classes feel like banquet tables piled with food—intimidating and delicious. I consume information until I'm so full that it hurts. I prepare before class and review notes after, until my mom claims that my hands will become grafted to my laptop. Still, she can't argue with results.

I contribute thoughtfully in class, though I'm careful not to make waves. In my AP Gov notes, I keep a sidebar of my rebuttals to Dailey's input instead of raising my hand. The one time he tries to spar with my commentary, the teacher clucks, "The devil can advocate for himself, Mr. Dailey."

The journalism lab quickly becomes my school nesting spot as I rework drafts for the *Insider*. Writing a tight, interesting article is somewhere between a puzzle and a painting—certain pieces have to interlock, but I have a little room to be artistic.

I volunteer to attend tennis, golf, and field hockey matches; I sit in on show choir rehearsal and pep band practice. Everywhere, I observe that Ingleside kids are, essentially, happy. They celebrate in a huddle after a winning goal; they film goofy videos, hamming it up. Sometimes their easy revelry hits like a smack.

Not a single person connects me to Sophie. I'm what they see: a quiet, blond nobody who moved from Vancouver, exactly as I'd hoped. Each passing day is an ever-bloating lie, and I'm not immune to the strain. But the tiny, gathered details are worth it. I smile more than I would naturally, quiet but always listening—in class, at the lunch table. People who were once outlines are filled in, paint-by-number style. With enough specks of color, they'll take shape.

Brooks and Warner chatter frequently about soccer. Sometimes, I hear snippets of weekend shenanigans, which seem like garden-variety parties. Zoe is well-connected, though most of her close friends graduated last year. *Being friends with the older kids: Cool when you're a freshman*, she quipped. *A bummer when you're a senior.* She talks a lot, narrating her inner life, though she sometimes pauses to involve me.

"You really don't have any social media?" Zoe asks. I'm scrolling through the Vancouver Art Museum photos she asked to see—a sketch of two squids, a pile of earthenware apples. "I can't tell if that's healthy or, like, out of touch?"

"Healthy," Brooks says through a mouthful of french fries at the same time Warner says, "Out of touch."

"It's the one thing my mom's strict about," I explain. This part is true. "I was forbidden until age thirteen. By then, it was like . . . eh."

"Damn, Mrs. MacLaren," Zoe says. "You *should* start an account though. This school's online ecosystem could really use more than drunk inside jokes."

Brooks snort-laughs, as if he's thinking of something specific.

"You live with your mom now, right?" Warner asks me. He's so enduringly pleasant that I can hardly reconcile him with the sick-faced boy from Sophie's visitation.

"Yep. My dad's work has picked up a lot, so he's traveling more. But I'll probably be back out in LA for college. He's based there."

"Jealous," Zoe says, sighing.

"You surf?" Brooks asks.

"Never have." I reach for my notebook before the questions can continue. "By the way, I'm supposed to survey you all for an article on up-and-coming tech. Any new gadgets or apps you're into?"

"That reminds me." Zoe snaps her fingers. "I have responses to your carnival questions in drafts. I'll polish them up tonight."

Catherine, the student editor, assigned me a feature story for the annual Fall Carnival, hoping I'll bring a first-timer's perspective. I asked to interview Zoe in her capacity as class president, and she's already crooned about the PTA–Student Council collaboration and how many school supply donations it generates for the county.

Across the table, Brooks dumps half a packet of vending machine Skittles into his hand. He plucks out the orange ones, puts them on Warner's plate, and then downs the palmful.

He catches me staring and holds out the bag. "Want some?"

"No thanks," I say quickly. I return my gaze to my food, desperately wishing Sophie were here to steal fries off my plate.

———————

The carnival spans from behind the school to the track, where most of the booths are set up, and I walk through, making notes on my phone. Beautiful day with some cloud cover—noted. Red vinyl tents make for a cheery, circus feel, and there's a low roar of conversation. I'm later than I wanted to be, after reporting on a Saturday cross-country invitational.

The crowd is mostly little kids and their parents, but I pass fellow seniors getting their National Honor Society hours. Christian Dailey, his best friend Jordy, and Jordy's twin sister, Jasmine, are managing the rowdy line for the bounce house. Up ahead, my first-period classmate Ben Ashby—who placed first in the cross-country meet this morning—is walking hand in hand with his junior girlfriend. I'm about to approach them for a quote when Warner's smiling face pops into view. "Hey, reporter on the prowl."

He's earnestly friendly, almost impossible not to like. This was always the impression I got from Sophie. But it's jarring, every day of the week, to see Warner Evans function with ease. When did he get over what happened at his house? Was it a lightning-flash moment or did the pain crawl to a halt?

I smile back. "Hey, guys."

Brooks sidles up beside him, as is usually the case. They're an odd couple—Warner making us laugh and Brooks being fairly serious for a jock type. And Brooks *is* the jock type, always on about The Game or whatever outdoor sport he did last weekend. But he also chimes in about music, with a much more alternative taste than I would have guessed.

"Pay the toll," I joke, poised with my notebook. They're used to me coming and going during lunch to collect quotes. "Senior Warner Evans. This is your last Fall Carnival. How does that feel?"

Warner surveys the booths with his arms behind him, like a lord and his landscape in a Romanticist painting. "Emotional. Profound. Affirming."

"I'm going to include that," I warn, jotting it down. "Brooks, as a student representative on council, what role did you play in the planning?"

Brooks scratches the back of his neck. "Well, I pushed for the empanada truck. The profit doesn't go right into our pockets the way the bake sale tent does, but I thought people would stay longer if they were well fed. And I like that place."

I scribble that down, a bit surprised. "That's a nice detail—thanks."

"I'd also like to add that Zoe did the heavy lifting, and we seniors are lucky to have her," Brooks says over my shoulder. "Oh, hey, Zo. Didn't see you there."

"Uh-huh." She gives a false smile, not falling for it. The September weather is still hot, but she's wearing a red blazer like a ringmaster. "The light has shifted, so we need help moving the photo booth backdrop."

Warner pretends to be offended. "Is that all we are to you? Brawn?"

"No," Zoe says sweetly. "You're also volunteers for the ring toss starting in five minutes. And, Warner, one of my studio friends is coming later, and he's—"

"No," Warner groans, tipping his head back to the sky. "No more set-ups with art boys when the only thing we have in common is being gay."

Zoe huffs at him. "That is *not* all. You're also both very cute."

Warner and Zoe face off for a moment, silent. I meet eyes with Brooks, who is struggling against a smile.

"Show me his picture," Warner concludes, his chin held proudly, and Brooks lets out the laugh.

With a smirk, Zoe says, "After you move the photo booth."

"That's on the record, right, Hannah?" Warner asks, as they start off toward their destination. "Bribery at the hands of upper management?"

"Fall Carnival," I say, in a solemn voice. "The dark side of one senior's struggle."

Warner laughs, waving as they meander down the main walkway. I stare for a moment, adjusting my idea of those two by a tiny click. Some days, I want to shake them so hard that answers fall out. But I've invested so much. Caving to impatience is not an option.

"How was the away meet?" Zoe asks.

"Really good, thanks." I'm pleased she would remember, with everything she's had going on here. "So, I have my face painting shift later. What else can I do?"

"Um." She glances around, a bit guiltily. "Come with me to get a shave ice, and, if anyone asks, say I'm giving an interview for the article?"

"Subterfuge? Absolutely." I follow her toward the blacktop, where the food and snacks lines begin.

Zoe's a funny one. She can be highbrow and almost pathologically out of touch. But I know this because she says most of her thoughts aloud. When she opens her mouth, she's equally likely to fret over homecoming schematics, declare someone "tacky" for getting puke-drunk at a party, or call a new MoMA sculpture acquisition "exhilarating."

75

She's not always nice. But what you see is what you get, and there's something comforting in that.

I've tried to mirror her casual friendliness without becoming a new-girl clinger. The social tightrope exhausts me, but I psych myself up on the drive to school each morning, becoming Ingleside Hannah somewhere between here and West Grove.

"Okay. Five minutes off-duty," Zoe says, settling into the bleachers with her raspberry ice.

A little kid streaks by us, screaming at his dad that he's never, ever leaving the carnival, and I smile, writing that down. Brooks and Warner pass by at a distance, and Warner yells, "Send me that pic!" Zoe gives him a thumbs-up.

"So," she says, "is there anyone at Ingleside you're into so far?"

Early in my lunch table tenure, she'd asked if I was single. I told her the truth: yes, and that I'd broken it off with someone in Vancouver. Who wants to do long-distance senior year of high school?

When I shrug, Zoe adds, "Liam Kendall was asking about you other day, but you can do better."

"See, that's what I need," I say. "Who's eligible? Who's bad news? You're my insider."

"Then best of luck to you." Zoe laughs, lifting her cup in a cheers.

"That sounds like a story."

"I have, like, horrendous taste in guys. There's no denying it at this point."

"Oh no."

"It's true." She gives me a grim smile. "Emotionally unavailable? *Bonjour*, I'm Zoe. Sulky? *Ooh-la-la*. Bad coping mechanisms? *Oui, oui*."

I'm laughing—I can't help it. "Sorry. It's not funny."

"No, it is a little. My taste in art translates to boys, which is regrettable. Give me hints of sadness, make me work for what it all *means*."

"At least you're self-aware," I offer.

"Lessons learned and all that," Zoe says. Her walkie-talkie crackles to life, and she lifts it to say, "Okay. On my way."

On our walk to the ticket booth, we pass a group of soccer girls in gray team T-shirts. My body tenses at the sight of Gabi, but she only smiles at Zoe and says, "Fine work here, Prez."

"Thanks," Zoe says. "Have you met Hannah?"

Gabi glances over with the blank-polite expression of someone who has never sobbed with me in a funeral home. "Yeah."

"We have second period together," I tell Zoe quickly.

"Enjoying the carnival?" Gabi asks.

"Definitely." I hold my phone up like evidence. "Taking notes for my first *Insider* feature."

"Best one yet," she says. "You can quote me."

"Thank you for the good press," Zoe says, as we start off.

What would someone who just met Gabi say? When we're out of earshot, I tell Zoe, "She seems cool."

"Oh, the greatest. She's going out with Catherine, you know. Total power couple. Nice to see her happy after last year." Zoe looks around to make sure no one's close by. "I'm sure you've heard about Sophie? The student who overdosed at Warner's house last year?"

My heart ticks like a jammed sewing machine. It's surreal to hear Zoe say her name. "Yeah. Terrible."

"It was. I feel so bad for Gabi." Zoe sighs, and it sounds genuine. Her tone lacks the breathlessness of good gossip. "I heard she carries that spray they use for overdoses. Like, her whole life, she'll be carrying around the trauma of finding her friend like that."

Of course, I also carry naloxone for the same reason and think everyone should.

"She's doing dual-enrollment class up at Yardley this semester," Zoe continues. "I think it's just to be away from Ingleside as much as she can."

"Mm." I stuff every screaming question down, down, down inside me. It feels like pressing my hands over a geyser, shaking with the force it takes to hold back.

"That's why I put so much into this event. The carnival last year was, like, so somber. Everyone was shell-shocked, parents freaking out, students in school counseling. The whole year was a mess, really." Zoe pressed her lips together. "I liked Sophie. But her choices hurt a lot of people."

It hits like spit in my face. I blink in the aftermath, too shocked for sputtering outrage. *Breathe, Hannah.* I grip onto my character—the bland Hannah of Ingleside CDS. That version of me chokes out, "Well, not on purpose."

Zoe sighs again, as if opioid use disorder is a small exasperation. "But everybody knows what drugs can do. If you don't want to die from them, like . . . don't start doing them? It's not rocket science."

No, it's neuroscience, psychology, health. I grit my teeth, holding in phrases like "trauma response" and "genetic markers." For a person like Zoe—so in control of her little world—it must seem simple.

"She left this grieving family and community—for what?" Zoe continues. We're nearly to the ticket booth. Then, finally glancing at me, "You'll have to just take my word for it. This year is going *much* better. Well, see you Monday!"

She flounces off to her duties, and I stand there holding a hand to my stomach, like I'd been drop-kicked in my very core.

— — — — — — —

On Monday, after my last class, I settle into what is now my usual spot in the journalism lab.

Other staff writers stay late on deadline days, but today, it's just Catherine at the helm. She's primarily a photojournalist, often seen with a giant camera around her neck, but she landed the editor-in-chief position because she's also a great writer. She and Sophie were friends, so I recognized her from the start. She has short-cropped hair, dark brown skin, and a retro, '70s style that she finesses into school uniform rules.

"Hey," I say, trying to announce my presence gently.

Catherine looks over from her computer screens. She's tall—a volleyball player—but I can still only see the top half of her face. "Hey. How'd the carnival go?"

"It was really fun! I'm about to take a pass at the draft."

"Great work with the football game story you filed yesterday," Catherine adds. "You've really been a star with all the extracurricular grunt work."

"No problem." This week, I've also watched fall play rehearsal and marching band practice. "It's a nice way to get to know the school."

No one is looking to make new friends during their final lap of school, but I still want Catherine to like me. She's forthright and easy to share space with—stretches of silence as she thinks and then bursts of tippy-tappy typing. In class, she talks a lot about "emerging media" and "disruption." She treats school like a job she enjoys being good at, but I can tell it's not the central thing her happiness rotates around.

I'm also eighty percent sure that Catherine knows who I am. But she's discreet—the picture of journalistic ethics.

"School year going okay so far?" Catherine asks.

"It's challenging," I admit. "But exciting."

"You have college plans?"

"Pre-law, hopefully at a school that gives me a scholarship. Will you major in photojournalism?"

She nods. "Hopefully in DC."

"Are you focusing on political photojournalism?" The words leave my mouth as I think better of them. "Well, I guess all photojournalism is political, isn't it?"

"Totally—both the subjects and whose lens you're seeing through." She reaches for a paper, fresh off the printer. "I basically want to follow in the footsteps of Ruby Washington and Michelle Agins at the *Times*. Politics, yes, but also art, protest, Black culture, joy, daily life."

No wonder Sophie liked you, I do not say. Sophie believed in saying goals out loud—the small ones and the huge, dare-to-dream ones.

"Speaking of which," Catherine says, lifting up from her desk. "I'm gonna head home to recharge before the school board meeting."

"Thrilling, I take it?"

"It'll be a long night of 'This is more of a comment than a question . . . ,'" she says, swinging her tote over shoulder, and I groan-laugh.

So, I'm alone, three attempts into reworking a lede line,

when Christian Dailey appears in the doorway. He leans, clearly waiting to be acknowledged.

I enjoy ignoring him for long enough that he realizes I'm doing it.

"Hey, MacLaren." He moves from one side of the door to the other, lazy and leonine. Whatever this is, it's not good. "Glad I caught you."

I train my eyes back to the screen, pretending to read. "What can I do for you?"

He strides in and settles into a nearby seat. I turn gamely, waiting for another appeal to join debate team. His tie is tugged a good inch from his collar, top button undone. We're supposed to stay in uniform on campus, even when we're done with classes, and as usual, Dailey walks a fine line.

"You," he says, one arm propped on another chair, "almost got me."

It's enough to toss my heart rate skyward, but Dailey has a flair for drama; this could be his introduction to almost any topic. I pinch my eyes closed through a labored sigh. "Okay . . . ?"

His eyes move fast across my face. "I had never seen Miss Logical—always so cool at the podium—make an emotional appeal before. So, the whole 'Please, Dailey, I need a new start' thing? It threw me."

Heat splits across my back. "I don't follow."

"A good play on sympathy, too," he continues. This conversation is moving too fast for me to clock his strategy or body language, to predict his next move. *Breathe, Hannah.* "But then you hang with Warner Evans and company?"

I shape my face into pure derision. "Oh, right. Because I definitely had my pick of friends on the first day at a new school."

"There she is." Dailey points at me, eyes bright. "Sarcastic. Rhetorical."

I roll my eyes, but my cheeks are hot.

"You show up almost unrecognizable, befriend kids you have nothing in common with." He ticks the points on his fingers just like he does onstage. "Tell no one you're related to Sophie. You quit debate, where you'd stand out enough that people might connect the dots. You're completely docile in class, even when people make rootless, ignorant comments."

That's five. He waggles his fingers. I need the room to freeze; I need the clock to halt in mid-tick. Dailey's peering at me, openly curious. "You're trying to figure out where Sophie got pills and who knew. That's what you're doing at this school you hate."

My tongue clogs the back of my throat, the half-swallowed air stuck.

He nods, sure of himself now. "And now you're blinking like I'm shining a flashlight in your eyes. Which is what you do in debate when you're caught off-guard."

My heart slams against my rib cage, muscle on bone. *It's okay; it's okay.* Before I walked into Ingleside that first day, I made contingency plans. But if he goes straight for blackmail, I might have a problem. "Well. That's quite a theory."

Christian studies me, probably clocking that I didn't deny it. "Relax, MacLaren—I'm not gonna blow your cover."

To my surprise, he looks earnest, and I would know, having spent years watching his various ways of bullshitting. Then why corner me like this? The satisfaction of besting me?

"But I want to help," he adds.

I blink rapidly again, even though he just pointed this out

as a tell. "Why, in the hypothetical world you are suggesting, would you do that?"

"Well, Soph was always nice to me." He glances to the side, embarrassed to flash sentiment at me. When his eyes return, they're intent. "But also? I don't like the wrong people being blamed for things. And when a rich white girl dies the way Sophie did, the whispers aren't about rich white party boys. The scrutiny isn't on them. Their lockers aren't 'randomly' searched more. I mean, I'm sorry to put it like that, but—"

"No, it's fine." There are plenty of things that offend me about the way people talk about Sophie's life and her death. That both are inextricable from race and privilege is not one of them. "So, what? You're the white knight?"

A muscle in his jaw clenches. "Do you remember last year? You asked me if I'd talked to Sophie that night."

I nod, immediately desperate to hear more. What I wouldn't give to see footage of that party—film reel from every angle.

"I was one of the last people to talk to her—I had to be. I've gone over it and over it . . ." Dailey scrubs at the back of his head, mussing his hair. I'll give him this: he looks sincerely frustrated. Is it survivor's guilt? The nagging frustration of a know-it-all who was ignorant at a key moment? "Someone knows more than they're saying, and it pisses me off, you know?"

"Yes," I say, though my face remains neutral. "I do know."

His mouth lifts into a half smile. "MacLaren. I don't mean to alarm you, but it seems like we're in agreement."

Not so fast. This is the trick with Dailey: never let the interpersonal distract you. He projects the good, moral guy so convincingly because he believes it himself.

"Well," I say, "It's nice to be seen as some vigilante with a master plan, instead of a sad girl bumbling around in a fog."

"Interesting." He sits back in his chair. "Going the denial route, redirecting to grief. Even though you know I could tell the whole school who you are."

My gamble now—as it has been since I decided to transfer here—is that Christian Dailey is too puffed-up on his own principles to stoop that low.

"But you know what?" Dailey says, grandly. "I think you trust that I won't. Why would I? I want the person found. And your personal animosity toward me aside . . . you know I value my principles."

"Oh, do you?" I ask, heavily sarcastic. That word comes up in every damn debate. The more principled stance, he'll say. But if we're centering the principle of the thing, he'll say.

Dailey grins. "You wouldn't snipe at me like that if you thought I'd tell your secret. So . . . you trust me to keep it, but not enough to loop me in? Even though I could help. Huh."

The axis has shifted entire degrees in only minutes, and still, I feel a physical tug to let the truth tumble out. *He could help.* I miss having someone to talk through everything with, and Christian Dailey is good at different things than I am.

Maybe I'm a fool; maybe he has a motive that will undercut me and ruin everything. But I'd be an even bigger fool not to know when he's got me cornered. So, I let the mask fall from my face and—I confess—it's a relief to move freely. "I need some time to think."

If I'm obvious with my blinking, then Dailey's tell is a wide-eyed look. For someone who acts like he knows everything, he sure looks surprised to find out that he's right.

"You and your preparations. All right—I have to get to debate practice anyway." He slides out the chair. "You know where to find me. Same number, if you still have it."

I do. I changed his name to Pompous Ass in my phone years ago. But I never deleted him.

And like that, he's out the door. My whole face smarts with renewed heat. I was fourteen, for God's sake. But no matter how many times I out-debate him, out-snark him, outsmart him, this will always be the underlying dynamic for us: the crush and the crushed.

Dailey leans back in the doorway. "Is Ben Ashby on your list? . . . actually, nope. Don't answer. I just wanted to see your face."

And then he disappears.

Junior Year

After the funeral, a fog crawled over my life—a gray dome span-ning several feet in each direction. It kept everything in and everything out.

There was only one match-strike flame of feeling, and I cradled it in my palm: burning curiosity. What happened that night and who knew? There was a Point A leading to a Point B; there was a series of events that led to Sophie dying in a base-ment bathroom.

In the daylight hours, I dragged myself through the school day. Information was absorbed, filtered onto notes, then output to papers and tests. I wrote debate positions, detached but focused. My mom set food in front of me; I chewed and swal-lowed. I texted my dad enough that he didn't worry. I tried—I really did—to go through the motions.

Lincoln and I kept training for our half-marathon, because

every stat was measurable progress. If I kept running, a destination would appear. Wouldn't it?

When I slept at all, I dream-wandered a hallway, rendered like Magritte paintings. Each door was ajar, a white puff of cloud lingering half in, half out. When I reached up, I grasped nothing. Cool vapor in my hands. If I walked through one of the doors— seemingly a portal to a blue sky or the beach—I arrived at another hallway, this one wallpapered with clouds or sand. I sat miserably on the floor, lucidly dreaming my own surrender.

At night, I sank into the blue glow on my laptop, searching: Do cops solve these cases, how do kids even get drugs, where did opioids even start? I took notes as if preparing to debate the universe for Sophie's life back.

I read about the fast-tracked FDA approval and the drug-makers in the 1990s, supposedly assuring the medical community that oxycodone wasn't addictive. Interesting, since reports say 80 percent of opioid users began with prescription painkillers.

Opioid deaths were on the rise, coinciding with synthetics— mainly fentanyl. Fucking fentanyl. In my state, overdoses mirrored racial demographics pretty closely, though white, non-Hispanic people accounted for more than their population size. Sophie was one of them now. I read about the probably underreported rise of overdose deaths in Black and Latine communities, and how systemic racism made people less likely to seek and receive treatment. One study claimed that nearly a million adults over age sixty-five have known substance use disorder.

My dad had always referred to himself as an "addict" or referenced his addiction. Those were his chosen words, comfortable for him. But Sophie wasn't around to decide. As I read and listened, "opioid use disorder" became the natural default.

Whatever I called it, it was everywhere. Everywhere.

So began my bargaining stage of grief. If I studied the ins and outs of medically assisted treatment, if I could explain why rehab facilities need better regulation, if I took an online course on how to administer naloxone, then what? If I could learn enough to create a plan that would have saved Sophie, would I get her back?

No. Of course not.

But I read on, with fervor.

Once confident in my basics, I took my search local. I'd already read the article about my uncle's State Senate campaign continuing after the death of his daughter. Andrew and Ginny had been public about the pills, which surprised me. This time, I forced myself to read the comments—sympathetic or soulless, or, in a few cases, impactful. *TerpMom02: It's tragic what happened. But I do think the media coverage is telling. How many people in our county died by overdose last year? Were any of them mentioned in the paper by name?*

Yes, it was telling—about who is considered to have potential. The deaths and disappearances of young white girls made headlines. That was not new to me, but it sent me reeling with fresh grief for people I did not know.

That's the wall I hit at every turn: dear God, there is so much pain. Not just physical, like Sophie's—but emotional pain too. Pain all the way down, connecting millions in near-translucent lines. I didn't even see the web until I'd walked smack into it.

I navigated to Ingleside's website, looking for reprieve. Instead, I found an article in the *Insider: Tensions Rise After Student Opioid Death.* I scanned through the student reporter's even-handed coverage. A few parents had pulled their kids from Ingleside for other private schools. The administration had instituted an anonymous tip line and, shortly after, a group of students walked out to protest its "unjust applications." Student quotes ran wild: pointing fingers at the administration or one another. The world of Ingleside had been rocked to its marble foundation.

Two nights later, I slipped into the school's "community forum" late, wearing a ballcap. From debate, I knew the auditorium, with its musty velvet and wood polish scent.

I couldn't see well from the back, but the police chief said an incredible number of words for not saying anything concrete. The school therapist talked about peer support groups and coping strategies. As she wound down, a deep voice called out, "But what are we going to *do* about this? We need to know what's happening under our noses."

"I hear you," the therapist said, trying to maintain her calm tone. "As a community, we're in shock. We're fearful."

We're mourning, I prompted in my mind. But this was already less about Sophie and more about everyone else's still-savable children. Tears wobbled across my vision.

"Liz," someone called. "What's the plan here?"

The Head of School took the mic. "Okay. Let's take a breath."

"We pay a damn fortune for this school," a voice rang out. "We deserve answers! How did this happen?"

Of course. Money makes you entitled to more knowledge, less pain. I crossed my arms tightly, willing myself not to scream.

"If there were answers, I would have given them to you," Dr. Ryan said. "Believe me. I'm suffering the same shock and fear as you all."

"How do we know what else this girl was into? There could be a whole network."

I pinched my eyes closed. This girl. Sophie did one thing they considered wrong, and she didn't even get a name. Some of those people had known her since kindergarten.

"Was she selling?" another voice called. "Who was she connected to?"

My jaw dropped, cheeks engulfed in heat.

"Excuse me," Dr. Ryan said, her voice sharp now. "I have detailed the steps the school is taking in multiple emails. And, to reiterate those now . . ."

The sound devolved to a roar, voices overlapping—a parent calling for more random drug testing, students crying out in protest.

I fled out the back door, unable to bear it for another moment.

On marathon day, Lincoln and I bested our training numbers, fueled in part by my fury. Steps past the finish line, I braced my hands on my knees and keened like a suffering animal. Somewhere, I could hear Elliott assuring my mom that this happened sometimes—exhaustion, catharsis, pride. Maybe. But mostly: what now? I'd done it, and Sophie was still gone. I could almost see her, a mirage in the dorky T-shirt she would have made to cheer me on.

Our parents left to refill water bottles, and I forced myself to make eye contact with Lincoln. "I'm sorry—I swear I'm happy, I just . . ."

"I know." He looked like he might cry on my behalf. "You wanna sign up for another half? Do a full this time?"

But I couldn't outrun it. Everyone else was moving forward, even if the pace was a slog through waist-deep grief. Andrew was campaigning, Ginny was already talking about making a foundation in Sophie's name, Maddie was doing group therapy, my mom kept the rest of us going. And then there was me: cavernously sad or else thrumming with anger, no one to understand. Well, almost no one.

Text Gabi. She said to. I stared at my phone, daring myself.

How are you holding up? I typed out. No equivocating, no small talk.

She replied immediately. *Not great. You?*

I blinked down at my phone. The truth, unvarnished. *Also not great.*

Are you around tomorrow? Gabi texted.

And just like that, a new door appeared.

———————

I'd always imagined Gabi living in a big subdivision house like Sophie's. Instead, I pulled up to an older stone home with a gabled roof and a front yard garden. I wondered, climbing out of my mom's car, if Gabi's parents would mention Sophie directly or politely step around her with platitudes.

Maybe Gabi saw the hesitation on my face when she answered the door because she said, "My parents are out."

She wore the glasses from the funeral and her hair in a slapdash knot. I nodded. "Okay."

"Thanks for coming over." Her smile seemed to take effort. To my surprise, I felt steadied by her presence, by her weary eyes and oversized gray sweatshirt. Grief calls to grief.

"Of course," I said, stepping inside.

"I hate being places where I expect to see Sophie," Gabi said. I followed her to the staircase. "So home is one of my only safe zones right now."

Just like that, I relaxed. I felt my lungs open, breathing deeply enough to shift my ribs. We were here to really vent.

It felt strange to step over a threshold that Sophie had crossed so many times. She loved it here—Gabi's dad's cooking, her grandma's visits. Whenever Gabi's two older sisters were home, Sophie seemed delighted, like the kid sister allowed at the sleepover.

I followed Gabi up to her room, with images of Sophie flickering like ghosts. She'd walked these halls, passed these family pictures.

Gabi's room was tidy, with a four-poster bed and built-in bookshelves along one side of the room, the cabinets painted glossy gunmetal. She settled onto her bed and nodded to the space beside her, implying I should climb aboard.

"Do you have a mental log of firsts?" I asked. "First Sunday without Sophie. First run since it happened. First new month. I want to crawl back through time."

"I know," Gabi said. "First soccer practice without her, I made it through five minutes of warm-up. Sobbed in the locker room, then drove home."

Oh, God. The way Gabi must look for her, instinctively, across the field.

"I wish I could quit, but Soph would be furious." Gabi sighed, then looked back to me. "What's it like at West Grove?"

Lonely. There was nothing materially different. I spoke enough in class to get participation credit; I stayed after with the debate team. But as I walked down the hallways, there was a hole punched into the center of my chest that no one could see. It wasn't that I wanted people to know or talk to me about it. I had Lincoln if I wanted that. "Quiet."

Gabi lifted her eyebrows, just briefly. The realization landed: some deep part of my brain could relax at West Grove High because I didn't expect to see Sophie. Gabi had no such luxury. "I saw the community forum, so I take it Ingleside is . . . ?"

"Brutal," Gabi finished, with a snort. "WASPs panicking because now opioids matter to them. Calling for random drug testing on all students. Forming a task force and hotline, which is going about like you'd expect."

I'd expect "random" suspicion to be pointed at scholarship kids and kids of color. "And the school's going along with it?"

"Of course. Anything to keep donors and alums happy, right? And there's the gossip, which makes me want to . . ." Gabi lifted her hands, forming them into a claw grip. "Scream."

"Gossip about Soph?" My voice sounded so small, like a little kid's.

Gabi flashed a look of surprise again. God—of course people talked shit about Sophie. Wouldn't it be the same at West Grove? Speculation was a blood sport.

"And about me," Gabi said, with fake cheerfulness. "Didn't you know Soph and I were secretly dating? Why else would I be taking this so hard?"

There'd been comments here and there over the years, even before Gabi came out as bi in eighth grade. "I know that's not true."

"Also not true: that my family has drug ties."

"Oh, good Lord." Of all the racist shit.

Gabi snorted. "Neither one is brand new. Just louder than usual."

If I'd walked in to find Gabi smiling, I might have switched to small talk. But the girl before me now—her tired eyes watching me with interest—was being dogged by the same question every night, with sleep circling and refusing to land. "Is anyone at school known for dealing drugs?"

"No," Gabi said, with a tinge of bitterness. "I mean, kids at school drink and smoke weed. People use study drugs they don't have prescriptions for, but it's not like there's a go-to person."

"Do you think her ankle flared up?" I continued, on a roll now. "I wondered if maybe she would hide it. She was so worried about her soccer playing time."

Gabi bit at her lower lip, where there was already a dry patch. "I think I would have noticed even a wince or favoring one side. But was she using the whole time, to cover it up?"

After years of playing together, Gabi and Soph knew each other's body language on the field. Sometimes, when they passed to one another—even on a breakaway—it was like they barely needed a glance. "Yeah."

I cleared my face. "Any idea where she kept her journal?"

"No," Gabi said. "But I remember the one Coach gave her— pale blue with a gold S."

"I've thought about going over to search her bedroom," I admitted. "And yes: I do hear myself. It sounds over the top, but . . ."

From somewhere in the blankets, Gabi pulled out a razor-thin laptop. "I want to show you something."

In that moment, I assumed she had spreadsheets like mine— links to articles about fentanyl and explanations of overdose demographics.

She typed in her password with confident keystrokes. "The night Sophie died, I came home from the hospital in shock—for days, really."

I didn't know exactly what Gabi had seen, though part of me wanted to stare every grisly detail in the face and let the suffering wash over me. Another part knew I couldn't have survived it. "I'm sure."

"I'd handed Soph's ID to an EMT," she continued, "but I still had the rest of her stuff in my bag."

Sophie's phone wound up in a police evidence locker—I'd asked my mom about that—so Gabi must have turned it over. I could conjure the image in my mind in such detail that I almost expected the phone to manifest—the floral cover with Sophie's initials in blocky sans serif. "Did you know her password?"

"No," Gabi said. "But I guessed it after getting locked out a few times."

There would be plenty of time for me to wonder if I, too, would have guessed Sophie's password. "And?"

"You can look for yourself." She reached into her nightstand and pulled out a flash drive. "I'm not the biggest techie, but I started clicking around—I took screenshots of pictures, cash app, browser history."

I stared at the girl beside me like she was glowing, iridescent. I'd been frantically googling, every thought glazed in shock. Gabi had the presence of mind to act. "Was there anything there?"

"One big thing." Gabi turned the laptop to me, with a document pulled up. "Soph had a burner app on her phone."

Gabi's bedroom went blurry around me. That's what I needed: proof that the pills weren't a one-night aberration. The reality was concrete, solid and painful to crash against.

"Keep going?" Gabi asked. I nodded, numb. "The only exchange was at 10:14 p.m. Almost definitely the person who gave her the drugs."

The blood in my face drained downward—to my core, to my feet. "How do you know?"

The screenshot pasted into a document had only three lines:

Are you still coming??

Yeah I'm here, where are you

Basement!

The number wasn't saved. "Area code 405. Where's that?"

"Oklahoma. Doesn't matter. It's another burner app or pre-paid phone. I tried to call it, search it—nothing."

"Then how does this tell us anything?" I asked, though I understood before the question fully left my mouth. "Soph hadn't seen the person earlier than 10:14 p.m."

"Exactly. And I was with her for most of the night. So, everyone I remember talking to with her? Even saying hi to? Can't be our guy."

"But couldn't this be from anyone? Not necessarily someone who gave her drugs."

"Then why use a burner app?"

I stared at the screen. Even seeing those six words, typed by the thumbs of Sophie's cause of death, made me furious. How could I have this trace of them and not a single bit of useable information? "Did you tell the police?"

"Of course." Gabi pushed the computer over, nodding at me to scroll for myself. I was staring at four columns: *People We Saw, There/ Did Not See Them, Definitely Not There, Could Have Been There.* "But the last column is almost infinite, you know? They think it could have been a total stranger who waltzed into the party unnoticed."

"But you don't," I guessed. Even I knew Warner's back-to-school party wasn't an open-door rager. It was an annual bash meant for their graduating class.

"The party was probably fifty, sixty people. Mostly kids in my grade. If the person were a total stranger, wouldn't Sophie have met them outside? Why have them come in? Needless risk."

I drank in the *People We Saw* column, which seemed to be a large chunk of Ingleside's junior class. Warner Evans, of course. Names that sounded vaguely familiar—her eighth-grade crush, a slacker lab partner from last year. Claire Hilson, the West Grove girl who had texted me that night. Christian Dailey. None of them hurt her.

"I've saved every post I could find from that night." Below the lists, Gabi had pasted photos from the party. The first few confirmed the people who saw Sophie. One picture featured almost a dozen girls in her grade. Some were not-very-subtly hiding spiked seltzer, others posed with lips pouted. Not Soph, on either count. She was grinning in the middle next to Gabi, who had barely pulled up her mouth.

I pressed one hand to my chest, where my heart threatened to flop out like a fish, dead and bloodied. All these people saw her that night, and I was across town, in the corner of Lincoln's couch, oblivious.

"Anyway," Gabi said. "Here's what I've got so far."

There/Did Not See Them

Brooks Van Doren (InCDS, soccer, Student Council)
Zoe Walsh (InCDS, Student Council president, swimming, Art Club)
Ben Ashby (InCDS, cross-country/track)
Jenny Lisk (St. Anne's), dating Sunita Kumar (InCDS, volleyball, Model UN)
Photo #5 White girl, black shaggy hair
Photo #6 White person, black shirt with rectangle symbol (?), birthmark

She'd accomplished all this while I lay in my bedroom, folding into myself like a paper star. My first selfish thought was that she should have looped me in. But when? A quick aside at the funeral? A text message afterward like, *Hey, by the way: I'm obsessively isolating when and how Sophie got into pills.*

"Here's where I'm hoping you can help me." Gabi taps the screen. "Any idea who this is? I'm thinking maybe West Grove."

The image only barely included the person in question. She was to the right of the frame, her face partially blocked by someone with his back to the camera. I could make out one side of a shaggy haircut—jet black, very punk rock—and a white tank top.

"Sorry it's so grainy," Gabi said. "Best I could do."

A feeling prickled at me. Maybe she worked somewhere I'd been—a coffee shop or grocery store. The association I felt was . . . somber. A little surprised. Somewhere crowded. "I can't place her. I don't know everyone at West Grove, obviously, but her hair is pretty distinctive."

Gabi nodded, expecting this. "And the last one's basically useless."

Picture #6 showed a girl kissing a guy's cheek. In the background, a slightly blurry person walked past. Black shirt, rectangle with some dots inside near-center. The one visible arm had pale pink skin and, above the elbow, a small birthmark.

"Huh," I muttered. "I take it the person hasn't shown up anywhere else?"

"Nope. I looked through everything, and there's no T-shirt like this."

"And you've never seen the shirt or birthmark at school?" I asked. But before Gabi could answer, I muttered, "Uniforms."

"Well, I see people outside of school and at soccer. But no."

A chill swept through me. There was something ghostly about the streak of color, this faceless stranger passing through a party unnoticed. "Shit."

"I know," Gabi said. "I also have some videos on my phone—stuff people posted from that night that I saved. Wanna take a look?"

Only more than anything. While Gabi navigated to the videos, I leaned back on a cumulus of pillows, trying to sort all the new information. "Wait. What if Soph already had the drugs on her? And the text, though very weird, is a coincidence?"

"She didn't," Gabi said, readjusting her bun. "I looked through her bag early in the night."

"Could've been hidden. Interior pocket."

"I turned that thing inside out." Before I could ask, Gabi added, "She said there was a tampon in there somewhere, but I couldn't find it."

"Tiny pills would fit in the pocket of her shorts, though."

Gabi's skeptical look could wither a plant. "True."

"Did you tell the cops you looked through her bag?" I asked.

"Yep. They said to let them handle it. But they did give me a brochure for a local support group."

I stared at her for a moment. "Well."

I scanned through the phone videos while Gabi kept scrolling through her laptop documents, noting when I asked a question she hadn't considered. My thoughts became a swirl of laughing, drunken faces. Two guys play-wrestling, the junior girls posing around Gabi and Soph, a girl trying to chug a beer and failing, liquid slopping down a tie-dye shirt—all tame and ordinary, and still I raged. The spoiled nothingness of it all.

Less than two months ago, Sophie was alive. How could that possibly be? Gabi and I had since warped into fun house mirror images of the girls we'd been—wobbly at the edges, something sinister in the distortion.

"Have you slept in the past few weeks?" I asked quietly.

"No," Gabi said. "Have you?"

Touché. "So, what next?"

She rubbed a line down her forehead with one finger. "I don't know. Everyone knows Soph was my best friend, so I can't do much asking around without tipping people off that I'm digging."

"Is there anyone else you trust with this stuff?"

"Catherine," Gabi said. I knew the name from Sophie's mentions, both in-person and online. "She's a good friend, but I don't want to involve her."

Gabi had a robust, solitary investigation going, and I felt the surge of competitiveness that pushed me to get to someone else's level. "I'll search for Soph's journal."

She whirled to me, pained with hope. "Yeah?"

"I've been putting off going over there." Sometimes, I caught myself imagining Sophie in her bedroom—still there, just across town. If nothing else, I needed closure. "But I'll do it. And I'll text you right away if there's—"

"No," Gabi said quickly. "I mean, text me about hanging out, and then you can come over here. I'd rather not leave a trail."

I studied her face—pursed lips and worried brows. "It's not illegal to look for something of Sophie's."

"I know," she said. "It's just how I am."

Sophie had always made Gabi sound steadfast and extremely careful, two traits that seemed more intense than the cool girl I'd observed. But maybe that was just it: total awareness. Of how she was being perceived, of what the risks and rewards were. A girl who had reason to be careful, as ugly rumors had shown just this week.

Gabi held out a small external drive. "Everything from the phone. I feel like I've exhausted it, but maybe you'll see something new."

My hand closed over it, tight. "Thanks."

I climbed down from her bed, even though I desperately wanted to stay. Gabi was the only other person burning with anger and loss. I wanted to huddle near it like warmth.

In an afternoon, Gabi had changed the shape of my grief, molded it into something useful. Something I could aim. "Do something else this week, yeah? Other than this. Even if it's just taking a walk or something."

"Okay." Her face reflected the blue light of the screen, and I closed the door behind me.

On the drive home, a focused, sweaty intensity fell over me. My heart pumped like I was a half-mile past the starting line. Eyes forward. One step at a time. Legs settling in for the long haul.

Senior Year

Several weeks into the school year, I spend a Saturday morning watching students race across the school grounds. The Ingleside cross-country course wends from open air to tree canopy, through the forest that brackets one side of campus. The leaves flicker with orange and red, which I note for my *Insider* article.

Ben Ashby flies into first place as if he has a rival on his heels. In fact, no one gets near him. Classroom Ben is mild-mannered, but this boy, with his perfect form and unflagging focus, smolders with intensity. My view of him has shifted, ever so slightly.

His girlfriend greets him afterward with, I assume, Ben's dad—a man as tall and lanky as his son, though with darker hair and a beard. I'm watching, waiting, even as I speak to other runners. When Ben strolls toward the water cooler, I make my move.

"Hey, Ben." In first period, I've managed only brief chit-chat about homework. "Great race."

He turns to me. "Oh, hey, Hannah. Thanks."

"Have a minute for a newbie reporter?" I hold up my notebook with a shy smile.

"Sure."

"First question," I say stiffly, as if reciting from notes. "Are negative splits always part of your strategy?"

There's a light behind his eyes that isn't on in class or walking the hallways. "You did your research."

"Eh." I smile, with a shrug. "I ran a half last year."

"You're a runner?" he asks, clearly cheered. There's a slight and charming gap between his front teeth. "Why didn't you join the team?"

"Oh, I don't know. It was always something I did with my best friend. And then—"

"You moved here," he finishes. "I get it. I was the new kid sophomore year."

A personal detail, unprovoked. "Oh, really? What brought you here?"

"My mom's job."

I ask how he got into running (his dad's a runner) and what his training is like (intense and always outside, weather permitting). And then, still with my even-toned fledgling reporter voice, "Have you ever been injured?"

"Not seriously," he says. "I've been lucky. Strength training, being conscious of your gait, good shoes—I think every factor counts."

"Agreed. Well, thank you so much for your time! And congrats again."

"Sure. See you Monday."

He heads back toward Violet, the girlfriend, and I pocket every detail for later examination. Someone will slip up eventually, with a tiny detail. If the machine is delicate enough, even a speck of dust will stall it.

Next stop: parking lot, where I'll wait for another match—this one inside the building—to be done. I text with my dad for a while to kill time, but the debate team still hasn't emerged. I wait in my car, seat pushed back and knees on the wheel, and I glare at Dailey's old truck, parked beside me.

The first few mornings after Dailey's confrontation, I walked into school expecting heads to swivel toward me: the girl who hid that she was Sophie Abbott's cousin. But Dailey didn't say a word—not to the gossiping masses and not to me. On day four, I made an intentionally flimsy argument in Gov and waited for him to roast me. He didn't even glance back, and then I knew for sure. This was a game of chicken. Whose curiosity will make them fold?

I thought it would be me. The same question echoed around my head: Why did he bring up Ben Ashby? But then Dailey caught up to me after class yesterday and said, "I could use your help on the, uh . . . project . . . we talked about."

No hello, no barely restrained glee in having something over me. He asked, and he waited. When I wanted to know what kind of help, he smiled and said, "The in-person kind."

So, here I am. Meeting where and when he asked. It's possible to acknowledge a clever play and resent it at the same time, and I do.

Even before yesterday, I've been studying Dailey's motivation from every angle I can think of. What does he stand to gain? Is he protecting someone? How much information can I safely hedge, in order to hear what he knows? Does he actually know anything at all?

When I let myself consider that he's telling the truth, I admit the temptation of Dailey as a teammate. There's no one better at poking holes in my way of thinking. Infuriating on the debate stage. Helpful when I am trying desperately to avoid mistakes.

He finally emerges, chatting with someone before they part ways. In my rearview mirror, I watch the moment he spots my car. His walk slows, like he's savoring the view. In ignoring me for two straight weeks, he gambled, and here I am—the payoff. I climb out.

"You showed." He sounds impressed with himself.

"Incisive as always."

Dailey smiles like this is all a weekend game of tennis and not everything I care about, dangled in front of me as bait. "Hostile even when I'm trying to help you."

"I thought you needed *my* help. So, let's hear it."

"All right, here's the deal," he says, stepping closer. "I'm going up to Yardley's campus right now to follow a long-shot lead. If it pans out, you let me help with what you're doing."

My heart skitters inside my chest. "What do you mean, a long-shot lead?"

"A guy at Yardley. Over the years, I've heard soccer guys talk about 'getting pizza from JJ'—that's how Jordy and I both remember it. Might just be weed, but it's definitely not just pizza. I figured we might as well try to rule him out."

I feel monstrous in this moment, ready to claw information from Dailey. If his lead is somehow connected to one of mine— if Person A intersects with someone from List B—I might have my answer. "So . . . I'm tagging along for what, exactly?"

Dailey pulls his phone from his pocket, glancing down.

"Well, he should be getting off work in the next half hour. He really does work at a pizza place, and—"

"You're going to confront him?"

"Nah. Just see where he goes after. Maybe try to get a last name somehow." Dailey nods toward the truck. "But I'm not sure if he walks or drives home from work. So, if I follow in the car and you jump out on foot, that should cover our bases."

I want to poke holes in this plan, but the thrill of new information is too strong. I'm in, and Dailey knows it. "I have more questions."

"Yeah, I've met you," he calls over the truck, tugging off his blazer.

Dammit. I stand there for a moment, just to be defiant, and then I yank open the passenger door.

The interior smells powerfully minty, like gum that has warmed in the sun. My view of Christian Dailey is so much imagination—the gaps filled in between former crush and current adversary. There's a strangeness to knowing, for a fact, that his car smells like toothpaste and binder plastic.

Despite our usual, hair-trigger dynamic, we stay quiet for the first few minutes, both adjusting to how quickly things have changed. Or perhaps the inside of a vehicle feels too small and combustible. We both need a moment to confirm our personalities fit safely inside.

I despise having to think fast, with less information than I want. This was an intentional fastball from Dailey, but I come back to my same instinct about him. He's an annoying person—a self-righteous show-off who was a real chickenshit to me freshman year—but he's not a *bad* person.

I would literally never admit this out loud.

When it comes to Sophie, my best guess is that Dailey hates the not-knowing as much as I do. It's the nagging feeling that you're a turn or two away from the lock clicking into place.

"So," I say, at the first stoplight. "How do you know what JJ looks like and when he'll be working?"

Dailey gives me a sidelong glance. "I don't have to reveal my methods."

My money's on Dailey popping in for a slice of pizza, scoping out name tags or eavesdropping on employees talking to each other. Maybe he called the pizza shop, posing as JJ forgetting his schedule. Or maybe Dailey simply struck up a conversation. He can be charming when he wants to be, bending his approach until he finds the connection. I have been both the mark and a witness.

"So, do you remember which soccer players you heard this guy's name from?" I say it in a more conversational tone, but it's not fooling him.

"I've answered, like, six of your questions," Dailey says. "Tit for tat, MacLaren."

I clear my throat and say, very calmly, "I have a short list of people that I'm keeping an eye on. It's based off two main things: someone gave Sophie pills at the party and whoever it was didn't see her before ten o'clock."

There: confirmation of three foundational things. Chewing on that should keep him happy for a while.

"How could you know that?" Dailey asks. I rest comfortably in my seat, unwilling to do the legwork for him. "A text? It would have to be. But then you'd know the number it came from . . . Unless it was a false number or a prepaid phone. Huh."

I tip my head, trying to look unaffected. "There you go."

The light turns green, and Dailey says, "I've heard JJ's name a few times, mostly from seniors last year."

The name is new to me. Of course, I'd wondered about the greater network of where drugs were coming from. But I had no foothold to even begin the climb.

"You've talked to Gabi," Dailey realizes out loud. It's an easy deduction. There's no other way I could know who Sophie did or didn't see that night. "That's great. I wanted to talk to her first, but—"

"No," I say quickly. "We're not on speaking terms. Believe me, she doesn't want in on this anymore."

"Anymore," Dailey repeats. He looks away from the road to stare at me. "Geez. Do you have bad blood with every person in your life?"

"No," I say, so defensively that I immediately regret it. Part of me wants to tell him that Gabi lied to me about something unforgivable, but that would beg more nosy questions. One slow breath through my nose, and I try again. "Why did you bring up Ben Ashby?"

"Ah. Well, I saw you talking to him one morning," he says. "But mostly, I was at the party. I remember him getting there."

I sit up, too invested to play it cool. "Who was he with?"

"No one, which is why I noticed. He's usually super-glued to his girlfriend, but he was alone."

In my mind, I project out of the truck. Oh my God. I've wondered that for almost a year now. It proves nothing at all, but it's interesting. "Who did he talk to?"

"That, I don't know," Dailey says. "I just saw him walk in, kind of late. He got there ten, maybe fifteen minutes before I left. Which is weird *and* it lines up with your info."

We settle back into the silence, both of us graphing the new information on to our own mental charts. This is tentative camaraderie—certainly not trust. I know Dailey too well for that. He's quick, and he's believable. What makes him great at debating makes him a faulty ally.

Despite his usual, charged-up frequency, Dailey drives with a casual calm. He keeps one hand on the wheel, one on the gearshift like he learned to drive on a manual. The radio is set to the local college station, playing an indie song I recognize for its drifting, mellow strings.

When we near Yardley's campus, I dig in my bag for my sunglasses. I flip down the mirror to see how much of my face they cover. They're not much, as disguises go.

"Do you like looking like that?" Dailey asks.

I spin to him, my view now sepia-toned. "What is that—some kind of negging?"

He grips the wheel harder. "I *meant* that I know the new look keeps anyone from placing you as Sophie's cousin. I just didn't know if you also prefer it, and I wondered. Sue me."

I'd feel bad for whirling at him, claws out, except that he's conditioned me for just that.

"It's both," I tell him, in a thank-you-very-much tone. "I feel . . . very far from the person I was before last August. It helps to look different too."

"Yeah, I get that." He sounds a little surprised that I told him the truth. After a moment, he adds, "You don't seem that different to me."

He has to be a know-it-all, even about my most interior self. It's almost funny. Though I suppose, to him, my hair color is different, but my animosity is still crystal clear.

The Yardley campus remains as quaint as I remember—old-fashioned lampposts and rows of shops. It's like a miniature Christmas village, if every other building was a dive bar. Dailey slides into the last available parking spot, giving us a decent angle on the pizza shop.

We're silent for first few minutes, ready to pounce. *Breathe.*

"So," Dailey says, when he begins to miss the sound of his own voice. "This works out and you'll tell me who else is on your list?"

I flick my eyes up to the ceiling of his truck. He already knows about Ben Ashby, which is honestly more than I'd prefer. "I'll tell you one additional name."

An irritated silence stretches between us, tense on both sides.

The shop door swings, and I rocket forward. But it's a girl, balancing a single slice on a paper plate.

Dailey clears his throat. "Obviously you suspect Warner. Wait—no. He saw Sophie early in the night."

"He's not on the list," I admit. "But I do wonder if he has information. You know him, right?"

"Eh. Only in the context of soccer."

I sigh loudly, exasperated. Dailey is the type of person who thinks he's an infallible judge of character. I want to hear those judgments for once, and he's reticent?

"And?" I prompt. "Does that give you any insight?"

"He's a really nice guy." Dailey shrugs. "Team player—good sport. He does take it hard when he messes up or misses an opportunity. More confident on the field than in the classroom."

"Family?"

"His parents seem great—always enthusiastic and nice at

games. Warner's older brother graduated Ingleside last year, and he's here at Yardley now. His older sister is too."

"Know anything about her?"

"I know that she graduated the year before I started Ingleside and that she's gorgeous. That's about it."

He's right. Audrey Evans has mile-long legs and a cascade of glossy hair, the same tiger-lily orange as Warner's. "So, you—the High King of Opinions—have no further thoughts on Warner?"

"I'm not the one withholding, MacLaren." He gives me a pointed look. Then, shaking his head, "I just don't know anymore. If someone would have asked me about Sophie, I *never* would have . . ."

Guessed she was becoming increasingly addicted to prescription painkillers. There's another tic in the column of Sophie rocking Dailey's know-it-all worldview. "Yeah. I know."

We're quiet for at least two minutes, though I can feel him glance over at me occasionally.

"Were you really on a movie set in Canada with your dad?" he asks.

"Yep."

He snorts. "Sparkling conversationalist."

"Closed-ended questioner."

The criticism lands like an invitation, and I scowl at myself. Dailey clears his throat. "Okay, then. How were the museums?"

God, this is what gets me. He *knows* things about me, same as I know his mom bakes him a German chocolate birthday cake every year and that he made a PowerPoint to convince his parents to adopt a dog. The summer we met, talking to Dailey felt like exploring an old house, full of nooks and surprising turns. I sensed him doing the same, pulling open the drawers in my mind. So, yes, I'm tempted to bar his entry out of spite. "One of the best parts of my summer. I saw First Nations art, Emily Carr, smaller galleries."

"Do you go alone?" he asks, and I flinch behind my glasses—pathetic, loner Hannah. Dailey seems to sense it, though, and he reroutes. "I mean, is your dad into art? Or do you prefer museum visits solo?"

Oh. I stare very hard at the pizza place's door, like I can conjure JJ out. "I do like to go alone, but I like to go with my dad, too. He doesn't mess with the energy."

"Yeah," Dailey says, after a moment. "I'm like that at history museums. I hate feeling like I have to rush because no one else wants to read all the placards."

He likes history because it's full of clues and patterns, often hidden by agendas. Another thing I know about Christian Dailey.

"That's him," Dailey says, urgently. The guy is white and skinny, with ruddy brown hair. He walks in a kind of bouncy way, his upper body curved. I want to leap from the car and grab him by the shoulders. In my peripheral vision, Dailey turns to me. "You good?"

I unbuckle my seat belt. "Meet back here if—"

"Yeah, go."

I'm on my feet, rocketed into a brisk walk. I look down at my phone as if I'm furiously texting. JJ walks past two more storefronts, then turns down an alleyway between the old buildings.

The walkway is mostly side doors and dumpsters, and I weave past the smell of frying oil and rot. He's an ambler, this guy, so I close in quickly with my nervous speed. When a waiter on a smoke break greets JJ, I slow my stride but still have to pass him. My shoulder is inches from his, and on some level, I'm surprised he doesn't turn to face me—the pull of my suspicion strong enough to compel him.

Emerging back into daylight, I lean against the building and hold my phone to my ear.

"Yeah," I say to no one. I can feel my pulse through my whole body, jugular to feet. "Uh-huh. Just take a left. I'm sort of between two trees, behind the building. How did the thing go? Mm-hmm. Yeah, I figured."

When JJ emerges, he makes a right turn onto the car-lined street. I make myself count to ten, so I've barely stepped forward when he reaches a maroon sedan, his key held out.

Shit. I don't think his license plate will help much, but I get close enough to snap a picture before he maneuvers out of the spot. He's losing me, and he didn't even know he was being followed. I breathe in, fighting a scream of frustration, when Dailey's truck noses up to a stop sign. He's on a street perpendicular to the main drag.

I pinwheel my arm toward the car, frantic.

Dailey turns after him, and my adrenaline whooshes in every tiny blood vessel. My legs ache as if I've had to halt midsprint, the energy desperate to burn. I last a minute, trying to calm my breathing, and then I call Dailey's phone.

"Hold on, he's turning," Dailey says.

I'm so charged up that I could rip trees from the ground, but I start walking back toward the storefronts. "Turning into where?"

"An apartment complex."

"Can you follow?"

"Of course I can." Then, muttering, "Give me *some* credit."

"I meant: is there a gate with a passcode or something?"

"Not that kinda place," Dailey assures me. "And . . . he's parked. I'll hang here another minute to make sure he goes in, and then swing back to get you."

The call beeps out, and I want to chuck my phone against the nearest building. Instead, I stalk back to a patio table and stare down the length of the street. Students in Yardley gear stroll by, bent over their phones or walking in tightly knit pairs.

Every minute grinds like a sustained record scratch.

There's a chance I just set eyes on the reason Sophie had pills. Of course, there's also a chance this guy had nothing to do with it, and we just followed an innocent stranger. But if I can figure out who he is? If I can find his social media and determine if someone from my list already follows him? This could be everything.

When Dailey finally cruises up, I nearly dive into the passenger's seat. "What happened?"

Dailey glances over his shoulder to his blind spot before pulling out. "He got into the apartment with his own keys, so I'm guessing it's his place. He might not leave again for hours, so unless you're up for a stakeout . . ."

"Did you notice the mailbox?" I asked. "Sometimes, with apartments, there are those metal lock boxes labeled with last names."

Dailey lifts his eyebrows. "Good point. Back we go."

The apartment complex is a two-story, mid-century deal, as outdated and impermanent as a motel. "Which one did he go into?"

"Right here," Dailey says, slowing to a stop. "First floor, on the left."

"Back in a sec." From here, I can tell that each apartment

has its own mailbox, and I get close enough to see that there's no label. Mailbox tampering is a federal crime, so the plan ends here.

However. I glance around the parking lot until my eyes land on the maroon car. Sometimes, my mom checks the mailbox as she leaves the house. Coupon booklets and other junk—all with her name—wind up in the passenger's seat.

JJ's front seat has wrappers strewn across the floor, a wad of flannel shirt, some old hiking boots. But in the console, beside a tin of mints, his face peeks out from a faded university ID. John J. Russo.

I clamp down a vindicated yelp, so thrilled that I almost raise my arms up in triumph. I'm so thrilled, in fact, that I almost miss it—an open cardboard box in the back seat.

It's full of black T-shirts, each with a smiley face encased in rectangle instead of a circle.

"Anything?" Christian asks, once I return.

"Russo," I tell him, still dazed. "His last name is Russo."

Junior Year

In the days after my visit to Gabi's house, I studied Gabi's flash drive. Lincoln let me choose our Saturday night movie, but I couldn't hear the dialogue—only questions bouncing around my mind. When I attempted my math homework, I saw names instead of numbers. When I tried to sleep, the party photos screened on my eyelids. Two guys roughhousing, a sea of smiles next to Sophie, Jenny Lisk chugging a beer badly, repeat. Did she do that and then find Sophie to pass off pills? The questions were corrosive.

I jogged to the library in cool autumn air and searched the names on Gabi's list, desperate to understand them better. Almost every return came from school websites—articles about service awards and field hockey championships. All the golden children and their golden trophies.

Gabi had firsthand knowledge—context, memories, photos. I had nothing but the chance to find Sophie's journal.

———————

"Take your time," my mom said quietly.

We sat in the driveway, staring at Sophie's house.

"Where's her car?" I asked. Sophie carpooled and rode her bike often but drove a ten-year-old hybrid when necessary. Ginny and Andrew had money, but not buy-a-sixteen-year-old-an-electric-car money.

I could feel my mom studying me. "In the garage."

That made sense. It would chip away at my sanity to see Sophie's car waiting every time I got home. And Maddie wouldn't even have her permit for two years—why keep the car around, taunting them? "Will they sell it?"

"I assume so," my mom said. "When everything calms down a little."

My mom had already assured me that Sophie's room was untouched, other than Ginny and Maddie taking a few special stuffed animals and pictures. So, it's not like I'd be walking into a half-erased space that used to be whole and hers. But honestly, entering the room without her seemed just as daunting. How ridiculous, that her possessions outlasted her.

Now down to the election wire, Andrew left before dawn to visit Lions Clubs, bingos in church basements, and fundraisers in six-bedroom houses. I wondered how he brought Sophie and grief and opioids into his campaigning, but no answer would have felt good to hear.

"Okay," I decided, and I unclicked my seat belt.

When my mom opened the front door, we were immediately

greeted with Andrew's face, blown up three times its actual size on a poster. He'd always had JFK hair, but in recent years, a band of gray wrapped around like Caesar's laurel wreath. His smile said: *Let's grab a beer, but don't forget—I have an Ivy League degree.*

"Good Lord," my mom said, under her breath, and I managed a laugh. Anything I ever borrowed from Sophie smelled like this house—that impossible-to-place, totally specific scent. Steam-cleaned carpets and three-wick vanilla candles. I clenched my teeth, willing myself not to cry.

"Gin?" my mom called.

Ginny's home design stretched the concept of neutral colors into a full palette—a lifestyle. Every room was painted French cream with birch-colored curtains, champagne linen chairs, rugs like swirls of sandy beach. As a kid, I assumed this was the height of elegance, a place where no spills would even be considered.

"Hello, hello," Ginny called, emerging from the kitchen. She looked the same as ever—or she should have, anyway. The paper doll parts were all there: smooth blond hair, nails like tidy pearls, a tight smile. But sadness clung, made her eyes look different. It changed the light around her.

"Sorry about the hubbub," she said, waving at the enormous Andrew Abbott face. "He has an office, but we still seem to wind up being headquarters."

She didn't seem sorry at all. This was a welcome reprieve—a project.

"Sure you don't want to knock on doors?" Ginny asked me. "Call it an internship for a political campaign on your college applications?"

I opened my mouth and closed it, hesitating.

"I know, I know," she said, with a smile. "You don't like politics."

Not exactly. I ruminated on politics in an exhaustive, exhausting way—how governance touches and connects, helps or ruins, everything. I didn't need to devote more time to it.

"Well, you're welcome to go up," Ginny said. "Please take anything special to you. She'd want that."

I swallowed, struggling against the lump in my throat. Ginny's this-is-hard-but-I'm-okay act was almost convincing, but I knew better. I'd heard my mom's voice two walls away, answering the phone at three a.m. Once, I tiptoed down the hall and crouched by the door. My mom's voice repeated, quiet and sure: *Oh, Gin. I know. No, I want you to tell me. Keep telling me.*

"You want company?" my mom asked, touching my arm.

I shook my head.

She made the kind of insistent eye contact that belied her genetic relation to Virginia Abbott. "I'll check on you in a bit."

On the way up the stairs, I tried to prepare myself. Sophie's walls and furniture were white, but Ginny let her choose the bedding—sky blue with clouds drifting across. Given total freedom, Sophie would have had an accent wall, photos tacked up all over, mismatched pillows, a colorful rug.

It was a silly, devastating thing to mourn: I'd never know what grown-up Sophie's room would look like, made entirely of her own vision.

Beyond the door, the full sensory experience flooded in. Ginny had certainly cleaned up, and that was a relief. If clothes were strewn all over, I'd expect Sophie to waltz in any minute. I inhaled the magnolia scent that lingered years after a body spritz spill.

I'd lived so much of my life in this room, and that part was over now.

For a moment, I let myself run a hand across clothes, books, the crystals on her windowsill. Eventually, I pulled her beloved denim jacket from the closet, stacked a few special books near it, and topped the pile with a framed photo of us. *Soph*, I thought at the picture. *Why didn't you tell me?* Soccer trophies; science fair ribbons; a Polaroid of her and Gabi from homecoming.

Then I shut the door. I hurried to the desk, riffling through school papers dating back to elementary school, but no journals. I searched her closet, digging in old backpacks, an empty suitcase, a pile of shoes meant for donation.

Even if I couldn't find the journal, I wanted evidence— not even of drugs, specifically. I wanted proof that Sophie had hidden major things from me. How could I understand what happened if I didn't fully understand who she *was*?

I looked in her nightstand drawer, under the bed, in her reading chair's cushions. I studied every spine on her bookshelf in case she kept the journal there. Nothing.

"You looking for pills?" a voice asked from the doorway. I startled up, hand flying to my chest. Maddie, who had silently pushed the door open a few inches, looked at me with sympathetic eyes.

"What?" I managed. "No—why?"

"My mom did," she said quietly. "The day after the toxicology report, she tore apart the closet, the bed, every drawer. My dad called your mom to come over and help her calm down."

I struggled to imagine my aunt frantic, out of control. "I was hoping to find some pictures of me and Soph on her laptop. Any chance that's around?"

"Yeah. My parents technically own it, so tech support helped them log in." Maddie had always taken after Andrew's side of the family, with darker hair and narrower face. But the eyes were Sophie's—twinkly, squinty when she really smiled.

"Bunny Blue and Greta are in my room," she continued, nodding down the hall. "And Mom took Sophie's T-shirts to have a quilt made. But other than that, let me know if there's something you want."

"I will." Part of me considered asking about the journal, but how could I possibly justify that? Besides, I couldn't bear Maddie's practical distribution of her sister's things for even one more second. "You doing okay?"

Maddie lifted one shoulder.

"Yeah. Same. What about your parents?"

"Who knows? Dad's never here. All election, all the time. Mom too, when she's not going to two workout classes a day and hovering around me. Reading every account of a parent who lost a child to opioids. She's talking about making a foundation in Sophie's name."

"I heard." And I felt tired just thinking about it.

Maddie moved to let me out of the room, and we both lingered near the banister at the top of the stairs, overlooking the foyer below. A recent Abbott family portrait smiled back at us, in subtly coordinated outfits. Maddie's photographed, six-months-ago face looked much younger than the girl beside me now.

"Can I ask you something?" I glanced over at my cousin, who nodded just once. "Did Sophie seem different this summer?"

Maddie rested her arms on the railing. "She seemed like Soph. Always with a project. Bickering with my mom, flouncing off to your house or Gabi's."

My eyes shot to the portrait above the stairs, the glint in Sophie's eyes—the peachy tone of her hair, refusing to fit into Ginny's color scheme. "Was she, like, irritable with Ginny?"

"Sure, sometimes. But my mom can be really uptight, especially compared to, like . . ."

"My mom?"

"Exactly."

I lower my voice. "Do you think the cops are getting anywhere? Or the school? Any time I ask my mom, she gives me platitudes."

Maddie sighed. "Based on my eavesdropping, I think the cops have no idea—how would they? Sophie could have been doing anything. I think the school is mostly worried about how it makes them look."

"Yeah," I said. "Sounds right."

Ginny, to my surprise, sent the laptop home with me. I promised to bring it back quickly, and she gave me a sad smile. To her, perhaps the computer was like the car—a shiny, painful reminder of who was not there to use it.

On the way home, the pile of Sophie's things in my lap, I looked at my mom. "You would tell me if any new information came in, right?"

She stayed quiet for too long, when a simple yes would have sufficed. "It's been theories at best. Ginny hoped that someone would send an anonymous email, explaining what they knew. But it's unlikely. Fear of litigation and all that, though that's not where Ginny's coming from."

"Are the cops treating this like a crime investigation?"

She glanced over at me, then back at the road. "Well, the police are always trying to figure out the drug supply chain, I suppose. I know they took witness statements, and obviously, there was a toxicology report."

That, I knew. My mom had to tell me exactly what was in Sophie's system for me to believe it. Oxycodone, laced with fentanyl.

"But I don't think it's considered an open investigation. Oh, honey. I know it's so hard not to know," my mom added. "We all feel it. But knowing won't—"

"Bring her back," I finished.

But trying to find answers brought *me* back into the world. I hugged my pile of mementos closer.

— — — — — — —

By my next visit to Gabi's house, purple mums had appeared on the front porch. I'd spent the days before wading through Sophie's laptop—mostly her schoolwork and cute graphics for pro-green social media efforts. There were older photos on her laptop than on her phone, which made me cry and did not help in any practical way. Her viewer history on YouTube was made up of vegetarian cooking channels and montages of favorite TV couples' best moments.

"I wondered if she kept a journal on the laptop," I told Gabi. "But I've opened every file."

Sophie had no consistent naming structure for school documents, either. It was maddening, but I'd clicked them all, AstronomyPaper3.doc to ZoraNealeHurstonQs.doc.

"And she definitely got a physical journal as a gift from our coach," Gabi murmured. "Before her ankle surgery."

We sat parallel on her bed, legs stretched out, as Gabi scoured caches and clouds. I eagerly pulled up the lists and photos, ready to revisit with fresh eyes. "Does everyone on this list have money?"

Gabi's typing stopped. "You thinking about motive?"

"Just trying to see the big picture."

"Brooks, yes. Zoe, yes," she said. "Ben Ashby's on a scholarship, so probably not. I don't know about Jenny Lisk."

I nodded, and we returned to silent focus. As I stared at the *There/Did Not See Them* list, one name would begin flashing. I zoomed in on pictures, studying the faces in backgrounds, cataloging the smallest details.

When I scrolled back to the shaggy, black-haired girl, I still didn't know her. But I'd studied the pictures well enough to recognize the chambray shirt in the frame—worn by Christian Dailey that night. He provided the context my memory needed.

Yes. That day was a tilt-a-whirl of memories, flashes of imagery as I spun out. But I could finally focus the lens. "I know where I've seen her."

Gabi jolted up. "Are you serious?"

"She came to Sophie's visitation. With Christian Dailey." I reached to my shoulder, twisting the end of my ponytail. My fingertips felt tingly, almost painful. "Which is . . . extremely weird. Are you one hundred percent sure Sophie saw Dailey that night?"

"A thousand percent sure. They were chatting while I talked Model UN with Jordy Green. This girl was not around." Gabi tapped her chin, right at the spot with the dimple. "Well, that's great. I'll ask Dailey if that's his girlfriend or what."

"You'll just ask him?"

She looked at me like I'd asked a far odder question. "Yeah?"

"And tip him off that you're looking into the party? What if Dailey's involved—or covering for her?"

Gabi gave me a look of extreme skepticism. "Dailey? The guy lives to point out wrongdoing. Believe me—I've had history class with him."

It was easy to imagine Dailey picking arguments, even with a teacher. Obviously, I could see him calling out a textbook's bias. But when it's personal—a girlfriend? Hard to say.

"He must be so annoying in class," I muttered, mostly as a little indulgence to myself.

Gabi snorted. "Sure, when he's arguing just to argue. But sometimes it's nice to have a squeaky wheel calling out bullshit. Half the faculty loves him for it, half would probably love to rescind his scholarship."

I blinked at her, sure I'd misheard. "He's not on scholarship."

Gabi was back to her computer, not even looking at me. "Yeah, he is. Lots of kids are."

Surely, there was a time when Dailey had told me, directly, that his rich family could afford Ingleside. Obviously they could—he went there. "Huh."

"But I won't ask him," Gabi said. "If that's your gut feeling."

"I'll find her name without Dailey," I said, reaching for Gabi's phone. Dailey didn't post often: Jordy on the soccer bus with an inside-joke caption, a friend posing with a statue near the Inner Harbor, Dailey cradling a dopey, mid-sized dog. That last one hit me square in the chest—I'd seen photos of that dog when he was a puppy.

And bingo. A trio of friends tagged at a state park, including that girl, black hair in a fringy ponytail. I hovered over his image, hoping for a tag. Kinstamatic's account was private, but the bio read: *kinsley / hhs softball*. Huh. His best friend. He'd mentioned her at the library years ago.

"Her name's Kinsley, and she goes to Hathaway," I announced.

Gabi typed *Kinsley softball* into Hathaway's website, and ahoy, a school newspaper article about a game last spring. Catcher Mary Kinsley, a sophomore at the time.

The other girl in the state park photo was a petite white girl—Mia, who seemed to be Dailey's girlfriend based on other photos. Beside her was a tall Black guy wearing a ballcap. His profile was private without a bio, but the username OmarLax9 helped. Lincoln probably knew him, as lacrosse seemingly connected every player in the state.

There/Did Not See
Brooks Van Doren (InCDS, soccer)
Zoe Walsh (InCDS, Student Council, swimming, Art Club)
Ben Ashby (InCDS, cross-country/track)
Jenny Lisk (St. Anne's), dating Sunita Kumar (InCDS, volleyball)
Photo #5 Mary Kinsley (HHS, softball)
Photo #6 White person, black shirt with rectangle symbol (?), birthmark

"Mystery T-shirt person," Gabi muttered, "is really starting to piss me off."

Senior Year

"You are a *saint*," Zoe says, sinking into her chair at the lunch table. She's been coming and going a lot during this period, dealing with final preparations for Spirit Week and homecoming. She wags a clipboard at me. "Thank you—for real. You're totally forgiven for ditching the dance."

I gesture magnanimously with my spoon.

"What'd you do?" Brooks asks from across the table.

"Volunteered for the Parent Pancake Breakfast, even though it's ungodly early." I smile, basking in my small act of kindness. "And even though the last spot was the worst one."

After a moment, Warner gasps, in horror and awe. "Mascot? You didn't."

"She did," Zoe says. "Because Calvin claims, as official school mascot, that he's only responsible for after-school activities. But whatever! Hannah solved it for me!"

"So really no homecoming dance?" Warner asks me.

It's a misstep, not going. I should be in the mix, glancing at my classmates in formalwear for any telling birthmark. Alas, an iconic senior night and the revelry of Sophie's peers is more than I can stand without openly sneering. Even the excited chatter makes me grind my teeth.

I fiddle with my bangs, which need a trim. "I'm taking the SATs near Maryland U's campus that day, so my mom and I are gonna do the whole shebang—campus tour, stay overnight."

"Smart move," Brooks says. He's taking a junior girl who I'm pretty sure is not his girlfriend, though not for lack of trying on her part. "Homecoming makes what could be a regular, fun Saturday an expensive dinner date with forced dancing."

"Do you *want* to die today?" Zoe asks icily. "You're on Student Council."

"You know what I mean. It's like . . . a girl always winds up mad at me for something."

"Yes." Warner, who is taking one of his friends from Hathaway, nods. "That's definitely homecoming's fault."

Brooks makes a face. "It is when she's mad that I'm not dancing enough."

"No more homecoming slander," Zoe says, one finger held up at him. "Suck it up, buttercup."

"Can we go back to how Hannah's not even going?" Brooks asks.

I jolt up. "Hey! Mascot patrol. *Mascot.*"

In my weeks at this table, I've slowly acquired a dossier on Brooks. He'll probably go to Yardley like his alumni parents, with a business major he seems to feel neutral about. He genuinely loves soccer; he and Warner can talk about it for the entire period. He asked me about skiing in Whistler, which I demurred by being a non-skier. He's moody—no more than anyone else, just more than I expected.

Sometimes, when he lands a good joke, I almost like him. Sometimes I don't like him at all—primarily when he treats Zoe like the things she cares about are silly. The goal of my presence is to get full, human pictures of these people. I didn't expect that it would be harder and harder to hear my gut feeling.

———————

The lion mascot yields nothing. I spend an hour staring through mesh eyes, inhaling the scents of maple and synthetic fur and perspiration. Meanwhile, Ben Ashby politely meanders through the tables, refilling coffee cups. His mouth barely moves, other than to reply to thanks with, "No problem." His girlfriend spoons scrambled eggs from a silver catering dish and smiles at parents.

Most of my time is spent posing for pictures in front of an Ingleside backdrop. I immediately recognize the dad from Sophie's fundraiser—Marty Van Doren—and almost laugh. He has no idea that Virginia Abbott's aspiring lawyer niece is beside him, the fool clapping her paws to the fight song. I linger when I can, trying to eavesdrop. He seems gregarious and boring, all golf outings and Ravens banter.

Once safely in the girls' locker room, I lift the head off. Sweet relief. Even the thick, powdery deodorant smell is an improvement. I slump onto one of the slatted wood benches, not quite ready for the plaid skirt and my good student face.

"Decent of you to volunteer as ol' Rex there," a voice says from the sink. It's Violet, Ben's omnipresent girlfriend, digging into her purse until she produces a face wipe. "Want one? I had to wear the suit once. Spent the week after fighting off a chin breakout."

"Thanks." I laugh, swiping the cloth across my jaw. "This is really not my thing, but . . . Zoe's a friend."

"Ah." She nods at me in the mirror. "You're new this year, right?"

"Yeah. I'm Hannah."

"Violet."

"I've covered some cross-country meets for the *Insider*," I say. "So I've seen you around."

"Ah, with Ben." Her smile has several dimples etched on either side. "We're so annoying, I know. People always call us an old married couple."

I get the impression, with her body angled toward me, that she doesn't think it's annoying at all. In a school full of hook-ups and unrequited crushes, she's smug in her happy commitment. Still, I smile. "I guess when it works, it works."

"Exactly. We're both introverts and just, like, not the big group or partying type. Being together is an easy fit for both of us, ya know?"

I do know, but platonically, with Lincoln. He texted yesterday, and I've put off replying. Even when all he sends is a stupid meme, I feel he's checking in to see if I've crashed and burned at Ingleside. That's probably the guilt talking. "Think you and Ben will stay together in college?"

"Oh, yeah." She waves a hand like it's old hat. "We've been apart for summers while I'm at camp. Not easy, but we manage."

I already knew that, of course, which makes me feel like a dire creep. "So, have you always been at Ingleside?"

"Only since freshman year." She gives me a sympathetic look. "It can be a lot, huh?"

I raise my eyebrows like that's an understatement. Here we go. "Sure can. But I heard last year was . . . well . . ."

"The Sophie Abbott stuff?" Violet asks. She leans forward, her eyes bright with interest. "Yeah, it felt like being on a Netflix show. A girl dying, everyone pointing fingers. High drama."

She's a theater kid, but still, the glibness stuns me. As if this wasn't Sophie's extremely real and necessary life. Blinking, I manage to get out, "I bet."

"You're lucky to have missed it," she assures me. "Half the kids were panicked they'd get expelled for so much as gargling with mouthwash. The other half were on a life-is-short bender. Things have leveled out. Be glad you missed it."

Oh, I want to scream. I want to pummel her with my stupid lion paws.

"Well." I turn away to toss the face wipe in the trash. "My complexion thanks you."

"Of course," Violet says, turning to go. "Nice to meet you."

I sit on the bench for a few moments longer, half me and half creature. Ben and Violet were together last year, but she wasn't at that party. She was at her last day of theater camp—she'd posted a photo that confirmed her as Not There on Gabi's list. In all the photos and videos I've seen, Ben Ashby only appears once and, if Dailey is to be trusted, he wasn't there for long. Why go without his safety blanket girlfriend, if he's such an introvert, no-big-groups type?

This is a question I thumbtack for my next meeting with Dailey. After our trip to campus, I gave him three provisional rules: no telling people what we're doing, no talking where classmates can see us, and no specific text messages. He's stuck to them so far, probably out of stubbornness. On this trait, at least, we're in sync.

— — — — — — —

The SATs are a hurdle I clear matter-of-factly. I studied hard, nothing threw me off, and I walked away: done.

When my mom gets home, I'm lounging on the couch at weird, splayed-out angles with a bag of chips and an art class essay on my laptop.

"How was it?" she asks, though I already responded to the same question via text.

"I feel good." I pause, taking stock of myself. "Yeah. How was the game?"

"Oh, fine. They lost, but they don't really care about that." Mitch, the boyfriend, plays softball on Saturdays, and apparently, my mom likes him enough to attend these games on occasion. I'm interested in meeting him, but not in a hurried way. We've been talking about a dinner next month. "Have you eaten a proper lunch?"

I hold up the chip bag and smile, all cheeks.

"No, ma'am. Tuna sandwich sound okay?"

"Sure. Thanks." I smile, waiting for her to walk through to the kitchen, but she sits on the edge of the couch instead.

"You've been cooped up in this house like Cinderella," she says, shaking her head. "Studying, stories for journalism, college applications. And I see your light on at all hours . . ."

"I have a lot going on. I'm supposed to. It's senior year."

"And you're meeting people at that school, right?"

She's been asking this since I was in kindergarten, and my responses have rarely been encouraging. "Yes, Mom. I have a group project tomorrow afternoon."

Meeting with my not-quite-trustworthy rival to discuss next moves in my continuing deception is technically a group project, right? Right.

"A group project is not socializing! This is your last year of being a kid—go to a party! Sneak out of this house."

"How?" I joke. "If you're telling me to go."

"Buddy," she says, not joking at all.

"Mom." I mimic her serious face.

I imagine this is the face she makes when examining propagated plants. Are the roots growing normally? She sighs. "Are we gonna talk about the house, Bug? Ginny's been asking, and I haven't been sure what to tell her. We have dinner with them next weekend and—"

"I know," I say irritably. "I've driven by, and I support Ginny's mission—really. But going in the house just feels . . ."

"Final," my mom guesses.

"Yes."

"I do understand that." She rises from the couch, apparently ready to concede. "All right. Tuna sandwich coming right up."

I watch my mom disappear into the kitchen, and then I turn my head back to my paper on sheer fabric rendering in realist painting. I've spent a paragraph on Kehinde Wiley's *The Two Sisters*, and now I move to Sir Frederic Leighton and *Flaming June*. The wild orange hums with patience and fixation and legacy. It's a while before I begin to type again.

———————

The Dailey family apartment is above a deli, in a freestanding, turn-of-the-century building on the older side of Hathaway. I parallel park on the street, which takes me three nervy attempts. It would be just like Dailey to watch out the window.

133

When he offered his place as our meeting spot, I balked. I'd never invite Dailey over. Where my house is cozy and interesting, he would see tiny and old. And there is no way he's setting sight on my childhood photos.

The stairwell smells like fresh sourdough, enough to make my mouth water. There's only one door at the top, painted deep sea blue, and I pause for a moment. In these moments, I wonder if I've lost my mind, to include him. *No, you haven't. Probably.*

I rap one knuckle on the door.

"It's open!" Dailey calls. Lovely—he can't even bother to get up. I turn the handle and push.

Inside, he's bent down, gripping the collar of a black lab mix, whose paws scramble in a futile attempt to rush at me.

"Forgot to ask if you're okay with dogs," Dailey says, craning to look up at me. "He can stay in my room if—"

"No, it's fine." I crouch down, hands held low for inspection, and Dailey releases him. The ears flop around on his way to me. "Hey there, Dodger boy."

Dodger's nose huffs hot air across my hands. Then he launches forward to lick my mouth, which I narrowly avoid by looking up.

"Dodge!" Dailey cries, pulling him back. "Manners—God."

Dailey reaches into a cabinet for treats and lures the dog toward the living room. The apartment surprises me—an open-floor-plan loft with exposed ducts and a brick wall on the far side. A piece of abstract art rests above the mantel, slashes of paint in a pleasing balance. The refrigerator is papered by invitations and last year's Christmas cards. I step closer, peering at a Polaroid. In it, Dailey and three friends are piled on a couch, with crooked party hats and New Year's glasses. Kinsley sticks her tongue out; Omar poses with a hand on his chin. Mia, Dailey's girlfriend, laughs as he blows a noisemaker.

"Sorry about that," Dailey says, returning alone. I nearly quip about attention neediness running in the family, but I'm taken aback. He's in navy joggers, which adds a weird dimension. I haven't seen him in anything but a uniform for years. "You can sit wherever."

He waves me toward the table, where his schoolwork—and the same SAT prep book that I have—is in disarray. On the wall above a credenza, there's a grid of family photographs: Dailey and his older brother, the boys with their mom, all four of them together. He looks about the age he was when we met.

"Want some water?" Dailey asks, jerking the refrigerator door open.

"No, thank you."

For years, I'd imagined him doing homework at a long, formal dining table, beneath a chandelier. Eating dinner on bone china and then clattering down to a finished basement to play video games on a wall-sized TV.

He returns to the table with a mason jar of water for himself, sitting at a right angle to my seat. For a moment, I feel almost woozy. I'm in Christian Dailey's apartment, which has rustic glassware and looks nothing like a lair.

This whole scene humanizes him. I feel the tug to lower my guard, which I absolutely will not.

"Cool place," I say. I, too, can be nice for sport.

"Oh. Thanks." He looks briefly surprised, like he'd forgotten, in day-to-day use, how cool it is.

"Does your family own the deli, then?"

"Nah. This place was my dad's midlife crisis. When he

135

bought it, it was an empty, cement cube that he kept calling 'an investment.' He meant to flip it."

"Is he a contractor or something?"

"Ha. A middle school teacher. But we hired some stuff out and worked nonstop the year my mom died. It was a good project."

I jerk my head toward him. His mom died? "I didn't know that."

"I know you didn't," he says mildly.

No—that can't be right. The mom who got her law degree once her kids were in school and made Dailey a special birthday cake? It must have been recent. Before or after Sophie died—I couldn't bear to ask.

"I'm so sorry," I say, though it's too much for three small words to hold. In the photos, his mom is smiling warmly, wrinkles fanned around her eyes. "She's lovely."

"Yeah," he replies, with a fast glance to the picture. "She was the best."

I want to ask about her. That's what I wished people would do with Sophie, so I could take a big breath and sing stories about her like one long ballad. But I've given enough clipped answers to read the room: Dailey doesn't want to talk about this.

I nod, more to myself than to him, and I try again. "So. A bachelor pad above the sandwich shop. There's a TV show in there somewhere."

"Yeah, we definitely existed on pastrami for a while there." He's stacking some papers on the kitchen table, making space for me. "Some of the smells take getting used to, but they bake bread starting super early in the morning. It's nice to wake up to."

We're quiet again for a few moments, off-kilter in a new place. There was friendly, quick-minded Dailey from summer camp. There was maddening Ingleside student Dailey, who I agreed to collaborate with. I did not expect the boy beside me to feel like a third version.

"Okay. So, let's talk about Ashby." I take out my notebook, which is more of a comfort object than a necessary tool. If I write down my thoughts on the investigation, I always rip them to shreds.

"I wish I could tell you more about the guy." Dailey reaches for a nearby pen and taps it on his book. "He's been here since sophomore year. Nice enough, but . . ."

"Enigmatic?" I offer. "Yeah. I've been chatting with him in first period."

"What about?"

"Classwork. Running." Ben Ashby has deep-set eyes and a pouty mouth—pretty and sullen as a French film. His smiles are small and rare, but he's not unkind. "I did get some face time with his girlfriend. She specifically mentioned that they're both homebodies—not into the party scene."

Dailey glances to an empty wall, like watching a projection. "I wonder if she showed up that night, after I saw Ashby arrive."

"She was out of town. So why does he arrive late, alone?"

The tap-tap of Dailey's pen loudens. "Maybe the cross-country guys got on his case to stop by. The whole, *C'mon, man, you're always with Violet, just come out* thing. Or maybe he was driving a drunk buddy home."

"Yeah, true."

Dailey leans back. Even in class, he always looks like he's a few seconds away from propping his feet up. "Most of this is guessing and speculation, huh?"

I frown at him, not even trying to hide it. "I mean, I didn't transfer schools on a lark. For every concrete item, there are a hundred ideas kicked around."

"So let me kick around ideas. Tell me the whole list so I can—"

I hold up a hand, stopping him. "I know you won't believe me, but I'm actually trying to—"

"Ugh," he says, tipping his head back. "I hate that trick. Now, if I do believe you, you get to feel superior for convincing me. And if I don't, you get the satisfaction of being correct about how I react."

"—look out for you," I finish haughtily.

"And for yourself."

"Yeah, of course. We're looking into a drug scene. Hopefully, it's small-time, but we don't know. It's safer to keep pieces separate." I cross my arms. "You won't change my mind."

Dailey full-on groans in exasperation. "Then what is the plan?"

"Slow and steady. I've been acquiring as much information as I can, hoping something pans out. I'll make a move if I have to, but for now, edging closer without risking much."

"Do you have a timetable?"

"Well, I want to get my college applications in. If I'm not making progress after that, I'll start . . . inciting." I lift my eyebrows pointedly. "I assume you'll have tips for me."

Half of Dailey's mouth tugs up. "After college apps, huh? Still LA?"

I nod and glance at my empty paper. "So. JJ. I can't find him online. Can you?"

"Not a trace," Dailey says, reaching for his phone.

It's infuriating. There are seventy-seven John Russos in Maryland, even more if I expand the search to Pennsylvania and DC. There's nothing on the Yardley website. All I have is a mysterious T-shirt.

I bite at the tip of my pen. Dailey looks off-guard, hair falling forward as he examines his phone. Foolish of me to consider him this way, with his family home as a background. Dammit.

"Have you ever noticed if anyone at school has a birthmark on their left arm?" I gesture above the crook of my elbow. "Right here, about the size of a quarter?"

Dailey looks between my face and my arm. "Is that some kind of riddle?"

"Am I a troll under a bridge?"

His mouth slips into a smile. Jerk. "Not that I've noticed, but I've never been looking. Wait. Is that why you're doing *Insider* write-ups for every single sport?"

I'd attended one of his soccer games, mostly to have an excuse to watch Brooks and ask the coach about history, including player injuries. After the game, Dailey asked smugly if I'd enjoyed the show. I smiled and told him he'd get better speed if he picked up his knees a bit more. He then asked if I wanted to race, and the soccer guys got quiet. They thought we were flirting, not engaging in a power struggle. "I'm more of a distance girl," I said meaningfully. "Short and quick doesn't really do it for me."

The guys howled, punching at him and laughing. Dailey shook his head, but he looked pleased. I was a fool for tripping into that dynamic.

"I'm a rookie staffer," I say, tucking a piece of hair behind my ear. "I go where I'm assigned."

"Fascinating," he murmurs. "So, there's someone on the list whose identity you don't know."

Ignoring him, I draw a rectangle with a smiley face within and push it over. "Do you know anything about this logo?"

Dailey glances at the paper and says, "Sure. Blockhead."

I part my lips to say: *Very helpful, Ding-dong.*

"The campus band?" he adds. "They're Yardley students."

Blockhead. Oh my God—of course. I press one hand to my chest, trying to ground myself in the dizzying adrenaline. I've heard of them, come to think of it. A band T-shirt. It was a band T-shirt.

"Pretty decent following, actually," Dailey continues. "My friend Kinsley thinks they'll get picked up by a label. Why?"

But I've already swan-dived into my phone, down and down with my hands reached out. Blockhead's website has a white background and graffiti font, complete with professional photos and article links. "Can you get on their social to see who from school follows them?"

"Okay . . ." he says, clicking around for a second, "Tons of people I follow also follow the band. They're popular. Why does it matter?"

"The night Sophie died," I say absently. I follow the trail through a world of ratty sneakers and smoky, low-light photos. "The birthmark person had a shirt with the logo on it. And JJ had a whole box of those same T-shirts in his car."

Dailey is stunned into silence, but only briefly. "Do you think it's JJ in the photo?"

"No—he doesn't have a birthmark." My heart races as I mutter, half to Dailey, half to myself: "Based on these pictures, JJ's not a band member, but maybe he sells merchandise for them? God—that makes so much sense, doesn't it? A merch table is cash-friendly, high foot traffic."

The day after Sophie died, the band posted a photo, presumably from the night before. All four band members are on an outdoor stage in the photo, captioned *Welcome back to the Yard, Rockheads*. Was the arm person coming to Warner's party from the show? Or leaving Warner's to head up to campus? Or it's totally unrelated and someone happens to own a shirt. "Dammit."

Dailey is craned in my direction, nosing toward my screen. "It could be a coincidence. They probably sell a ton of those shirts."

"Right, but we know where to find JJ next, don't we? Where we can easily strike up a conversation." I'm frantically clicking, on the hunt for band member names. "Is there an Ingleside connection in the band?"

"Um, I think the drummer's a Hathaway grad." Dailey's on his own phone again. "Kinsley will know."

On the tour page, Blockhead's next local show is listed for November, a last hurrah before Yardley's holiday break. Soon, but not soon enough for me.

I'm navigating back to the band's website when Dailey asks, "What are you doing?"

"Hopefully," I say, clicking the contact page, "I'm interviewing Blockhead."

Junior Year

The first week of November, my uncle won his campaign. I was holed up in my room doing debate prep when my mom texted: *They're calling it for Andrew! Wish you were here!* She let me skip the party, of course. No one likes a crier during the balloon drop.

The second week of November, I had my last debate of the regular season, against Ingleside. I prepared equally for the topic and for a conversation with Dailey.

As the JV teams began their matches, the Ingleside varsity team sat in the back of the auditorium, spaced out. A few of them scrolled on their phones, but Dailey sat a bit apart, watching the stage.

We never talked before debating—not since that first time. But here I was, dropping into the velvet seat right next to him. "Hey, Dailey."

He sat up, his eyes springing wide. "MacLaren, hey. How are you?"

"Oh, okay."

"Good. You haven't been around, so I wasn't sure you'd—I mean, I worried that you'd bow out."

My debate coach had let me skip every fall scrimmage—anything on the schedule that was unofficial. Most of my energy was burnt up on tasks like continuing to breathe and speaking without sobbing.

"Worry about me, do you?"

"Sure." His voice puffed up, the persona returning. "'Will there be anyone even close to my level on the debate stage?' is a legit concern."

I watched the stage without really seeing it, but I could feel Dailey looking my way.

"For real, though," he said. "I'm so sorry about Sophie. Sorrier than I can even say."

"Thank you." I'd had enough practice, by then, that I could say the words neutrally. "And thank you for coming to Sophie's visitation. The day was a blur, but I do remember seeing you there with someone."

"Yeah, with Kinsley." Two summers before, we'd both griped about the constant assumption of crushes on our best friends and "like a sibling" comments.

"I didn't realize she knew Soph."

"She didn't," he said. "But Omar had theater class that morning, and Mia and I had just broken up. So, Kins kept me company in line."

Hmm. I sneaked that revelation into my suit pocket. "Sorry to hear that. About Mia."

"Eh, we're back together now. Kind of a thing with us." He smiled sheepishly. "So, how's your family doing?"

"Um. I'm not sure. Busy," I said distractedly. I'd finished the part of the conversation I planned. I should walk away. But the ember I carried with me everywhere flared. "Hey, were you at the party? Did you see Soph that night?"

I wanted to hear what he'd say—how he'd say it.

His face went pained. Guilty? "Yeah, I did. And Hannah, I—"

"Hannah?" I joked, to cut him off. My throat ached with rising emotion. Bringing this up was a mistake. "It's fine. I just find it darkly funny that my rival saw Sophie closer to her death than I did."

"Rival," Dailey repeated. "Not worthy adversary?"

"On a good day," I said, offering him a half smile. "Well, see you out there."

"Yeah." His eyes followed me as I rose from my seat, watching for something. The softness of it—the consideration—made me feel feeble and irritated.

I looked back at his loose-limbed posture and the expectant look on his face. "Don't go easy on me out of pity."

"And go from rival to enemy?" he asked, one eyebrow arched. "Never."

In the end, I landed the easier-to-defend position. Dailey, clearly relishing the underdog role, brought his A-game, and I lacked any real heat. I was using all my fire for something far more important.

— — — — — —

"Mom!" I gripped the banister, swinging a little in a way that irritated her. "I'm going down the street!"

"Pause," she said from the kitchen. "Reverse. I would like to see my child's face at least once this weekend."

The night before, I'd holed up in my room with sewing orders and homework, while my mom went to Ginny's. I'd left early for a morning run by myself, and I stayed at Sophie's graveside for a while. By the time I got home, my mom had left for errands, and I'd been back studying since.

I backed up into the kitchen, where my mom was putting away groceries, and gave her a cheesy, little kid smile. "Hello, Mother."

She snorted, gesturing for me to put the fruit into the bowls on our countertop. "How was your evening?"

"Fine. I finished that monogram order for the bridal party robes and packaged them up."

"I saw that," she said, a bit thinly. "You also fell asleep with your light on, your history notes spread out, and your laptop open to a TV show."

"You were at Ginny's late," I said, sidestepping the accusation. "Is she doing okay?"

"Your aunt is . . . managing." My mom and Ginny flew together like magnets when one of them needed help, and I wanted them to. But every time my mom left for Ginny's house, my heart split with wanting Sophie. All my life, I'd had someone to show up for, no matter the hour. Now I was the only one left, still trying to make good on it.

"Ginny said she emailed you?" my mom continued.

"She did, yes." About the foundation she's starting in Sophie's name. She'd asked for feedback on the name—The Sophie Abbott Foundation, no feat of creativity but solid nonetheless. She'd asked me to edit Sophie's bio, the mission statement, and the foundation's "About Us." *I can get information across clearly,* Ginny told me, *but not with the kind of "voice" I'd like. Old journalism habits die hard, I suppose. If you have any suggestions for punching it up, I'm all ears!*

My mom tossed me a loaf of bread, which hit my hands with a thud. "And have you replied to her?"

"It's in my drafts. I just have homework, and—"

"Not rushing you," my mom insisted. She leaned a hip against the counter. "So, listen. Ginny and Andrew have decided they'll spend Christmas with his family in Florida."

"Oh," I said. We'd never really celebrated together formally anyway. Still, I stood there with the bread in my hands for another moment. "Okay."

"Gin's thinking it'll be a nice distraction for Maddie—cousins, the beach."

"Sure." I rose to my tiptoes, stretching to reach a higher shelf.

"But your aunt would like to host a girls' winter luncheon for the four of us." The look in her eyes said: just hear me out because we are going along with this.

"And what is that?" I asked delicately.

"Well," she said. "I don't quite know. But she perked up while talking about a 'festive meal' and whatever else this idea entails."

Our holiday traditions involved jammies, fleece blankets, baking, and eating. But Ginny, I suspected, was trying to give Maddie more memories from this year than the canyon of loss and its echoes.

"Okay," I decided. "Good."

"Good," my mom agreed. She reached into the fridge and

held out a pan half-full of leftover spaghetti bake. "Take this with you."

Carrying the casserole down the street, I drew up my happy face. Days before, Lincoln was offered a partial lacrosse scholarship at a D-3 school a few hours away. It was everything he wanted, and so I wanted it too. But with Linc, I could briefly pretend that my life resembled the one I'd lived until August. He ran beside me, mused about movies endlessly, let me go quiet for long stretches without being weird. Next year was unfathomable, so I hid from the thought.

Instead, obsession about Sophie's last night grew inside me like a slow and spreading sickness. It had begun to overtake the remaining healthy parts of my life, just beneath my notice.

After the credits rolled on our first movie selection, Lincoln and I debated a second—possibly from our list of inspirational sports movies.

"Is there such a thing as a lacrosse movie?" I asked, through a mouthful of popcorn. "Or are they all football?"

"There's a documentary about the Iroquois Nationals on their path to a championship," Lincoln said, sitting up. "You'd like it."

"Pull it up, then," I said. Lincoln looked very pleased as he searched for streaming rentals. "Hey, this movie might be your way to bridge future lacrosse teammates and the film studies kids. Who wants to watch a lax documentary in my dorm?"

He rolled his eyes at me, grinning over.

"I'm not making fun!" I insisted. "It's a useful idea!"

"Watch the trailer if you want," he said, as he rose from the couch. "Be right back."

He closed the hallway bathroom door behind him, and, as if I'd planned it, my hand shot out to grab Lincoln's phone. It was still lit up, warm from his hand. In my ears, *You can't* and *you have to* screamed at equal pitch. If I'd asked, he probably would have let me, so what was the difference, right? Besides, I wasn't snooping through *his* life.

I was snooping through Dailey's friend Omar's life. A few lacrosse videos, lip-synchs of dramatic TV monologues, and general tomfoolery with theater friends. I clicked a few, including one called FIRST DAY, which seemed to be at a restaurant. As Dolly Parton's "9 to 5" played, the video panned beyond Dailey's shoulder to Kinsley behind a cash register. Her apron was embroidered with a few scattered coffee beans, the logo of a café in Hathaway. When she spotted them, one hand shot to her hip, giving me a clear view of her elbow. No mark.

The toilet flushed, followed by the sound of running water—my warning. When the faucet creaked off, I dropped Lincoln's phone as if I'd never touched it.

"You ready?" he asked.

"Yep." My brain offered excuses for what I'd done—valid points that I could build a case on. But there was no tricking my body, now feverish. "Let's do it."

———————

"So," Gabi said the next day, as she closed her bedroom door behind us. "Any luck?"

I plunked myself down on the rug, which had ropey lines I walked when I needed to pace. I'd become very well acquainted with Gabi's room—the photo of her family beside one of her and Sophie, the meticulously organized bookshelf full of magical realism and famous leaders' memoirs. "Kinsley is not the arm person."

Gabi spun in her desk chair. She often started there but eventually shifted to the floor. "Do I want to know how you know that?"

"One of her friend's videos. Lincoln knows him."

"Damn." Gabi tapped at her chin, taking in the small disappointment. Both of us hoped we could consolidate two suspects to one. "You want to hear my news?"

"*Please.*"

She gave me jazz hands. "I ruled out Jenny Lisk."

"Really! How?"

"Well . . ." Her tone careened from happiness to hesitation. She pressed her palms to her cheeks. "I have maybe been doing something ethically questionable."

At least it wasn't just me, then. "Okay . . ."

"The school brought in a counselor whose specialty is 'loss in teen communities,' right? And I've been going to the group session."

I let this sit for a moment, figuring out to say this gently. "Well, that's good. That night was horrendous for you and—"

"Oh, I'm very screwed up from it. But I'm going to sessions mostly to hear what people are saying." She grimaced at me. "I know. But Sunita talked about how Sophie had only met Jenny one other time and still remembered her name that night to say hi."

I imagined Warner's house as I'd seen it in pictures—two stories and a basement. My mind moved the players around like dolls. "How much of the time were you and Sophie apart?"

"We each did a bathroom break earlier in the night—probably

ten minutes apiece since you get stuck chatting with people along the way. Those were the only two times she wasn't nearby. Except, obviously, later . . . when . . ."

"We don't have to go there," I said quickly.

Five people left: Brooks, Zoe, Ben, Kinsley, and T-shirt person. Not that many, all things considered . . . and yet still too many.

"So, let's say this is all the information we're ever going to have." Gabi stretched her legs out, toes pointed. At home, her body language relaxed, sometimes to the point of terrible posture. "What can we do with it?"

Thus far, my ideas made for a hefty scrap pile: Confront each person and hope they break open, the truth spilling out freely? No—the accusation was too easy to deny, and we didn't have proof. Place trackers on their cars to see if they go anywhere shady? Illegal and also faulty—shady dealings could happen anywhere. Take our information to Ingleside's Head of School? It wasn't enough to go on, and what could she do anyway? Tell our parents, who would be horrified.

"So, I thought I could create a fake profile," I admitted. "Use a stock photo and generic pictures from around town, clearly a girl from . . . say, Hathaway."

"Oh, that's not bad," Gabi said, perking up. "And follow people on the list?"

"Right. Eventually strike up a rapport, ask about the party scene." I shook my head. "But it would be so suspicious. I'd have to get followers they might know. And a newly created account? It would only work on a sucker."

"This person had a burner account," Gabi said. "They're not careless."

150

True. The hate reared up inside me—the person who gave Sophie drugs could have emailed Ginny and Andrew anonymously. Given my family peace. "I guess we could tail each person? See if they have any shady dealings."

"Maybe." Gabi frowned, picking at a loose thread at her cuff. She sounded genuinely defeated. "But three of them know me, so that's tricky."

For months now, Gabi had run at this list with everything she had, through the wilds of grief. So, now that her energy was flagging, the least I could do was summon the morale.

"Well, I could do it," I said, wiggling my eyebrows. "Or we could go in disguise."

That was when the Halloween costume tub got dragged out of her closet. Honestly, it got silly for a while, both of us desperate for reprieve. Gabi wound up in a sparkly cape and a gray-haired wig from a *Golden Girls* costume. Holding up a glittery purple bodysuit, she smiled. "Ah, my Selena costume. Eighth-grade Gabi was trying to get out of 'the sporty one' stereotype."

"How's this for a stakeout?" I flipped my head upside down to tug on a blond, mid-length wig. Adjusting the elastic around the bump of my ponytail, I popped up.

"Holy shit." Gabi gave a befuddled laugh and jabbed a finger at her mirror. "Go look. How does that completely change your *face?*"

Staring at blond me, I touched my face to confirm I was still in my body. "That is . . . bizarre."

"Maybe it's that you never wear your hair down." Gabi cocked her head, examining the effect. "And the bangs change your face shape or something."

"It's my coloring, too." The blond hair created contrast to my brown eyes and brows. "Wild."

Gabi pointed between us. "So, the blond girl and the old lady do . . . what? Tail Ben Ashby one weekend, see what he gets up to?"

"I don't know." Following is a legal gray area, at best. I pulled the wig off. "I'm just realizing we could have used Halloween to throw a party here. I could have dressed up beyond recognition and tried to score drugs."

Gabi slumped, cape shimmering in the light, and dropped her wig back into the tub. "Yes, in a parallel universe where my parents are clueless, and you couldn't get in serious trouble for even attempting that, we could have."

"Good point."

"I'm out of ideas," Gabi admitted. "And I can't be out of ideas because then I'll have to deal with my life."

I knew the feeling well, but it still socked me in the gut to hear Gabi say it. "Which part?"

"The 'what comes next' part. Soph and I had all these plans." Gabi twisted her hands together. Talking about Sophie had come bit by bit, both of us tiptoeing. "If I go through with them, am I clinging to my old life in an unhealthy way? Will that always make me sad? Or is it honoring her and not letting her death stop me? I have no idea."

I leaned back against the foot of Gabi's bed. "DC?"

"Yeah." She ran the bodysuit through her fingers, sequins rustling. "I'd major in public policy, Sophie in environmental engineering. We'd volunteer, work in our communities. Then grad school for me, lobbying for Soph. Maybe found our own nonprofit. After that, who knows?"

"Oh, c'mon," I said, joking. "Next stop: secretary of state and head of the EPA."

She laughed a little, clearly struggling against the rising tears. Yes, I felt jealous. Sophie had never detailed how her specific ambitions were tethered to Gabi's—surely to spare my feelings. But mostly, I wanted that vision too: Sophie taking on the world with a friend beside her. Softly, I said, "It's a good dream."

"Thanks." Gabi looked at her nails. "She made the big dreams sound . . . not even possible, but *inevitable*."

"Yeah, I made her mad in that way. She wanted me to want— I don't know—the Supreme Court. She thought I was thinking small."

"Well, you are."

I let the comment settle for a moment, absorbing it. "Thanks *so* much for that."

"No offense," Gabi said lightly. "If you think you'll be happy with whatever law job you can get, no criticism—genuinely."

I gritted my teeth. This again, huh? "Calling my life 'small' isn't criticism?"

"I don't mean it to be." She smiled at me, a bit curiously. "Maybe it's jealousy talking. I'm good at policy in Model UN, and I'm a confident-enough public speaker. But I'm not as strong with rhetoric or written argument. *You* have that."

"I know," I said thinly. "That's why I'm planning to be a lawyer."

"Which is great. I'm just saying: you really could shoot big. You could be an investigative journalist or a linchpin strategist or comms person for important causes or—"

"Maybe I will." I raised one eyebrow. "But you could also

believe—as I do—that practicing law, even small-scale, gives you a great capacity to make the world better or worse."

One side of Gabi's mouth slid up. "Natural debater."

"Not to mention," I continued, "I'll likely go into deep debt for following my interests, even considering a traditionally lucrative field."

"All right, all right," she said good-naturedly. "Sorry—idealist."

And I, truth be told, was a cynic who needed a push sometimes. "It's fine. I actually miss Soph nagging me."

"God, me too. Even though I can't get near steak without hearing the words 'carbon footprint' in my mind."

I laughed, the sound low in my throat. "You know what else I miss? How she'd fall in full-scale love with someone she'd just met. And we both knew she'd forget him the next week. But the way she'd talk in whisper voice?"

"Thinking big even with crushes," Gabi said.

"To be fair, it did annoy me sometimes," I added. "Like, here we go again: Sophie has a crush. But now I can appreciate the romanticism."

She should have gotten more loves. The thought ripped through my rib cage.

Fortunately, Gabi was still going. "There was literally no one better at wallowing. After my first girlfriend broke up with me, Soph charged in here with a *kit*. Tissues, baked goods, beauty products, plans for a movie marathon that would have taken three days straight."

Soph did that when I split with my sophomore year boyfriend. Well, she tried anyway. I enjoyed the cookies and the movie, sure, but I simply wasn't that broken up about breaking up. I liked him; he was good to me. Sophie could never have a relationship like that—good enough for a while.

"All or nothing," I murmured. "No meat, no alcohol, but a joyous consumer of literally all other food."

"Don't you miss eating with her? How excited she was to try new things." Gabi stared up at the ceiling, where the fan spun air all around us. "But there was also this . . . melancholy deep down, wasn't there? The projects, the whirlwind, the ideas. I loved her for all that. But sometimes it felt like she couldn't let down for a moment."

"Yeah." I glanced at the artwork above Gabi's desk—a string of moons in all phases, changing only by how the light hit. "I always admired her for having a hard line on not drinking. Our grandparents weren't diagnosed or anything, but there was definitely substance use disorder there. Now I wonder if Soph had a sense, even subconsciously, that stopping wouldn't be simple for her."

"She got blackout wasted at the first-ever high school soccer party," Gabi said. "Did she ever tell you that?"

My instinct was to snap at Gabi that this couldn't be true. I hated to think there were more things I didn't know. "She didn't, no."

"She was nervous around all the older girls and overdid it." Gabi finally tugged off the gray wig, her hair now rumpled beneath it. "She was so embarrassed after."

When I tried beer for the first time, I told Sophie the next day. I reported that I found it easy to stop after one drink. No wonder she hadn't countered with her blackout story. "My dad's in recovery," I said, surprising myself. "Has been for a long time. Sophie probably thought I'd be mad or something."

Gabi nodded, staying quiet.

"That's the confusing part about the pill situation. I adore my dad, and Sophie knew it." I wiped away a tear. "Did she think I only love him because he's not drinking?"

"I don't know," Gabi said. "I hate the what-ifs. They feel infinite."

Yes. "But our list feels concrete."

"Agreed." Gabi threw a handful of dress-up pieces into the storage container.

I traced our Ingleside lineup in my mind. Brooks Van Doren and his collegiate athletics brochure vibe. Ben Ashby, all speed and angles. Zoe Walsh, with ice-queen eyes and chic, art-girl outfits. Gabi's knowledge of them made them much fuller profiles than snippets of articles about Jenny Lisk's swim team stats or the fact that Mary Kinsley worked at the coffee shop.

"What do you make of Zoe Walsh?" I asked. She wasn't in that picture of a half-dozen girls in Sophie's grade. But she posted a photo that night, wearing a bright red top and posing with two friends.

"I find her unlikely," Gabi admitted. "I've known her for years, and she's Type-A—very driven, annoyed by shenanigans. Tends to say whatever she's thinking."

Sounds like a treat, I thought, wrinkling my nose. "But?"

Gabi slid a worried look my way. "But I've been wrong before."

Senior Year

Just past dinnertime, the sky outside George and Elliott's kitchen is already dark. The windows reflect a full table. I wish my life were as simple as it seems tonight. I met my mom's boyfriend, who came to our house and asked me about school; I asked about his eleven-year-old twins. Then we all trekked down the street, dessert offering in hand, for Friendsgiving. Lincoln's home for break, and he invited Parker over for dinner.

I revel in hearing Lincoln's college stories that I suspect are edited for parents. I notice the blush and good-natured smile on Mitch's face when George teases him. I answer Parker's polite questions about Ingleside and almost let Elliott talk me into a 10K.

"So, you're really okay at that school?" Lincoln asks, so that only I can hear.

"I really am."

Of course, I'm also lying by omission to everyone at this table.

"Well," I say, placing my napkin beside my empty plate. "I can honestly say this is the most I've ever enjoyed being seventh wheel . . ."

"Oh, stop," my mom says, with a laugh.

I grin around the table, making sure the comment landed as a joke. "But I've gotta get going."

"Oh, yeah," George says. I'd already told him I'd have to duck out early. "What are these hot plans tonight?"

"Seeing a band play on campus with a friend."

When it came to the Blockhead show, Dailey and I agreed for once. We can't be there together since we might run into Inglesiders. So, he's bringing his Hathaway friends, and we'll each take a shot at approaching JJ separately.

"Is this the band you're doing the article on?" Lincoln asks, looking up. "Blockhead?"

"Oh, I like them!" Parker chimes in.

I do too, truthfully. After Catherine green-lit my pitch, I interviewed Blockhead via email. The drummer responded to my questions about their history and inspiration, which ranged from an ex-girlfriend muse to bathroom graffiti. Those were just a warmup for: How does band merchandise work? She explained that a business major friend has always coordinated for them. Freshman roommates with the bassist. JJ.

"Do you get to go backstage?" Mitch asks.

"Nah. I want to be in the audience—hear what people are saying, that kind of thing."

"A journalist of the people," George says, and Elliott gives an approving nod.

"Thank you for dinner," I say, standing. Then, to Mitch and Parker, "Look forward to seeing you again sometime."

"Have fun," my mom calls, "of the non-drinking variety, Hannah Louise."

"I'm driving," I singsong back. Then I give a pointed glance at the wine glass resting in her hand.

"Very funny. Be home at a reasonable hour." She smiles at Mitch. "But not too reasonable."

Well, good for them and also yuck.

Before I'm out the door, I smile back specifically at Lincoln. He seems to be waiting for that quick connection, and he smiles back, reassured. I like Parker. I don't feel left out. And everything is totally fine.

— — — — — — —

"Verdict." Zoe scans the venue, ruby lips pressed in consideration. "Much stickier floors than an Ingleside party, but a much more interesting crowd."

I'm bent over my phone, taking preliminary notes. The campus venue is called the Waverly, and it has a kind of crumbly, once-great ambiance. Outside, the November air is chilly, but a crowded room of bodies heats up quickly. I shrug off my thrift store leather coat, draping it over one arm. "Almost done here."

"Good." Zoe cranes her neck around, taking a sip of her raspberry seltzer. I'm pleased that she feels comfortable enough with me to use her fake ID for a drink. "How are you as a wingman?"

I pocket my phone, and she tucks her arm through mine in that girls-at-a-party way. There's a pang of guilt—of course there is, and I ask, "What are we looking for in a guy?"

"Well, I have no physical criteria," she says as we settle in a decent spot. "It's more a vibe. Like, does this guy seem like the protagonist of an indie film with a depressing soundtrack? Should he be in an Edward Hopper painting?"

"Elegant? Moody?"

She shrieks out a little laugh, patting my arm. "You get it."

I waited to text Zoe until last night, pitching this outing as a girl's night. If Brooks and Warner show up, I want it to be for their own reasons, not because Zoe mentioned the concert at lunch.

JJ's behind the merch table as expected, and somewhere, Dailey has hopefully arrived with friends. I could hardly sleep last night, daydreaming that someone from my list might really show tonight and stroll right up to JJ. Unlikely. But possible. *Dream big.*

"What about you?" Zoe asks, and I realize we're still talking about boys. "In your little vixen outfit over there."

"Vixen!" I glance down at myself, surprised. "I just always wear black. It's easier."

"Trés chic, too." Then, sighing, "Okay. Should we embargo college talk on girl's night or can I vent?"

"Go for it," I say.

We switch to talking about her ever-shifting portfolio for art school applications. She holds her phone out, and we consider a grid of four self-portraits.

Zoe's still musing when I spot two familiar silhouettes and tune her out. Gabi's hair is pulled halfway back, and she's wearing faded blackwash jeans; Catherine's in high-waisted pants the color of marigolds. Instead of holding hands, they link pointer fingers at their sides. I shift to block Zoe's view, but not quickly enough.

"Gabi!" Zoe calls out. "Catherine!"

My lips circle to form the word *Wait*, but no believable excuse follows. Zoe is tugging me by the elbow.

"Hey, girls!" Zoe says, cozying in to make a little chat circle. "Fancy seeing you! Is Blockhead, like, a trendy thing I didn't know about?"

Gabi's smile is stiff for only a moment. "It's my first show."

"Mine too," Catherine says. "Hannah got me interested with the story she pitched."

"Oh," I joke, trying to sound casual. "Are you here in a supervisory capacity?"

"Never. When I'm off the clock, I'm off the clock."

Gabi gives her an affectionate smile. "Aw. What an egregious lie."

"Yeah, guilty." Catherine grins at us.

At school, they swap conspiratorial, admiring glances, but neither is the public display type. I could never begrudge Gabi this happiness, like little stars all around them. But what must that be like, to move on even one step?

"How's class going up here?" Zoe asks Gabi. "Like a sneak peek of college life? Tell me everything."

"Freshman English is a big lecture class," she says. "So, the professor doesn't know me, which is strange compared to Ingleside."

"Weird," Zoe agrees. "You think you'll apply for undergrad?"

"Nah," Gabi says. "I want to be close to home, but not this close."

The college conversation rolls along—Catherine landed on early decision to George Washington; Zoe is shooting for RISD and MICA.

161

"Hannah, you're doing West Coast schools, right?" Catherine asks, and I nod.

"But a few closer, right?" Zoe adds. "Maryland U, Wythe, et al."

Gabi's eyes flick to me, her careful guard dropped. "Really. Wythe?"

"My counselor basically insisted." I stare down at the black gloss of my boots. Last Gabi knew, I swore up and down that I'd only apply to large, faraway colleges. Wythe is small, prestigious, and located in Virginia. They're known for their writing track and student paper. "I probably won't get in."

"Of course you will," Catherine says. "Well, I should try to finagle my way toward the front to get some photos—yes, I flashed the press pass, judge me."

"Never," I say, and we all wish one another a good night. My exhale of relief is entirely too loud, even in this crowded room.

Zoe and I settle back into our spots. She gives me a few seconds before asking, "Was I sensing some weirdness there with you and Gabi?"

I just had to befriend the vibes queen of the Eastern seaboard. "I don't think so?"

Zoe eyes me. "Huh."

It's too much of a lie; I can feel it. We both can.

"There's something about her that kicks up my competitive drive," I say. "Not a cute quality, I know."

"Well, not if you act in an ugly way." Zoe pauses for a sip of her drink. "But envy can be revealing, right? Shows you what you want, deep down."

So, I guess I'll be spending the rest of the night unpacking that one. This is not what I needed, to be thrown off by a Gabi conversation and then called out on it. I'm here for a reason, and that reason is staffing the merchandise booth. Maybe handing off pills wrapped in folded T-shirts right this minute.

I glance behind us. "I'm gonna hit the bathroom real quick. Hold our spot?"

"Yep," Zoe says. "Hurry—band should be on soon."

A minute later in fact, to booming cheers. I move upstream through the closing-in crowds, and I emerge near a quieter spot. JJ's staring down at his phone, no longer contending with a line. His face is somehow both bored and friendly.

"Do you have anything else for sale?" I ask, trying for doe eyes. I raise my voice over the first chorus of "Blown Fuse"— one of my favorites. *Her mood is blue, and her hair is red / One smile from her, and I lose my head.*

"Pretty much what you see." JJ surveys his table. "Did you have something specific in mind?"

Is this where I'd use a code word, if I knew one? "Like . . . something smaller?"

He scratches the back of his neck. "We did a limited run of keychains, but we've been out of those a while. Something cheaper like that?"

I have no idea if this is doublespeak. "Not necessarily. I mean, I can pay."

"Oh, okay. So, just not a T-shirt situation." He ducks beneath. I wipe my clammy hands on my jeans. When he emerges, he has a logo sticker between two fingers. "Got a neon-pink one left!"

Dailey and I anticipated that my attempt with JJ—a more

subtle approach—might not land. Time to trust Dailey's bullshitting. "Sure. Great."

I hand JJ three bucks that I really do not want to part with. In return, he hands me the pink sticker—a twisted memento of my time chasing ghosts. "Thanks."

"Enjoy the show," he says.

The disappointment lands like a weight on my shoulders. I'm not a fool—this was always a long shot. But I lost my favorite person in the world, and I still don't understand how. When there's even a half-a-percent chance of information, my hopes can't help but rise toward it.

I fire off a thumb's down to Dailey. After a few more songs, he'll approach JJ with a more direct ask.

And then I'm swallowed into a sea of people, still singing: *Blown fuse, blown fuse, but you're still my muse. You're the one, you're the one, you're the one that I choose.*

— — — — — — —

I drop Zoe off at her beautiful house—stately brick with a bright red door—and I drive home in the quiet. I've just parked on the street outside my house when Dailey calls. He already texted at the venue: *Nada.* I deflated for only a moment, then bucked up for the sake of Zoe's perceptiveness.

I press the phone to my ear. "Hey."

"Hey," Dailey says. "I bombed. In fact, our friend JJ kind of chewed me out. Did not have 'getting scolded by a stranger at a concert' on my bucket list."

My brows tug down. "What do you mean?"

"I started with the whole: 'Hey, I'm visiting a friend; any idea where I can get some stuff?' And JJ was like: 'You looking more for energy or chill?' But when he realized I was talking about pills, he shut it down. So, I said, 'Oh really? Because a friend said . . .' and then he got pissed."

"Like defensive? Caught?"

"I don't think so." Dailey's voice sounds deeper through the speaker, but also familiar. I don't talk on the phone much, so this feels overly personal. Both of us sitting in the darkness of our separate cars, connected by invisible waves. "More confused and annoyed. He said if I wanted good weed, sure—he knows a guy. But oxy's a sore spot because he had a childhood friend overdose a few years ago."

I lean forward, resting my forehead on the steering wheel. Epidemic. There's a weight to the word, but it gets used so flip-pantly that the syllables turn to mush for me. "God, it's freaking everywhere."

"Yeah," Dailey says, solemn. "Sounds like what I overheard about 'pizza from JJ' was always a weed hook-up."

"Maybe he used to deal pills? But got out of the game after Sophie?"

"Maybe," Dailey says, with a resigned sigh. "But even if that's the case, I don't know what our next move would be."

Me neither. I sit up even though I'm suddenly so, so tired. "So, that's it. JJ trail cold."

"I guess so." There's an apology in Dailey's voice—maybe even guilt. "I really thought it might be something, with the T-shirt connection."

I cross my arms. The sleeves of my leather jacket are warm from the car heater blasting. "It's better that we know."

"Music was great though."

There were a few moments, swallowed up in the crowd,

when I felt suspended above reality. Nothing to do but let the music seep into me. "It really was."

"So," Dailey says. "What next?"

I stare out at my street, the yellow light cast over car roofs and the moon hung above treetops. "I have to get closer to some people at school."

Junior Year

"So, this could go a few different ways," my mom said, staring at a magnolia wreath on the wide, wooden door. In my arms, I balanced three gifts wrapped in holly leaf paper.

"Yep," I said. It was a comfort, actually, that Ginny could summon the energy to decorate for Christmas. Still, we stood.

"It's what Ginny wants," my mom added.

"Yep."

What awaited us was, perhaps, two hours of forced smiles and pretending everything was okay. Or maybe we'd all devolve into crying while Judy Garland sang about muddling through. Maybe we'd sob from the start—that might be healthiest.

The house smelled like clove and citrus. Ginny entered the foyer in a winter white sweater, waving with both hands. "Hello, hello."

Her delicate snowflake earrings glinted in the window can-dlelight. So, the winter dinner was really a full theme, huh? At least I'd worn my nice white cable knit, though it was more "old mariner" than Junior League.

The table was set, complete with taper candles, and Maddie stood at the end, filling glasses.

"Hey." I tried to smile in a way that suggested I was on her side. Whatever side that was: I hate this fancy dinner or I love it.

Maddie gave a just-going-with-it smile. "Hey. Thanks for coming."

Ginny and my mom facilitated conversation in this overea-ger way that broke my heart. So, between bites of roasted duck that Sophie would have been angry about and Brussels sprouts so fancy that they tasted only vaguely of Brussels sprouts, I played along. After a while, the pretending felt warm at the edges. If we could act okay enough to almost convince one another, perhaps we could almost convince ourselves.

"So," Ginny said, setting down a linen napkin. "I have some exciting news to share. As you know, I've had a few meetings with Yardley's administration." She smiled around the table, ascertaining eye contact. "A student brought to my attention that they could use an on-campus house for students in recovery. I think I've got school leadership on board, including a live-in residence advisor trained in substance use disorder counseling. I'll raise the vast majority of the funding with donations and grants, hopefully."

Several seconds of surprised silence followed. My mom spoke first. "Gin—wow. They went for it?"

"They did. Starting college is a total lifestyle change, so destabilizing—the new responsibility, the academic stress, the parties. So, having support and a social life built around recovery . . ." Ginny paused, looking between Maddie and me.

"It's great," I said. In addition to meetings, my dad had relied on routine and his local AA friends, especially in early days. And Ginny, I knew, was imagining the parallel world where Sophie was still here. Maybe she'd be in recovery and on to college. "I didn't know that's what you were doing with the foundation."

"It was the hope. And it's preliminary—the earliest the house would have students is fall after next. But I'm very motivated, and Yardley has agreed to collaborate as I move forward. We'll have a board of community members and college administration. So! Really exciting."

Maddie looked like she might cry. "That's incredible, Mom."

"Thank you," Ginny said. "But I'm telling you, in part, because I need your ideas. I want us all to imagine what this could be. Hannah, your edits to the initial materials were inspired, and I'd love to consult with you along the way."

"Sure." The word came out, but I felt numb. It had been less than five months. Why did Ginny's project make me feel so far away from Sophie?

"Will there be scholarships for the residents?" my mom asked. "And prioritizing students who might not otherwise be able to afford Yardley?"

Ginny nodded. "Absolutely. Eliminating financial burden is a cornerstone."

"You should help kids who are first in their families to go to college," Maddie said. "Soph would like that."

My mom and Ginny glanced at each other with sad smiles. Ginny was that person, once upon a time. "Completely agree."

"The house itself," I said, in a quiet voice. "It should have the smallest possible eco-footprint. Solar panels. Garden, compost, that kind of thing."

Ginny's eyes went downcast for a moment, then rose back to me with a determined glint. "Of course. I should have thought of that."

I gave a wan smile because I'd never add to her pain on purpose. But yes, I sometimes thought she was grieving the girl she wanted Sophie to be. I was grieving the real thing—the Sophie whose local eating was not a phase, who loved her worn denim jacket over cute dresses, who, if you listened, had some real insight with that "astrology stuff," as Ginny put it.

"We're going to host a gala in late winter!" Ginny said. "Kick off the fundraising while searching for a property. Andrew and I will cover the down payment and renovation."

Staring across the low flames, I wondered if Ginny was smothering her grief with busyness. Once the house's doors were open, all would be well: Sophie's life made into monument and meaning. But Sophie wasn't a project or an idea or even a cause. She was many projects and many ideas and many causes and also more than all those parts of herself.

Shortly after the snowflake ornament painting began, I excused myself.

I curled up on Sophie's bed upstairs. Part of me still believed she'd climb in the window and, with a grin, ask what she missed. And worse, I treasured that delusion. I feared being farther away from it, in a place I never expected her at all.

I stood up before the tears could surge into sobbing, and something made me pause by the bookshelf. Winter sunlight hit the silver lettering on the widest spine—*Look to the Sky: A Modern*

Guide for the Ancient Zodiac. I pulled out the tome of a book, hoping she'd underlined or earmarked something in Aries that felt like a message just for me. But shoved beneath its front cover? A slim volume slipped loose, then dropped to the floor. My heart followed it down. I crouched, gripped the journal like it was my own life, and fled on a shaky legs.

I crept into the hall closet and slid the journal into my bag.

"Everything okay?" my mom asked when I returned.

I could barely pluck words from my mind to speak them. My train of thought was primarily: *Oh my God, oh my God. What if it's nothing? What if it's everything?*

"Actually," I said, "I don't think the duck is sitting right with me."

— — — — — —

At home, I burrowed into my room, my eyes adjusting to Sophie's slapdash penmanship. The journal started off simply enough: a straightforward log of her physical therapy exercises or some new facet of recovery. *G met me at the park, and it helped to kick the ball around without an audience.* A sentence or two about her sadness in missing games, her frustration about people not understanding. Almost nothing social or personal. My name appeared only once. *H keeps reminding me that the training process isn't linear, so of course healing isn't either. Which I guess is true. But she'd go nuts if she couldn't run.*

I didn't start to cry until the entry that read: *Coach keeps telling me to be patient but come on. I'm not getting into a really good college without soccer. No one says it, but we all know.*

I wanted to tear back through time and insist this wasn't

true. Or maybe it was, but God—who cares? There were so many good lives without top-tier universities.

The whole thing presented a far angrier and more scared Sophie than the one I knew. Yes, she was a little low last winter and into the spring. I sat next to her right here in my room, talking it out. She felt her feelings; she had perspective. How had I been so wrong?

Where was the Sophie of bold declarations? This was a girl grappling for any sense of self-worth. Had she been spinning out even before the ankle setback?

After I was done, I held a cold washcloth to my face, trying to chase away the puffiness. I returned downstairs, where my mom was knitting on the couch with her cozy English mystery show.

"Hey," I said, leaning a hip against the banister.

"You feeling better?"

"Much. And, um, I just got a text from Gabi."

She sat up a little. "Everything okay?"

"Yeah. Sounds like she could use a shoulder, though."

My mom gave a sad smile. "The holidays kick up all kinds of feelings, don't they?"

"They do," I said. "So, I'm gonna take the car, if that's okay."

"Of course," she said. "Drive safe."

There were at least a dozen cars parked in Gabi's curved driveway, and all the windows were lit up. I'd texted only to say I was on my way, to which she replied: *I'm here.* Closer to the house, I heard the low bass line of music and the high notes of laughter.

Gabi stood waiting on the porch, arms hugged across a smoky velvet blazer. She stepped forward. "Tell me."

"I'm sorry to just show up, but . . ." I held up the journal, gripping at the spine so the gold S could catch the Christmas lights.

Gabi's eyes bounced back up to mine. "How?"

"Her room. I looked again."

"Holy shit." She pushed the door open, motioning me inside. Voices filled the entryway, conversations overlapping. "Does it have . . . ?"

"Yes. Not definite, but it narrows it down." The whole house smelled like fruit, sweet and spiced. "I didn't know there was a party. Your parents must—"

"They understand." Gabi was already on the steps. "Holidays. It's tough."

We hurried up to her room, and I sank onto the reading chair. "Okay, so. Soph uses initials for everyone. You're G; I'm H. Obviously not meant to be code—just shorthand while she was quickly scribbling."

"Okay . . ." Gabi all but waved her hand, hurrying me forward.

"There's someone she calls B."

"B," she said, trying it out. "And it's pretty clear that this person is . . . ?"

"Clear enough." I thrust the journal at her, open to last March. *I have another doctor's appointment and hopefully he will* <u>*listen*</u> *this time. Like, just because you think it should be better by now doesn't mean it is! I'm trying not to complain because I'm sure people are sick of it at this point. When B asked today, I blurted it all out. So at least I have a backup plan.*

Gabi frowned. "I mean, that's a bit of a stretch for—"

"I know. But here . . ." I flipped to the other page, from

173

June, and pointed: *I'm curious to see what the scan will say tomorrow. Feeling so much better thanks to B. Not ideal, obviously, but works till my ankle can catch up. My run time is improving!*

"B," Gabi repeated. Brooks Van Doren. Ben Ashby. She bit at her lower lip. "If I didn't know about the pills, I'd never read this and think: oh yeah, definitely oxy. I'd think they talked. But considering what we know, I think it's a decent assumption."

"Right. And after this, the entries are bizarrely cheery," I said. "Is there *anyone* else who would qualify as B? A soccer friend, a coach, a trainer? I guess there's a chance B wasn't the person at the party, but—"

"Did connect her with that person," Gabi finished. "I don't know. The fact that we have two options feels too coincidental."

Our eyes connected above the pages. So. The list was down to two. Well, two with a rectangle T-shirt bullet.

"There's nothing else concrete?" Gabi asked.

"Not that I can tell. At first, the entries are raw. She seems panicked—not just by the ankle. In the later pages, she's brief and chipper. It's like she's insisting, even to a private journal, that everything is under control. It's, um . . . hard to read, actually."

Gabi nodded, mouth pressed tight. "I still want to, though."

"Yeah, of course." I handed the journal over. "Make sure I didn't miss anything."

"Here." She pulled her phone from her blazer pocket. "Find Brooks's and Ben's social media from the journal days. Just in case they were obviously out of town or something."

I nodded. "Then we should look through our texts and photos. Maybe one of us was with Sophie on the days she mentioned."

We both sat there for a moment, still adjusting to the wind

change. This was the most concrete thing we'd had since the text message, months ago.

"Do we tell someone?" Gabi asked quietly. "Do we show Sophie's mom? Or give this to Dr. Ryan Something?"

I stared at the journal, now resting in her hands. "Do you think they'd take it seriously? Ginny's all hyped about this house, and I'm not sure she'd even want this drudged up."

Gabi ran her thumb across the cover. "And school has finally calmed down a tiny bit."

Neither of us spoke our big fear: that these adults would see two lost girls, thrashing in the maelstrom of grief. They'd see delusion; they'd see obsession over something beside the point. This was more than that.

We nodded, yet another pact between us.

I was mid-journey through Brooks's many outdoor sport vignettes when a text dropped down on Gabi's phone. Her mom, asking *Need anything? Will bring a plate of food up shortly—can leave outside door. XOXO.*

"Here," I said, shoving the phone at Gabi. "Text came in."

She glanced at it. "You hungry? . . . Actually, my mom will bring up a mountain of food regardless. So, any requests? Have you ever tried Oaxacan food?"

"Nope."

"Sample plate it is."

"Thanks," I said, with a flash of embarrassment. I'd been so single-minded, charging over here. "Please tell your mom I'm sorry I just barged in like this—"

"Oh, stop." Gabi glanced up from the phone. "Even if it *had* been about holiday feelings, I'd have stepped away. Just like you would have for me."

Yes, I would have, in a heartbeat. Somewhere in these past few months, this had become a real friendship. At least, it had for me.

"All the nativity and kid stuff was earlier anyway," Gabi continued. "By now, I'm usually stuck refereeing my little cousins as they come down from sugar highs."

"Okay," I said, convinced enough.

"Holy shit." Gabi reached out to grip my arm. "Barrett."

"Barrett?"

Gabi pressed her hands to the side of her head, like preventing her mind from exploding. "Warner's older brother. He's a senior at Ingleside this year."

Warner, who hosted the party where Sophie died.

"The T-shirt," Gabi continued. "Maybe Barrett was home, staying out of the way in his room. Or maybe he was out and got home, texted Soph."

It sounded much more likely than anything else. My body felt frozen in place, shallow breathing my only movement.

"He tutored her," Gabi whispered, fierce. "In pre-calc. Second semester."

"That was him?" My voice sounded more like breath than words. Last year, Sophie's perfectly fine grades made Ginny nervous about the SATs. Sophie rolled her eyes when she told me. *Oh well*, she said. *It's just one morning a week.*

Gabi reached her hands to her laptop, navigating to Ingleside's school paper. The search returned an article that showed Barrett Evans in uniform, posing with a robotics creation. But the third or fourth golf team picture Gabi clicked had Barrett in a polo shirt, his left arm showing and without a birthmark. "Okay. So, it's not him in the picture. But it doesn't mean he wasn't there."

"No, it doesn't." I settled in, crossing my legs. "What do you know about him?"

"Not a lot." Gabi pressed her hands together. "Warner has always been our class's unofficial social chair. I've never seen Barrett out anywhere but, like, events with parents around. He seems very school-focused."

This, I surmised, was Gabi's delicate way of saying that Barrett was not the cool older brother.

I could still see Warner's face at the funeral, slack and gray-tinged. Did he know? "Okay, then! Looks like I'm flubbing my next math test after break."

Gabi looked troubled. "Do you have to screw up your math grade to set up tutoring?"

"I doubt Barrett has, like, a website. It's probably just word-of-mouth. I'll need his contact info from Ginny."

"Mm," Gabi said. "True. So, how do you play it with him?"

I bent forward, stretching my legs. "If I can set up tutoring myself, he doesn't have to know I'm Sophie's cousin. Maybe I make up a running injury, talk about the pain."

We stopped discussion when Gabi's mom brought us two plates of delicious food. With her kind face smiling at me, I should have felt guilty. I'd spent the back end of this year conspiring with Gabi, while her mom believed us to be commiserating—healing. Which we were, in our own way.

It was hard to feel bad about it with the journal shoved under the bed, real and waiting.

After her mom had gone, I looked at Gabi. "You're out of town till after New Year's?"

"Yeah," she said. "But that gives us some time to strategize."

I walked out into the cold, burning with possibilities: the letter B, a birthmark on an arm, so many faces. At the end of

Gabi's street, I took a left, driving deeper into Eastmoore. The Evans family's address was easy enough to find in property records, and I'd looked at the street view online. But idling a few houses down, I finally set eyes on the place where Sophie died. Each window had a plastic candle, illuminating evergreen boughs on the sills. When I closed my eyes, the images from inside swirled: the junior girls posing, two guys roughhousing, Jenny Lisk laughing as beer dribbles down her chin.

Someone walked through that door with death in his pocket. *His*—I could say that now. With only four people left, I should have felt exhilarated. Instead, I stared at the house in the mid-December dark, and I wiped away a tear.

DECEMBER

- - - - - - - - - -

Senior Year

The second annual Girls' Winter Holiday Luncheon is held on the first truly cold day of December. When Ginny asks about Ingleside, I gush about my classes. I tell her that my feature story on a local band was accepted with enthusiasm, and I rode that success onto a new pitch: *Seniors Confidential: The Uncertainty and Regrets Behind the Perfect CVs.*

"People actually seem eager to share," I explained. "With anonymity, of course."

"That sounds interesting," Ginny says, fork and knife poised for a delicate bite of halibut. "What are the common responses?"

"Well, they're contradictory. Some people wish they'd loosened up a little." Specifically, Zoe, who announced that she'd been a bit uptight. Her uncertainty about college is making friends. She said, very neutrally, *I get the impression I'm an acquired taste.*

"Others wish they would have applied themselves better. With uncertainties, it's mostly school choice and major."

"What do you think the piece's takeaway will be?" Ginny asks, her journalist gears whirling. "Balance? The merits of choosing a path and following it through?"

"Good question," I say. "I guess I'll find out as I keep working."

I'd moved on from my JJ disappointment with a long Sunday walk. I left the season's last good sunflowers on Sophie's grave and reworked the plan.

On our side of the table, Maddie and I swap stories about being the new girl. She likes St. Anne's more than she expected. I choose benign Ingleside stories like the senior prank in which students drop everything and break into the fight song each day—the time of day changes, posted by a football player the night before.

Eventually, in a brief lull, my mom announces, "Hannah's going to a party tonight."

"How wonderful!" Ginny looks at me like I'm a dog dancing on its hind legs. Honestly—I'm a homebody, not a hermit. "I'm so glad that you're connecting with your classmates. Any names I would know?"

"Zoe, right?" my mom says.

"Zoe Walsh, of course." Ginny says. "Sharp gal. Very 'together.' Her parents always had the most interesting stories of their travels."

"Mm-hmm." In my desperation to change the subject, I ask, "How's the house coming?"

Ginny and my mom go still in the candlelight, transparently surprised by my interest. Ginny recovers first. "Oh, great. Thank you for asking."

She rattles on for a while about the bathroom "gut job" and construction timelines. I nod along politely, spearing my Brussels sprouts. My least generous thought remains: Ginny can fix up the house to her liking in a way she could never quite fix up Sophie.

For the rest of dinner, I let myself imagine that Sophie is just upstairs in her room, taking too long to get ready. Never so far away from me and never fully gone.

———————

Zoe is a neurotic host armed with absurd amounts of charcuterie. I arrive early to help with setup, since I'm the one who talked her into this "petite soirée." She wished she'd loosened up, so I nudged.

"Pause," I tell her. She's wearing a red headband, which makes her look like a long-haired Snow White. "Sip."

She accepts a cup of the punch that she asked me to fine-tune. She wanted something wintery, but clear in case of spills. Her parents are in Aspen till Sunday night, but no amount of time can fix cranberry juice on an antique rug. "Oh, that's it! What did you add?"

"Ginger ale."

"Perfect. *Fin.*"

Her friends, who graduated Ingleside last year, arrive early, bubbling over with excitement. At school, I know Zoe as a one-woman show, so it's nice to see her with a comfortable group. Her friends complain about being home for break—the boredom of this town—but, in truth, they seem happily inside their comfort zone.

Two hours into the party, I drop onto the couch next to Warner, who is finally alone after his mingling. In our interview earlier this week, he admitted to feeling unsure about his major, which I commiserated with deeply. I didn't have the guts to ask about regret.

"All I Want for Christmas is You" comes on as part of the meticulous playlist. Brooks, in front of the kitchen island, spins a senior girl in an impromptu dance.

"Oh, wow," I say. "Good moves for a drunk person."

Warner laughs, lifting a cup of the punch. "It's his turn to drive, actually."

Blinking at the scene before me, I try to reconcile that information. Brooks seems so different—body looser, quicker to smile.

"He doesn't really like school," Warner adds. "Or home."

"So he's happy at parties and . . . ?"

"At soccer. Skiing, doing outdoor stuff. At my house. And that's actually a lot of the time."

Brooks remains a collage of athleisure ads and cologne samples. He can be witty and good-natured. But occasionally, I feel a pulse of something sinister. I'll look across the lunch table at this boy the world wouldn't dare touch. Maybe it's that he looks like he'd play a frat guy in an *SVU* episode. Or maybe it's more than that.

When I tried to interview Brooks, he told me that he didn't have any regrets or uncertainty. To Warner, I say, "Think I should try for an interview again, now that he's relaxed?"

Warner snorts. "Don't take that personally. His real answer about uncertainty is, like . . . everything."

"Really? Seems pretty confident to me."

"I know how it seems," Warner says. "But his dad's, like, really hard on him."

"Well," I say, considering jolly Mr. Van Doren. "Brooks has a lot of advantages, right? It makes sense that his parents would want him to take those things seriously."

"Sure. But his dad doesn't care if he's succeeding or failing except for how it reflects on their family. It's like . . . he wants to be the dad of a son who drives an Audi. He didn't get Brooks that car to be nice."

"I know the type." Though I hardly consider that the worst fate in the world.

When I look over at Warner, he's watching my expression like he senses a skeptical audience. He's in a rust-colored sweater, and the warm color suits him. "When we were ten, I turned my ankle pretty bad on the way back from playing in the woods near Brooks's house. He wouldn't leave me to go get help because the sun was setting. I never would have admitted it, but I was still terrified of the dark. So, he piggybacked me until we found a stick big enough to be a crutch. Never told anyone I cried."

"Mm." What I can't say out loud is that people can be a lot of things: a cousin with a heart on her sleeve and a secret in her back pocket. But I take Warner's point, and I understand that he told me out of loyalty. "Sounds like a good friend."

"You have no idea," Warner says flatly. He takes a long drink. "Can I ask you something?"

I swallow so hard that I expect to hear a *gulp* noise. "Sure."

"Do you know what happened last year?"

Okay, here we go. My awareness hums to life. "Yeah. And I'm so sorry, Warner. It must have flipped your life upside down."

"It did. And Brooks just . . . stayed with me. When parents blamed me—turned on my parents, the whole thing—and I

183

definitely blamed myself, he wouldn't hear it. He talked me down a hundred times. Slept on my floor some nights."

"Wow," I say, sounding duly impressed. But this tells me something: if Brooks was the person who texted Sophie that night, Warner doesn't know about it. He couldn't. Because that unflagging friendship wouldn't be so impressive; it would be guilt. But his own brother, on the other hand . . .

"Anyway!" Warner says brightly. Then, glancing over the rim of his plastic cup with a grin, "God, what is in this punch that even my meds can't keep me from being a bummer? Red wine?"

His meds. Maybe that's part of how he crawled out of the pit of last year's August. I smile back, though, and we move along.

After another hour, I abscond to the all-season room off the side of the house, and I relax into a couch there, running my hand over the persimmon fabric. The window reflects a translucent girl, and I face off with her. If I let myself think about it too much, my life now feels like two walls closing in on either side. One is the Hannah I used to be, and one is the Hannah I will have to be after this year. I hold my arms out, shaking with the effort to keep both of them away from me.

I see Dailey's reflection first, sauntering with a plate in hand. There's a spark of relief at the sight of him, which I resent. Pathetic, how quickly I've warmed to an ally.

He settles onto the couch, keeping a few inches between us.

"I didn't know you were coming to this," I say.

Through a bite of cracker he says, "Jordy's plus-one."

"Right." Jordy is one of the more beloved figures of the Ingleside social scene. I interviewed him for my article yesterday and walked away rather charmed. He has questionable taste in friends, of course.

"So. You're hiding?" Dailey asks, gesturing at the couch.

"I guess." Regrouping. Sorting through my conversation with Warner. "Are you?"

"Oh, definitely." He holds the plate in my direction, offering one of the many cheese options. I take one with a dill sprig on it. "I'm mostly used to the rich kid stuff. As you forced me to point out last year, I'm the one who made the ethically controversial decision to attend private school."

I pause my chewing to smile. Our topic was: *Private schools should not exist.* After I won the coin toss, I chose to argue against the measure, just to watch Dailey take an ardently anti-private school stance while wearing a school crest.

"But sometimes," he continues, "the flippant way they talk about college stuff pushes me toward the edge."

"A cross to bear for the middle-class white guy with a scholarship."

"Fair enough." He offers me the plate again, but I demur. "So, update me on the seniors article. Anything new?"

"Not really." I turn over my shoulder, even though I can see behind us in the windows. I drop my voice all the same. "I did talk to Ashby."

"Oh yeah?"

"Don't get too excited. His regret was underestimating an opponent at State sophomore year. His uncertainty about college is being a small fish in a big pond, running D-1."

"All running related," Dailey says glumly.

"Exactly. And I even teased him about it, like *Nothing personal? Must be nice.*" For just a flash, I swear he went somewhere else in his mind. There was an answer knocking on his door, and he pretended like he couldn't hear it. "But, as he pointed out, he's always gone out with Violet. No relationship regrets."

"Hmm. Have other people been confessing their relationship woes to you?"

"A few." I like to think I'm a good interviewer who makes people feel comfortable. But also, I'm a mostly unknown new kid, and school's almost over. Why not vent? "No one gives specifics. They'll say they missed a shot with someone or dated a real loser."

"Mm." He nods knowingly.

"You dated a real loser?" I ask, joking right past my genuine interest.

"Oh, no way." He's perfectly relaxed in this topic, selecting another cracker. "Had some good runs with Mia, on and off since freshman year. And we're still friends."

Past tense, then. The buzz from testing punch recipes is long gone, but I still feel emboldened. Maybe the reporter stuff is sinking in. "Why are you off now?"

"Because we were on and off since freshman year." He shoots me a wry smile. "The good stuff that brings us back together isn't enough to last long. So, we broke the cycle."

"Sorry," I say. It seems like a sad thing, to try your best and still have to cut your losses.

"Don't be. It's good. I like her new boyfriend, even."

"*Very* big of you," I say, with mock solemnity.

He gives me a nose-wrinkled, play-snooty face, and I smile. The beats of silence are a comfort level. We are two people who know each other now.

I stand abruptly. "I should get back in there."

I've become fond of Dailey, and it rips at my seams. Old ideas of him splitting. Old ideas of myself. But I've damn well learned my lesson about warm feelings and this particular boy.

I'm halfway gone before he calls, "Okay, see ya."

———————

At the party's end, I clear cups and trays with Zoe. A few of her college freshmen friends are still here, tucked into their catch-up conversations in the living room. Zoe is pleasantly buzzed and we're back, once more, to her portfolio.

"Here," she says, handing me her phone. "The last six in my favorites. How do they look together? Be honest."

I've *been* honest about her portfolio choices, but Zoe tends to fixate. I can't exactly throw stones, considering that my whole life is a glass house. "Perfect."

"Ugh. Really?" She sprays a platter. "Scroll up and tell me if there are any others you'd consider."

"Wait, I've never seen this one!" I say. The background is a landscape, warm light cast on summer trees. Painted across the canvas, however, are four crimson words: YOU BROKE MY HEART. "Holy shit."

"Oh, that." Zoe glances over and snorts. "Should *not* be in favorites. Garbage."

"Not to me." This piece is beautiful and strange, full of anger. Did nature break her heart? Did the world? "There's so clearly a story here."

She laughs darkly. "It's how I met my last-year boyfriend."

"The jerk?" I ask. A peal of laughter comes from the other room.

"Mm-hmm," Zoe says, with perhaps a little satisfaction at

the tasty gossip. "My professor said I should work on a landscape for my portfolio, so I trekked up to the nature preserve to paint *en plein air*, right?"

"Of course you did," I say.

"I'm intense. It is known." She brushes her hair back. "So, a cute guy was passing by on the trails and stopped to chat. We talked again the next day, and . . . well, I got really great at tree brushwork after a week of that."

I can imagine Zoe in the woods—a pretty oddity with her easel, brows furrowed over the tiniest detail. "Wow."

"It's like a movie, right?" she muses. "A boy who came to follow the path through the woods; a girl who stands in one place to paint them. We were admiring the same place, but in different ways. We talked about things like that."

"Romantic," I admit.

"So, you can see why I fell for it." Zoe smiles, and then, mocking her own voice: " 'Oh, of course I'll meet you for dinner. Yes, please do tell me about your painful past. *I* understand you.' Ninny behavior."

"And then . . ."

"A cheater." She drops her hand like a gavel. With a sigh, she says, "So many, many weasels in this world, Hannah."

Something inside of me—maybe my conscience—flinches. Here I am, lying by omission, over and over. "What if you became a prolific painter of weasels? Like Hunt Slonem and rabbits—hundreds of canvases, all colors and sizes."

Zoe shrieks out a laugh. "Stop! Oh my gosh. And I name each piece after a different, rotten boy. I'll fill a gallery! I'll do commissions."

"But this," I say, waving the painting on her phone, "is good. It's not just realism. It's *real*."

"Zo!" someone calls from the next room. "We need paper towels!"

"For God's sake," Zoe mutters, ducking to open a cabinet. Then, loudly, "It had better be the clear punch!"

She disappears with a roll of paper towels and a bottle of vinegar, and I realize there's a smile on my face. This is another person that I genuinely like.

And then I realize I have Zoe's phone in my hand, open to her photos. Before I can second-guess myself, I scroll to pictures from August last year, her every snapshot a blur beneath my thumb.

Finally, my eye catches the cherry-colored top Zoe wore the night Sophie died. There are a few photos of her with two friends. These are Zoe's only pictures from that night—before then, two hands interlocked over a car console and after that, a sunset. The party picture from 9:47 p.m. is familiar—the trio in a flattering selfie. But four minutes before, they'd had someone else take the photo. That pose shows far more people on the periphery. And the couch.

On it, Sophie is angled toward Christian Dailey. My hands begin to shake, cradling a new photo of my cousin. I'd always figured they talked for a minute in passing, about soccer or classwork. I never imagined a seated conversation that is so . . . locked in. I zoom in to Sophie's active listening face. Dailey's expression is blocked by the angle. What the hell were they talking about? My entire view of him flops upside down.

"Hannah?" Zoe calls, and I startle, nearly dropping her phone. "Can you grab baking soda out of the bottom left drawer?"

I set the phone down with trembling fingers. "On it!"

———————

The day after the party, I stay at Sophie's grave for longer than usual, debating. Do I confront Dailey head-on? No—too volatile. I'll move to a slow play: say nothing and buy myself time to consider motives and next moves.

It's easy enough to sidestep Dailey during our last week before break. I give him tight, cursory smiles in the hallway like any other classmate. We're all buzzing with an antsy energy—collective obsession about term papers and finalizing college applications. After my biology exam, I'll be home free—a brief Christmas with my mom and then off to California.

I'm walking to my lunch period, talking with Warner about our bio final over the bustle, when a girl I don't know approaches.

"Hannah MacLaren?" she asks.

"Yeah?"

"I'm a runner for the office." She hands me a small piece of paper. "The Head of School needs to see you."

"Now?"

"Yep."

My eyes dart down the hallway, as if the reason will appear. "Did she say why?"

"Nope. Mrs. Modi is with her."

My nose goes cold, blood draining from my face. "That's weird."

"Oh, stop. You're probably getting an award for most impressive new student ever," Warner says. "Go. I'll grab you a yogurt."

"Thanks," I say, absently, and I shove my biology flash cards at him.

After the fastest walk before an outright jog, I arrive in the office, breathing heavily. The administrator behind a computer glances up with alarm.

"What's wrong—is it my mom?" I ask. "Hannah MacLaren. I'm Hannah."

"No, sweets. They always tell me if it's family stuff." She raps lightly on the door and then opens it for me. "Go on in."

Dr. Ryan wears a festive Scotch plaid blazer and a tense, white-lipped expression. Beside her, my English teacher gestures to something on the computer screen. Mrs. Modi is an Ingleside institution—tough but funny. Right now, there is no humor on her face.

"Hannah," the Head of School says, gesturing out to the chair. "Please sit."

I truly might yak on my dress shoes. I sit.

"I'll cut right to the chase." Both sets of eyes study me. "We received an anonymous tip that led to a search of your locker."

I stare, blinking as the words register. "An anonymous tip about me?"

Dr. Ryan hands over a short stack of papers. I stare down, leafing quickly—essays, all related to the required reading from Mrs. Modi's class. "They're . . . English papers?"

"Two of them," Mrs. Modi says. "Not great ones, but solid. B, B+."

"I'm sorry," I say, shaking my head. "I'm not sure what this has to do with me? I wrote my final paper on artistic rendering in *The House of Mirth*."

The Head of School clears her throat. "The anonymous tip suggested that you've been offering your essay-writing services for a fee. Using your locker as an exchange drop box."

"Um, nope." My face crumples into blatant confusion. What the hell? "Exchange? Exchange for what?"

"Money," Dr. Ryan says simply.

I'm shaking my head, as much in confusion as denial. "Are you sure it was the locker assigned to me? This has to be a mistake."

But it's not. The realization lands like a boulder, and it rattles the earth at my feet. Someone's trying to get me kicked out of Ingleside, and he's treacherously close to succeeding. I grip both arms of the chair. That clever little jerk.

"It was your locker," Mrs. Modi says. Then, with a sincere look of hope, "Is there any explanation for this, Hannah?"

I set the essays down with a trembling hand. My brain pings in every direction. They think my motivation is money. The Head of School knows my aunt and uncle pay my tuition. Luckily, I have one solid fact to fall back on. "No. This is bizarre for several reasons, but one of them is that I don't use my locker. Ever."

The two women exchange a quick glance. Dr. Ryan looks back to me. "And why not?"

"It's in the sophomore hallway. I was a late addition, so I assume the senior hallway lockers were taken." I'm speaking too fast, sounding too desperate for absolution. "I don't have time to get there between bells. You can ask anyone who knows me. You can ask the sophomores who have lockers near mine. I haven't opened it since the first week of school. Security footage would prove that. And would maybe show who *did* put this in the locker."

Dr. Ryan's jaw clenches. "The locker is around a bend in the hallway that isn't monitored. But cameras can confirm who's heading toward or away from that hallway."

"It won't be me," I assure her. I need to poke more holes, cast reasonable doubt. "Someone must have noticed the locker is never used and decided to use it themselves. And why would I devise a locker system when all this could be done online, anonymously?"

"So that the transactions could happen in cash," the Head of School suggests. She tosses a stack of twenties, which land on the essays. "This was also found in your locker."

"Does anyone else know your lock combination?" Mrs. Modi asks.

"No," I say, glancing down at the pile of evidence before me. I need an alternative theory, fast. The papers are creased, folded in half. "Wait. Couldn't anyone have shoved these into the locker vents and called in the tip?"

Both women grimace in tandem. But I can see I have a foothold. How can I explain to them why someone would frame me? *Well, you see, I'm here to hunt down a pill dealer, and it seems I've rattled him . . .*

"My last appointment with my counselor . . ." I say slowly. "She told me, if I hold my mid-term grades, I'm poised to crack the top ten."

Dr. Ryan squints at me. "Bumping another student— possibly several—who have been at Ingleside for longer."

It does occur to me in this moment that Christian Dailey could be one of them. The counselor never mentioned names, but Dailey swans around like top ten is a given for him.

"This is a lot to take in." The Head of School takes the money and essays back. "I do believe you, Ms. MacLaren, and we'll be reviewing the hallway cameras. But we've had issues with a similar cheating scandal a couple years ago, so this is very unfortunate déjà vu for us."

"You're a wonderful student, Hannah," Mrs. Modi says. "I hope you can understand that we had no choice but to . . ."

"I do."

Dr. Ryan gives me one more troubled look. "Please get a pass if you need."

As I walk the empty hallways of Ingleside Country Day School, I fume. But there is also something electrifying in this contact. He knows who I am; he has guessed what I'm doing. And that means he's real, and he's guilty, and I am not boxing with shadows, panting alone in the dark.

This little stunt could have easily worked for him. But I also might be able to smoke him out. The more he acts, the likelier he is to make a mistake.

I divert my path to the journalism lab and pace around there. It only takes Catherine a few minutes to show up.

"Hey, Hannah." She strides in with a binder tucked under her arm. At the sight of my expression, she stalls out. "What's wrong?"

It's a game time decision, but I trust her. And more important, I need her. "I just got pulled into the headmaster's office and accused of running an essay-writing ring. They found two English papers and cash in my locker."

Her eyes widen. "You're kidding."

"No. There's not enough evidence for me to be in real trouble, fortunately."

"But someone's got it out for you." Catherine's gaze moves across the white board as if she's mapping possibilities. "You think it's Sophie-related?"

Well, there it is. The printer fans hum between us, the only sound.

"So you did know," I say.

Catherine shrugs, as if we'd mutually agreed to this knowledge and her silence. "You have your reasons for keeping it quiet, I assume."

"Did Gabi tell you?"

"Ha. No. I mean, she told me after you had that . . ." Falling out. Catherine is too polite to say it. She lands on, "Tough conversation. Otherwise, she doesn't want to talk about it."

Right. Well. Neither do I. "So, here's the thing. Dr. Ryan made a comment about this being a problem in the past. I figured, if anyone would know . . ."

"I would," Catherine finishes. She smiles. "And in fact, I do."

I pull up a chair. Sophomore year, the *Insider* editor at the time got a scoop: someone was running an essay-writing service. A kid got caught because he didn't even read the paper he turned in—couldn't answer a single question about it. When the administration interrogated him, he talked.

"His English grades were sinking—he was doing extra credit, tutoring, all of that," Catherine explains. "Then an anonymous emailer reaches out to him, offering a paper for a price. The kid had another huge test to study for that week, so he took it."

"Presumably paid anonymously?"

"Yep. Two hundred bucks to a cash app they couldn't trace."

"Oh my God," I mutter, the disdain rising from my chest. Two hundred dollars.

Catherine gives me a knowing look. "Yep."

"So you think the person stopped after that kid blabbed? Or . . . ?" Oh, man. The thought pierces me down the center. "He kept at it, but the administration was focused on Sophie."

Catherine strums her nails, painted an orangey-red. "I'm not sure. After the article, Ingleside teachers revamped paper topics. The board paid for a detection system that saves all student papers in a database for searching. Maybe that's why it stopped. Or maybe the person running it graduated. Who knows?"

There's a little spark in this for Catherine—the thrill of a journalistic chase. I like her for it.

"But I didn't go here, so I obviously wasn't involved then," I reason. This feels sloppy, desperate. "Maybe he picked the essay thing because he knew it was a sore spot for the administration."

Catherine's eyes shoot back to mine, clocking the word choice. "He."

The precipice is before us, but the last inch is not mine to cross. "I don't want to get you wrapped up in this."

Catherine gives me an arch look. We both know what I mean: Gabi.

"She doesn't get to decide what I risk." Then, more quietly, "Sophie was my friend, too."

God, it still aches like hell—the depth of love and the breadth of loss. Every day that I walk into the mouth of this beastly school, I barricade my feelings off as best I can. They still find me.

The bell sounds overhead, and I spin to the clock, disbelieving. "Shit. I have to go take a biology exam."

"We'll figure something out," Catherine says, with her usual calm command. "Meet up after break?"

It feels so good to have another person—someone sharp, with new energy—on my team. The guilt is only a tiny flame. "Thank you. Really."

On the way out, my shoulder connects with someone else's, and I step back. "Sorry."

I'm staring at Gabi, her face fallen in surprise. "My fault. You okay?"

"Yeah, fine."

"You seem . . ." She's unspooling every possibility, taking in my body language. "Not fine."

I draw myself up. "Just handling a little issue."

She glances beyond me, probably reading Catherine's expression. "Oh?"

"Disagreement about an Oxford comma," I say, as lightly as I can. "So, you know . . . code red journalism emergency."

"Code red journalism emergency," Gabi repeats slowly. She knows it's made up, of course. We hold eye contact for another moment and she says, "Okay, then. Well, happy holidays."

I think of last year, shared plates of food on her bedroom floor and the sounds of singing from downstairs. I still don't know who B is, and now he's hunting me back.

"Yeah," I say, already past her. "You too."

- - - - - - - - - -

Junior Year

My mom and I spent a low-key Christmas at home, same as always. A days-long movie marathon. Delivering cookies to neighbors. Claiming that we would organize the downstairs closet only to remove half the items and mostly give up.

It had always been important to my mom that we had family traditions separate from anyone else, so I didn't feel Sophie's absence as acutely. Even the impending plans with Gabi were, necessarily, on hold.

Two days after Christmas, my mom and I were halfway through our bracket, ranking worst new holiday movies. My mom glanced at her phone and then motioned to for me to come outside.

"Outside?"

"Yep. C'mon. There's a late present on the porch."

I followed her to the front door, which she threw open with unusual panache.

A tall figure stood with his hands clasped, looking a bit sheepish under the porch light.

"What?" I screeched, flying forward. "Dad!"

Over appetizers at my favorite Mexican restaurant, my dad and I talked about my college plans. He pried about my love life (nonexistent); I pried about his love life (recent breakup—a bummer but the right choice).

When our entrees arrived, he really settled in. "Tell me about Sophie stuff."

Sophie loomed so large in all my childhood stories—my eternal conspirator. But my dad had only been around her a few times. "Um. Which stuff?"

"All of it. How you're feeling, how other people in her life are coping. Your mom said you've been spending some time with Sophie's other good friend?"

"Yeah." I pushed at my mountain of rice. "Gabi."

"Mm," he said, chewing slowly. "Are you and Gabi are helping each other heal? Because it's also easy to get trapped in a loop of the past with someone."

This was the thing with my dad. He'd worked the steps, done the moral inventory. The topics that made everyone else clench up? He set them into conversation like model sailboats on a pond.

I pressed my fork into my enchilada, oozing sauce. "Can it be both?"

"Like two steps forward, one step back? Yeah, I think it can be like that."

More like: Talking with Gabi gives me peace, but so does

single-mindedly winnowing down the pool of possible pill-mongers.

"We laughed about Sophie the other day," I said. "Like, really laughed. I didn't realize we were doing it until we caught our breath, you know?"

"Did it feel good?" he asked.

"Yeah. Until it didn't."

"Sure." Under the table, he shifted his legs. I was so used to hearing his voice, seeing his face on video chat. Sometimes, his body language was surprising—his hand gestures, the adjustments made for his height. "Letting the pain go feels like letting her go."

I nodded, swallowing around the lump in my throat.

"You mad at her?" he asked gently.

"At Soph?" My voice arrived as a raspy whisper. "No. I'm mad at myself."

His eyes went softer. "Why, kid?"

"I could have helped. I *would* have. Why didn't she tell me?"

My dad looked so terribly sad, watching me tread a path to nowhere. Tracing and retracing the steps. "There are so many reasons, and not a single one is your fault."

Adults said this a lot, and I was starting to find it very unlikely. How could so many things be my responsibility—my schoolwork, the plans for my future—but Sophie somehow wasn't? "Give me one example, then."

"Shame."

"But I don't think it's shameful!" I said, louder than I intended. "Sophie knew that!"

"You can't vanish an entire cultural mindset by yourself," he pointed out. "Here's another reason: I didn't even attempt recovery—for years—because I believed I was better drunk. With booze, I could tolerate myself, so the people in my life probably felt the same, right? Does that make any sense?"

It did, as much as anything could.

"Not actual sense," he amended. "But in my mind, I saw no problem."

I considered him, across from me. "Can you describe it to me?"

"What it felt like for me and drinking?" He took another bite, as casually as if I'd asked him to describe his meal. "Well, I only know my own stuff. But I can tell you quitting is like doing the hardest thing you've ever done, while feeling sick as shit— excuse me—crap. And you know you could get quick relief for the second one, but only by failing at the first. So, once you get to that point of needing to quit, it's just more . . ."

"Pain," I said quietly.

"Yep. Not physical, for me. But I had a lot of mess from childhood." He teetered his hand, pausing as he thought. "Plenty of people manage that without getting into a substance cycle. Your mom, for example. Who knows what the difference is? Community, safety, access to care."

I looked down at my hands, lacing my fingers in and out. "Sophie wasn't all sunshine, obviously. But Gabi recently mentioned that Soph had this melancholy side. She never stopped moving, like if she did, something would catch her."

"Mm. Do you agree?"

"Yeah." I dabbed at a tear, coughing as if the spice got to me. "But I don't have the same impulse. I keep wondering if that's why she didn't tell me."

My dad gave me a soft smile. "Even if that were true, could you change that about yourself?"

"No," I said quietly. The question was rhetorical, of course, and a reminder of the serenity prayer. Serenity felt miles away, behind a labyrinth of endless doors. "Could we talk about your job stuff now?"

He nodded, and I felt the buzz of something—his excitement traveling from his side of the table to mine. "Well, kid. There's actually news there. I landed a gaffer gig."

"Dad!" He'd wanted to lead the lighting department on-set for years, but it was the kind of thing you worked up to. "That's amazing!"

"Thank you, thank you. Someone I worked with a few years ago is the director of photography seat, and his first hire bailed. But the movie films in Vancouver, so I'll get to be up north for the summer."

"That's so cool. A whole nother country!"

"Salary bump, too," he said. "I mean, nothing major. Still piddly for LA. But I've got a bit earmarked for you to get a passport and a flight to visit Canada. If you'd like that."

I leapt from my seat, hugging my dad as soon as he stood. And my first thought—my first foolish, hard-wired thought: I can't wait to tell Sophie.

Senior Year

I spend the end of holiday break in LA, catching up with my dad. Over dinner at his favorite hole-in-the-wall, he asks me about Sophie, and I tell him the truth. In love and anger and sadness, she is never far from my mind.

From across the country, I stare at my game pieces. What to do about this person framing me? Will he get more desperate? And is Dailey lying to my face, hiding something I can't yet fathom? He texted me *Merry Christmas*, and I replied *You too*. I turn him over in my hands like a Rubik's cube, irritated but always returning.

My dad and I wander LACMA, and, when I try to imagine living in the city, the image feels dreamy, hazed over. One afternoon, we drive to the beach and eat french fries as the wind whips our hair. I think of the Magritte paintings that still haunt my sleep with oceans and the sky beyond half-open doors.

When I strip off my socks, stepping pale feet toward the water, my dad yells, "You're gonna freeze!" But it feels comforting. I plunge my hands in too, proof of what is real.

On the plane home, I consider what it would feel like to move to California and leave my entire Maryland life behind. Not my family, obviously, or Lincoln's family. But everything else—scrape down the canvas and begin painting anew. Could I leave the neighborhoods where I see memories of Sophie like old film reel? Could I visit her grave only on holidays?

I stare out at clouds suspended just beyond my reach.

Junior Year

As the winter winds swirled on, Sophie did not turn seventeen. I started her birthday with a nice, cleansing sob in the shower, and I emerged with an idea.

What are you doing right now? I texted Gabi. She'd convinced her parents to let her stay home from school by telling them I was allowed to. Little did they know about my mom's "It's your life, Bug" parenting philosophy.

Gabi replied in seconds. *Being miserable?*

Let's go somewhere. Then, in case it sounded like investigation talk, I added, *Like, for fun.*

The dots appeared then disappeared, clearly Gabi processing the idea. Finally: *Pick you up in fifteen.*

We drove around the outer belt to the indoor skydiving place that opened a month after Sophie died. She loved trampolines and park swings—anything that felt like flying without any real risk of falling. She'd planned to be first in line at this place.

I handed over my credit card, numb to the cost. It was a small exchange for surviving the day. Next came waivers and instructions and jumpsuits, with Gabi and I swapping nervous smiles.

The vertical wind tunnel looked straight out of a sci-fi movie set—a wide cylindrical tube, from floor to ceiling.

Gabi was chewing at one side of her lower lip.

"You okay?" I asked.

"I prefer being earthbound," she admitted, with a quick smile. "But this is good."

Still, I went first. I stood at the small entrance with arms up, palms flat, and elbows at an angle. The instructor waved me forward, her arms out ready to guide. She gave me the nod to tip gently forward, and I left the ground.

My body lifted against the column of air, limbs wobbling. Then flying.

The grin must have covered half my face. I screamed inside of my helmet, the sound of it lost to 120 mph wind. *Soph*, I thought. *Soph, you should be here.*

After Gabi's turn, she suggested we stop at a nearby bakery. We couldn't drop the momentum or we'd remember why we needed it.

When the server appeared, Gabi glanced at him over the top of a considerable menu. I was expecting her to politely ask for more time. Instead, she said, "Could we have one piece of every type of cake, please?"

I clamped a hand over my mouth. Yes—that was exactly right. The only way.

"Sure thing," the waiter said, smiling at our glee.

The plates filled the circular tabletop—vintage china rosettes and filigree. Gabi and I took bites from them all, reaching over each other and laughing. Neither of us whispered happy birthday; neither of us mentioned Sophie at all. Instead, we sat by the drafty window and talked about everything else, celebrating like Sophie was right beside us.

"Can you believe that, a year from now, we'll be done applying for college?" Gabi asked.

I gave her a sour look, mouth full of ganache.

"Isn't it a relief, in a way?" she asked. "There will come a day where that part is done. You still fleeing the tri-state?"

I sipped my water, buying time. Honestly, I'd hardly thought about it. Leaving Maryland felt like leaving Sophie. Staying felt like being conquered by loss. "Probably LA."

We moved on to other topics, and I only cried later, when I thought to check Gabi's social media. She'd posted for the first time in months—a picture of the table, with triangles of cake like a Wayne Thiebaud painting. *Happy 17*, it read. Comments turned off. *I miss you every minute.*

———————

"What's on your mind, Bug?" my mom asked. She was dicing vegetables for soup while I scrubbed at dishes. For the first two weeks of January, I'd been back to school and working toward this conversation.

"Eh." I waved one hand. "I bombed a pre-calc quiz—that's all."

"Really?" The chopping sound—knife to wooden cutting board—stopped. "Well, I'm sure you're just getting in the swing of things after break."

"Maybe." I dipped the sponge into a mug, working a coffee stain at the rim. "But I can't get integrals to click for me."

"You may not realize it, little wunderkind, but it's actually perfectly normal to not be great at something, even if you try hard." She leaned close enough to bump me with her hip. "You sleeping okay? They say most teenagers need ten hours."

"I'm sleeping," I said. And I was, some nights. "Better than in the fall anyway."

I could feel my mom staring as I stacked now-scrubbed forks.

"My beloved sister," she said, "thinks I should send you to a head shrinker."

Well, that was a left turn. My face stung with heat. "Why are you talking to Ginny about me?"

A ridiculous question. I used to see my mom and I as a duo, a two-person household doing things our own way. But when the chips were down, my mom chose her sister every time.

"Because, my love," my mom said gently. "There's a lot of your aunt in you, and when I want to understand—"

"Then ask me!" I said, forks clattering to the counter. "Ginny has no idea how I feel."

"I'm sorry." Her shoulders slumped. "That was the wrong way to bring it up. This isn't my forte, Bug—you know that. I don't know how therapy and all of that works."

I could never quite place my mom's stance on therapy. Extremely pro-AA and Al-Anon. Open about depression and anxiety and medication since I was little. But sometimes, when a TV episode mentioned talk therapy, she snorted from her side of the couch. To her, all therapists were white collar folks, looking at real problems like bugs pinned under glass. She could handle her own business.

"And yet, you've offered to set up an appointment for me," I reminded her. "Multiple times."

She studied my face. "Should I be insisting, though? That

doesn't seem right, since I've never done it myself. But Ginny says that Maddie is doing so well. She's become close with a few kids from her group session, and she's really voicing her feelings to Ginny."

"So, I'm supposed to 'voice my feelings' to you?"

"Hannah." She reached to touch my cheek, but I swerved. "You haven't mentioned Sophie in weeks—months."

Was that true? I thought about her constantly, but those thoughts were often pointed toward action. Maybe I'd trained myself to silence in front of my mom, afraid I'd reveal too much. "There isn't anything new to say. I miss her constantly."

"I know you do. Did you talk about her with your dad?"

"Yeah. You know how he is." Calm demeanor, with questions that probe your very soul.

Her expression changed to a careful neutral. "Do you think you'd feel better staying with him for a little while?"

I'd thought about it—of course I had. But that would mean walking away from my momentum with Gabi. Walking away from Sophie. "I'm not sure running from it would help."

She gave me her huffy, *who's-the-parent-here?* laugh. "Maybe not, Bug. I don't know. That's the truth: I don't know how to help you. Should I be asking more direct questions? Should I—"

"Mom," I said. "I'm really okay. Gabi and I talk about Soph all the time."

"And that's great. But here? I see you silent, I see you running miles and miles—"

"That's a healthy activity."

"To a point," she said sharply. "Floundering on math tests, though? Now, I don't care about the grades—you know that. But I care that it's a difference for *you*."

All solid points. On the debate stage, I'd be flipping through my notes, praying a helpful detail would jump out at me. "I feel about as good as I think you can expect, six months after. But I might need a little more help with this stretch of calc. That's all."

The staring continued—a piercing, green-eyed beam.

"If you say so," my mom decided.

I looked away and left the room before the guilt could catch me.

————————

I showed up early at the library for my tutoring session with Barrett Evans, settling in. Gabi had briefed me on him as best she could, but I still had no idea what to expect. A varsity golfer. Coding Club and Robotics. Middle child. In between two tall, redheaded siblings, Barrett stood average height with average brown hair.

In person, he was one of those guys you could immediately picture as a thirtysomething. The clothes weren't to blame—he wore his Ingleside uniform—but still, I saw him with a closet full of khakis and two kids at home. I raised one hand, motioning to him, and we made our introductions.

"So, Hannah." Barrett spoke like a guidance counselor, instead of someone a year older than me. "You said in your message that you've felt solid on everything so far, but integrals are tripping you up. You're all good with the quadratic formula?"

"Yes." I nodded, confident.

"Cool. Mind writing it out and explaining it to me?"

It was a strange hour. Sound tutoring, but with a very subtle smugness. I knew his type from being a shy girl in honors classes my whole life. Barrett seemed fairly run-of-the-mill smart, but he'd decided Genius was his identity. There was more than a whiff of misogyny to it.

I wondered if he'd made Sophie feel small. If she'd surprised him or wanted to. Maybe she was above all of that.

"Seems like you've got a decent grip on it," Barrett said, as the hour was winding down.

"Thanks," I said, lining up my shot. "I think I've been distracted in class. I'm a runner, and my shin splints have been acting up."

He glanced at his phone. "Bummer."

"Pretty common," I continued, despite his obvious disinterest. "And sometimes fine! But sometimes the pain pulls my attention away from class."

"I'm sure."

Huh. Nothing. Not even eye contact.

"Well, thanks for your help," I said brightly. "You applying for colleges and stuff?"

Barrett gave me a pitying smile, this naive junior who didn't understand the timeline. "All set. I did early acceptance."

"Oh, congrats!" I said, fiddling with my ponytail.

"I got into Yardley with an academic scholarship, so . . . yeah." Barrett smiled, letting this land for me. "It'd be a bad move to pass on that."

My smile became genuine. "So you're staying in town!"

"Yeah. I mean, I'm sure I could have gotten into an Ivy, but . . . why pay so much more?"

"Totally." *Keep him talking.* "Your parents must be so excited. My mom is a nervous wreck about my college stuff."

"Yeah." His gaze lifted past me, briefly, and I wondered if he was thinking of what his family had been through this year.

"Well, hit me up if you need any further help. You okay in your other classes? English?"

Resist the eye roll. "Totally solid there."

He nodded. "I usually find it's one or the other with math and English."

There was absolutely no reason for me to engage with this. But something inside me flared, refusing to quell.

"Yeah, it's so interesting, isn't it?" I said, through my smile. "Since Descartes was a writer and philosopher."

Barrett laughed, in that way people do when they don't have a response. It was a familiar sound on the debate stage—a low chuckle that makes derision seem good-natured. "Sorry— didn't mean to offend you."

Ah. Making this about my emotions instead of his wrongness. I wanted to say: *I'm not offended, just aware of the intricate links between fields that we're told are disparate.* I wanted to place my hands on either side of my mouth and holler *Polykleitoooos* into the quiet library. But I had to focus on the big picture, even if it made me sweat with repressed rage.

"You didn't," I bit out, through my too-toothy smile.

After that charade, I drove straight back to Gabi's, wringing the steering wheel like a neck. I reported the entire interaction, ranting despite myself. "So, he's staying local, which might be good for us. I do think it's relevant that he seems high on his own cleverness."

Gabi spun in her chair, a hundred and eighty degrees and then back. "Yet absolutely no reaction when you vented about pain."

"Nothing." I coiled the end of my ponytail around one finger.

"I wish I'd inherited the tech-building gene," Gabi mused. "I could talk robotics with Barrett."

Gabi's grandfather was a chemist who became a serious computer hobbyist and eventual patent holder. Mrs. Reyes grew up building electronics with him.

"That was your Lita's husband, right?" I asked. I'd met her Lita twice now. Both times, she spoke to me directly about Sophie, which I appreciated.

Gabi smiled at his memory. "Yeah. Gone since I was eleven."

"She must miss him a lot."

"She does. But he's also very present for her. Last week, I caught her muttering at him, 'You just wait till I get there,'" Gabi said. Then, quickly, "I mean, she's not, like, out of touch with reality."

With a privately amused smile, I said, "I get it."

All these months, I'd learned about Gabi in the spaces between our investigation. She used to dance, but the strain of all-weekend-long competitions and travel became too much. She can't resist a nature documentary, and she idolizes her older sisters, even when they annoy her.

"You okay?" Gabi asked.

"Um," I said, rubbing at my temples. "Yeah. I just thought we were closer."

"Me too." Gabi sighed, leaning back. "The journal seemed like the key to everything."

Truthfully, I was raging inside, fully done with delicate information gathering. What had been a contained fire was crawling out across the floorboards. "I'm ready to confront them."

Senior Year

The first day back, I get to school early with two double lattes in my hand. I stride the floors in my black Mary Janes, feet firmly on the path. Now that it's second semester, class periods will shift to accommodate new electives. I'll no longer share first period with Ben Ashby.

Catherine's at her seat in the journalism lab, where I knew she'd be starting her Monday with the editorial schedule. I hand her one of the coffees and announce, "I need to plan a nuclear option, and I'm hoping you can help."

She takes a sip of the latte, eyes closed in contentment, and then rolls her chair out. Her trousers are technically school regulation—that heavy chino fabric—but they've been tailored into high-waisted flares. "Say more."

I settle in the seat nearest to her. "It may get to the point that my only move is to make everything I know public. Set the whole school on the chase."

Catherine's exhale becomes a low whistle. "Chaos option."

It's true—the school would descend, again, into rumors and finger-pointing. It might cloud the facts even more. "Only as a last-ditch effort. I'll just feel better having a plan to do it— anonymously."

She rests her chin on one hand. "Publish something in the *Insider*, you mean?"

Part of me expects the floorboards to shake—Gabi sensing the suggestion and rushing to shut it down. "That would get linked to you. But what else? A throwaway email account sending info to the whole school?"

"A dummy social media account that sends info to a few targeted gossips." Catherine crosses her legs. "Do you want it to be flashy? Matter-of-fact? Do we want info reaching students before teachers or at the same time?"

"Good questions. I'll mull them over, but let me know if you have any genius ideas."

"Want to put a deadline on it?" Catherine asks. She returns the smile that has quirked up on my face. "Yes, I'm an editor to my core."

May is too late—too close to the last day for seniors. If I turn my classmates into a search party, I need school to be in session for at least a few weeks. "Late April."

Catherine turns to the school calendar mounted on the wall. "Around prom time?"

"Yeah," I decide. "Around prom time."

— — — — — —

Dailey's waiting outside my second period class, and despite preparing for this moment, I nearly stumble in the emotion of it. After two weeks, I've accepted that I'm back at the starting line with him, questioning every interaction. Mortifyingly, it still hurts.

"Hey," he says, pushing off the wall. "How was LA?"

"Fine, thanks." I give him as much of a smile as I can manage. All I see is the boy from freshman year, spurning me in front of his fancy schoolmates.

The beat of silence stretches into a full pause. Dailey, peering at me, tries again. "My break was good too. Thanks for asking."

A breathy laugh leaves my throat. "Sorry. I'm kind of in my head about being a second semester senior. It's more intense than I thought."

"Yeah," he says. "Like relief *and* pressure? We're supposed to just keep learning as if our fates won't be sent by colleges at any random moment from now till Spring Break?"

"Exactly." I glance beyond him, to my usual seat. "Talk later?"

"Sure." He almost walks off, but he turns back—maybe trying to catch me in a hidden emotion. "Sure you're okay?"

Dailey's maddening face looks so earnest. Is he a very good actor? Or am I simply weak?

I nod and take my seat.

— — — — — —

Over the weekend, Zoe invites me to an art gallery and brunch with one of her studio friends. I should appreciate the reprieve from school, but of course I stare quietly at surrealist portraiture and curse my ticking clock. I'll have to incite—more than prying with my *Insider* senior questions but less than my public-tell-all, nuclear option.

This is what I'm debating on my drive home, when I notice the car behind me. There's no straightforward path from the east side brunch place to my street in West Grove.

That means this guy behind me, in a silver car, just made an unusual turn.

I try to laugh at myself. To ease my mind, I pull into the next public lot—a gas station with plenty of people coming and going—without signaling. There's an open spot near the door, and I brake too hard, my instincts knocked off by nerves.

The car behind me slides up to one of the gas pumps. Okay. He probably took that side street because he needed gas. Honestly, Hannah.

Still, I walk inside, stalling for time. I grab some gum next to the register and pay for it, with one eye trained on the man.

He is not pumping gas. He hasn't gotten out of his car.

So what? I tell myself. *He's texting someone. Checking email.*

Walking back outside, I bite the plastic wrap on my pack of gum. I move toward a nearby trash can, which takes me a few steps closer to the silver car.

The guy remains behind the wheel, difficult to see clearly—particularly with sunglasses on. He's white and, from here, has no stand-out facial features. He's the guy working at the bank or in the grocery store or any number of my uncle Andrew's friends.

Just pull out of the spot and prove how silly this, I tell myself. But in the past year, I've learned to catch the scent of anything even slightly out of place. This is a book shoved in the wrong spot, a door left unlocked, an item returned but askew. I grip the wheel tight.

When I'm back onto the street, he's behind me, and now I have decisions to make. I can't drive home—that much is clear. Do I try to lose him? Drive to the police station and park in the lot? That will communicate to my stalker that I noticed—does that change anything? I'm on the edge of Hathaway, and I can only think of one option. Too panicked to question it, I reach for my phone, dialing with shaky hands.

Dailey answers by saying, "Always hot and cold with you, MacLaren."

"Where are you?"

"Walking into my apartment." The mockery has dropped from his voice. "Why? What's wrong?"

"I'm driving home, and I think I'm being followed." I glance back for confirmation. There would be some irony in the car peeling off only after I make a dramatic call to Dailey. "What's my move, you think?"

"Um, okay," he says. "Let me think. Put me on speaker so you can keep both hands on the wheel."

As if I hadn't already. I'd roll my eyes, but I have to keep them on the road. "It's a silver sedan. A Toyota, driven by a white guy with sunglasses on. Maryland plates. Can't quite make out the license number, but maybe if I catch a long stoplight."

"Where are you?" His breathing gets louder, like he's hurrying.

"Larabee, by the laundromat."

"Head toward my place," Dailey says. "Take the turn onto Hudson. I'm getting in my car right now, and I'll drive toward you. If he's still following at McMillan, I'll try to get between."

I exhale. That, at least, is a plan. I won't be leading this stranger to my home or anywhere else. "He's keeping pretty close."

On Dailey's end, I hear an engine turn. "Then, I'll at least pull behind him and get his plates."

My hands shake against the wheel, and I grip harder, trying to calm them by force. "What if I make it all the way to your street and he's still on me?"

"One sec," Dailey says. "Let me make this turn, and . . ."

How nice for him, that he can tackle one issue at a time. "Better put me on speaker so you can keep both hands on the wheel."

He is, I'm sure, giving a deadpan look to no one. "It's reassuring, actually, that you're calm enough to bust my balls."

I glance to my rearview mirror again. "I just took another left. He's still there."

"Okay," Dailey says. "It's okay."

I swallow down the bile rising in my throat. How can something feel both shocking and inevitable? I've been courting this escalation, summoning it. With the senior interviews, I was standing at the center of the arena, screaming: *Someone come and face me!*

"Hey, Dailey? If you were trying to get me kicked out of school, how would you do it?"

There's a long pause. "Am I a version of myself with different principles?"

"Oh my God," I mutter.

"Fine. I guess I'd . . . try to get photo or video of you doing something illegal or against honor code."

"Yeah," I say, glancing at my rearview mirror. "That's what I'd do too."

This guy on my tail is getting down the routine, maybe. Figuring out where I spend my time. If I hadn't noticed him, would he be staring at my bedroom window while I study or sew?

For another minute, I steer in a driving-test-perfect way: alert, hands in position, eyes moving from the road ahead of me to any possible threat.

"I'm coming up on Fern," I tell Dailey. McMillan is next.

"I'm here," Dailey says. His truck idles, turn signal blinking, and I inhale more easily, past the tight feeling in my lungs. This is bizarre and scary, but now someone can see me.

In my rearview, I watch Dailey's truck get behind the silver sedan. "Okay, clearly, I couldn't cut him off. But we've got two four-way stops ahead, so I should be able to get plates."

"Where should I go?" I brake at the first stop sign.

"Head to my apartment," Dailey says. "I'll meet you there."

"And lead this guy to your place? That makes no sense."

"Trust me—it'll take me ten, maybe fifteen minutes."

"To do what, Dailey? What does your apartment change about this?" It's my turn at the four-way, and I have to go.

"Hannah, I've got it, okay?" The line clicks out.

"Christian!" I yell into the empty quiet of the car. "Shit!"

Another car turns behind me, and I lose my view of the silver sedan. At the first stoplight, I call his phone again, but he doesn't pick up. *What is going on???* I type. The light turns green before I can smash my finger on the pissed emoji at least ten times. This is what I get for the badly wired instinct to call Dailey for help.

It's all good, he texts back, a few minutes later. *Be there soon.*

I park behind his building, finally wiping my clammy hands. What the hell just happened? Some unrecognizable man following me? He could be a dealer or an enforcer—is that TV show drama? Or is that real and my life? My frustrated tears are stoppered by annoyance at Dailey, who is out there commandeering the situation.

When his truck bumps into the lot, I spring out of my car. He appears unharmed, though his hurried gait lacks its usual swagger.

"What's wrong with you?" I yell, swatting his arm. The hit makes only a soft pat on the corduroy sleeve of his coat.

Dailey holds his phone out to me. The picture is the car's license plate, from a closer angle than Dailey could have gotten from inside his car. "It's fine. I just tapped his bumper at the stop sign."

Words won't come out right away, so I lift my hands. "You did *what?*"

"It's fine. Worked perfectly." While I'm taking the long breath it will require to yell more, Dailey adds, "Well, not perfectly. The scratch wiped right off, so he didn't want to exchange names and insurance information. But I got him off your tail, and I got this."

It's a picture of the guy's face, though it's from a weird angle. He has a reddish, angry face and a plaid button-down. I don't recognize him, and I'm still reeling. "What if he'd had a gun?"

"Well, he didn't." Dailey pockets his phone and turns to study me. "You okay? Honestly, MacLaren."

"I guess." I run a hand through my hair. No, I'm not okay, and I got Dailey mixed up in this. Entirely to myself, I mutter, "I shouldn't have called."

A muscle in his jaw flexes. "You needed help; I helped."

I wave, as if he is beside the point of this conversation. "And I appreciate it, but I've been trying to spare you this stuff."

"There's been more shit like this?"

"Well, I—" I rub my palm over my face, cold skin on cold skin. "The day before holiday break. Someone told the administration that I'm writing other students' essays for a fee, and he stuffed my locker to make me look guilty."

Dailey stares at me, brown eyes unblinking. "And you didn't mention that escalation to me because . . . ?"

"What could you have done?"

He rolls his eyes at me, then points to the apartment. "Okay. Inside. We'll start searching for headshots of local private investigators."

Crossing my arms tight, I rock onto the balls of my feet. "You think the guy following me was a PI?"

"He had a long lens camera on his front seat. Now that I know someone's trying to get you kicked out of school? Yeah, I think a PI is tailing you for misdeeds." Dailey ducks a little to look me in the eyes. "But we'll come up with a plan. Okay?"

What does it mean that, in my scrambled panic, I called Dailey? On some deep, cellular level, I trust him. I believe the picture with Sophie has an explanation. That Mary Kinsley's presence was a weird coincidence. "Okay."

"But this time, you clue me in all the way." He crosses his arms too, drawing the line. "Which Ingleside kids do you suspect?"

"Just Ben Ashby and Brooks Van Doren. And I guess the Blockhead T-shirt person could be an Ingleside kid, though I've ruled out dozens."

He's surprised, by both my quick delivery and the shortness of the list. "Really."

"Really."

"Good," he says, gesturing toward the building.

I follow him inside, where the smell of fresh-baked bread makes my stomach growl audibly. But at the top of the stairs, I hesitate, staring at Dailey's shoulders and the indigo door. I lean against the railing, unwilling to go a step farther. "Wait."

Dailey lifts the key to the lock and then turns back to me.

"I recently saw a photo from the night Sophie died. In the background, you were talking to her on the couch." I watch his face for alarm, for defensiveness, for anything suspicious.

He stares back, confused. "Right . . ."

"It appears to be a fairly serious conversation." I'm trying for calm, but the words are spitting heat. "What did you talk about?"

The sconce beside the door flickers. Dailey frowns and then says, like it is obvious, "Uh . . . you."

I blink at him once, then again.

"I'd just found out you and Soph were cousins—you know that."

Yes. And I also know Sophie's expressions, including her passionate, keyed-in face. Whatever she and Christian were talking about was not light-hearted. "What, specifically, was said?"

He runs one hand through his hair, buying time. It must be clear by now that I'm not moving forward without a solid answer. "All right. I didn't want to go there, but . . . Sophie, um. She thought you liked me, okay? Or . . . could like me."

I recoil, one hand gripping the rail for balance. No way. Nope. Sophie would never, ever betray me like that. She knew how I felt about Christian and why. I hold out a finger in warning. "Okay, now I *know* you're lying."

Christian laughs, the sound edged in spite. "*Why* would I make that up?"

"To hide whatever you were really talking about with her!"

He held his arms out, as if to be examined. "Jesus, Hannah. There's no ace up my sleeve! There's no trick. What else can I say?"

I steel myself. "Her exact words. Surely you recall the last time you spoke to her. Or are you going to claim you were too drunk?"

"I remember perfectly," Dailey says. "She was very interested to know that I'm a Scorpio. She said you're hard-headed and only come around on your own terms, like a typical—"

"Ram," I finish, a whisper.

"Yeah." I can't see Dailey's features through my watery vision, but he better not look smug. "And that you are motivated by treats."

I'm helpless to the laugh that erupts, even in my embarrassment. My mind plays a montage of Sophie, traipsing into my room with a bakery bag in hand—the heart cookies to cheer me up, the pistachio muffin for favors. I could almost hear the low-pitched bleating sound she would make until I laughed.

The picture on Zoe's phone is a different scene than I imagined. Sophie's serious face, insistent on engineering my love life on the night she died. I wipe my cheek. That perfect, maddening busybody.

"You believe me?" Christian asks quietly. A lock of hair falls into his eye, and he pushes it back.

I nod, wiping my eyes. "Sophie saw us talking at her fundraiser. I don't know why she latched on to the idea, but it was her imagination. To be clear."

His jaw works for a second before he says, "I got that."

I expect him to push the door open and get on with it—I made an accusation; I was handily, embarrassingly put in my place. Let's move along. But Christian stays where he is.

"You knew I talked to her," he says. "I was clearly never the guy in her text messages. So, what would I have been hiding?"

"I don't know." We're right at the edge of it anyway, and I am so tired of in-betweens. I run my tongue against my canine teeth, pressing hard enough hurt a little. "There was a time that I wondered if you were covering for Kinsley."

There's a stretch of silence as Christian breathes in all the air he'll need to yell, incredulous, "You thought *Kinsley* gave Sophie drugs?"

"See here's the thing." I contain my anger, but just barely—my fingers shake as I press pointer to thumb. "The level of indignation you feel right now? That's how I would have reacted to the idea of Sophie using drugs up until the moment I knew she'd died from them. No—even *after* I knew. Sometimes the people we love hide things. So if you could just spare me the dramatic—"

"Fine," Dailey snaps. "Kinsley swung by the party to drive me home because I'd had a couple beers. She came in to say hi to Jordy; we left."

"But you can see where I'm coming from, right? She got there late in the evening." I count this on one finger and then, raising another, "And Sophie didn't see her. Then she showed up to the visitation with you."

"Yeah, because I was messed up! Sophie died half an hour after we talked! I couldn't stand in that line alone, and my dad isn't great with funerals." Dailey touches his temple, exasperated.

"You thought Kinsley was an arsonist watching the fire? That's . . . sinister."

I lift my shoulders like: Yeah, welcome to my past year. "This whole thing *is* sinister. I just got followed."

"All this time," Dailey says slowly. "Months now. You thought my friend might have given Sophie drugs and that I was helping cover for her?"

"I ruled her out last year," I admit. "But when I saw that photo of you and Soph, it made me question everything. So, if you could not act like it's ridiculous to think through every possibility because—"

"Fine." He holds up his hands, a frequent gesture around me. "You were presented with new information; you reexamined your existing beliefs. But is that the last of it? Seriously, MacLaren."

A brawler till the bitter end, I almost spit out: *Depends on whether I get new primary sources.* "That's it."

The apology is in my mouth, but I hold it there. We look at each other, a few feet apart, as the pressurized feeling of argument fades. There's this flash-bang second where I almost step forward to hug him. It's nothing—just the muscle memory of calming down from a fight.

"Well!" Dailey says, clapping his hands together with false cheer. "Being interrogated makes me hungry, so I'm gonna pop down to get us some turkey clubs, and—"

"I'll do it." Possibly I feel a little guilty. It will pass.

He quirks an eyebrow. "Do *you* have a free sandwich on your punch card from being an extremely frequent customer?"

"No."

"Come with me if you want." Pushing the front door open,

he nods inside. "Or just chill for a second. Get a glass of water, pet the dog."

I open my mouth to disagree, but, on cue, Dodger appears, tail wagging. Never in my life did I imagine I'd find myself alone in Dailey's apartment. And never did I imagine I'd stay right in the entry, petting a zealously happy Labrador and not snooping even a little.

Someone followed me. Was that even legal? Sitting on the floor next to Dodger, I search on my phone. When does following become stalking? Can a PI follow a minor?

I text my mom that a group project came up and I'll be home later.

Dailey returns in a few minutes, and we set to work over our sandwiches. Of the six best-reviewed local private investigators online, three have headshots somewhere on their websites. Another PI uses a logo only, but searching his name shows a smiling face—next to wife and baby—on social media. None of them are my stalker from this morning. So, that leaves us with Cerberus Solutions and Old Line State Investigations.

"I can call and schedule a meeting as a potential client," Dailey offers, crunching down on a pickle. "Wait, no I can't. The guy saw me. And you can't go in there because—"

I hold up one finger, slowing him. "Why do we have to go in at all? We just need to see his face to confirm it was a PI. So, couldn't we coincidentally have a very long conversation in my car outside his office?"

"You know what?" Dailey smiles. "I think we could."

Junior Year

My mom dropped me off at Ginny's house with an approving look. "Thanks for this, Bug. I'll be back after my appointment."

Because I had, once again, rebuffed my aunt's request to make a speech, I volunteered for gala prep. The whole endeavor seemed extremely silly—an opulent evening where thousands would be spent for more thousands to be made. Wealthy donors would buy very expensive tables, where they'd be served a meal. There would be speeches and more money donated.

The invitations were cream-colored, with embossed vines curling around the sides. I'd studied mine with tear-glazed eyes: *The So Far Foundation invites you to its inaugural event.* I'd suggested the play on Sophie's first and middle names. Booking the botanical gardens was a nice touch on Ginny's part—and without my reminder to think about what Sophie would have liked.

Maddie let me in with a harried smile. "Hey. Thanks for coming over!"

I followed her into the dining room, which had been overtaken with papers and various examples of table settings. "This is quite the undertaking."

"Yep." Maddie gestured to a pile of envelopes. "Some people sent the paper RSVPs and some did online—I think my mom wants someone to check her spreadsheet to make sure she didn't miss anyone."

"I love spreadsheets." Then, gently, "You okay?"

"Yeah, okay." Maddie ran a hand through her hair, which had grown past her shoulders for the first time in years. I swallowed, pushing away the thought: Sophie would never see her this age or any older. "Good news, actually. My parents are letting me transfer to St. Anne's in the fall."

"Oh?" I couldn't recover fast enough to hide my surprise. Andrew and Ginny were always so into Ingleside; I'd never considered another private school as an option. "I didn't know you were thinking about it. That's great, if you're happy."

"I am. One of my friends from group therapy goes there. I couldn't stand the idea of Upper School at Ingleside, you know? Everyone seeing me through tragedy glasses."

"Sure," I said. A feeling of certainty washed over me: Maddie was going to be okay. She'd lost her sister, and that grief would always be part of her, its shape warping with time. But Maddie could still hear her own voice and ask for what she needed.

"Hannah!" Ginny called from the doorway. "I didn't hear you come in. Did you show her, Maddie?"

"Not yet!"

Ginny bustled in with a single sheet of paper—a beige, four-square house with weathered siding. 11 Caldwell Street. "Oh. Is this—?"

"The campus house we've offered on, yes!" Ginny said, clasping her hands. "It needs some renovation and a major spruce, but the location is on a quieter street. And there's a studio for a resident advisor to live on-site."

"Wow," I said, blinking at the image.

"I know!" Ginny tilted her head to admire the photo. "I'm thinking a Chantilly or a light fawn for exterior paint."

Oh, Lord. "Maybe a cheerful front door?"

Ginny smiled as if she'd barely heard me. "Your mom is lobbying for a sage green, which might be on-theme. You were so wise to imagine an eco-friendly mission. One of the botany professors is planning garden beds already!"

"That's nice. And the street number is perfect."

"Oh? Is eleven lucky?"

"I think it's, like . . . well. Hold on a sec." I hurried up to Sophie's room and lifted the giant astrology book from her shelf. This was the third time I'd been in her room and, for some reason, the most heartbreaking. Perhaps because I felt, now, like I was failing her. Grief reached out with smoke curl arms, beckoning me into darker spaces, and I hurried away before I could be dragged down.

Laying the book open, I pushed it toward Ginny.

"Eleventh house." I pointed to the wheel illustration. "It's the house of community, social life, goals, and causes."

"Eleventh House," Ginny repeated. She ran her finger over that spoke of the circle. "And that's affiliated with—?"

"Aquarius," I said quietly. "Yeah."

"Well!" Ginny set her shoulders back with perky stoicism. "That seems meant to be then, doesn't it?"

Nodding toward the computer, I said, "I'm happy to check the RSVPs, if you want."

"Yes!" Ginny said. "Wonderful. So, there's a color system . . ."

Her voice trailed off in my head as I took in the spreadsheet. I saw not only the colors but an opportunity, pulling together before my eyes.

———————

The next day, Gabi came over to my house for the first time. My mom had made a rare Sunday outing for a coworker's baby shower, leaving me without a car. I liked Gabi's house—a retreat from my everyday life—but this seemed like a natural progression.

Once in my room, Gabi spun, taking in the full three-sixty. "It looks like you."

Did I look like a black chalkboard wall and simple white bedding on a low-to-the-floor mattress? An industrial garment rack for sewing projects? The art tacked up around my bed: a black and gold Art Deco print, a few postcards, and a poster of my favorite Julie Mehretu piece.

"Thanks," I decided, sitting on the edge of my bed.

"All right." Gabi plopped down on my rug and crossed her legs. "So, you have an idea?"

"I do. The gala."

"What about it?"

"All three of them will be there." The Van Dorens bought a table, of course. Warner's family table meant Barrett's mandatory appearance. And Violet Atwell's family also bought a table, which would almost certainly include Ben Ashby. This wasn't so different for Gabi—our three suspects were at school every day. But this was a Sophie-related event, where the implication would be heavy. And I would be there.

"Okay," she said. "What can we do with that?"

I took a deep breath. We would send an anonymous message to all three of them: *I've been waiting for you to be honest on your own, but I'm about ready to tell the truth for you. If you'd rather work it out privately, wear a green tie to the Sophie Abbott gala, and I'll pull you aside discreetly to talk. Any other color, and I'll assume you'd rather I go public.*

"I'm hoping you can track down their numbers, because I already bought a burner phone." I reached under my bed for the box, which I'd bought with cash at a superstore. I also grabbed some discounted Christmas chocolate, to stress eat while contemplating how my life had come to this.

"You bought a burner," Gabi repeated. She stayed very still, considering. "But why wait for the gala? Why not just text them now?"

"It's way too easy to text back 'I have no idea what you're talking about' or ignore. The gala construct forces them into a more active choice."

Gabi bites at her lip. "What if he just ditches the gala?"

"Then that'd be a gamble too, wouldn't it? Would we go public at the gala in his absence?"

Gabi lifts her eyebrows. "Huh. Okay. So, ideally, we'll know which one is guilty as soon as he walks in the room. Then we can confront him."

"Or not. Once we know, we can decide how to proceed." I nodded at Gabi's uncertain look, encouraging her. "But keep talking—I want to think this through from every angle."

She leaned back, staring up at the ceiling now. "The two who aren't involved would see the third wearing the tie."

"Maybe. But the event's at a botanical garden—there will be tons of green ties."

"True." She pointed her toes, legs aligned with the lines on my rug. "And they might not assume anyone else got the text."

"Right. And we obviously can't contact the arm person, but that still leaves us a seventy-five percent chance."

Her attention snapped back to me. "If you got a message like that and you were innocent, what would you do?"

"Hmm." I hadn't considered that. "Think it was weird— maybe a prank—and be sure to wear a blue tie. Why? What would you do?"

"I'm not sure . . ." Gabi said. "Maybe I would tell someone. Like, if I didn't have anything to hide, I might ask around to see if anyone else got one."

A valid point. "If any of the guys do that, you'd probably hear about that at school, right? We can adjust accordingly."

Gabi looked out my window, her mind scanning my plan for holes.

"Here's the worst-case scenario, I think." I held out my hands, balancing the ideas. "B will know someone suspects him, but he might guess that we're not sure enough to make a public accusation."

"And he might not wear the tie, so we're no better off. Plus, he'll know it's someone at the gala," Gabi added. "But I guess it's, like, two hundred people closest to the Abbotts. So that doesn't really narrow the pool."

"Right."

"What about Barrett?" Gabi asked. "If he sees that the girl from tutoring is related to the Abbotts, that's a red flag."

"I don't think he'll know. Ginny and Andrew are sitting with the rest of the board. I'm with my mom, my best friend and his dads, and a few Yardley people. Barrett will probably think I'm Lincoln's date, nothing more." Running my ponytail through my hands, I added, "And I'll wear my hair down."

I met Gabi's eyes, a more golden brown in the direct stream of light. She nodded. "Okay. I'm sold. We just have to figure out how to send the message."

"Right. And if we think we might confront him, should one of us wear a wire?"

"A wire? Why?"

"Hard evidence." Given the look on Gabi's face, this was over-the-top. Maybe wearing a wire was strictly a *Law & Order* type of thing. "We'd probably need it to bring formal charges, right?"

"Charges." Gabi's mouth moved strangely over the word. "Like criminal charges?"

"Yeah."

Gabi squinted like I'd become difficult to see. "Soph committed a crime too. Is that how you think of it?"

I rolled my eyes. "Maybe technically, but she was—"

"Not maybe, Hannah." Gabi's whole body had gone stony, only her eyes moving over me. "She was trying to handle something alone, which we sympathize with because we know that and love her. But every addict has those people in their life."

"Don't call her that," I snapped.

Gabi eyed me coolly. That had been bait.

But then, Gabi knew that. She tilted her head. "So, Sophie is different than all those other bad drug users who do belong in jail?"

"I'm talking about selling something laced with fentanyl! It's literally a different charge. You're telling me you don't want accountability?"

"Of course I do!" Gabi says. "But I don't know the circumstances. It's not crazy to think he's also using. What if Sophie had passed drugs to a friend? Or if she sold pills to pay for her own because that's how far it had gone? Your first solution for Sophie would be jail?"

"She wouldn't have done that!"

"Hannah!" Gabi yelled, flinging her hands. "She really, honestly might have! But there's accountability that isn't 'put a kid in prison.'"

"These guys are practically adults!" I insisted. "And if that's what it takes for an entitled asshole to learn his lesson?"

Gabi sat with her arms crossed, refusing to shape further argument. She knew I'd play it out on my own anyway.

Maybe I could have agreed with her if the guy had turned himself in after the party. If he'd mourned, apologized from his guts, explained that it was a horrible accident. Given Sophie's family a few crumbs of closure instead of leaving me to hunt traces of what happened, in disbelief.

But I knew a badly reasoned argument when I heard one, even in my own head.

"He's the reason Sophie's dead," I said—not to further the argument, but because I needed to say it out loud.

"There are a *hundred* reasons Sophie's dead." Gabi leaned forward, putting her hands on my knees. "He's just the closest to it, the easiest to blame. But all it takes is a quick Google of 'the war on drugs' to see how—"

"Stop. I know." I squeezed my eyes closed, tears dribbling out.

And I did know. I could have made the argument without a single note card, without a moment's preparation.

"Hannah," Gabi said from somewhere. The word floated above us, like in a bubble. "Talk to me."

"If he was knowingly selling fentanyl-laced pills, I think jail should be on the table," I said. I clutched my chest where I could feel the anger, like tree rot, still spreading through me. I knew my positions—logical and moral—and these past months, I'd chucked them for revenge fantasy. "I'm so angry all the time."

"Me too." Gabi dug her fingers into my knees, keeping me on the ground with her. "We just have to aim our anger in the right place. If we can figure out who did this, we'll know better about accountability, right?"

Through tears, I nodded. Above all, I couldn't let my cousin go without understanding what happened that night. Not with her voice in my ear, so close and so far.

I sat back, clearing my face. "Okay."

Gabi's eyes met mine, now with more flame-flicker than sadness. "I'll get the phone numbers."

Senior Year

Dailey and I idle outside Cerberus Solutions after school on a Thursday. We're in his dad's car, although I have no idea what Dailey said to justify the swap. In forming this stakeout plan, I tried to map every possible outcome while Dailey pushed for action, confident he could think on his feet. We landed on a solid plan within days.

This particular idea sprouted after we searched Cerberus's address—the first floor of a multi-family house, shared with an accountancy business. In other words, a place you can deliver—or easily mis-deliver—food to.

"This is not how I saw my senior year going," Dailey mutters, closing the flip mirror. A beanie, tugged low, hides most of his hair, and he's wearing a pair of drugstore reading glasses. I drove by the house earlier this week, clocking a doorbell camera. With this minimal disguise, we roll the dice. "Pulled into your web of lies."

As if he didn't beg for entry. I roll my eyes, passing him the bag of burritos with a mittened hand. Just for good measure, I'm wearing a brunette, bobbed wig and a big scarf wrapped around me. As Dailey climbs out of the car, I hiss, "Slouch your shoulders so your body language is different."

I pretend to stare down at my phone as he approaches the door and knocks. We found the name of a neighbor via public property records. So, if my stalker does answer the door, Dailey will simply say, "Delivery for Ken?" and thank the PI for directing him next door.

If it's not our guy, Dailey will try to work in a few questions. I suggested starting with a comment on the business name, as shown on the sign—*Greek mythology, right? Cool! You're a PI, like in the movies? Do you work with anyone? I think I could be good at investigations.*

When it comes to Dailey's ability to bullshit, I have as much faith as I do for anything in this broken world.

Someone opens the door, but Dailey's position blocks my view. They chat for long enough that I increasingly doubt it's the man who followed me. When Dailey finally leaves, he walks to the house next door in case the PI is watching, discreetly tucks the food bag in his coat, and returns to the car.

"All right!" Dailey says. "Not our guy, and he does work alone."

"Okay." I ball my clammy hands inside my mittens. "Okay."

He reaches for his seat belt and says, in a higher pitch, "*Great job, Dailey! Really came in clutch.*"

I turn to him and coo in my dog voice, "Who's a good boy?"

He fights a smile—he wanted a reaction, the sadist—and flops his tongue out of his mouth, panting.

"I already got you a treat." I gesture to the burritos, which I paid for because I don't like owing him.

Dailey steers the car away from our parking spot. "You want to call it a day? Or head home and start a plan for Old Line?"

Old Line State Investigations is a harder mark—located in an old office building where we can't simply knock on the door. There are several large parking lots surrounding the complex, so the silver sedan would be a needle in the haystack—and maybe he rides the bus to work or carpools. We've batted around ideas, but so far, looking for the car and settling in for an hours-long stakeout is the best one.

But now that Cerberus has been ruled out, I find I'm scared that the man wasn't a PI at all. Every other option seems worse. "Let's go to Old Line now. Do you have anywhere to be?"

"Nope," Dailey says, though he sounds surprised. I'm always the one demanding time to make a plan.

"We're already in a car he wouldn't know," I explain. "And it's almost four. People might start leaving for the day soon, so maybe we'll get lucky."

After circling in a fruitless search for the car that followed me, we park in a spot near the main doors. We eat the burritos and listen to music on low. We complain about classwork feeling increasingly pointless; we talk college plans.

More than once, I think about Dailey needling Sophie into saying I might like him. My cheeks feel hot then, and not just from the car vents blowing warm, dry air.

The sky is going pink around us, and I have my knees on

the dashboard. I'm sick of squinting at the door, heart leaping every time it opens to another unfamiliar face.

But when the playlist switches to a Blockhead tune, I have to smile. Sophie would have liked the band. Something about their music makes her feel close by. "Did you see that Blockhead signed with a label?"

"Yeah. Good for them—well-deserved." Dailey takes a drink of his fountain soda and slides his gaze over. "Why are you making that face?"

"I feel uneasy when we agree on something."

"We almost always agree on principle," he informs me. He sticks the straw in his mouth again, and it rattles on the last sip. "Just not on methodology."

Is that true? Despite myself, I'm a little pleased that he has made a study of our contention. I stare at the door. "If people flood out right after five o'clock, I might jump out and pretend to be pacing, talking on the phone. It's hard to see with people bundled in scarfs and hats."

"Sure thing." But when Dailey pauses, a hesitation transmits through the space between us. My shoulders tense on instinct. "Um. So, hey. I need to come clean about something."

I sink my teeth into my lower lip, holding in a rage scream. Somehow, I've always known I'd hear those words from this boy's mouth, and yet here I am. Of course he does this while I'm trapped in a car with him, reliant on a ride home. "Great."

"At the party last year, when Sophie and I talked." He turns, trying to make eye contact, and I stare harder at the door. "She *did* say that she thought you might like me. But only because I told her I was kind of into you."

I pivot toward him, blinking so hard that I create a strobe

effect. Just when I think we've reached fair play, both of us disarmed. "You what?"

"I was buzzed and stupid—I don't know. Sophie mentioned she saw us talking at the fundraiser . . ." He scrubs at the knit hat covering his hair, clearly hating every moment of this. My heart crams itself into my throat. "So, the Hannah's-an-Aries thing? She was telling me she thought I had a shot."

I try to swallow and find I can't. The Sophie part, at least, makes total sense. She didn't waltz up to my enemy and fabricate my supposed crush on him. But the rest?

Dailey's got a hangdog look to him, penitent. "I shouldn't have let you think Soph was gossiping about you or something. I didn't realize it might land like that till later."

"So, you're telling me that you liked me?" It doesn't sound any more believable spoken aloud.

He gives me a contemptuous look. "I thought about it for a split-second, so you can relax."

"Relax?" God—only Dailey would pick a fight over this. He's acting like I'm dancing around, delighted with myself. "From my state of blank surprise?"

He rolls his eyes. "Oh, like it's *such* an insane thought. Cool."

"I'm sorry," I say, heavily sarcastic. "A week before that, you were antagonizing me at the library debate, so forgive me if I'm—"

"O-kay." He gives me a thumbs-up. "Sure. That's what that was. I'm the bad guy, when you're the one who started it."

"I absolutely did not."

He whirls, his upper body turned to face me. "Our first time onstage together, you went after me like a junkyard dog. It wasn't tough, friendly competition, Hannah, and you know that. It was *spiteful*."

"Of course it was!" I shrill at him. "After what a jerk you were?"

"*What?*" he crows. "When?"

It's the shock that pisses me off. Like, in wondering why I treated him with scorn, Christian Dailey had never bothered to reflect on his own behavior. "The first time our schools competed against each other. Freshman year."

His brows tug inward. "The September match?"

Mortifyingly, I think I might cry. Fourteen-year-old Hannah sits beside me, a gangly specter still feeling a pain that has long dulled. "You treated me like gum beneath your shoe, Christian. You know you did."

"I—" He's staring in genuine disbelief. "No, I didn't."

As if I couldn't remember the exact moment our eyes met and he looked away, ashamed. His hesitation, the way he glanced at his Ingleside friends in their starched white shirts. It was one of those moments that imprints on your brain. I was sentenced to replay the humiliation on nights I couldn't sleep.

After all these years, the least he could do is not gaslight me. "You never texted me back after debate camp, and that was fine. But you stood there with your Ingleside buddies like you'd never seen me in your life. And when that guy was so nasty to me? Crickets!"

"I was an awkward fourteen-year-old, Hannah! I was out of my mind with grief." He tosses his hands up. "Which I'd planned to tell you, but you walked up to me when all those people were around, and I short-circuited."

Grief? I stared at him. He mentioned that his mom died a while ago, and I hadn't asked follow-up questions because he seemed done with the topic. In my mind, I replay the memory through the eyes of a boy whose world shattered all around him.

Dailey watches my realization and looks away, annoyed. I can almost see time warp, a blur around me. "Your mom died at the end of the summer. After we met."

"Yeah."

I grip the tassels of my scarf, knotting them around and around. Never once did I guess that, in the few weeks between summer and our first match, that something terrible happened to him. If his mom was sick, he hadn't told me, and I think he would have. "It was sudden."

He stares out the front window. "Yes."

Good Lord. I press my lips together. "I didn't know."

"I know you didn't," he says, a bit thinly. He's got his arms crossed petulantly, but in this case, I think I might deserve it.

"Well, Sophie should have told me. She knew how I . . . felt, after . . ."

"Sophie didn't know. It was my first year at Ingleside. Believe me, I wasn't advertising my tragedy." With a wry smile he adds, "Perhaps you understand the impulse."

The Blockhead song croons its final lyrics, and then the car feels very quiet. "I'm sorry. I really am."

There: a palms-open, best-I-know-how apology. I've had plenty of practice accepting them, like so many casseroles.

"It's fine." He nods, swiping his fist over his mouth. "I could have told you somehow. I *should* have. I tried to write it out, I just . . ."

"Couldn't text a girl you'd just met something so heavy?" I ask gently. Seeing it, finally, from his side. "*Hey, the rest of summer was okay. My mom died unexpectedly. So, how are you?*"

"Well." He softens, maybe pleased to hear me make an argument on his behalf. And like that, he's back. A side grin and a tip of his head. "Water, bridge, et cetera."

But I'm still staring. We'd built all this voltage over nothing—perceived slights and unacknowledged loss.

Dailey looks back up. "Wait. You said some guy was nasty to you?"

I return to staring at the door, where two women exit, chatting. "Your debate captain."

"What did he say?"

Maybe I'm just being soft now that I glimpsed Dailey's sadness, but I don't think he'd lie. "Standard rudeness. West Grove stuff."

I wonder if he's staring in the glazed-over way I'd just experienced. Rewatching the past four years with new information like a lens laid over the memories. My chest aches from how fast my heart is beating.

"If I'd heard him," Dailey says, "I might not have called him out. Not as a new-kid freshman. But I would now."

I watch his face closely, as I always do—God, it's like studying a cipher, hoping for a shift to understandable language. "I know that, actually. But thank you."

"The only person allowed to mess with you," he adds, "is me."

I give him a humorless smirk. "Wait. If you had no idea about that . . . why did you think I came at you so hard in spring quarterlies?"

"I thought you were an incredibly sore loser! You were competitive at debate camp, and Ingleside won that fall match, so . . ."

I press my face into my hands, laughing to fight the tears. It feels like absolute heartbreak, the impulse to tell Sophie all of this. I want to call her and start with "Soph, you're not going to believe this . . ." and I want her to hear it. That call would go straight to voice mail on a long-dead phone, collecting dust on a police precinct shelf. I wipe my eyes.

"Hannah," Christian says.

"No, it's fine." I wave one hand, motioning him off the subject. "It's Sophie stuff. Sorry—kicks up at weird times."

"I get it," he says. And he does. He genuinely knows what it's like to lose someone in a shocking, instantaneous way. "But you need to look up."

I do. That's him walking out of the office—the man from Dailey's picture. He's not tall or short; he's neither skinny nor fat. His hair is starting to thin. He looks like a man buying milk and eggs behind me at the grocery store. Like someone's dad at a T-ball game. I take a picture with my phone, just as proof to myself.

"So, someone has a PI on me." I considered many consequences in my switch to Ingleside. This was not one of them. "I guess it's better than a dealer, eh?"

Dailey has his hand on the door, and the muscle in his jaw flexes. I should have seen the hero complex coming.

"Hey," I say. "There's nothing we can do."

"Mm . . . I think I could definitely call this creep out on tailing a minor," Dailey says. "Maybe scare a name out of him."

"Yeah, you could," I say quietly. "But not here."

———————

After school on Friday, we set up in Dailey's apartment. I take a page's worth of reference notes while Dailey makes himself tea with honey—preparing for his role like a true diva. We practice twice, with me playing the PI, and then Dailey nods. We're calling from my good old burner phone.

It rings loudly, on speaker. "Old Line State Investigations."

Christian's eyebrows jump up, but he recovers quick, landing in his lower intonation. "'ey there. I'm looking for Tom Forsythe."

"Speaking."

"Tom. This is Hank Serrano from Maryland Investigators Coalition," Christian says. This association of PIs actually does exist—easily searchable. I'd called Hank to ask about an article I'm not actually writing, just so Christian could hear his voice. "How's everything?"

"Uh—it's fine . . ."

"Great! Listen, just wanted to give you a heads-up that we've got a report of you tailing a kid." Christian's turned away from me, focusing, but I'm poised with a pen.

"You mean the custody case?" Tom asks, sounding confused. "Mom thinks Dad's getting a babysitter on all his weekends with the kid—standard stuff."

"Hold on, I'm looking at my notes . . . says you were clocked following a teenage minor, female."

On the other end, computer keys tap. "What did you say your name is?"

"Hank Serrano, from the MIC board." When my stalker Tom searches the name, the real Hank really will pop up, on leadership at their professional organization. "Well, FYI, the girl reported your plates to local police. Fortunately, I've got a buddy in the department who gave me a shout."

"Oh my *God*. The girl in the Cabrio?" Tom says, annoyed. Me. "That was nothing. Some kid away at college suspects his girlfriend's cheating—easy cash. Wanted photos of her partying or out with other guys."

Christian locks eyes with me. Who's lying? Tom Forsythe, PI? Or the guy who paid him? I wave Christian on. "Well, no sweat. Just a fair warning because the girl's mom sounds pret-ty litigious."

"Good to know. I'll confirm to the boyfriend there's nothing going on and call it a day. Thanks."

"Yeeup. Take it easy, man."

Dailey ends the call, and we stare at each other. Did we really just get away with that? "Oh my God," I whisper, shoving his arm. "The Oscar goes to you and your extremely fortysomething man lingo."

He laughs, hand on his heart. "Whew. Kind of a rush."

From here, maybe Tom Forsythe will call my "boyfriend" and tell him the case is closed. Or maybe Tom calls Hank Serrano back and discovers that someone impersonated him. But either way, I just became a complication that no one would want to pursue.

But the high of success mellows quickly. I glance down at my hands. The phone call gives my specter a more corporeal form. The boy I'm chasing is on the move, changing strategy. "So. B wants to catch me in the act of something. Get me expelled from school, right?"

"I think so. He probably did what I did—called a PI, pretended to be someone else." Dailey murmurs to himself. "B. Ben or Brooks. Are we leaning toward Brooks, since PIs cost a lot of money?"

I blow out a breath. "Not necessarily. Ben has so much money on the line for college, and we don't really know his whole situation."

"True."

I glance around his apartment, the pictures of Dailey's mom sending a stab through my chest. "God. I shouldn't be here. That was the first time I noticed being followed, but not necessarily the first time it happened."

"Would he have seen you anywhere but home and school?" Dailey asks. "Library? Coffee shop once or twice?"

I scowl because: yes. And Sophie's grave, though it's a bit of a walk into the cemetery from the parking lot, and I'm aware of everyone I pass. "You don't know me."

"Sure I do." He hits backspace on his keyboard, deleting something. His refusal to make eye contact brings out a canine instinct, a need to settle dominance. "I know the exact expression on your face right now."

"Oh, do you?" I ask, with sarcastic interest.

"It's a personal favorite. Probably how you look at art—undecided whether you like it or hate it."

Wrong. I'm giving my most belittling stare. "It's your favorite when a girl looks at you with what might ultimately be hatred?"

"Well," he says. "Keeps you looking, doesn't it?"

He flashes the quickest look above his laptop, just long enough to clock my surprise. His mouth doesn't even move, but he gets this goddamn twinkle in his eyes.

For several days now, I have known that he briefly entertained the idea of liking me. Now, he's trying to fluster me—even out the power balance.

And fine: I do consider leaning across the table for a single, solid kiss. He would be shocked and silent, and I would sit back with haughty smile. I'd say, "*You got me, Dailey. I'm besotted! Swooning.*"

Instead, I think of a night last year when I did not expect to see him.

Junior Year

The conservatory looked like a vintage jewel box, greenhouse glass bursting with color. Outside, February blustered, but the lobby's tropical humidity wrapped around us.

"Here we go," my mom said. She looked beautiful in a long, floral dress, a summer favorite made fancier by heels and earrings. I wore a dress borrowed from Gabi, a simple slip of black fabric. My hair fell nearly to my waist, and, already, I was batting at it, desperate for a hair tie.

My mom's role tonight, I knew, would be watching over her sister. Was Ginny's energy flagging from all these conversations? Did she stop to eat?

My role would be to find the boy who gave my cousin pills.

A few steps led down to the event space, where circular tables were dressed in black tablecloths and battery-operated tea lights. The dimness and canopy of leaves made for a glinting moodiness that Sophie would have loved. And in the center, a small woman in a champagne-colored dress commanded caterers like a maestro.

Ginny put me to work with place cards, and I took careful note of the calligraphy names. I'd relax as soon as Gabi arrived, both of us made braver in the other's presence.

"Second time I've wound up in a blazer for you this year," Lincoln said mildly, when he showed up with George and Elliott. This was less a complaint and more checking in with me. Was I overwhelmed? Or up for joking a little?

I gave him a wry smile. "More like the second time I've landed you free catered food."

He smiled back. "And I will do my duty."

"C'mon," my mom said, shooing all of us toward the desert room. "Let's do a little tour before it gets crowded."

I tried to act normal—to say enough words about cactuses that I appeared mentally present—but my mind spun in circles. Tonight, I could come to face-to-face with the person who had pocketed the last puzzle piece of Sophie's story.

Gabi arrived on the early side in a gray, houndstooth suit. Her parents finally met my mom, and Mr. Reyes politely talked to me about law. All the while, I kept catching Gabi's eye, unable to think beyond the next half hour. I forgot, after all these months holed up in her room—the way her presence changed in public. Her body, drawn up with a dancer's poise, looked taller.

Attendees began to trickle in and then swarm, and I glanced at any exposed left arms—a scan that had become habit in recent weeks. Brooks Van Doren entered first, with his gelled hair and bored expression. The room swayed, flickers of candlelight, as my eyes adjusted. At first, I saw a black tie. And then, as I pretended to text while walking past: forest green. I was certain. I pressed one hand to my chest, trying to contain the flurry within.

That asshole. That absolute asshole.

Tears—from rage and adrenaline build-up and relief—filled my eyes. We got him. Now, Gabi and I could decide what comes next. A quiet confrontation and the truth. I could finally close the door.

Weaving through the crowd as quickly as I could without drawing attention, I searched for Gabi. A handsome couple dodged around me, and I spotted her, wearing the exact same blazing expression I imagined on my own face. Had she already seen Brooks?

She held my gaze and then, purposefully, looked to her left. Ben Ashby stood next to Violet and two people I assumed to be her parents. His tie? A mellow spring green.

No. But that would mean . . . were they both involved?

Gabi and I both twisted around, searching for Barrett. As if waiting for this exact moment, the Evans family appeared at the top of the steps. Warner stood between his parents—his dad, tall like him, and his mom shorter with auburn hair. Audrey, the older sister, was unmistakable with long hair, orange as sunset. A jade dress with a short hemline made her look even leggier.

For a split-second, I panicked that Barrett ditched the gala, but then he stepped into view. He tugged at his collar, scanning the room—for me, in all likelihood, though he didn't know it. His tie had blue stripes across kelly green, and I turned back to Gabi, full of silent questions.

"Fuck," I whispered. An older woman snapped her head

toward me, mouth in a disapproving purse, and I hurried toward our Orchid House meeting point. The whole room smelled of petals and champagne.

"What do we do?" Gabi asked quietly. A purple orchid arched right behind her head, like one of Frida Kahlo's self-portraits.

"I don't know." I could hardly hear for the blood pumping in my ears. The human body was not meant to withstand anticipation spiked so high, only to be thrown back down into despair. "God, of course they're all guilty of something. They're probably cheating on homework, drinking at parties. Literally anything."

Gabi lifted one hand to her forehead. "I cannot believe I let myself think we'd have an answer tonight."

"Wait . . ." I said slowly. My eyes landed on a creamy white orchid, its identical blooms cascading down the stem. "I think this means we can use the process of elimination."

Gabi crossed her arms. "What do you mean?"

"Say we tail Brooks, and we discover he's one of those rich kids who shoplifts. That doesn't totally rule him out for pills, but . . ."

"But it does tell us something."

"It means no matter who we look into, we have a chance of finding out something that helps us."

Hope renewed, we nodded at each other and parted ways before we could be noticed.

We sat down to dinner, then speeches—all of them forgettable—and everyone returned to mingling. All the while, I stewed in my own failing. I should have anticipated this; I should have been more specific in my message. They're all guilty. All of them.

Lincoln's fork hit the plate, slice of almond cake officially polished off. "I'm gonna go say hi to Parker. You wanna come?"

"Do you want me to come?" I countered, arching an eyebrow. "Flying solo comes across as more self-assured."

"I don't like her," he said, with absolutely no attempt at sincerity.

"I know," I said. "You love her."

He gave me a mean smile. "*Now* I don't want you to come."

I waved him away. "If you seem to be flailing, I'll approach you with some kind of emergency."

"Thanks for the vote of confidence."

Now alone at the table, I rested on my elbows, trying to keep track of relevant parties. Brooks, along with some other Ingleside guys, had decamped to the lobby area, killing time on TikTok until parents said their goodbyes. Barrett and his family had left without my notice—perhaps even during speeches. Ben and Violet, last I saw, were whispering in the Orchid Room. My mom was allowing a nice-looking man to flirt with her near the bar. Gabi, politely making the rounds with her parents. Me, rethinking the game board alone.

The LED tea lights flickered close to the centerpieces, and I pressed my fingertip to the plastic flame.

"Hey, MacLaren."

I looked up, blinking at my sudden return to human contact. "Dailey. I didn't know you'd be here."

That was true, at least, until I put his name card down on the table Jordy Green's parents purchased.

"Jordy's plus-one," he said, settling into my mom's chair. The suit and tie weren't so different than his uniform: black instead of blue, his tie still pawed at. "Nice event."

"It is." And then, as if I hadn't looked up Ingleside's results online, "How's debate going?"

"Good. Your family doing okay?"

My eyes found Ginny, her hand resting on an older woman's arm delicately as they spoke in hushed tones.

"This is good for my aunt," I said, surprised to find that I meant it. "I barely see my uncle. Maddie's coping okay, all things considered."

"And you?"

And me. "I'm . . . here."

Dailey gave a slow nod. "Yeah. It's like that at first, isn't it?"

Lacing my fingers together, I turned toward him. "Can I ask you something?"

"Sure."

"What's it like at Ingleside these days? Have things calmed down?"

"Somewhat. It was a shitshow early on—parents descending on the place, screeching. Rich people trying to fix a two-decade abyss overnight."

I leaned back, crossing one leg over the other. "I know what kids tell teachers and parents: *No, of course we don't know anything about opioids.* But . . . is it true, do you think?"

He lagged his head to one side, with a half smile. "It may shock you to know that I'm not exactly the center of Ingleside's social scene. I mostly hang with my Hathaway friends. Apparently making consistent, valid criticisms of the school curriculum gives you a 'narc vibe.'"

I laughed—a single ha!—that surprised both of us. Dailey didn't have that vibe to me, but then, I knew how much he wanted to be a public defender, like his mom. For all his faults and bravado, Dailey faced off best against bad systems, not human beings.

"Nobody at school has forgotten Sophie, though," he said gently. "The administration is less panicky, but she's still on everyone's minds."

I should have felt grateful, but no. I wanted to snatch the thoughts of Sophie out of those kids' heads. One of them placed destruction in her outstretched hand.

With a quick inhale, I summoned a smile. This night had become screwed up enough without me crying in front of Christian Dailey. "Thanks for telling me. But, um, I actually have to go make sure my best friend is being cool in front of the girl he likes."

Dailey's expression shifted, thrown by my abrupt departure. "Yeah, of course. I—yeah. See you in May."

"See you." I was already out of my chair, hoping he couldn't see my tears glinting in the low light.

But my next stop wasn't Lincoln's conversation with Parker. No, I fled to the restroom, desperate to pull myself together. What about Christian Dailey being perfectly nice to me made me fray at my edges? I'd hardly glimpsed my reflection before a beautiful brunette emerged, dabbing her eyes with a three-square stream of toilet paper.

"You all right?" I asked. The words left at the same moment I realized who I'd given them to.

"Oh, sure. Boy stuff." Zoe Walsh, lovely in a burgundy dress, sighed in my direction. "My grandma calls this being a ninny, which I'm sure isn't very feminist. But the word feels right at the moment."

I felt a stab of guilt. I'd once suspected this girl of covering up her knowledge of Sophie's death. "Well, I hope he gets a pop-corn kernel stuck in his teeth for, like, two full days."

She laughed, sinking the balled-up paper into the trash bin. Before she left, we smiled at each other, our reflections in the same frame. "Thank you."

Senior Year

On Monday, Zoe beelines to me right at the art class bell. "We're going off-campus for lunch, 'kay?"

"Oh, I—" My careful school facade is not quite as pinned-up as usual, but Zoe doesn't seem to notice. "Is that allowed?"

"It's fine." She flashes her Student Body president smile. "Warner needs a breather from this place."

My eyes briefly lose focus. Am I about to be confronted? "Senioritis flaring up?"

"He said it's family stuff," Zoe whispers.

Heat flashes to my face and neck.

The teacher calls, "Okay, people! I want to see meaningful progress on your paintings today. Silence or headphones in as you work, but no chatter. I'll be walking around to discuss senior projects individually, so be ready!"

I'm nearly shaking from Zoe's announcement, but fortunately, I've taken photos of my gown's progress. I show our teacher the precise cuts of muslin laid out on my sewing table. She coos over the fabric sample I brought and praises the essay outline I turned in last week.

It's a tightrope balance: being an exemplary student and also a giant phony in constant risk of exposure.

I return to my painting with Blockhead playing in my ears: *She's smart and vain and flighty / And I think I met my match / She's just like poison ivy / Like an itch I cannot scratch.* I bob my head, painting Prussian blue onto my rendering of a vase.

After class, Zoe, Brooks, and I wait on the curb for Warner's Jeep to pull up. When I text Dailey that I'm going out for lunch, I tell myself it's because he might worry. Not because I want someone to know where I am.

But Warner pulls up wearing sunglasses and blasting pop-punk—apparently leaning into the drama. Brooks salutes at us, blasé in the passenger seat. I wipe my sweaty hands on my uniform skirt and settle into the backseat next to Zoe.

"Don't judge me," Warner calls over the music. "My family's being dysfunctional, and I want to get Dairy Queen."

"How suburban," Zoe says. Warner hits the gas.

Almost immediately, I realize there's no anger in Warner's energy. He's yell-singing along, Brooks air-drumming near the dashboard. This is a Ferris Bueller breakout, not a confrontation—I'm almost sure. Zoe elbows me, prodding me to join the sing-along. I fake the senior year, near-freedom bliss like I have everything else. Inside, my gut gurgles with unease. These three seem carefree, dancing on the cusp of their promising lives.

I bide my time until we have four red trays of food between us.

"So what's going on?" I ask Warner.

"Can you keep something quiet?" Warner asks me. He flicks his eyes to Zoe. "I know *you* can."

She smiles coyly, but I'm taken aback. Zoe can't even keep small observations hidden.

"Yeah," I tell him. "Vault-level. What's up?"

"Well, my brother, Barrett, is a dumbass," Warner begins. Brooks snorts like this is an understatement.

I sip my milkshake, trying to appear unfazed.

Zoe jabs another fry into the ketchup. "Not news, babe."

Warner snorts. "He got caught cheating at Yardley."

Both our heads rocket up. I get to words first. "Oh my God."

Zoe's in open-mouthed shock. "How? Like sneaking glances at his phone kind of thing?"

"Worse," Brooks says, through a bite of chicken tenders.

Warner nods reluctantly. "Selling essays."

I can feel my cheeks going warm, surely turning pink. It's a conscious effort to slow my breathing, which I cover with another sip.

"Shut up," Zoe says breathily. "You think he was doing that at Ingleside?"

"Oh, he absolutely was, through his tutoring gig," Warner says. "But he got away with it. Why start back up at college? It's so fucking stupid. As if we haven't heard our mom sniffle-crying in her room enough for a lifetime."

Well, that gets me. And I'm not the only one—Brooks stares down at his food, too stricken to keep eating. I imagine the woman I saw at the gala curled up on her bed. Wondering how her lovely life got upended by one high school party.

"Is he getting kicked out of school?" I ask.

"Nah." Warner reaches for his drink, unphased. "My parents know everyone at Yardley, so they negotiated down to him failing the class and being on probation."

And there it is. The Evans family is so connected that their child gets special treatment.

"At least it can stay private," Zoe says.

"I guess," Warner says, sighing. "But after everything my family's been through!"

"Barrett's always been like that, though," Brooks says. "Middle child shit."

"Did he do it for the money?" I ask, unable to resist.

"Ha. No," Warner says. That little laugh almost makes me sneer. "My brother tries to get away with things to prove he's the cleverest person in the room. Anyway. What a shit week. And on top of that, the guy I met at that coffee shop ghosted."

"No!" Zoe says. "That little weasel!"

"Right?" He sighs. "Anyway. Hannah, do you have a prom date?"

The topic change has spun me out. I'm struggling for my bearings. "Oh, I—no."

"So . . . can I be that person?" Warner smiles winningly, but this is a bridge too far: my senior prom spent on the arm of a boy I've hidden from? I'm sitting across from Brooks Van Doren, who is staring at his plate, inscrutable. What can I do—say no?

Zoe's clapping her hands. "This makes our group perfect!"

"Yeah," I say vaguely. I lift my mouth to a smile. "Perfect."

———————

When Dailey and I made our meeting plan, I wasn't thinking about the calendar. So, sitting in his apartment that Saturday,

I'm so hyperaware of the fact that it's February fourteenth that I act especially grumpy toward him.

I say nothing about my Barrett revelation because I don't have to. When Dailey asked me about Ingleside kids, I dodged that name on a technicality.

Dailey stretches his arms, his rib cage pulling up, and I glance away. "Every idea I come up with is either minuscule or way too big of a swing. Is there anything left to do with the *Insider?*"

"Well, I did interview Violet Atwell about the school play."

"And?"

"Nothing usable." I led her as near to Ben as I could without being obvious. Turns out, she has an encyclopedic knowledge of theater history and plans to become a speech therapist, since practicing monologues helped her learn to manage her stutter. She'll apply to schools in North Carolina, where Ben has committed to run cross-country, but other places too.

Turning to my phone, I find a post from earlier this week—an advertisement for a Valentine's Day Blockhead show on campus tonight. The smiley face logo's eyes are replaced with hearts below spray-painted letters: *Love rocks.*

Dailey peers over. "You're looping back to JJ?"

"I keep wondering if we missed something with him. We wanted to know if he sells pills, right?" I pause, the idea formulating. "And we don't think he does."

"Right."

"But you heard a rumor from older soccer guys that JJ was the go-to for *something*. That means Inglesiders might have heard that rumor."

Dailey's eyes move around the room, as if tracking a

wayward thought. "You think people have tried to buy pills off him before?"

"Or since." I tap one finger against my chin. "Okay, I'm thinking out loud here, but what if I just . . . ask him?"

Dailey serves a look of skepticism, but that's what I want. He's a one-man vetting process for my ideas. "Ask him what?"

"If he's ever been approached about pills, other than us. Do we have anything to lose?"

Dailey sticks out his lower lip, considering. "Let's go ask."

"I'll go." God, now it looks like I'm roping him into plans on Valentine's Day, the stupidest holiday on Earth. "You have that party."

"I just have to stop by," he says. "We can do that now and then head to campus. It's Hathaway people, so we can be seen together."

"I'm good on my own," I say, gathering my things.

"I'm the one who asked JJ about pills," Dailey points out. "Here, I'll do both sides of the argument to speed this up: *I dunno, Dailey. I'm pretty tired, and I don't—*"

"Is that supposed to be me?" I give a withering look to his pitched-up voice. "That's what you think of my counterargument skills? *I'm tired?*"

"Fine," he says. "What have you got, then?"

The dog nudges my leg, jostled awake from beneath the table. "Why would I go to a party where I don't know anyone?"

"You'll like my friends," he says. "For real—I'm the worst of them, by far."

"Well." I lift my eyebrows.

"And they'll like you. God, meeting you will be a dream come true for Kinsley."

"What? Why?"

By the look on Christian's face, I can tell that he's about to sacrifice some kind of information, an offering to convince me. "She came to one of our sophomore year debates. Fall, at Sentinel."

I think back to that one. "You won."

"Oh, I know," he says. "But she loved watching you 'take me down a few pegs,' as she put it. She's been banned since."

"So she didn't get to see me dominate you that spring?" I smile at the memory.

He sighs. "So?"

I hitch my bag onto my shoulder and give the dog one last scratch. "Yeah, okay."

— — — — — — —

Dailey parks on a car-lined street and gestures toward the ranch-style house we're approaching. On the quick ride over, he chattered more than usual, to my amusement. I've never seen him nervous. "This is Natasha's house. She's close with my best friend, Kinsley."

"Better not let Jordy hear you say that."

He smiles crookedly. "Yes, it's very hard for them to share me."

A few people are outside smoking, and he does a backslap hug with one of them. To someone he doesn't name, he says, "This is my friend, Hannah."

I guess it's more succinct than saying *This is my rival, turned co-conspirator with grudging mutual respect, Hannah.*

When Dailey pushes the front door open, I follow him, heart hammering. We weave through the crowd to the basement stairs, and finally to a couch, where two people are turned in to one another and laughing.

"Hey," Dailey says.

His friends look up and stare, still as a Rembrandt. Instead of formal black hats and white collars, they're a palette of worn denim and small metals—buttons and boot buckles that catch the lamplight.

Dailey holds up one hand, a demonstration. "This is Hannah."

I feel like a middle schooler at the edge of the lunchroom. "Hey."

A guy with dark-brown skin and a tunic-length white shirt gets there first. "I scarcely believe my eyes. The nemesis, in the flesh."

From beside me, Christian sighs. "Omar just finished a run as Hamlet. It's been exhausting for all of us."

I nod, shocked into silence. The nemesis. I'm a known entity to his friends.

A white girl with shaggy black hair leans forward for a brief handshake. A few rings press against my fingers. "Kinsley— big fan."

Christian mutters, "Yeah, I told her you enjoyed that debate sophomore year."

She does a chef's kiss. "It was delicious."

"Despite me actually winning," Christian adds.

Kinsley shifts to him, sly. "And yet you sulked around, fixated on it for a week. Why is that?"

When I sneak a glance, he looks young and a little embarrassed. It's possibly the least I've ever hated him.

"Drink?" Omar asks me, hopping up.

"Sure. Thanks."

"Kins? Refill?"

"Please." She holds out her cup and then angles toward me. "Sit!"

I obey, lowering myself onto Omar's former spot on the couch.

With a glance up at Christian, Kinsley says, "Since you're not staying, you should really go say hi to Tash."

He holds eye contact with her for a beat too long. "Yeah, I should. And *you* should—"

"Be on my best behavior?" She flutters her eyelashes. "Always. Go! Bye!"

Christian appears to be gritting his teeth. Glancing at me, he says, "MacLaren? You okay if I—"

"Fine." I say it breezily, like my heart is not pounding at a possible interrogation by Christian Dailey's longtime best friend.

As he backs away, Kinsley turns into me. "So! Library Hannah. Or—wait, you go by MacLaren?"

Library Hannah, huh? "Only Dailey calls me that."

"Gotcha. My first name's Mary, but everyone calls me by my last name. In middle school, I thought Kinsley was *different*." Her face is so animated, every tiny muscle is engaged—eyebrows ready to jump up, mouth waiting to bend toward a smile. "Now, I'm like . . . Mary is a *classic* and edgy in its own way, right? But too late. I spent years making everyone say Kinsley. Maybe I'll be Mary in college."

"I like both," I tell her. "So, you guys have known each other a long time?"

"Eternity. Me and Christian since birth. Omar moved to the neighborhood in third grade; Mia in fifth." Kinsley pauses, catching herself. "She's the fourth person in our group, generally. But she's doing her own thing a little more this year."

"Which one of you did she break up with?" I joke, though I know the answer.

Kinsley laughs happily. "Christian. They're cool, though."

Mia has popped up on Christian's social media through the years. She's very pretty, with big eyes and chestnut hair cut pixie-short. I used to look at her and wonder why someone so cute would choose Dailey, of all people. I don't wonder that anymore.

After a pause, Kinsley says, "Hey, I know there's no non-awkward way, so whatever; let's just do it! I'm really, really sorry about your cousin. Christian spoke highly of her."

"Thank you," I say sincerely.

"So! How's Ingleside treating you?"

How to sum up the frustrating, satisfying challenge of the classwork and the infuriating institution? "Ingleside . . . is what it is. I'm almost done, and I'm grateful for the opportunity."

"That's pretty much Christian's take, too."

"Really? He seems very at-home."

"He's used to it now. He never really relaxes there, I don't think."

My eyes find him over her shoulder. He's deep in conversation, hands gesturing. "Yeah. I see that."

"I mean, it's totally worth it for him, obviously! He's already in at some amazing universities, and he'll wind up—"

"Taking over the world?" I guess.

"Nah." Kinsley grins. "Just changing it. You have school plans?"

"Eh, I'm a renegade for the scholarship money. What about you?"

"Education," she says. "I want to teach art. Or be an artist. Or both."

"What kind of art?" I'm sitting up taller now, leaning in.

As we sip our drinks, Kinsley tells me about her mixed-media work. I realize, aloud, that the painting above Dailey's mantel is one of hers. We swap the museums we dream of visiting, and she shows me more of her work—bold, bright, balanced—on her phone. Omar offers us refills at some point, but I decline. Kinsley sips another drink as I show her the inspiration and sketches for my black capstone gown.

"Shut. Up." She zooms in. "Have you made a gown before?"

"Not from scratch. My inspiration started with *Portrait of Madame X*. But then I saw this 1855 painting of women in off-the-shoulder dresses, which made me think of the black velvet drape they use for girls' senior pictures. Then there's the pop culture moments—Bardot, Princess Diana's revenge dress." I cut myself off from further blabbering. I haven't shown these plans to anyone but my teacher, Zoe, and my mom. "Anyway. A rich history."

Kinsley returns my phone and says, "I like you."

It's a tipsy pronouncement, to be sure. Still, I admit, "I like you too. I was curious about you."

"Really?" She looks delighted. "What did he tell you?"

"Nothing at all—that's why. Just that his best friend is a girl, and I guess I wondered, like . . ."

"Who is the long-suffering angel who has tolerated him for years?"

"Pretty much exactly that. Yep."

"I've *always* been curious about you," she says. "When he told us you were at Ingleside, we were all like: Oh, this is gonna be fun."

"A puddle and a sparking wire, now in close proximity?"

"Totally. He's so freakin' touchy about you! I mean, look at this," she says, tipping her phone toward me. My eyes follow a string of texts on group chat. Kinsley scrolls up to Christian, saying: *Hannah's coming with me, pretend to be normal.* Omar sent back

WHAAAT and Kinsley, three wink emojis with their tongues out and OMG *it's happening.*

I swear to God, you clowns, Christian had typed.

Kinsley beams. "He's horrified that we'll embarrass him."

"Will you?" I ask hopefully.

Like he can sense this disturbance, Christian glances away from his conversation a couple yards away. His face, watching us, goes very still.

"Kins," he calls, pulling out the syllable. "Whatcha doin'?"

She smiles sweetly. "What am I ever doing? Showing off pictures of Sourdough."

When I glance back down at the phone, Kinsley has navigated to a photo of a cylindrical cat, sunning its golden tummy near a storm door. She flashes the picture to Christian.

"So cute," I add.

Kinsley nods solemnly. "Love of my life."

Christian narrows his eyes at us and mumbles something that looks like, "Worse than I thought."

Kinsley tips forward, giggling. "See? *So* touchy. I have this theory that he's stalled out at age fourteen when it comes to you. The mere mention of your name, and he's, like, awkward and defensive over nothing. And he can't resist bugging you! Hilarious."

The booze feels hot in my stomach. Our rivalry is a wicked, living thing between us—a carnivorous plant that we both tend in our spare time.

Omar plops down with a game expression. "Okay! What are we talking about?"

"How Dailey had a big, giant boner for Hannah freshman year."

My mouth drops open in full, fly-catching shock. Omar looks between us, like perhaps he can grab the words from the air before they reach my ears. Realizing what's done is done, he lifts one finger from his grip on a beer and points to Kinsley. "He's gonna kill you. RIP. Done."

"I accept my fate," she says, her chin held proudly. "It was a lifetime ago—who cares? And hello? Senior year. Ticking clock on making this happen."

"Well, she's here," Omar says, gesturing toward me. "Seems like he's doing okay on his own."

I feel detached from the party—from the planet—and not just because I'm being spoken about as if I'm not sitting here. The nemesis, the conspirator, the *she*. I take a long sip of my neglected beer, tepid and sour.

"It's fine," Kinsley is telling Omar. "I'm sober enough to see that Hannah's into him too."

"You're cut off is what you are," Omar replies. Then, eyes on me, "Sorry about Tipsy Kins. Notorious bigmouth."

"It's okay," I say as Kinsley huffs. Then, with defiant calmness, "She's not wrong."

I cannot believe I've said it. I was trying the words out—daring myself. But with almost sickening certainty, I know how much I mean them. Kinsley slumps back against the couch, smiling as if her work here is done.

"You little chaos agent," Omar grumbles at her. "You had no way of knowing that would work out."

"Nah, I knew."

They continue bickering while my entire worldview spins out, a globe off its axis. Christian liked me that first summer, when I was so stupidly smitten with him. Maybe that's why his freshman year behavior upset me so much—I *knew* he liked me; I could feel it. That's why his brush-off sent me into social self-doubt, right as I entered West Grove High.

I watch across the room as a girl approaches him. They hug briefly, chat for a few moments.

"He's a really good guy," Kinsley says.

I glance away, feeling caught. "Oh. Yeah."

"I mean, he's argumentative as hell—self-righteous, too. A good-hearted shithead." She drains the last of her drink, with a smack of her lips. "But he always shows up for the people he loves."

Did Christian bring me here knowing Kinsley would meddle? Knowing she'd give him a sparkling character reference?

"Sophie would have liked you," I mutter at Kinsley.

In an over-loud voice, she asks, "What?"

"Nothing."

When Omar jumps up to play flip cup, Kinsley announces she needs the restroom. I almost tag along, just to avoid staring at the wall while I rethink the past four years. Dear God—I told Christian Dailey's friends that I kind of like him, and I meant it. Kinsley is barely out of view when he drops into the seat beside me and says, "Whatever she told you is probably a lie."

I've sat beside him plenty of times this year. Just now, it feels brand new. "She *did* mention you're a really good guy."

His expression is wary, clearly waiting to have some tidbit of personal information volleyed back in his face. "So this was fine?"

"This was lovely."

He gives it another beat, in case I'm winding up criticism or a joke. "Oh. Good. Well, we should—"

"Get going. Yeah."

I'm quiet in the truck, staring out the passenger window as the neighborhoods fly by. For all I know, Kinsley has already texted him: *Hannah likes you.* But God, isn't it obvious by now? To everyone but me. Even in our worst moments, I have felt some claim over him—my partner at debate camp, my enemy, my collaborator these past months. The link has never disconnected, only changed.

Why is that, Hannah?

"You're not micromanaging the plan for talking to JJ," Christian observes. "Everything okay?"

"Yeah." I twist my hands in my lap. They want to reach for him. "I'm just a little nervous."

"Oh." What he's thinking is that I've never admitted that before. That I am fallible and I doubt myself and, sometimes, I can even say it. "Sure. But like you said. We've got so little to lose with JJ at this point."

We're quiet for the rest of the drive. I don't trust myself to speak. I'm afraid I've unlocked a door that, once opened, will flood us out. Electricity and sea, meadow flower and right hook.

When Christian parks the car, he looks over. "Hey. What's going on over there?"

"Nothing," I say, though, in truth, I'm thinking about Van Gogh—specifically *Still life with meadow flowers and roses.* The background is lagoon blue, the petals lush red and fresh white. For years, art historians only suspected it was Van Gogh's work. They couldn't confirm until they X-rayed it. Beneath the saturated, dreamy florals, they found that a different painting had once occupied the canvas: a wrestling match, men with bare torsos and hands braced in combat. Van Gogh had written about it in a letter once, but it had never been found.

The canvas has two lives: fighters and flowers.

It will always be both things.

"Let's go," I say.

— — — — — — —

In line outside the venue, I'm shivery with cold and anticipation, frustrated to feel so rattled. I want to be calm and clear with JJ, but here I am considering Christian Dailey in the marquee light. I'm quiet, and he knows better than to push the conversation, so we shuffle through the line with hands jammed in our coat pockets.

Inside, we head straight to the merchandise table. Dawdling would only spike my nerves higher, and there's no reason to wait, with JJ straightening up the T-shirt display.

"Hi," I say, sounding as abrupt as I feel. "Do you remember me?"

"Um . . . should I?" JJ asks, wincing. But then he looks beside me. "You. Pill guy."

Christian looks pleased. "That's me."

JJ doesn't smile back, but I step forward. "I approached you the same night he did. We were both trying to figure out how and when my cousin started using drugs."

"Oh." He looks between us, suddenly uncomfortable. "Wait. You thought I had something to do with that?"

"Well, we don't anymore," I say. "But we'd heard at school that you might have the hook-up for something."

JJ peers with heavy-lidded eyes. "What school?"

"Ingleside Country Day."

He considers this for a beat. "One of my buddies went there. But he'd never start a rumor like that."

"What's his name?" Christian asks.

"Callum O'Donnell."

Christian turns to me, looking vindicated. "Younger brother on the soccer team, graduated last year."

JJ scoffs. "Callum's brother said I sold *pills?*"

"No," Christian says. "The rumor wasn't clear."

"Well, pass the word," JJ says, one finger pointed. "I'm not your guy for that shit."

He clearly wants to end the conversation, but I'm still grappling for ground. "Has anyone else ever asked you? We can't be the only people who heard the rumor."

"I mean, people ask about weed since I know a guy," JJ says. At this point, I am one hundred percent sure that JJ *is* the guy. "But no one has ever tried to buy pills off me."

I nodded. "Okay. Thanks."

"No big," he says. "I get it. The closure part."

I turn away before I think better of it. The talk of older siblings, the way the Ingleside web touches everything at Yardley—it begs one more question. "You don't know Barrett Evans, do you? Freshman here?"

"Nope." JJ thinks for a moment. "Don't think I know any freshmen at all. I know Audrey Evans. Any relation?"

Yes. "How do you know her?"

"I mean . . ." He gestures around us. "From going here? She went out with Logan."

I glance from him to the empty stage, lit hot pink and waiting. "The lead singer?"

I'd been so careful not to mention the concert in front of Warner, and he hadn't said a word about my article. But, then again, beyond the paper's staff, what busy senior is reading the *Insider* cover-to-cover?

"Yeah. Audrey was the inspiration for some of their best songs," JJ says.

My heart is pounding so hard that it almost hurts. "When did they break up?"

"I dunno. While back. Why does it matter?"

"It doesn't," I tell him, and I tug Christian's arm toward where a crowd is forming. "Thanks, though."

"Holy shit," Christian whispers, as soon as we're a few yards from JJ. "She was the one in the T-shirt that night."

"No." On the surface, it looks obvious: Audrey Evans was at home for part of Warner's party but left for campus wearing a Blockhead shirt. "She doesn't have a birthmark."

"You're sure?"

"Positive." I saw her at the gala.

"Well, shit," Christian mutters. We stop at the edge of the crowd, waiting. "You wanna tell me why you asked about Warner's older brother?"

"He's someone I've eliminated from the list. Just had to ask, you know?" Then I nod to the stage. "Um, I'm gonna hang around to hear the band. So, I'll get a car home if—"

"I'll stay," Christian says. "If that's okay."

"Yeah." I cross my arms, doing battle against myself. And losing. "That's okay."

I follow him through the crowd. He's more willing to be pushy than I am, which is an obnoxious quality until that person is doing it partially on your behalf. He gestures for me to stand in front of him, a gallantry I don't expect from someone only a few inches taller.

The band leads off with "Cinematic," a crowd favorite that belongs on the radio. No one really dances, but there's swaying and singing along. *Yeah, I know we ended tragic / but baby, weren't we cinematic?*

A few songs in, someone worms their way past me, and I'm jostled—the right side of my body thunked into Dailey's chest. He grips my arm, bracing in case I'm further knocked off balance. I right myself quickly. So why does the touch linger, heat tracing up my back?

They play my favorite song—one of their only ballads—earlier than I expected, which is for the best. I cry silent, stonefaced tears that I don't wipe until the last chord fades out. The whole time, I think: if Christian notices and tries to comfort me, I will push through the crowd to watch from somewhere else.

So, I don't know how the next thing happens, exactly.

I reach behind me, knowing his hand will be there. He laces his fingers through mine like it's an old habit, as well-worn as bickering. The music washes over me, and I'm holding Christian Dailey's hand. It feels absurd and inevitable. Song after song, I don't turn around; he doesn't lean forward to whisper to me.

The final piano outro sounds like Sophie's laugh.

After the encore, my ears still ring with reverb. I'm bobbing underwater, crowds swarming past by like schools of fish. Christian guides me out the door with a glancing touch to my lower back. Neither of us says a single word on our path back to the car, but we clasp hands again.

We round the corner, by a brick building with a giant octopus mural, and then we're kissing as if we'd agreed upon this exact spot earlier. On my eyelids, images spin out like a kaleidoscope: streetlights and concert crowds and Christian's face. My shoulders settle against the wall behind us; he gets his hands in my hair. He kisses me with a certainty, like he has known exactly how he would do this. It's staggering, to be touched with such intent. I dig my nails into his shirt, the impulse to claw at him finally realized, after all these years.

My mind, normally so busy around him, falls quiet. There's only sharp, familiar spearmint scent and the comfort of having known several versions of him through the years.

I'm the one who parts my lips more, escalating. It feels like wordlessly arguing with him, like proving a point and conceding. Do I want to impress him, overtake him, yield strategically, make him buckle at the knees? Yes. All. Help.

We ease off somehow, and now he'll break the spell—say something know-it-all or so earnest that it triggers my gag reflex. I'll be reminded of the truth: he's still Dailey, vexation in human form.

Instead, he links our hands again and says, "We should go."

I stand there, dazed and still staring at a problem that needs to be solved. Mostly to myself, I mumble, "That wasn't supposed to happen."

Christian succumbs to a smug, lopsided smile. "Agree to disagree."

I narrow my eyes, offended. "I would *never*."

He laughs, muttering that yeah—he knows. But he kisses me again beside his truck, both of us clinging to the moment. After this, there's only the mess for us to pick through.

When we're buckled in, I press myself into the passenger door. The reality of what just happened sits, invisible and hulking, between us. I clear my throat. "Well! We are literally never going to talk about that."

He holds up both hands like *Whatever you say*. But I catch the smile as he shifts into drive. I turn my face to the window so he won't see mine.

MARCH

Junior Year

In the gala's aftermath, I spent hours at my sewing machine with hemlines and my thoughts. I prepared obsessively for my spring debate tournament. I went to one of Lincoln's lacrosse games with his dads and to the farmers' market with my mom. And, of course, Gabi and I retraced our steps, lobbing options back and forth.

Short of tailing our suspects—legally questionable and risky in terms of exposure—I faltered. Every idea would be a major escalation: stick a tracker on a car, steal their phones, hire a hacker. So, mostly, we lounged in Gabi's room watching *Real Housewives* while I swiped through her phone. Another ski video from Brooks: a thrill.

"I can't believe Sophie finally got us into this show," Gabi mused, waving a hand toward the wine-fueled showdown on the screen. "So dramatic, but somehow also soothing."

Like Soph. My phone buzzed, and I stretched to reach it—Lincoln, saying they were ordering Thai food later and did I want to come over? *Sure,* I typed. Now that we were in March, his graduation felt too close. Then summer, then gone.

I glanced over at Gabi. "You ever wish you could just close your eyes and wake up when you're moving into a dorm?"

"Constantly," Gabi said. She flexed her feet in their fuzzy gray socks. "I'd happily skip every senior thing—my last soccer season, prom, graduation. I've actually thought about doing dual-credit classes at Yardley just to spend time away from the Ingleside microscope."

"You wanna transfer to West Grove?" I joked. "It's so over-crowded that you can just blend."

Actually, she probably couldn't—not with her stylish, understated wardrobe and easy beauty.

Gabi gave me a faint smile. "Or you could transfer to Ingleside."

I snorted loudly "Yeah. Me in tartan."

"It's not a bad idea." She paused, thinking through the facets. "Your neighbor friend's graduating, right? Ingleside would be great on a transcript."

"Wow, you're really playing for Team Ginny over there."

Gabi made a face. "Yeah, yeah. Just had to try. Saying big dreams out loud, right?"

She has a point. By all appearances, Gabi wasn't joking. She seemed vaguely hopeful that I'd latch onto the idea.

"Then we'd both be under the microscope," I pointed out, as lightly as I could. Maddie wanted to dodge the Ingleside scrutiny so much that she was switching schools.

Gabi frowned, really considering. She had her hair in a low

ponytail, as she often did at home. "Yeah, but we'd have each other."

We began as teammates, irrevocably linked by loss, but our real selves had spilled through the cracks. We shared Sophie memories, of course, but also family histories, resentments, fears. Our time together was the relief from everything else.

"You know . . ." I said slowly. "Maybe I'd think about it."

Gabi sat up. "Really? I'd write the *best* peer recommendation."

At the time, it felt like meaningless daydreaming. It was just nice to know someone wanted me there.

———————

There was one non-rainy day in the early March forecast, so Lincoln and I planned a six-miler. I ran like flames were licking at my heels, like—with enough speed—I could push through an invisible barrier. All the while, I imagined Brooks and Barrett and Ben Ashby, holed up in their bedrooms and guilty.

We stopped at a park water fountain before a mile cooldown home. Lincoln pulled his shirt up to wipe his face and groaned, dropping down to stretch. I did the same, both of us silent until our panting became regular breaths.

"So," he said, squinting at me. "What was that about?"

"Me crushing you on that run?"

He frowned. "You wanna talk about Sophie stuff? Like, the gala and everything?"

This was the first time he'd ever asked me straightforwardly, though he'd circled the subject. I could feel his stomach clenching so acutely that mine did too. "Um, they raised a ton of money. Ginny's happy."

Lincoln stared at me, then gave a disappointed sigh. "All right."

"What?" The word came out in a lash, defensive.

"Am I asking wrong?" He looked genuinely perplexed. "Or not enough?"

All these months, Lincoln had been a safe harbor. Yes, sometimes I wished he had some great insight on my grief, after six years of observation. Sometimes not having that felt like a small indignity, like I wasn't as known as I wanted to be. But only when I was already cranky and lining up his faults like a pool table shot. "It's not you."

"You didn't say a word about Sophie to me," he continued, "Not before the event or while we were there."

I flushed at the criticism. "Well, I thought about her, obviously."

"I know," he said gently. "Which is why it feels like you're keeping something important from me."

He was right, of course. I'd trained myself not to mention Sophie for fear of slipping up—referencing the clues that filled my time with Gabi.

"Well, actually . . ." I paused, daring myself to actually say the words. If ever I was going to float my plan, Lincoln was the right prep round before facing the big boss: my mother. "I've kind of been thinking about transferring to Ingleside."

"Okay. Ha-ha."

"No, Linc. I'm serious. You're graduating, and . . ."

He went still. The silence thumped like a slow heartbeat.

"I need to get out of the rut I'm in," I continued. "At Ingleside, I wouldn't be the only person who misses her."

"Ingleside?" he burst out. "Come on. That's not *you*, Hannah."

"Well, neither is West Grove."

"And whose fault is that? You have the debate team and you have me, and that's all you've ever seemed to want. You could have joined cross-country or track! I invite you to stuff! You've always wanted to hang at home or—"

"With Soph," I finished.

He inhaled sharply. "That's not what I meant. You're not some great outcast at West Grove. You could decide to branch out."

"Maybe. But Ingleside—"

He shook his head vehemently. "No. Stop acting like this isn't weird. You don't talk to me about Sophie for months, and then you announce you want to transfer to private school? *What* is going on?"

"Well, I've *been* feeling like—"

"And how would I know that? It's like I'm blocked off from that part of your life," he said, using swipes of his hands to demonstrate. "Why? What did I do?"

"Nothing! That's just how friendships are—we bring out certain things in each other. You talk to Kyle about lacrosse, not me."

"That's not the same. We talked about Sophie all the time when she was alive." His eyes flashed with frustration. "Did I shut you out when my grandma died?"

No—the opposite. He was thirteen, and neither of us had lost someone close to us before. Between mourners, Lincoln kept looking up for me—the one person there specifically for him. He didn't cry until everyone else left. I could give him quiet presence, which is what he wanted. These days, I wanted action, which he wouldn't approve of.

"Exactly," Lincoln said, to my ashamed silence.

"We were a lot younger," I said feebly.

"What the fuck does that have to do with it?"

I pivoted to him, shocked that he would escalate. "It means I have better coping mechanisms!"

"You *really* do not," he said. "You went from thinking about what happened constantly to never mentioning Sophie's name."

"Oh, I'm sorry," I said, sarcastic. "My mourning is being graded now. Excuse me for—"

"God, you are the *worst* person to argue with."

"Now I'm being graded on arguing too?"

"That!" He stabbed a finger in my direction. "You flash every weapon. You prod me on purpose so that I—the least yell-y person on Earth!—wind up yelling at my sad friend, like an absolute asshole! And then I feel guilty, so I drop it, but no. I won't, Hannah. God—you have to talk about it!"

"I do!" I shot back. "I talk to Gabi."

I got the briefest look at his hurt expression before he turned away. "All right. Well, there it is. At least you can admit it."

"Admit what?"

"You'd consider Ingleside because of Gabi. Your new best friend."

"Is that so wrong, Linc? I can't stand being the World's Most Depressing Girl one hundred percent of the time," I said, hands open in pleading. "Gabi's already low, so I'm not dragging her there with me."

It was a good argument, and it wasn't a lie. It just wasn't the whole truth. All the same, I felt the rift widen. He gave me a moment to come clean, and I'd made a bigger mess.

"I need to take the long way back," he said, climbing to his feet. I stood too, my mouth hanging open. Quiet and over his shoulder, he said, "I'm sorry I yelled."

Then he was gone, his bright T-shirt and familiar gait disappearing down the path.

———————

For my debate tournament, I pulled my hair back in an especially tight ponytail. It made me feel steeled, ready to compete. After my early matches, I lingered near the auditorium door, watching a JV match. It didn't surprise me when Dailey joined me in the shadow of the entryway.

"I sat in for you versus Porter," he said. My first match went well—a solid win, but not a gimme. "It's nice to see you lit back up."

I wrinkled my nose. Hard pass on being spoken to like he's my guidance counselor. "Don't know why that's nice for you, considering that we face off next round."

"Oh, c'mon," Dailey said. "You know I prefer winning when you're on your game."

"Mm. So sorry my grief spoiled your fall victory."

"I didn't—" he began, but I couldn't fight a sly smile. "You're screwing with me."

Yes. We watched a few beats of counterargument, and I tried to imagine Dailey and I practicing together at Ingleside.

"If we were ever on the same team . . ." I ventured. His eyes widened at this break in our usual script. "You think we'd kill each other?"

"Very possible," he said. "But we'd definitely smoke everyone else."

Ultimately, the judges called our match in my favor, but I could have accepted a loss for how good it felt. All week, I'd been reliving my argument with Lincoln, where defensiveness and anger rose so fast. Here, I only felt exhilaration in every lunge, parry, riposte. Dailey and I clanged swords across the stage until I felt pleasantly winded.

Before we left with our teams, he gave me a quick salute, and I nodded back.

That night, Magritte's doors lined my dreamscapes, so real that the handles felt smooth on my palm. I wandered a hallway full of choices, full of sky and ocean and land, full of nothing.

MARCH
- - - - - - - -

Senior Year

I knock, expecting Dodger sounds and Christian's voice calling for me to come in. Instead, the door opens, and I almost startle back. Christian has never actually answered before. "Hey."

"Hey," I reply. He backs up to make way for me, and I am entirely too aware of where his body is in relation to mine. "No Dodger today?"

"He's in my room with a treat." Christian pushes the door shut. He's trying to read me, which is a problem because my thoughts are blaring—against my will: *again, again, again.* "I thought we might want to talk for a sec."

Nowhere in my plans did I prepare for Christian offering, bluntly, to talk it out. I also didn't prepare for the energy between us, so bright and obvious that I think the air will crackle. "About what?"

He frowns, perplexed. "Okay. Maybe not, then. We're good?"

"Yeah, we're good."

There's a single beat of accord and then my bag drops to the floor. I don't even realize I've stepped forward to kiss him until I'm pressed against him.

This time, I pull away after only seconds, as abruptly as I'd thrown my arms around his neck.

I can feel the shock on my face, even though I'm the one who started it. "Sorry. Bad idea."

"Really?" Christian sounds genuinely surprised. Honestly, how did I wind up *liking* this pompous ass? "I think we should have been doing that for months."

I shake my head, struggling to remember what I planned to say. The pull of him has always lured me—it is wide and very dark blue, and I have no idea what happens if I release myself. Maybe I float, lighter than I have ever been. Maybe it swallows me whole. "We're in the thick of searching for these guys. Is this some twisted extension of that?"

"Oh, come on." He shoots me an annoyed look, like I'm better than that. "This has been something for years."

Well. Yes. "Did you invite me to that party knowing Kinsley would blab?"

"Now, why would I do that?" he asks, trying to flatten his smile.

"Because I wouldn't have believed it coming from you."

"Hmm." He glances to the floor, where his socks nearly touch my boots. "I asked you to that party because I like when you're around. But yeah, I knew she might say something."

It is entirely possible that I'm a case study in unhealthy attachments. Maybe I need the first boy who ever really hurt me to like me. "How much of this is about winning?"

"You tell me," Christian says, stepping closer with a laugh. He knows what I mean: do we both want to prove that we were never the bad guy? "With us? It's probably always going to be a tiny bit about winning. I don't know if that's such a bad thing."

A good, honest answer. Dammit. I almost push his hand from my waist because I'm too aware that it's there.

He faces me head-on, working up to something. "Is any of this about Sophie?"

I know what he means. In the days before her death, Sophie was rallying me to give Christian another chance. She saw through my defenses, as always. "She was just pointing out what was already there."

He nods, satisfied, but the direct mention of Sophie sends a flare of guilt up my throat.

"There are only a few months until graduation," I continue. "I can't get distracted."

After a few beats, Christian says, "Okay. That's fair."

I huff out a laugh. When, in Dailey's whole life, has he conceded so quickly?

"What?" Half his mouth lifts into a smile. "I'm not going to debate you into this, MacLaren. Not great for the ol' ego."

There's a feeling inside me that rises like a gale, insistent and pushing. "I don't want people at school to know, in case someone tries to sabotage you, too."

His eyes sweep across me quickly, the spark of a disagreement. "Okay. But outside of school, can we just hang out and start fresh? Kinsley is already asking if you'll come to some art show opening, which obviously you don't have to, but . . ."

I'm not sure a fresh start is possible. There are second chances, but no do-overs. The memory of what came before exists alongside the new version.

"Hannah," Christian says. "What are you thinking?"

"Um." My gaze dips to his mouth. "About Van Gogh."

He grimaces. "That can't be good."

"Actually," I say, reaching for his hand. "I think it is."

— — — — — — —

It's good for weeks. I thought we might flame out quickly, nothing left when the pent-up tension clears. But he's obnoxiously smart, and he makes me laugh. We play board games with his friends, who love him and give him so much shit. He always has an arm behind my chair, not touching but still close. At school, we exchange quick, knowing looks, and it feels nice to have a good secret. When I catch my mouth smiling on the drive home from his place, I feel annoyed—at myself, at him, at the whole thing.

Of course, I bluster at him when he presumes to know what I'm thinking, and I struggle against my instinct to believe the worst. Yes, he'll pick a petty fight because something else is bothering him. Once, in mid-March, I storm out of his apartment, but he catches me by the bottom of the stairwell.

We're in his living room when I get the email from Maryland U. I'm swept into Christian's arms, spun clumsily as the words FULL ACADEMIC SCHOLARSHIP sink in. I'm awash in relief, though not as happy as I am during the lunch period when the Wythe email comes in. I call my mom from the bathroom, teary-eyed, and Christian—who locked in George Washington and American acceptances—drives us to celebratory ice cream.

When I kiss him, I imagine a single deep-sea diver, stark white on a canvas of ocean depths. I hear only breath and heartbeat and the timer I know is ticking. In every moment I linger, something is risked. But finally—finally—the space around me falls quiet. Did I have to go this far to find it? I don't know, but I'm already here.

Told you. The words swoop through my mind like a breeze.

———————

In other words, I get distracted, just as I feared. My mind, usually easy to direct in the classroom, wanders away without permission.

"Something is up with you," Zoe pronounces. "You're smiling at your yogurt."

"Well, I've gotten into several colleges," I reason. "Senior year's winding down. Prom is soon!"

"How's the gown coming?" Warner asks.

"Great," I say. It's currently on my dress form, waiting for a hem. "How are plans, Zo?"

Warner flashes me a look of despair because Zoe, of course, launches into décor and budget considerations. Warner excuses himself, muttering something about getting Pop-Tarts before next period.

"Can you keep a secret?" Zoe asks me, leaning in.

I almost bleat out a high-pitched laugh. "Sure."

"I'm doing this surprise video for our class at prom," she says. "Like a montage."

"Oh?"

"Once I announce prom royalty . . . well, let's be honest, once I crown Gabi and Catherine, I'll play this whole beautiful thing so everyone can remember the good parts of our four years."

"That's nice," I say reflexively. Sure—paste over Sophie and the attendant sadness. But even in bitterness, my diabolical brain whirs to life.

"Anyway," Zoe says, flipping her starlet hair. "I want pictures most people haven't seen before. Do you think you could get me some photos from the journalism archives? Catherine gets a lot of shots for the paper and yearbook, but I know she takes great personal photos too."

There we have it: my opportunity, handed up on a platter. "I'll ask her. She takes journalistic ethics super seriously, so she won't tell."

"Yeah, okay." Then, with a happy little trio of claps, "This is going to be so fun."

Would I really hijack Zoe's beautiful event to pull attention to Sophie's case? Earlier in the year, I wouldn't have given it a second thought. I still dislike Ingleside as an institution, and I dislike many of the kids too. They're uncritical—of themselves, of their position in the world, of the information presented to them. But I've been well-challenged in class, and there are classmates I like and even admire. It's all so much murkier than I planned.

As if he can sense me debating, Christian texts from across the cafeteria. I glance at my phone while *mm-hmm*ing at Zoe, who has moved on to weather panic.

Study for AP Gov test tonight?

No way. I have to actually study.

Excuse me! That's what I'm suggesting.

Fine. My place?

I get to come to your place?

Will you behave?

He sends a dog emoji.

I've been laying the groundwork with my mom, mentioning Christian's name. The first time, her face soured. She'd only heard his name in my debate complaints. But when I explain that he's been a good friend to me this year, she concedes.

My mom greets him very neutrally and then goes back upstairs. Christian and I really do study the entire time, both of us refusing to be the one who breaks. I expand my collection of flash cards, and Christian uses his uncanny memory to my great annoyance.

I walk him out, keeping things stubbornly platonic. It's a mild night, spring's first song in the air.

"Well," Christian says. "See you at school."

"Yep, see ya."

He turns just before opening the car door. "How was that for good behavior?"

"A very convincing impression."

"I like your house," he adds, which makes me feel squirmy. I'm used to his bravado and rhetoric; it's the directness that feels shockingly personal.

"Good."

"And I like you." He smiles sneakily, knowing this will make me avert my eyes. In that obnoxious, higher voice, he says, "*I like you too, Christian.*"

I kiss him to shut him up, aware that I've been played.

As he drives off, I stay there for a moment, shaking my head. The glow lingers around me like fireflies. Beneath the giddiness, I register the metallic jangle of a dog collar nearby, and it takes me a moment to notice a tall figure on the sidewalk.

My smitten smile drops. "Linc. Hey."

His spring break starts tomorrow—I knew that, actually.

He's standing totally still, jacket zipped to his throat. On her leash, Thea strains to get close to me, and I step forward to pet her on instinct.

"That was just, um—" I hitch a thumb at where Christian's car had been.

"Your pal, Dailey. Yeah." His expression is boarded up, unreadable. I'm scrambling for the right words, but Lincoln's shaking his head. "I can feel you about to lie, okay? Save it."

Above us, thunder rolls through the sky. Or is it below? Or am I imagining it? The sidewalk feels tremulous beneath my boots. "What's that supposed to mean? The thing with Dailey is just . . . I don't know what it *is* yet, so—"

"I bet," Lincoln says, stepping past me. He tugs Thea gently, leaving several feet between us. The sky is still and cloudless. So why do I feel the pattering on my shoulders?

"Why are you acting mad about this?" I call, over winds that push us apart. "You didn't tell me about Parker for a month!"

Lincoln spins back. "Oh, quit it, Hannah."

"Quit what?"

"This," he says, swiping a hand across me. "You want to hide shit from me? Fine. But don't act like it's normal."

Before I can reply, he takes off faster toward his house. "It's a new development. I haven't told *anyone*."

He whirls back, yelling, "Dailey was an asshole to you for years, and you knew I'd hate it."

We're partway down the block now, facing off in front of Mrs. Studebaker's house. "And it seems I was right!"

"Yay, your favorite thing!"

Ouch. Thea looks between us, troubled.

"He's different than I thought, Linc."

"Which I would know, if you'd mentioned it." Shaking his head like that, he doesn't look like goofy Lincoln, my childhood friend. I see glimpses of him as a grown-up, not so many years from now. "But do you text me? Have you made plans to come to even one of my lacrosse games? Has it ever occurred to you that going off to college is scary and I could have used my best friend?"

No. Nope. I felt jealous of Lincoln, able to flee to his new start. It didn't occur to me that he'd need support. But my pride rears up, an ugly, winged thing. "I've been a little busy trying to keep up at my new school."

"And you know exactly how I feel about that," he says. Then, shaking his head, "It's the same old shit, Hannah. Things get hard, and you shove people away."

Well, there's no denying *that* in good faith. "It's not how I want it to be, I just—"

"Well, sorry the bed's uncomfortable, Han," he snaps. "But you're the one who made it."

With that, he storms down the street at the fastest clip before a run. He turns back at the last moment that I'd be able to hear him, his voice carried on the wind roaring in my head. "I broke up with Parker, by the way. Not that you've asked!"

I wrap my arms, and I let the feeling soak me to the bone.

Junior Year

On the night before my seventeenth birthday, I stayed up past midnight, and then I cried myself to sleep. Part of me wished my mom would sense the pain and crawl into bed beside me, holding me without a word spoken or expected.

Instead, she gave me a car the next morning. She and George had secretly driven two hundred miles to inspect, purchase, and drive home a white '90s Cabriolet.

I stood in the driveway in my pajamas, having several conflicting reactions in the same moment. Elated that I could come and go as I pleased. Deeply worried that my mom had taken a loan or made some ruinous credit card decision. Frustrated that she felt a car would actually help anything. Furious at myself because I *did* feel excited somewhere in all of that.

"Anything over twenty-five years is considered vintage," she said brightly. I wished to pause the whole scene and process my emotions without her hopeful face waiting. Inside the house, box brownies were already in the oven—the traditional birthday breakfast in our household. "So, it isn't an *old* car. It's vintage. Only one owner! There's no AC, but you can put the top down when it's nice!"

This just didn't seem like my mom, who criticized Ginny for spending her way past emotions. To be fair, my mom did this too sometimes. The year she got laid off from the dry-cleaning company, she bought herself a nice coat for Christmas. Sometimes it feels like things are coming apart anyway—might as well have one nice thing.

"Well?" my mom asked. "You're still in shock?"

"I'm still in shock," I said, which was maybe truer than either of us knew. "But, Mom. Can we do this? Is this okay?"

Her eyes went stormy. "If I say it's okay, it's okay."

I had to wonder, though, if this was in some way related to Ingleside. Our preliminary conversation had been rocky, though my mom seemed relieved to hear me talk openly about Sophie and my feelings. She agreed, unhappily, to talk to Ginny for basic information. Perhaps this car was meant to be a compromise: a novelty, a freedom.

Later that day, I drove the car to Gabi's, and it felt alarmingly good to steer something of my own. Perhaps I was a more materialistic person than I thought.

"Whoa," Gabi said, when she opened the door. She pointed at the car. I'd always borrowed my mom's to drive over here.

"Birthday present," I said.

She pressed one hand to her forehead. "April second. I knew that, actually. Soph told me once—the story of your mom and April Fool's Day."

"Ah, yes." I was born on 12:03 a.m. on April second. My mom claimed that she held off intentionally, despite the pain. *I spared you a lifetime of people pranking you at your birthday party!* she'd say.

"You okay?" Gabi asked. "My birthday was in September, and I pretty much disassociated when my family sang to me. They were trying so hard to make things seem normal, but . . ."

It wasn't. We'd become older than Sophie would ever get to be. "So far it's had good and bad moments."

"Let's take the car to go get cupcakes or something," she said. "My treat."

After stopping at a bakery Sophie always loved, I glanced at Gabi over the to-go box. "Any chance you want to go see her?"

"Always."

Sophie was buried in a particularly nice spot in the graveyard—surely expensive, which was ridiculous to even think about. Now that trees were beginning to bloom, the scene was much gentler than the black branches of winter.

Maybe it should have felt disrespectful to eat a heart-shaped cookie while sitting on fresh grave sod. But it felt as normal as anything had in over six months now. I wondered if anyone ever strolled past here and noticed the etched letters—Sophie Farris Abbott. Did they glance at the dates and think what a shame it was?

Gabi leaned back on the headstone a little, looking very at home, and I wondered how often she came here. "How's Ginny and everyone?"

"Okay," I said. "Their offer on the campus house was accepted. Sounds like it's moving ahead."

"And things with Lincoln?" she asked.

"Icy," I admitted. He'd mumbled "hey" while walking the dog past my house, but that's it. "But I brought up Ingleside to my mom, and she took it better than Lincoln did."

Gabi smiled. "I can't believe this might actually happen."

After Sophie died, my imagining of the future dropped off. Senior year still felt like a distant shore. "Do kids at school talk about Soph still?"

"Not to me. They sort of stay away, like trauma's contagious." Gabi gave a shrug, as if she had not just dropped the bedrock truth of the matter: what happened to her that night was traumatic. "Which is fine. I don't want to pretend I'm okay or talk about it with people who don't get it. Catherine's been amazing, at least."

She said it so reverently that I had to ask. "Amazing in a . . . friend way?"

Gabi smiled down at her hands. "Good question. I'm not sure."

Once she said it, I couldn't believe I missed it before—a glittery crush in the gloom. Gabi had seemed a bit lighter. I felt happy for her and also farther away from Sophie—too far.

At first, losing Sophie painted my whole world in grayscale. But there in that cemetery, with early spring greens and blues, I thought of Chagall paintings. Parts of the world were recognizable again but out of place, the color too bright. "Will you tell me about that night?"

"Which night?"

"The night Sophie died."

"What?" Gabi turned her head sharply. "No! You don't want that in your head—believe me."

Maybe. But how could I bear not knowing yet another thing

about Sophie? And besides, she would hate for Gabi to be alone with it. "It's already in my head. I'd rather have the truth than my imagination."

Gabi was looking away, her eyes swimming.

"Have you told anyone all the details?" I asked.

"Of course not!" Twin tears raced down her cheeks. "No one should have to imagine it. And I don't want to relive it."

"If that's the reason, then okay," I said firmly. "But I can go there with you. I wouldn't say it if I didn't mean it. The not-knowing . . . it's too much."

"Hannah," Gabi said, and the word sounded small.

I placed my hand over hers. "Start when you couldn't find her."

Gabi shook her head, truly crying now. But her mind was already moving, recounting the night.

We'd reached the place, finally. No more secrets. Gabi told me how she found her, what she did, what it was like—all the images that closed in like hungry ghosts.

"When I remember it," Gabi whispered toward the end. We'd both stopped even trying to wipe the tears from our faces. "I see it from above. Like I left my body. I see myself kneeling on the floor, head tipped back and wailing. But I don't think that happened. I never stopped moving."

"I'm so sorry," I whispered again. Again.

We wept a puddle into the new grass, and we floated there for a while, staring up at bright blue.

"My dad says he can't have secrets," I told Gabi. "I think it's an AA thing. Secrets mean shame or resentment, which make it harder not to drink."

"Makes sense," she said.

"I think it's better," I decided. "To drag things out into the light."

When I remember it now, I see the scene from above: two girls clinging to something they can't quite name, only one of them realizing that it was not the final secret.

Senior Year

On the day of my eighteenth birthday, I get to Sophie's grave early, with a few simple crocuses in hand. Two ages without her now.

Today, I think of all the people who would have loved her— the college roommates, the friends she would have made for life there. She'll never know them. They'll never know what they missed.

I suspect that every year, I'll mourn some new facet of loss.

While I'm there, Lincoln texts me happy birthday, with the reminder that I can legally place bets on horses or—more my speed—sue someone. It's a jab, maybe, but at least he didn't ignore my birthday. My dad sends flowers, and my mom and I eat leftover brownies for lunch.

Christian takes me out for tacos later, after I've made it

clear our relationship depends on him not singing to me in public. When we're idling in his car outside my house, he announces, "I got you a present."

If the roles were reversed, I would have no idea what to get for his birthday. We're only six weeks into this thing. "Bold."

"I thought so," he says, reaching to the backseat.

It's a T-shirt with my name scrawled in neon airbrush—the kind you get at the boardwalk in Ocean City. Ginny always thought they were tacky, and my mom thought they were too expensive. I smile, running my thumb over the *H*. "I've always wanted one of these."

But then, Christian knew that. We talked about it the summer we met.

I twist in my seat to face him, gripping the T-shirt. "I have to tell you something."

Christian mimics my posture. "I'm a great gift-giver—yes, I know."

"I've decided to make my information public on prom night."

His eyes widen. "Wow. Okay."

"It's my last chance," I explain. "At the end of Zoe's slideshow, I'm adding a slide with the time parameters, the fact that Sophie hadn't seen that person, and the birthmark."

"Not the B thing?" Christian asks.

"I've debated that." I spin the T-shirt's hem around my finger. "I think people will fixate on it, right? And I don't want the people who are ultimately innocent to get pilloried."

"The school will go nuts," he says evenly. "Your aunt and uncle will hear about it."

"I know."

"Are you going to tell everyone you're Sophie's cousin, then?"

"The slide will give a burner phone number for any tips." When I talk about this plan, I feel removed, like I'm planning it for someone else—the Hannah I've constructed. These days, she's more real than any previous version. "But yes, it'll probably get out."

Christian nods, working through the many possibilities here.

"No one will know you have anything to do with it," I add. That's a vital part of this. Zoe might be implicated as the prom event planner, but I trust her to deny it vehemently.

"Okay," he says, reaching for my hand.

I give him another moment. "That's it? No preaching caution?"

"I got onboard with my eyes open." His smile is faint. "I've always known you're gonna ride it to the end of the line."

———————

The evening of prom, I do a lap around the lobby, with a dress bag over one arm. The Fairchild is a boutique hotel, full of trendy vignettes for photo ops. For every traditionally ostentatious feature—the marble floors, the tufted couches—there's something irreverent. Ceramic Dalmatian statues by the doors, a formal portrait of a solemn old white guy, but with a pink swipe across his mouth labeled *Shhh*. Everything seems to say: *We're so rich, lol*. Of course it's the venue Ingleside chose for prom.

The Walshes rented a suite for Zoe and her group to get ready in. The parents will come by to take pictures and then,

I'm sure, treat themselves to a fancy dinner while we eat catered chicken at eight tops in the ballroom. I suppose the parenting philosophy is that they'd rather keep the drunkenness on-site.

My mom is having her own night on the town with Mitch. When he asked me for Christmas gift help months ago, I suggested tickets for the local Shakespeare company's spring run of *A Midsummer Night's Dream*—the only assigned reading she ever liked in school. She cried when she opened the envelope, and the fact that she's not around to make a big deal out of prom is merely a bonus.

The elevators are framed by tall, spiky ferns, and a neon sign above me blares, in acid pink, GOING UP? I press the button and stare at my reflection in the mirrored doors, thinking how Sophie would have loved this trippy, Miami Beach deco thing. She would have posed everywhere.

I stop jamming my finger against the button only when someone approaches. Even in my peripheral vision, I know her gait, her height, the subtle swing of her hair. So poised, so cool with a garment bag over her arm—the perfect outfit for the perfect prom queen.

The moment Gabi reaches me, both elevators slide open in sync. Of course. I laugh under my breath as the mirrors push our reflections apart. We're barely inside when an arm juts out, keeping the door from closing. Violet Atwell, smiling brightly, bustles in. "Hey!"

Violet doesn't seem to notice the weird barometric pressure of words left unsaid. Gabi recovers into a friendly smile. "Sorry— didn't see you or I would have held it."

The doors close.

"No worries!" Violet tells Gabi. "Are you so excited for tonight? I voted for you—you're totally going to win."

"Thank you," Gabi says.

Floor 2, Floor 3.

Violet turns to me, with a glittery excitement that I wish I could feel. "You getting ready with Zoe and everyone?"

"Yep." My brain scrambles for what I can ask that would reveal something about Ben Ashby.

Floor 4. "Cool. Tell her this venue was a great choice!"

"I will." Ding: Floor 5. I step out and force a smile back. "See you out there."

"Have fun!" Violet calls.

As the doors close, Gabi gives me a long look. "See you."

———————

The parents take a thousand pictures and after they're gone, Zoe pops a bottle of champagne with a sly expression. She's been a little more devil-may-care since getting accepted to MICA. I sip one glass of bubbly, hoping for bravery. I only feel light-headedness. How can this be my life, here at Ingleside's fancy prom? Maybe I fell asleep last spring, a fairy-tale maiden poisoned by grief, and everything since has been a dream.

How else could I have wound up in the same prom photos as Brooks Van Doren, with his best friend's arm looped through mine? With his sweet mom calling out various poses and his dad's big, round laugh as he talks with Warner's parents? This is all so twisted.

Brooks's adorable date talks a mile a minute, to his obvious chagrin. Warner refills champagne glasses and asks me to take a photo.

"It's the last school dance you ever have to go to," Warner tells Brooks. "Smile."

So, I take a picture of two boys—longtime best friends—on

their prom night. My view of them, captured forever. It's possible that they both know who I am, and we're playing a 3D chess of denial. It's possible that they still have no idea.

We take more pictures throughout the ballroom, squealing over everyone's formalwear. Most of the dresses are sexy and forgettable, with jewel tone fabric cut at acute angles—sliced-out necklines down, leg slits up.

I'm in my senior project gown, black with an off-the-shoulder neckline that dips at my breastbone. I kept my hair down, one side clipped back with a knife-thin barrette. The look is boring or it's timeless. Either way, I'm wearing a shadow, and that's what I need for the night.

On the way to our table, Catherine shimmers over in a bronze lamé gown like a '70s queen. Gabi stands beside her, statuesque in that elegant, moon-silver suit, and we all exchange compliments. Catherine admires Warner's tux jacket, which he wears with easy confidence.

Every course of dinner tastes like butter and rosemary, and I bob along in the conversation. Zoe is up and back several times, basking in compliments. Brooks sits nearby with his sweet, still-chattering date, and my guard is never lowered. Ben Ashby and Violet—in an aptly purple gown—share a nearby table with the cross-country guys.

Christian and I are staying apart of course, but I watch him. He and Jasmine make the rounds, sometimes ducking in to whisper and laugh. It's the cozy conspiracy of old friendship. I still feel a tiny flame of jealousy.

When we're well into the night, our original group disperses—some of them well beyond tipsy, to Zoe's irritation. A teacher calls to her for some official business, and, standing alone, I begin to spiral. The clock is counting down, and I don't have time for doubt.

When I turn away, Christian is waiting. His tux is midnight blue, with satin lapels that catch the light. For someone who did not grow up in this world, he can wear it well when he wants to.

"Think we can get away with one dance?" he asks.

My false lashes weigh heavily as I scan the room. Couples are pressed close, lost in the gauzy world of self-reverence. These moments—right now—will be the memory this song calls up, when it's heard at a bar years from now. They'll laugh and say to their new friends, in a new city: *Oh my God. This was my prom song.*

And I would like to give myself this one moment.

At the edge of the dance floor, I drape an arm around Christian's neck. He tucks one hand over mine and holds it against his chest, near-center where his heart thumps. He's a solid dance partner. I would have guessed that, had I ever thought about it.

"You made this dress," he says. There's an appreciation in his voice, and I soak in the feeling of being looked at this way. Zoe would call it ninny behavior, but I can't help it. Yes, Christian can gaze at me with consternation or annoyance. But most often, he looks at me with blatant interest. Soft marvel. Even in our ugliest exchanges, there's a shared, small thrill of dancing with a worthy partner.

Where will he be, when we're old enough to laugh about our prom song? Maybe in DC, carrying a briefcase to his public defender job.

"You're worrying," he says. "Second thoughts?"

"About dancing with you or the slideshow?" I give him a

half smile, the best I can do. "Complicated feelings, but no second thoughts."

"So, hey," he says, voice intent now. "I'm confirming at George Washington."

This isn't a surprise, as I've watched him circle it, debating. "Good. I think that's right for you."

He thinks I should go to Wythe. I can tell in his careful restraint, in the way he presses his mouth into a line when we talk about it. He's trapping the opinion inside. On my pro-and-con lists, I write out undergrad enrollment, location, best-ranked majors. But my real indecision is more emotional than practical. Why had I always insisted I'd move to the West Coast for school? Was it really about connecting with my dad? Or was it about the desire to flee, alone, as my primary problem-solving method?

At West Grove, I could hide on the outskirts of the crowds and ace classes with relative ease. Ingleside, for all its entitlement, forced me into the public sphere and into a new echelon of academic pursuit. It's so annoying to admit, but . . . this way is better for me. And would it be so bad to stay close to home, to the relationships I've managed to forge?

"Whatever you decide," Christian continues, "I want to keep doing this. You and me, I mean."

God, the tailspin of this boy. I glance up the ceiling, blinking at a light fixture with dozens of exposed bulbs. "You want to have this conversation right now?"

"If the investigation comes up empty by graduation," he continues, as if I hadn't hesitated. "Can we call it? Say we gave it our best shot, and just spend the summer together?"

"It's not a school project for me, Christian," I whisper,

denying my impulse to step away and put space between us to argue.

"I know that," he says. "And I want you to have closure. But outside of all the investigation stuff, you seem pretty happy."

"Yeah," I say tightly. "If I could separate out the grief and anger of losing Soph, I'm sure I *would* be happy."

"You know I didn't mean it like that," he says. "But don't you think Soph would want you to move on and—"

"Don't," I snap, fiercer than I meant to. "You don't know what she'd say."

He tips his head, conceding. "You're right. But I can tell you from experience, letting yourself be happy can feel like honoring the person you lost."

It's an excellent pivot to ethos—a reminder of his expertise. My hackles lower, body relaxing against his once more.

Christian doesn't know what Sophie would say, but I do. Wherever spirits live, hers would throw a party if I let myself be happy with him for a summer. Not because a boyfriend is some better version of my existence, but because in this case, I've toppled a labyrinth's worth of walls to arrive here. She would also, of course, delight in being correct.

The problem is that I also hear her telling me to press on in my search.

"I want to keep doing this too," I tell him. It's the closest I've ever come to admitting the depth of my feelings for him. He probably sees the wild-eyed look sometimes, when I'm torn between clinging to him and darting off, spooked.

"Good." He leans forward an inch before catching himself. I feel the kiss as if it had landed on my mouth. "Let's just have this one minute."

We dance in silence, and I try to memorize the brush of my cheek against his. I'll be grateful for this moment later, when everything goes to shit.

The song dips out, replaced by the pulsing intro of a Top 40 song remix. I look at Christian intently. "Whatever happens, stay with Jasmine, okay? I don't want people—"

"I know," he says, arms tight on my waist for just a second before he releases me. "See you after."

On instinct, I sweep my gaze around the ballroom, looking for my chess pieces. Brooks is laughing with soccer guys. Ben and Violet are still in slow dance formation on the dance floor.

I slump into my seat. The anticipation is real now. I'm about to detonate the fragile peace this school has found. In the process, I'll probably show myself as the liar I have been.

But even in the blur of it, something catches my eye. At dinner, I'd set my satin handbag above my plate, near the flower arrangement, to make room for all the utensils and elbows. The little silver clasp had faced upward, reflecting in the centerpiece's glass. Now it faces toward me.

Great end to prom night: someone stealing my stuff. My mom taught me better than to leave a purse lying around, but that's what a year at Ingleside gets me. My phone is still in there—thank God—and my ID and credit card. Maybe a server moved the bag while clearing plates, but I feel the prickling at my neck.

Standing, I move to the back exit. I need better light and fewer prying eyes, and I find both outside the ballroom doors. In the bag's side pocket, I feel for my naloxone spray, but there's something else, beneath the folded tissues my mom packed for blotting.

Pills—three flat circles that I press with the pad of my finger. The hallway goes wobbly around me, and I rush into the bathroom, dodging several girls and a cloud of perfume. When I slam the stall door, one of them says, laughing, "Yikes. Someone did beer before liquor."

The crowd of faces registers a second too late, and I back right out of the stall. Sunita Kumar—stunning in a deep, jeweled pink—is leaned toward the mirror, reapplying lipstick. Beside her, a familiar brunette is perched on the sink, taking a photo. Jenny Lisk is glammed-up, but I recognize her from the sloppy beer-chugging video I watched a thousand times. Gabi ruled her out—I know this. Sophie saw Sunita that night and remembered her girlfriend's name. Jenny.

They both turn to look at me, this silent girl who is staring.

I lick my lips. "Um. Do either of you have a tampon?"

Sunita shoots me a look of sympathy, and Jenny says, "Yeah, I've got you."

As she unsnaps her evening bag, my eyes pull downward. She's in a strapless dress, exposing her whole shoulder and arm—including a distinct birthmark above her elbow.

I accept the tampon, unable to move my expression from shock.

"It'll be okay," Jenny tells me, uncertainly. "Your dress is black, so even if it stained, no one will be able to tell."

"Right." Fake smile as I return to the stall. "Thank you."

Jenny Lisk spilled the beer she was trying to chug. Warner probably grabbed her a clean shirt from his sister's room—a Blockhead shirt.

It's too much at once. Finally, the arm person appeared, which almost doesn't feel real. I'm down to Brooks and Ben.

And, somehow, there are pills in my possession. They're white—oxycodone is my guess. Or could they be generic brand aspirin, meant to freak me out? I can't exactly find a teacher and tell them that someone—God, it sounds insane—planted pills on me, only to discover they're aspirin. Then I'm blamed for a prank or made to seem paranoid.

Or these pills are real. Maybe someone is out there, telling a teacher they saw me take something. Maybe he's saying he saw me pass meds to another student.

I unfurl my hand. The pills plink into the toilet water, and I watch them spin. If they're gone, does that cover all my bases? The person could still accuse me, but there would be no proof of wrongdoing. What am I missing? I pinch my eyes closed, trying to visualize the jumbled game board. This is a chaotic move, and I can't place it.

What if someone planted pills on Christian? In his jacket pocket, when it was slung over the back of his chair? What if this guy has watched me with Zoe or with Catherine at the paper? If he knows I'm Sophie's cousin, maybe he guessed that I know Gabi better than either of us lets on. Anyone who corroborates my story—surprise, they've got pills on them too. A network, right under the administration's noses. Me at the center.

"Hurry up," I hear one of the girls tell the other. "They're about to do prom court."

Brooks or Ben. Brooks or Ben.

I stare at my phone, about to type: *Someone might have planted pills on you. Check your pockets and purses now, discreetly.* But—God—what if the person has already pulled a teacher aside? Gabi and Catherine will be lined up awaiting crowns, their phones left behind. Zoe will be ready to announce the queens.

My shaky legs carry me to the hallway. From just behind the double doors, I stare into the ballroom, the sea of black tuxes and shiny satin. The kids Sophie grew up with. One of them gave her the drugs that killed her, and he knows I'm close.

Breathe.

I pull the fire alarm so hard that my knuckles ache.

Junior Year

As soon as my mom agreed to take a meeting with the Head of School, I bounded over to Gabi's house like a Labrador retriever, holding my good news like a giant stick. Mrs. Reyes let me in and pointed me upstairs to Gabi's room, where I threw my arms wide, triumphant, "I think Ingleside might really happen!"

Gabi looked up from her seat on the bed.

"That's great," she said, but she couldn't muster any enthusiasm into her voice.

My defensiveness rose—that old self-consciousness with her sneaking in. Now that Ingleside was becoming a reality, she'd changed her mind? It was her idea. "I mean. I don't have to go through with it . . ."

"I want you to. It's just . . . it's such a big change in your life. And I . . ." She pressed her face into her hands, voice a whisper. "I need to tell you something."

I sank down beside her, hands gone cold with worry. "Okay . . ."

"So, I . . . well—" The words were choked off by a proper sob. Gabi pressed her hands to her cheeks, hiding as much as she could.

This crying seemed more tortured than our recent graveyard cry. "Gabi."

"I knew Sophie was using," she blurted out.

I blinked, struggling to connect the words with reality. "No, you didn't."

"There was a day in July when she was acting *too* chill at the pool. Dreamy, in a weird way. I made some stupid joke about her eating an edible, and she didn't laugh. She got cagey."

"Is that all?" My voice sounds like someone else's, tinny and faraway. "That's not *knowing*."

"She kept checking the time," Gabi continued. "Then went to the bathroom right at noon, with her tote. I confronted her in the car on the way home."

"And?"

Gabi blew out a breath. "Um, she cried. Acted shocked and betrayed that I'd think that about her. By the time I dropped her off, I felt two inches tall."

The journal entries returned to my mind—the way Sophie lied even on a page meant for her eyes alone. I imagined her, her eyes red in the passenger seat of Gabi's car.

"She apologized the next day," Gabi continued, staring at her hands. "And admitted that, a few times, she doubled a dose. She knew it was stupid, and her prescription was out anyway. It was, like, enough of the truth to placate me, you know?"

Yes. And Soph was always good at apologies. "That was the last of it?"

"Yeah." She didn't lift her head to look at me. "But I could have said something. I *should* have. It seemed too minor to tell Ginny, and . . ."

Sure, I almost said. But then it hit: since the day Gabi pulled me aside in the funeral home, her persistent support had been driven by guilt. She didn't need a friend as much as I did. She needed to make amends. God—who had I been in this room with, week after week?

"When you told me you searched Sophie's purse for a tampon at the party," I said slowly. "You were looking for pills."

She held very still, and it all settled—the truth, which would not budge, and the hurt, which only grew.

"You have to tell Ginny," I said. All these months of feeling like there were no warning signs, like the drug thing couldn't possibly be *true.* "Like, today."

"I told her a few weeks after the funeral. Once the shock wore off."

My jaw lowered. "Oh."

"I thought you might blame me," Gabi said, back to fully crying. "I mean, I blame myself! And I didn't want to lose you."

I nearly snarled. "You lied so you could have an assistant for your investigation?"

"No!" She looked genuinely hurt. "Don't do that. I mean—be mad. But don't do that."

Don't act like we haven't needed each other to survive losing Sophie. Don't act like this hasn't meant everything to both of us, solid ground in the tempest of grief.

But that was the problem. For months, Gabi's steady presence in my life—her clear-eyed motivation, her willingness to talk about Sophie—kept me hanging on. And all this time, I was her penitence.

I stared at her, like looking at a stranger. I'd shown her more of myself than anyone had seen in months. "You used me."

Gabi's jaw dropped. "Whoa. That's not fair."

Wasn't it? I let a few tears fall, swept away by my pitiful hurt feelings.

"Hannah." Gabi climbed off the bed, reaching toward me. "I'm so sorry. But honestly, I—"

"*Honestly?*" I repeated, stepping back to wipe my cheeks. "I'm about to transfer to a school where you're the only person I know!"

For a few moments, we both sat there, staring with wet eyes. I kept trying to speak, and instead, I'd shake my head, throat aching.

"You'll never be able to forgive me," Gabi said quietly. "Will you?"

I stared up, my lashes sticky and wet. Words flew across the ceiling—*no* and *yes* and *how could you do this?* None of them felt entirely true except, "I don't know."

I respected her, however begrudgingly, for not sinking into dramatics. She'd been stretching our friendship as far as it could go, knowing we'd reach this point.

"I need to leave," I said.

"Hannah."

I turned back, stricken by how ruined everything felt. Gabi's sleeves covered her hands as she wiped at tears. She'd let me spill my guts while she held back, but I still didn't want to hurt her. "I will never—for one second—think it was your fault. And you know I mean it because I'm *so* pissed that you lied. If I was ever going to try to hurt you, it would be right now."

"It *is* my fault," she said bitterly.

"Sophie hid things from you. From all of us, maybe from herself." I pressed a hand to my chest, already feeling the crack in my voice. "But then you hid things from me too. What am I supposed to do with that?"

"I'm sorry," she said. "I wish I could go back to the start."

"Yeah," I said, reaching for the door handle. "Me too."

APRIL

- - - - - - -

Senior Year

I dab a tear from my eye. Dr. Ryan, too, seems to be struggling against emotion, though she certainly looked angry at several points.

"And that was that," I finish. "Gabi and I fought and called off the plan. Which is for the best—it was rash and childish. I decided Ingleside was too good an opportunity to pass up. Gabi kept her promise for a peer recommendation."

She nods slowly. "But tonight, you saw Ms. Reyes not only continuing her senior year at Ingleside but being celebrated by her peers? Possibly including someone you believed to be involved."

"Yes," I say. I could tell her about this year, right down to the pills from tonight, but I won't—not yet and maybe not ever. I'm down to only two players, and I need more time to decide what comes next. "The fire alarm was a split-second, terrible decision, and I sincerely apologize. I'm prepared to accept consequences."

"Well." The Head of School clears her throat. "This is a lot to take in, but I do appreciate your candor. I'm not a stranger to the way grief can make you desperate for an answer."

It's generous. I nod, again trying to clear my streaked mascara.

"And you never discovered the identity of the student you sought?" she asks.

"No." I twist my hands in my lap. "Because it was always true, wasn't it? The last column—people who might have been there—is infinite."

There's a light tap on the door, surely signifying that my mom has finally arrived.

Dr. Ryan nods. "I'm going to touch base with your mother. Hopefully, we can move forward, but I do need to be fair. That fairness might include a brief suspension."

Outside the office, my mother paces the hallway. She's still in her pretty dress from the theater, and I feel like the worst daughter who has ever lived.

"What in all of hell, Hannah?" my mom demands.

I make myself meet her blazing eyes.

"Well," Dr. Ryan tells my mother. "Hannah and I have had a very edifying conversation."

"Oh?"

"It seems that Hannah and Gabi Reyes had something of a falling out last year, and tonight kicked up some old feelings."

My mom narrows her eyes at me. Good God, I am in so much trouble.

Dr. Ryan gestures toward the door. "If you'd like to step in for just a moment so we can get on the same page . . ."

I stare at the worn, intricate patterns on the Persian rug. My mom sweeps past me, and I hope for mercy.

Alone in the hall, I take one slow breath, then glance at my phone. I intend to type my "everything is okay" texts and then move on to the apologies. But a string of messages from Zoe stalls me out.

I've told you things.

Like, personal things.

You've been to my house!

What is wrong with you?

You knew what this prom meant to me!!!

Psycho behavior, truly.

I'm done. Blocked.

The tears give way. All of a sudden, I truly cannot stand to be within Ingleside's hallowed halls. I burst through the same doors I entered my first day, desperate for air. It's no longer raining, but the atmosphere is wet with humidity. I sink onto the bench outside, gulping air that feels far too thin.

— — — — — —

The ride home is chillingly quiet, except for my earnest apology to Mitch. He says, "Oh, don't you worry about me." My mom's anger is silent but thrumming, a current below the engine rumble.

When Mitch parks on the street outside our house, I peer to the porch, where someone is waiting. Ginny is standing under the thin light, arms crossed over a raincoat.

"What's Aunt Ginny doing here?" I ask.

"We're having a little family conversation." My mom's voice is eerily even. She leans over to peck Mitch on the cheek. "Sorry about all this, love. You've been a prince."

"No trouble at all," he says. "Call tomorrow."

I get out of the car in case my mom wants to say anything else in private. But she's right behind me, ushering me forward. Maybe she called Ginny for backup. Maybe I deserve a two-on-one scolding, like the kids whose parents live together.

Mitch's SUV backs out, headlights bending across the three of us.

"Hannah, you okay, sweetie?" Ginny asks, and I nod. She looks perplexed, trying to read my defeated posture and my mom's coiled anger. "What happened?"

"Both of you," my mom says, "Inside."

The porch light rests on Ginny's hair like a halo. "Okay. I'm a little confused here . . ."

"You two are cut from the same cloth," my mom mutters. "I should have known."

Now I'm the one staring. Still, Ginny and I file inside, knowing better than to cross my mom at this moment. We troop through the house and wordlessly seat ourselves at the kitchen table. My mom fills the kettle and plunks it onto the stove.

"I would appreciate an explanation now," Ginny says firmly.

My mom looks between us, her stare a pendulum of scrutiny. I want to shrink to the floor and skitter away like a beetle. "It seems that last year, Hannah and Gabi Reyes were doing their own little investigation into what happened with Sophie."

Ginny stares at me in blank shock. One hand travels to her mouth, fingers laid across her lips.

"I need you to tell her, Gin," my mom says.

The two of them lock eyes, exchanging something in sister telepathy.

"Tell me what?" I demand.

My aunt clears her throat. "For a stretch of time last year, I also became preoccupied with getting to the bottom of it."

I stare at this woman. She is still my aunt, but she is also something else entirely. Virginia Farris Abbott, former reporter and fearsome mother. Why had I never guessed?

"At first, I worried a teacher or coach could be involved." Ginny sits very straight, hands delicate on the table. "You see things on TV—I don't know. I just wanted to make sure other kids were okay. And I was so, so angry."

I stare at my aunt, barely registering her words. Behind her, the kettle begins to rattle, and my mom pulls three mugs from the cabinets.

"Oh, honey." Ginny sighs. "Sophie bought pills shortly before the night she died."

No—that wasn't right. The questions bombard me: Was she certain? Why hadn't she told me? My mouth hangs open, not a single word airborne. "How do you know?"

"Educated guess," Ginny says. "There were a few expensive items missing from her room, and I found the designer purse at a consignment shop in Eastmoore. She sold it to them less than a week before she died—and some nice jewelry the month before. I . . . I didn't want it to change how you saw her."

It doesn't. Or it does, but in a way that expands both my love and pain.

"So, you don't know where she got the pills?"

"No," Ginny admits, though there's a quick glance to my mother that makes me wonder. "But the purse snapped me out of it. Sophie was seeking out cash in a way I couldn't trace to her credit card."

I look to my mom, scowling. "You said no secrets."

My mom places tea in front of us. Steam rises like a smoke screen between our faces. "I was trying to protect you."

I turn back to Ginny, still processing her revelation. "But Sophie texted someone that night, with a burner app."

"Yes," Ginny says quietly. She wraps her hands around the mug. "Maybe there was someone else involved. I don't know. But I've made my peace with it."

Then she looks to my mom for permission once more.

"Around January last year," Ginny says slowly. She's choosing her words carefully. "A local woman emailed me anonymously. Her teenage son had finished an in-patient detox, and she wondered if I had any contacts who might help with next steps. This poor woman's husband didn't even want her to attend support meetings in person, in case someone saw her."

I lace my fingers together, anticipating. Teenage son. The Van Dorens seemed to care about appearances, and drug use would disqualify Ben from cross-country. Secrecy would be important.

"I don't know if he was an Ingleside student," Ginny continues, "but it was easy to imagine. So I did. And that scenario freed me."

"Wait." I stare between my mom and aunt. "That's it?"

"Hannah," my mom warns, voice low.

Ginny smiles, sadly. "Oh, sweetie. I was never out to punish a sick kid. And Lord knows being in the system doesn't fix a damn thing."

The two of them share a loaded glance that means they're referencing their parents. It hits me—with a clear and sinking certainty—that there is no real answer coming to me. All this information, and no closure.

I'm near-bursting with desperation, to be so close without touching. "But . . . but what if this guy is still selling to kids?"

"And what if Sophie sold to him?" Ginny asks gently. "The boy's mom emailed me once more, a few months later. She'd gotten him continued treatment without the father realizing, and her son had months of recovery. I won't disrupt it to demand answers, and I doubt she'd reply anyway."

I shake my head furiously, eyes brimming with tears. How nice for Ginny and my mom, that they've had each other to talk it through. "You don't get it."

"Don't get what, Bug?" my mom asks. I resent the pity in her voice. I'd rather her be angry at me—as angry as I am.

"The two of you have each other," I snap. The tears stream down my face now, a steady fall of water. "And I had Soph. Now, I have no one. I can't just be okay with that."

"No one wants you to be okay with it," my mom says. "No one."

Ginny shakes her head, forehead crinkling with emotion. "I'll never be okay with it, Hannah. Ever. I will mourn for Sophie until my dying day."

"But someone out there knows what happened!" I insist, shrill and losing control. It feels like my lungs are on fire. "How do I live with that?"

My mom reaches to stroke my arm, but I pull away, glaring at her. No—I won't be pacified like a little kid after a grade-school slight. This is literally life and death.

My aunt's eyes, teary now, look laser-beam green. "Here's how I see it: I could obsess about how, specifically, my child got drugs. Or I could champion something that students asked for as support."

The campus house. This giant project that I'd written off as a monument to Ginny's idea of her daughter. Here, I wanted to destroy something bad, and that's not always the wrong impulse. But Ginny had begun to build something good. I press my hands to my face.

I'd been wanting to set fires, let myself and everything around me be consumed. Ginny used her fire to power the engine and move forward. It feels humiliatingly obvious.

That, as much as anything, is why I let myself burst into hiccup-y tears, like the small child I'm trying so hard not to be.

"Hannah," my mom says quietly. She rests her hand on one arm, Ginny on my other.

Oh, Soph. How did I make such a mess of all this?

"I hear you," I manage. And I finally do.

———————

When the last tea has been sipped and the last tears cried, we walk Ginny to the door. I'm still in my dress, shifting uncomfortably. As my aunt climbs into her car, I hear my mom's quiet voice. "Looks like you have company."

Christian's waiting outside, pacing the walkway to the porch. His tie is gone, collar unbuttoned. When he looks up, I expect him to charge toward me and ask if I'm okay. But he hangs back, expression hard.

"Five minutes," my mom says, severely. The door shuts behind her.

I step off the porch, hitching up my skirt. "So, my plan went a little sideways."

"You pulled the fire alarm because something went wrong, and you needed to bail on the slideshow," Christian guesses.

"Yes." I press my lips together, confused. If he understands my reasoning, why is he frenetic and seething on my lawn?

He stops for long enough to face me. "You made me think I knew the whole story."

I blink a few times, confused. "You do. Other than what happened tonight, you know everything that's relevant."

"Ah," he says, with a knowing nod. "'Everything that's relevant.' That's pretty subjective, wouldn't you say? Covers a multitude of omissions."

My stomach twists with dread. The dam is splitting, a crack down the center.

Christian looks at me dead-on. "Has Gabi been in on it the whole time?"

Yes, is the answer. But then, Christian knows that. Blood beats in my ears, like rushing water.

"It didn't make sense for her to call you out like that or for you to just stand there and take it. There was this look on your face . . . like . . ." He shakes his head, trying to find the words. "Like you two were on the same team."

The less he knew, the safer he was. But I know better than to blurt out my rebuttal. This is an interrogation.

"Here's what I think," Christian says, pacing again. "I think Barrett Evans was a bigger piece than you let on. I think Gabi did dual credit at Yardley to get close to him, while you took on Brooks and Ben Ashby. Am I in the ballpark?"

I swallow thickly. "Yes."

"So, it was a lie, that you and Gabi had a falling out."

"No, we did. It just . . . wasn't the whole story." With the wince of betrayal on his face, I can't hold back. "I was trying to protect you! The less you knew, the—"

"I was *clear*," he says, near-yelling now. "I was clear that I wanted in regardless of risk. I've told you that what happened to Sophie matters to me, for many reasons, and one of them is you. Yet here I am, some chump you don't even trust."

My eyes flood with tears. "I do, though."

"This is why," he says. "This is why I wanted us to call it at the end of the school year. You care about this investigation more than you care about me, and that's fine."

"Christian—"

He flashes a don't-try-me look. "But you also care about it more than you care about yourself. About your future, your safety. And that's the problem for me."

"There's just more to it than you realize—"

"Well, that I believe," he snaps. "Tell you what. How 'bout you figure out if you can actually be in this with me, and—"

"I can," I say, stepping forward. "I just—"

"No." He holds up a hand, keeping me back. My own hands are raised into a pleading pose, desperate. I lower them. "Really think about it, Hannah. Don't call me until you have an honest answer."

My mouth wants to spit out every justification, but he's being clear about what he needs from me. For once, I take it on the chin. "Okay."

"Okay." He nods, once, and stalks back to his car.

I slump onto the porch step, crumpling my fancy dress, and I press my face into my hands.

But I wasn't lying before. There really is more than he realizes.

Junior Year

After Gabi's confession, I drove away slowly, struggling to see the road through my tears. Gabi had become a cornerstone in my life after Sophie. Without her, my grief toppled like a city inside me. Rubble. Ruin.

My mom and Lincoln had accused me of shutting them out, and I had denied it. But they must have been right because how else could I have felt so abandoned? Gabi was the only person I'd allowed to truly see me these past six months: blazing, desperate, unable to loosen my grip.

I parked at the cemetery and hurried to her headstone. Sophie Farris Abbott. Beloved daughter and sister. And cousin and niece and best friend and budding environmentalist. And I cried more than I had since the week she died. I cried remembering sitting here with Gabi on my birthday, cried so hard I scared the cemetery birds to a different tree.

"You just left me here, Soph!" I yelled into the air, hitting my fists against the grass. Then, immediately guilty, I skimmed my palms across the blades gently. "I don't know what to do."

And then, as quick as the confession, I did know. I felt left behind, and, in that moment, I wanted to leave. For months, I'd stayed, faithfully, in a life that dealt me relentless reminders of Sophie's absence. But there had always been another option.

At home, I found my mom in her room, hanging up clean clothes.

"I want to go to Vancouver for the summer," I announced, before I could lose my nerve. "Stay with Dad, clear my head."

My mom hung up one more dress and stepped back from the closet to study me.

"It's like you said," I continued. This was a hastily assembled argument, underpinned by my desperate energy. "He's good at talking about all the AA stuff, and I could use that. Plus, I think a change of scenery would make me feel less . . . haunted."

Like I might see Sophie at any turn. Like I can hear her voice whispering in my ear.

My mom gave a long sigh, her eyes cast up to the ceiling as she considered. "Okay. Let's slow down a minute. Have you talked to your dad?"

"Not yet."

This was hurting her—I'd have been oblivious not to sense it. Whatever was wrong with me, she couldn't fix it. "I'll call him to discuss whether it's a possibility. You're sure?"

I nodded, with a relieved smile. "Thanks, Mom. This feels right. I need a break from the everyday, where nothing has changed except Sophie is dead."

She winced at my bluntness. "I know. And I've been thinking about Ingleside, too. Ever since Lincoln said you're like a ghost at school and—"

My calm, persuasive voice fell immediately. "Lincoln said *what?*"

"Don't be mad at him, Bug," she said, with an admonishing look. "He worries too, you know."

"He's . . . I'm . . ." I could feel my face flushing with anger. I wanted to argue that, because Gabi had a similar relationship with Soph, it makes sense that I talk to her. I don't get worried when Lincoln talks lacrosse with Kyle instead of me. But no matter how much I dislike Lincoln and my mom gossiping about my emotional response, this works in my favor. "Yeah. I mean, he's not wrong."

My mom nods at me. "Then we'll change things up. I appreciate you telling me."

Satisfied, I strode down the hall with renewed purpose. My whole year was a bust? Fine. I'll run. I'll disconnect, abandon it all. My whole friendship with Gabi was built on a lie? No problem. I'll leave it behind, along with the investigation that started from a bog of guilt.

There wasn't much evidence of our quest. My mom wasn't the snooping type, but I'd take Sophie's journal with me to Canada and dispose of the burner phone before I left. I reached between my bed and the wall, feeling for the phone. Why did I power it on? I don't know. Sixth sense.

There was a message waiting from number: Unknown.

Consider this an informal cease and desist warning for your threats against my son, who had no part in that girl's tragic choices. I won't hesitate to formalize the complaint with my lawyers if you contact him again.

I stared, frozen, at the words. I should have felt a shrill of fear, being threatened by someone sharp and assured. But I could only feel the heart-pounding exhilaration, the new facts clutched in my palm.

One: this was the real B. When we texted the boys on our list, we didn't mention Sophie directly. And yet, this message understood the accusation perfectly.

Two: his parents knew. Or, at least, one of them did. Maybe he'd denied his involvement, but there's no way his family would hit back this hard over absolutely nothing.

The rage began low, near my feet, but it crawled up like flames. A kid who stayed silent after screwing up so badly? I resented it enough to chase him down. But a full-grown adult keeping their child from accountability? That made me sick.

Sophie was someone's kid too.

I flipped the phone around in my hand, considering. This changed everything.

Only then, after hours of silence at the graveyard, did I hear the whoosh of a familiar voice.

Mehhhh. Go talk to Gabi.

— — — — — — —

The next day, I stood on the Reyes's porch for the last time, between cement planters full of violets, and I knocked.

Gabi answered, her face fallen in surprise. "Hannah."

"I'm not over it," I said. By then, she knew me well enough to expect that. She also knew me well enough to know that it was simply an opening statement. Our eyes connected. "But I have to show you something."

Ensconced in her room, I explained with the phone in

hand. Gabi's eyes went huge, then ticked across the floor as she played out the implications. "That *asshole*. You think the gala spooked him and he confessed to a parent?"

"Who threatened us instead of holding him accountable?" I finished. "It's one theory."

She sat back, her lower teeth digging into her upper lip. "I thought I was ready to let it go. But I don't think I can."

"Me either," I said. "And I have an idea."

We'd stay apart so no one at Ingleside—and not even our parents—could connect us. I'd return from Vancouver the new girl, I'd chip away at Brooks and Ben Ashby, and Gabi would take a dual-credit Yardley class, trying to get close to Barrett. In case of an emergency, we'd use a simple code. Green: this person knows I'm Sophie's cousin or we need to tell them. Yellow: this person knows one of us is up to something. Red: this person knows everything or we need to tell them.

We parted with a tight embrace, despite my lingering anger. "Are we okay?" Gabi whispered.

"We're okay," I said, releasing her. Sophie wouldn't tolerate anything less. "Have a good summer. And, if it gets too hard . . . you can call."

She gave a sad smile, like she knew just what I meant. "Back at you."

With a nod, I walked away—the last time I'd see her until the first day of school. I missed her right away.

All those boys were guilty of something. We just had to figure out what.

Senior Year

The morning after prom, I dress in my oldest leggings and a white shirt. I push my bangs back with a folded-over, black bandana, and I walk downstairs.

My mom is in her robe, reading with a cup of coffee beside her.

"I know I'm probably grounded," I say quietly. "But can I go to the Caldwell house?"

She gives me a once-over with tired eyes. "I suppose. You good with the door code?"

I am. The drive is silent, in golden light breaking through trees and buildings. I park in the driveway and take in the full effect of the house. The color is equal parts gray and green, like eucalyptus leaves, and the front door is a soft, denim blue. I have to give Ginny credit—it's a more whimsical palette than I expected.

There's a figure waiting, leaning on the porch's pillar. Her face has been scrubbed of prom night makeup, hair pulled back but still parted in the middle. She's in gray coveralls, white paint specks freckling the fabric. I haven't seen her anywhere but school and at Sophie's gravesite for almost a year. Far, far too long.

Gabi meets me halfway, opening her arms. I hug her, and we stay that way for a minute, quiet and held tight. We've tried to be efficient at our meetings, but we also alternated who brought treats and, on weeks with little news, sat together for the rest of the hour.

"You okay?" she asks finally.

"I'm okay." We release each other, smiling weakly. It's a sad, heavy calm, but it is still calm. "I can't believe it's done."

She nods. All along, she's been more prepared to walk away than I have been. Possibly because she's been coming to this house, helping my aunt Ginny. "I hated last night. Was it the right call?"

"It was exactly what I wanted you to do." When I looked at Gabi head-on in the rain outside of prom, I chose my words carefully: green with envy. In other words: tell them I'm Sophie's cousin. It was the alibi I needed for my behavior. "I think B, whoever he is, has to know that I folded, right? Exposed at school, in trouble. I'm clearly done."

Gabi nods. "I think that's right. How bad is it?"

"Not sure. Dr. Ryan was kind of sympathetic. I told her a lot of the story, but I ended with our fight last year. So she doesn't know you're still involved."

"I know," Gabi says softly. We were so careful to keep the pieces separate. "But I still hate it."

It could have easily gone the other way. If Barrett had been our guy and not just a cheater Gabi could rat out anonymously, she might have been in the hot seat.

"Christian pieced it together," I say, sighing. "He's furious, of course—*don't* say I told you so."

She zips her lips together. More than once, she'd admonished me to just tell him the whole plan. Catherine knew, after all, and had known since before holiday break. "You'll work it out."

I'm not so sure. Of all the havoc I'd wreaked yesterday, Christian's pained expression was the one that kept me awake last night. And Zoe's texts. My mom's horror at my behavior. And failing, after everything.

"So," Gabi says, nodding toward the house. "You ready?"

"I am." Finally, this is what feels right. I need to get my hands dirty and work my way back. Action and not words.

I watch Gabi's finger on the keypad—7674—and I pause. "Hey. I've always meant to ask. Was that the password to Sophie's phone?"

"I tried that at first," Gabi says. "But it was 4299."

My birthday and Gabi's, together. How will I ever live with the unknowns?

Gabi pushes open the door and glances back. "Here we go."

MAY

Junior Year

A day later, Lincoln showed up with a bag of donuts and a guilty wince. I was on the front porch, lacing my running shoes and considering a sprint away from him. Instead, I gestured, offering the floor for an opening statement.

"You're so mad I talked to your mom that you're leaving for *Canada?*" he blurted out. "She just asked if you were okay, and what could I do? Lie?"

No. He never could.

For all I was willing to do, I couldn't gaslight Lincoln. I'd played out the arguments, all of them flimsy. And besides, this new plan worked. "I'm going because I miss my dad, and I think it'll be good for me."

He sat on the stoop beside me, offering me the open bag. "I can't believe you won't be here for my last summer before college."

I gave him a grim smile. "I know. But I get a real summer vacation away, somewhere I've never been. Like that Audrey Hepburn movie."

"*Sabrina*," he said automatically. We did a marathon a few summers back, but I always mixed them up. "She's gone for two years, though."

"True," I said. "But I'll definitely be changing my hair before Ingleside, so stay tuned."

I'd meant this as a peace offering: relating my situation to film, changing to a favorable subject. But Lincoln—I could feel in the tension between us—was not buying.

"You're still going to Ingleside," he said flatly.

It was clear, in that moment, Lincoln suspected something. There's no way I'd be disloyal to Sophie, and there's no way I'd lose a battle I walked into knowingly.

He'd answered my mom honestly to save me from myself. Alas.

"Goddammit," he said, waving one hand as he stood up. "No—you know what? Make your own bed. But I'm saying this one last thing. It's only going to hurt you. Leave it be, Hannah."

I will, I almost said. Debate had trained me to see all sides, to argue each with equal fervor. Sometimes I worried that I'd lost my instinct for the real, ethical truth. But not that day with Lincoln.

So I didn't say another word. I let him go.

MAY

Senior Year

In the week after prom, I write a letter to the hotel manager, sincerely apologizing. I lean more on earnestness than rhetorical device. That—and whatever the Head of School says to him—turns out to be enough. He won't press charges.

In my back pocket, I keep two facts: I have the list narrowed down to Brooks and Ben, and that an adult is aware—and complacent—in his involvement with Sophie's death.

I'm suspended from Ingleside for two weeks, though I'll take AP exams under the school counselor's watchful eye. It's just as well. My presence is a sideshow, and I'd rather the gossip exhaust itself without me. Once I'm back from suspension, I'll only have a week before the last day of school for seniors. So, I study for exams and panic that Wythe will revoke my scholarship, which illuminates the path I want the most. I confirm there, and, just in case, I draft an email—this time, my most rhetorical writing—about why my suspension actually affirms the reasons they want me as a student.

I think about Christian constantly, but I don't call. The problem is that I remember exactly how it felt to stand in that bathroom stall on prom night. To think he might lose everything he's worked for because I'm a ship who steers herself toward the rocks.

While my mom goes to work, I go to 11 Caldwell with my headphones blasting miserable love songs. Ginny comes and goes, along with a few other volunteers. I spend two days on the ancient staircase, sanding down hard-to-reach woodwork detail and retouching it in fresh white. With every paint stroke, I consider the past year and a half of my life.

"I'll do it," I tell Ginny, on Day Four. "I'll speak at the dedication ceremony. If you still want me to."

Ginny cries a little as she hugs me. We didn't used to do either of those things.

On the Friday of my first week at home, my mom leaves me a note to weed our garden, a punishment I enjoy. The pieces that don't belong are obvious and easy to tug out. When I'm done, I lean back on the one patch of grass in our yard, watching the clouds shift.

"Well, this is quite a scene."

A wet nose connects with my arm, and I startle to an inspection by Thea. I'm looking up at Lincoln's face, shielded by a ball cap. "Lying in the bed I made. I thought you weren't home till tomorrow."

He sits beside me. "Your mom told my dads what happened."

We're a few feet from where we met, eight years ago. The

little girl I was—lonely, hopeful, ferocious in a quiet way—wouldn't believe I've wrecked our plans.

Actually, that's not true. If I'd leaned in and told her, *We ruin everything, but it's for Sophie,* she would simply nod. "I didn't leave it be, Linc."

"Yeah, no shit," he says, with a near-laugh. Then, gravely, "How bad is it? Think colleges would drop you?"

I drape my arms across my face, blocking the sun and also my shame-ridden face. "Possibly. And you wanna know the real mind-boggler here?"

"Hmm?"

"If I could time-travel to last year, I'm not sure I'd do anything differently." I hear Thea behind us, huffing at my mom's seedlings, and the jangle of her collar as Lincoln gently tugs back. "Figuring out what happened felt like the only door that might lead forward. I was sick of the hallway."

"Yeah, I know," he says. "I was there."

Behind the blockade of my arms, the tears circle like a storm cell. Lincoln was always there, waiting.

"So, what now?" he asks. When I peek out, he's got his arms resting on his knees. "Honest question."

"Well. Everyone hates me." I try to say it glibly, but I do wish Zoe and Warner would respond to my texts. They're probably bonding over what a liar that Hannah girl was, and I deserve it. "I'm suspended from school, put my college plans in jeopardy, I was a big jerk to you, and my mother's furious. And I messed everything up with Christian, which is probably better for him. It's like I'm radioactive, Linc. Anything that gets close to me turns toxic."

"I don't believe that," he says, frowning. "They're your choices, Han. Make different ones."

"I am." I drop my arms so he can see my earnest expression.

Lincoln gives an exaggerated eye roll. I missed the way his cowlick splats out under the brim of his hat. "No, you're lone-wolfing. Again. Things are hard, so you're looking for an excuse to sprint off to the woods."

I scowl at him. "You're taking the pro-Dailey position?"

"I'm taking a pro-Hannah position," he says. "Apologize to him. Say you'll do better. And mean it."

Oh boy. I roll to one side, really facing him. "Linc, I'm so sorry. Really."

He nods, and I feel bowled over by what an absence he's been this past year. I just couldn't let myself feel it before, for fear of an emotional avalanche. "This investigation. You're done?"

"I am," I say. "And I understand if you don't want to hang out after the way I've acted, but—"

"Okay, drama queen." He spins his hat around. "I'm obviously going to hang out with you. You're, like . . . well, honestly, you're—"

"Don't."

"Like a sibling to me," he finishes, with a smile. "And you're running a 5K, at least, with me this summer."

"Fine." I sit up on my elbows. "Will you tell me about college now? And Parker?"

"Will you tell me about Sophie?" he counters.

What would it look like to unpack my year truthfully? Out of that box, my worst decisions will scream like ravens. Lincoln will see cloud bursts of lingering grief and the bright-red hearts of people I've hurt. Those things will be there whether he sees them or not, and maybe they could use some air. What was it that my dad said about secrets? "Yeah. I will."

— — — — — —

On Saturday, my mom announces that she's going to Mitch's place. I prefer the quiet anyway, though I secretly accuse her of childishness—fleeing the problem or flouncing off to punish me. There is a small, wriggling part of me that considers telling her about the private investigator, about the pills. But for what? Sympathy? She'd just be angrier.

When there's a knock at the door, I expect Christian, who I'm not ready to see yet. I still can't get the apology speech right.

So, I'm surprised when I find myself facing Zoe, her arms crossed over a satin bomber jacket.

"I got this address from your school file," she says, pushing up heart-framed sunglasses. "Guess you're not the only one who can be a creep."

Suppose I deserve that, though I flinch.

"I need closure," she says thinly. "And I think it's the least you can do."

That much, I understand. I hold the door open wider. "Would you like to come in?"

She nods once and steps inside, taking in the living room. "The wallpaper really works as an accent for the Art Nouveau piece."

Her tone is flat and observational. As always, she's not intentionally being nice; she simply made her opinion audible.

"Thanks," I say. "It's all my mom."

"Good taste." Zoe sits in the olive velvet chair, and I lower myself to the couch. I have absolutely no idea what is about to happen here. She crosses her arms. "So! You were lying to me the whole time. That's fun."

"I was trying to figure out what happened to Sophie. That doesn't it excuse it, I know, but—"

Zoe is unmoved, staring at me. "Did you befriend me on purpose? To get close to someone? Warner?"

"No," I say, adamant. "I swear."

She narrows her eyes. "That first day in class . . . what did you know about me?"

"I knew you were into art, like me." I lean back, trying to relax my body. How can I tell her the truth without dragging her further into this mess? "I knew you were Student Council president."

"Did you want to use that for clout?" she interjects. "Access?"

"No." I hold the eye contact, letting her search my face.

She clutches a tasseled throw pillow like she's bracing for impact. "Did you think I was hiding something about Sophie?"

I press my lips together, wishing I could deny it. "Yes, but only before we met. I ruled you out last year."

"How?" Zoe demands. "Why suspect me; why rule me out?"

I teeter on my next answer, trying to walk the line. "There was a text suggesting someone met her that night but got to the party late. I ruled you out because Sophie referred to whoever got her pills as 'he.'"

"So why talk to me that first day?"

"There wasn't a plan. I liked your painting. You were nice and interesting."

"Yeah, right," she huffs. "Anything else I don't know?"

Tears build behind my eyes as I nock the arrow. I wish so badly that I didn't have to release it. "I looked at your phone once. Late fall. I scrolled back through pictures to see if you'd taken any the night Sophie died."

Zoe's gaze shoots to the window, unable to look at me. There's some internal conversation happening, as she nods a little. "Well! What a disturbing violation of privacy."

"I know." I wring my hands, restless on my lap. "I'm sorry. I justified some shitty stuff, believing it was for Sophie."

"The part that sucks so, so bad," Zoe says, fanning her watery eyes, "is that I would have showed you my pictures if you'd asked. I would have helped! You were my friend."

The past tense knocks the wind from my lungs. I'm my own force field. Anyone who gets close enough is jolted backward, dropped to the ground.

"Zo," I say quietly. Now or never. "Someone knew I was digging around and tried to get me kicked out of school. And prom night? He planted pills on me—that's why I pulled the alarm. Because I didn't know if he'd also done that to you or someone else."

Her face contorts in disbelief. "I'm sorry—what? Planted *pills* on you?"

"Trying to get me kicked out of Ingleside—or discredit me. So, part of me was relieved when you confronted me on prom night. At least word would get around that you didn't know anything." I nod out the front window to the garden. "And when you leave, I want you to storm out. I'll sleep better."

She lifts a sculpted eyebrow, trying to discern if I'm dramatic or delusional. Or if, possibly, the threat is real, and I care about her. "You think someone would be watching the house?"

"Probably not," I admit. "But someone had me followed a while back."

"Hannah!" Zoe shrills. "That is beyond messed up. Why didn't you tell the cops? Or the Head of School?"

Because they would have made me stop. "I was handling it."

Suddenly, she narrows her eyes. "You didn't suspect Ben, did you?"

I stare at her—the dark hair curled gently, the prim way she sits with ankles crossed. "Why would you ask that?"

"He got to the party even later than I did," she says. "And didn't see Sophie."

My mouth goes dry. "How can you be sure?"

Zoe's eyes shift past my shoulder, to where my mom's favorite photo of Sophie and me hangs. "Not that you deserve to know this, but . . . Ben only came to see me because I was ignoring his texts. I'd posted a photo from the party to make him jealous."

I sit very, very still, with hands slack on my lap. She'd met her ex while painting at the nature preserve, where he had been passing by. Running by.

There's a look of grim triumph across her face, getting to be the one with the secret this time. "Yep. That sad boy who jerked me around?"

Ben Ashby. "But he was going out with Violet."

"Why yes, he was," Zoe says wryly. "He told me they were 'taking some time away' while she was at theater camp. For him, it was over. But he owed her a final, in-person breakup conversation, right? Noble."

"Zoe," I say quietly.

"He really sold it," she says, drawing herself up. "Then Violet posts this photo from camp—a stack of letters. And the caption is, like: *Can't wait to get home to the sweetest pen pal tomorrow!* Blah, blah, blah."

All that broken trust, and here I'd been lying to her all year. "That weasel," I mutter.

"Yeah, well." She wipes her cheek. "I know better now."

"You're sure he didn't see Sophie?"

"Yeah. I saw him from the moment he walked in—my big,

romantic gesture. I thought he'd come to tell me he broke up with Violet. We went out to his car to talk, so he could convince me to hang in there till he could end things gently. That's where we were when the ambulance showed up."

I imagine Zoe and Ben in the car, spinning to face the pealing siren with red light cast across their faces. Their classmates would be dispersing; would they be noticed? Inside, Warner and Gabi hauled Sophie up, screaming for help.

But that means . . .

"Oh my God," I murmur. My face has gone tingly, almost painful.

"Yeah, well." Zoe stands, straightening her skirt. She hasn't clocked my world-warping shock. "Thanks for your time, I guess? I'm not great at ending things, as history has shown."

I can't speak, my lips parted and dry. Zoe lets herself out, and maybe I say goodbye. I'm dimly aware that I've braced my hands on the coffee table. I kneel on the rug for some time, staring at nothing. My worldview splits open to make room for the truth I've been hunting for: it was Brooks. It's Brooks. The arm person was always Jenny, and Ben was with Zoe, and Barrett is a cheater but nothing more.

A previous version of me might have torn over to Brooks's house, ready to burn everything down. Another might have paraded around town with a bullhorn, screaming the truth. The girl I am today has a different impulse, and no one is more surprised than me.

They're your choices, Han, Lincoln had said. *Make different ones.*

— — — — — —

On some level, I'm surprised that Christian let me stew in my bad choices—never charging over to save me from myself. Personal growth, I guess. And so it is for me, when I stand in front of that familiar, inky door. I have no strategy, no big speech.

The second I can see his whole face, I blurt out, "You were right."

"Mm," he says, as if savoring the words. "About . . . ?"

I want to fling myself into his arms—beg, if I have to. "Everything. That I cared more about finding the truth than anything else. That I held back. I push people away when things get hard, but I'm trying to change. And I'm sorry—I'm really sorry."

He makes me sweat for a few seconds. Then, opening the door wider, he says, "C'mon, then."

"I want to tell you everything," I continue, following him in. Dodger trots over to me, and I place a hand on his head to placate him. "But it's a lot. Is that okay?"

Christian guides me to the couch, where the truth floods out. It's the full story of Gabi and me, plus everything that happened at prom—and since. Finally, there's Brooks. Christian's eyes go wide, and he murmurs "Holy shit" a few times, but he lets me finish.

"Mr. Van Doren is on the school board," Christian says quietly. "And something tells me Brooks didn't hire a PI alone. We have to tell someone."

He's right, of course, but it won't be anyone I used to picture involving—not the police and not Ingleside higher-ups. Would Dr. Ryan, all tweed and decorum, even confront the Van Dorens? Power protects power. "I don't want to ruin the Caldwell house opening for Ginny."

Christian retracts his head a little, surprised. "Okay. Fair enough."

"I need to tell Gabi and get her take," I continue. "Then, I'll tell my mom, who will want to tell Ginny with me. We'll go from there. That's what feels right."

"Then that's what you do," he says simply.

Only then can I feel it—the crushing weight. The adrenaline come-down, the finally knowing, the crooked trail of right and wrong choices in my wake.

Was it worth it? I want Sophie so much that I could scream, rend my clothes, beat the floorboards with my fists. When I tip forward into my sob, Christian's waiting.

"Yeah, I know," he says softly, as I wail against his chest. "I know."

Junior Year

My first meeting at Ingleside went as well as could be expected. Though the Head of School had my transcript, Ginny rattled off my GPA, PSATs, and debate rankings in a chipper voice. My mom asked a few pointed questions. Then, I made my argument: Ingleside is an academic challenge and advantage that I'm ready to accept. I want a fresh start. My best friend is graduating from West Grove, and I'd like to be with Gabi here at Ingleside. And though I don't want Sophie to be my whole identity, I do want to be where other people knew her.

My mom sighed for what felt like the whole walk to the car. "Is this really what you want, Bug?"

Outside the windshield, students streamed out in blocks of plaid. They walked in packs, chattering. One guy jumped on another's back, goofing around. A couple linked hands, swinging their arms. Everyone looked happy, and why shouldn't they be?

Everyone but Sophie.

When I got home, I stared at my hair in the bathroom mirror. No going back now. I raised my sewing shears and made the first cut.

MAY

- - - - - -

Senior Year

The ribbon-cutting for 11 Caldwell happens on a warm Saturday. My mom planted sunflowers that will, come Leo season, rocket skyward and gate the house in yellow. There's more work to be done on the house this summer, but Ginny scheduled the dedication so Sophie's classmates could attend before scattering postgraduation.

And attend they do—the people I've spent the past week avoiding in the hallways. The front lawn, past the few rows of folding chairs, has people on every square inch. I refuse to focus my eyes, for fear I'll spot Brooks or his family. Catherine has her biggest camera lens, shooting the house and crowd from various angles, while Gabi chats with people in the front row.

I stand on the steps of the house, nearing the microphone. *All right. You're already in it.* A single paper shakes in my hands.

Good afternoon. My name is Hannah MacLaren. As some of you know by now, I'm Sophie Abbott's cousin. For over a year, I've been hiding that fact in some way or another, and, for that, I owe my classmates an apology. Secrets, shame, and resentment have so much power. I'm trying to give them a little less by talking to you today.

Sophie was my best friend. Living without her feels like being trapped in a thick fog. I can't see far ahead of me, or well. Sometimes I want to sit down and let the gloom overtake me. Sometimes it makes me want to sprint forward, screaming.

It will always be a tragedy that Sophie lost so many years of her interesting, passionate life. I used to think that figuring out what happened would clear my path forward. How could I grieve my cousin if I didn't truly know her? But I did know her. She was a lot of things, some of them seemingly contradictory. She was kind and angry, transparent and hidden; she was smart and silly. She was into both science and the mystical. I truly loved her, and I know that many of you did too.

Sophie had just about every advantage. She had a safe home and stable, caring adults in her life. She had medical care and many privileges. Interests and opportunities, family and friends. She also had pain—physical, yes, but maybe other kinds too.

In our family, we talk about substance use disorder like we do any other serious illness—a medical challenge that requires support. And still, I was shocked by Sophie's use and death. I wonder about that reaction now. From inside my two-years-long haze, I've had moments of clarity about a huge, ruinous system and my own views. I've stumbled through self-blame, blame of others, and regret. These days, I mostly feel resolve. And that is because I finally see the people around me.

My aunt, Virginia Farris Abbott, has taken her grief and her skills and her position in the world to make something concrete. She knows what I'm learning: recovery from anything requires support—through medical help, yes, but also through sustained connection. Community. And you can't have that with judgment, shame, and punishment. Those things plainly—statistically and morally—don't work. They never will.

With this event, Yardley College and the So Far Foundation have created a beam of light so bright that I can see it through my fog. I'm not out of it—and I think it will always trail me. But I finally see a path, and, now that I do, I can't believe I ever locked myself into one hallway, fixated on retribution. I could have rallied to expand local access to fentanyl test strips. I could have fought for naloxone training in schools, founded a student club, written letters to the editor about harm reduction.

In my early research, I read articles about how people are fighting back—against stigma, policy failures, racial inequity, in ways both local and far-reaching. But the problems felt so dauntingly, impossibly huge. Now all I can think is: Yes. Better start chipping away, then.

To anyone sitting in these seats who is suffering from hidden pain, I hope you trust someone with it. Everyone else, I hope you can be worth trusting. And to anyone sitting in these seats blaming yourself, as I have done, I hope you can release that.

Most of all, I hope 11 Caldwell offers its future students a place to be their entire, contradictory, beloved, battling selves. The residents—who I hope will become a community—will only ever have love, admiration, and support from my family.

And if you ever want to share your Sophie memories with me, I'd love to hear them. I will always miss her. But I will not miss any more opportunities to chip away toward a better world, which she did with every such enviable, Eleventh House flair. Thank you.

I step back to polite applause, and my mom wraps an arm around my shoulder, securing me in place.

After the ribbon is cut, the lines of guests become swarms. Through them, I see Gabi. She smiles at me through the shifting sea of people, then looks down at her phone. Mine buzzes in the purse at my side.

If I ever run for office, you're consulting on my speeches. I smile back, rolling my eyes.

Some of the people who approach me get teary about pain in their own lives. Some of them share Sophie memories, and I cry a little too, though not only from sadness.

My feet are beginning to ache when a familiar hand takes mine. I smile, tapping the second-highest button of Christian's shirt. "Hi."

"You did it."

"Yep." I let myself lean into his shoulder. The word "love" buzzes at the edge of my thoughts, as it sometimes does, and I swat it away. It will return eventually. "Now, please get me out of here."

We're ditching the annual senior bonfire because I'm a pariah, and an exhausted one at that. I have burned more than enough this year.

Instead, we made a reservation for dinner on campus with Gabi and Catherine, and then we'll enjoy Blockhead's final Yardley concert. It felt like the perfect bookend—a few gems I discovered this year, while looking for trouble. By the time we leave dinner, the end-of-year celebrations are well underway, revelers spilling onto bar patios. Some are still in Yardley graduation caps, posing for pictures.

The concert is outdoors, with a big stage spanning the quad.

Vendor tents line one side, selling food and raffle tickets for student groups. As we settle in for the opening band, I feel as peaceful as I have in long time. Christian, Gabi, and Catherine all know the secret we'll need to tell in the coming days. For now, we can joke and talk about our big plans. I'm not alone in any of it.

Blockhead is about to go on when someone hurtles through the crowd, directly toward us. I know that auburn hair and the slouchy posture. The rage in his eyes is new.

"You two," JJ says. He stares at Christian, then at me. "I thought I told you to pass the word to your Ingleside buddies."

"Sorry?" I say, taking half a step back. "What?"

"Some kid!" he bursts out, "From your fuckin' school, just a couple hours ago. Stops by my last ever shift at the pizza place. We're celebrating, saying goodbye, and he just charges in, asking for oxy."

My lips feel numb as I grapple for the right follow-up questions. Gabi grabs my arm, nails digging into skin.

Christian's already got his phone out, pulling up Brooks's social media. "Is this him?"

JJ leans forward for only a second. "Yeah—he was a real dick about it, too. My buddy pointed him to campus services, but he stormed off."

Everything warps around us. The beat slows to a groan, the crowd sways in half time. It seems he's using—or at least trying to.

I spin to my friends.

"What if Brooks . . . ?" Relapses. Overdoses. I can't make the words come out, but no one needs to hear them.

We all move at the same time, leaving JJ behind. We're

weaving through the crowd despite scoffs and swears, and I can't get enough air into my throat. The main drag of campus has become a block party, with shouted versions of the fight song and the yeasty smell of spilled beer.

Christian turns back to me when we reach the first empty sidewalk. My cheeks are wet with tears.

"We're going to find him," Christian says. He glances at Catherine and Gabi, whose faces have gone slack. "Bonfire?"

"You go there," Catherine says. "We'll head to his house, then Warner's next."

For a moment, my eyes connect with Gabi's, and we nod before parting ways.

"I'm gonna call Warner." With shaking hands, I grip the phone.

We're nearing Christian's truck as the call rings and rings in my ear. I settle into the passenger seat, the minty smell reaching my senses. I dial again.

Christian reaches over and clicks my seat belt into place. The ringing becomes voice mail, and I want to throw my phone at the windshield. I want to break everything. I want to keep everything from breaking.

You have to breathe.

"Okay," I whisper, and then I dive back into my contacts, reliving the worst night of my life. I text Zoe CALL ME RIGHT NOW, and then wait as long as I can before dialing. Ten seconds, maybe fifteen.

"Probably shitty signal in the woods," Christian says. He shifts into reverse, but I reach for his hand, stopping him.

The lights are still on at 11 Caldwell, and I can make out my aunt's car in the driveway. That makes sense—surely she'd be overseeing cleanup. But I know. Something in me knows. It lifts me out of the car.

"Hannah?" Christian asks, but I'm propelled forward, my legs picking up to a sprint.

There's a figure on the porch swing, watching his feet kick off cement. His hair is incandescently red in the dusky light.

My feet clatter up the steps. "Is he okay?"

Warner startles up from his thoughts. "Yeah. And kind of not. But he's inside."

I know his expression so well—when you have been walking your everyday path and your foot plunges through the earth, dropping you into another dimension. You can't even process that you've fallen. There's only lying there, bones singing with pain, and the words: *This cannot be right. This cannot be right.*

I join him on the swing, leaving a foot of space between us.

"We left the dedication thing." Warner casts his eyes off like he's watching the memory. "And Brooks wanted to stop by our soccer buddy's house. No one was home, so then he insisted on stopping for food. But he came out of the shop without any pizza, and just . . . lost his shit in my car."

Christian has reached the porch, but he hangs back. I nod back to the road and mouth *Gabi*. He walks back the way he came, phone in hand.

I reach a hand to Warner's arm, gentle.

He doesn't shrug me off. His slack expression is trance-like, half in the world and half out. "I begged him to tell me what was going on, and he kept muttering that he couldn't. I thought he'd failed a class or something—that he wasn't getting his diploma. But he said I'd hate him. I told him I could never."

"So he told you?"

"Everything." He finally looks up at me. "And I'm thinking . . . Do I drive him to the emergency room? Is this a call-my-parents thing? Like, what's my move? It's my one chance, and I can't fuck it up."

"Warner," I say, pained.

"He's my best friend," Warner says, eyes intent on mine. "He's always been my best friend."

"I know," I whisper. "Believe me."

Warner swipes one hand toward the house. "He let me drive him here. It was like a lid had loosened, and he had to keep spilling out. Your aunt and mom are calling around, trying to find a program that will take him before they contact Mrs. Van Doren. My dad is with Brooks now. Your uncle was here at first, but he took Maddie home. It's . . . a lot."

"Okay," I say. "I'll stay out here with you."

"He wants to talk to you," Warner says. "Or, at least, he did."

This is not the last conversation Warner and I will have about this. For him, I can be the person I did not have after Sophie died. It is no consolation at all.

"He told me," Warner whispers. "He told me he tried to get you kicked out of school."

My eye travels to the street, where Christian is hurrying back with Gabi and Catherine.

"Yeah," I said quietly.

Warner gives me one more severe look. "His dad knew. About everything. God, I hate that guy."

I nodded, unsurprised, and the three others reach the swing, murmuring to Warner. Good. He needs better support than I can give right now.

Going inside is a blur—past the staircase I detailed with my own hands. Ginny's sitting at the kitchen table with a laptop and notebook open. My mom stands, placing a hand on my arm and, at first, I see her mouth moving without hearing a sound.

"What?" I ask, blinking.

"Are you okay?" she repeats.

Of course not. And also yes. "Warner said Brooks wanted to talk to me."

She exchanges a look with Ginny, whose blazer is draped over the chair now. "He may be talked out, honey."

"This is a very charged situation," my mom said. "But he's done a brave thing here."

"I know." This is what I'm capable of now: I can squint my eyes shut and pretend Brooks is Sophie. In a different world, their roles may have been swapped. It doesn't change the facts, just how I see him.

Brooks is on a deck chair next to Warner's dad, who whispers something and then moves back toward the house. Mr. Evans gives me a nod, an acknowledgment but also a warning.

Brooks's face is swollen from crying, his hair sticking up at odd angles. This is all I've wanted for almost two years: a conversation that replaces a question mark with a period. And now that I'm here, I hesitate. Am I allowed to feel angry? Should I feel penitent—do I?

His voice comes out exhausted and harsh. "You must be pretty happy about this."

I almost laugh at the idea that I did any of this for happiness. I did it for infinitesimally less suffering. "Sophie's still dead, so . . . weirdly, no."

He huffs, as if that was a low blow. Then, as if I'd demanded the information, he says, "I only got pills for her a couple times early on, from out-of-town friends. Every other time, she's the one who got them, from who-knows-where."

The tears flood my eyes in an instant, as I imagine the loneliness Sophie must have felt. *Try to feel that for Brooks.* "Okay. I'm glad to know that."

There's a silence I read as skepticism. But I won't escalate, even if he comes at me swinging.

"If she just would have waited," Brooks said, voice cracking. "I got to the party late, and I guess she got impatient. But if I would have been there, I might have died too."

My aunt had told me that Sophie bought pills, but I didn't fully believe it. I do now. It's physically painful, the truth slicing down my chest.

Brooks takes a deep breath, and this is what I learn: They got high together a couple times. Back then, he could do it as a one-off, chill thing.

After she died, everything lost shape. Brooks overdosed that Christmas break while skiing, but one of his friends had naloxone.

"Oh my God," I whisper. While I was finding Sophie's journal, Brooks was having a near-death experience.

"Yeah. Scared me straight. I told my parents and did inpatient detox. Four days over break and back home." He laces his fingers together. "My dad told me he wouldn't pay for college if I used again. There. Solved, right? But my mom found me treatment."

I imagine gregarious Mr. Van Doren, landing on that supposed solution. "You told your dad about Sophie."

He nods. "After the gala. I assume that was your little stunt?"

I nod once in return.

"I thought my dad would know what to do. He said confessing would ruin my family's life—and for what? It wouldn't bring Sophie back."

Good God, these Ingleside parents. They'll do anything but let their kids accept the consequences of their actions. "I'm assuming you didn't tell my aunt that part?"

"I did, actually." Brooks stares down at the wooden planks on the porch.

I blink at him, openly surprised. I have no idea what that will mean for him. But I know that secrets are poison. Sooner or later, they flood out every good that is trying to grow.

Brooks asks a few questions about what I knew and how. I'm forthright about my actions, though not my collaborators. When I'm nearly wrung out, I ask, "Why now?"

"I've just been trying to get to graduation," Brooks admits. "But I'm basically there, and now what? At home, my mom's on top of me. Warner's always nearby. On my own? There's no way."

I look up, taking in the back of the house, its paint gray in the moonlight. "You think you could be in a place like this?"

He looks down at his sneakers. "I dunno."

I can't keep up with the swings here: he's reticent and bristly, then honest and regretful.

"You had naloxone in your purse," he says quietly. "The night of prom."

When he planted pills on me. "Yeah."

Brooks nods, like I'd confirmed something more telling. Half of his face is lit by the porch light. "How did it feel, when everyone found out you were lying the whole time?"

The past two years drop down before me like a drive-in movie screen. I watch myself lie to my mom and Lincoln, vow to do better, and then double-down anyway. I mislead Zoe and Warner; I hide things from Christian, always leaning on my justifications.

"Like absolute shit," I say. It felt like shivering outside in a wet dress on prom night as Zoe looked at me with disgust. My mom's worry and fury at the kitchen table, unsure of who she'd raised all these years. "And also much, much better."

"Yeah," Brooks says. Then, quietly, "It seemed like that."

There are probably more questions, but I can't find them. "My aunt is a terrifyingly persistent person. She'll find a program and get your parents onboard."

"Maybe," he says. "Still feels like shit."

"So did the other way. At least this route leads somewhere worth going."

He nods, and that's all I've got. I do not have it in me to be profound or pretend like I know what he's facing. Am I allowed to be angry and to admire him? I want him to sustain recovery, and I also never want to see his face again, in this world where I will never again see Sophie's.

The moment I walk inside, Warner's dad pops back out.

My mom searches my face, looking for signs of distress. "Christian and Catherine took Warner to go get food. He needed a moment away, I think."

"Gabi?"

"Outside."

On some level, I knew that. It's like I can feel Gabi's pain emanating through the front door. I follow the trail down the hallway, still ripe with new paint smell. How much had been lost and restored within these walls? A hundred years of silent weeping into pillows, a hundred years of quiet morning joy.

I walk away from the half-dozen people buzzing around the house. A network has formed, several people deep in each direction. Brooks is supported by Ginny, who is supported by my mom. Brooks is supported by Warner, who is supported by his dad and friends. This is as it should be. But God—it takes so much. So many people, so many tries, with resources and time and back-up measures. Almost everyone gets far less.

Outside, Gabi is huddled on the top step of the porch, where I spoke just hours ago. The May breeze carries, wrapping around me, and in the distance, I can hear the low bass of a familiar song.

There is just so much pain. How can anyone hold it? Once you've seen it, how can you do anything but buckle under its weight?

I settle in close, my arm reaching around Gabi's shoulder, and she curls in to be held. There's a feeling like we might tip away from the world—somersault backward through time, like the past two years have been a bad and bleary dream.

Sophie is still gone. Those are the words that snake through everything, like the air itself. Nothing will bring her back.

Tears reach my chin, and I drop my head back, lines of water tracing down my throat. I open my mouth to tell Gabi—what? That there is a little less pain than there might have been? Brooks is here, and this is not the end. She knows.

So, we cry until we're emptied out, tethering each other to the broken world. We cry until I begin to wonder if nothing really matters; we cry until I wonder if that somehow means that everything does. I cannot explain it, how both things can be true.

Junior Year

Lincoln graduated from high school the day before I left for Vancouver. I sat next to my mom with my newly short hair, and I did not cry, though the pressure rose. At home, I packed my bags, socks balled up inside sneakers and feelings stuffed down deep.

On the plane's ascent, my palms went clammy. I wanted to reassure myself with other passengers' calm expressions, but I forced my gaze out the window. The two other times I'd flown, I marveled. This time, I felt paper thin on a too-strong wind.

I reached one hand into my sweater pocket, my thumb finding an already-wilted flower. That morning, I'd stopped by Sophie's grave. On either side of the headstone, early summer flowers swayed like a concert crowd. I'd chosen a bloom and made a promise.

That's what I repeated now—to her memory, to who she was and will not be, to the widest stretch of sky I'd ever seen.

I'm going to figure it out, Soph, I thought again and again.

I know you are. The voice was fond but resigned. *Little Aries nightmare.*

Senior Year

Sophie's voice is harder to hear now. I miss it, and I need it less.

In the days afterward, everything around me goes quiet. The first June sunlight peeks in my bedroom window, and I drift back to sleep in its warmth. I nod off on a deck lounger as my mom bustles among her plants. I fall asleep on Christian's couch, my feet resting in his lap.

It is not exactly peace—or maybe it is, and peace is grayer than I thought.

When Warner comes to my door, we sit on the porch step, my hand spread on his heaving back. There is a lot to say, and we have all summer.

Mr. Van Doren resigns from the school board to "focus on his family." My mom won't tell me what else transpired between Brooks's parents and my aunt and uncle. Brooks and his mom are staying with a relative in DC while he does outpatient treatment.

The anger still glows, warm in the pit of my stomach. It's hard to face that most of my enemies are giant, broken systems and also concepts: greed, profiteering, human nature, apathy, pain. But I do have to face them, if I'm going to pick a spot and aim the things I am good at—the things I am capable of.

When my mother thinks I'm asleep, I sit at the tippy top of the staircase with my knees tucked up. She's on the couch with Ginny, whose crying is muffled by her hands or my mom's shoulder. *I want her back*, Ginny wails.

I do too. It's the truth at the heart of every stupid thing I did this year, and every good thing too. I press my mouth into the crook of my elbow, muffling the sob.

— — — — — — —

The universe scrounges up some nice weather for graduation day. With puffed-out clouds across blue sky, the world looks wrapped in cheerful wallpaper. I stare up while the choir, from raised bleachers on the podium, sings an acoustic arrangement of an already outdated pop song. The breeze stirs gently, carrying the smell of cut grass and expensive perfume.

I wear the white dress I once wore to the country club. I'm a different girl in some ways, but just as committed to showing up for Sophie. This summer, that will look like campaigning for better local naloxone access and also trying to have the carefree summer days that Soph would have wanted for me.

After Grant Aarons walks across the stage, the announcer requests a moment of silence for Sophie Abbott. I'm glad to get it over with early. I close my eyes and pretend she's here, her laugh a perfect, played-back recording in my mind. I pretend none of my classmates are sneaking glances at me. I pretend I can't feel Ginny's broken heart radiating from a dozen rows behind me, where she sits with my parents.

I feel the glances again when we reach the end of the alphabet, after Emily Vale. Though he's not here, Brooks will be awarded his diploma. I think of him often.

In the end, I place ninth in the class, to Christian's sixth. When we got that news, I pointed my finger at him and said, "Don't. I swear to God."

"Ninth is a freakin' triumph! Your first year at Ingleside? After everything you've been through?"

I made a face at him, though I secretly like when he argues on my behalf. "I'm uncomfortable with this dynamic. Go back to gloating."

He laughed and kissed me once, quick. Sometimes, I suspect he does this to remind me that we're on the same team. He pulled away, eyes narrowed. "You thinking about how your college GPA will be higher than mine?"

I lean in close, whispering right by his earlobe, "Oh, it will be."

After the caps are tossed, the crowd disperses to take a thousand more pictures in different combinations of family, of friends, of school groups. My mom and I did pictures before so she could leave with Ginny, who knew her limits. Ceremony: difficult but possible. Staying to chitchat with other parents: unbearable. So, I pose with Lincoln, a companion to our mantel photo from his graduation. Our summer plans include me getting him into hiking and watching every *Star Wars* movie in order.

The school paper team assembles for a picture in front of the building, then I help Catherine wrangle groups for yearbook end paper photos. Zoe poses with her Student Council, sans

Brooks. Even after wearing the mortarboard, her hair is perfectly in place. She eyes me just before I turn to go.

"Maybe I'll see you around the Baltimore art scene," she says. Curt, but not unkind.

"I hope so."

She studies me, openly considering the prospect. "Yeah, I think I do too."

I turn to go, carrying that smudge of hope with me.

Christian and I agreed to meet back by the stage, so I wander that way, hoping everyone has cleared out. A teacher is picking up stray programs between the seats and, on the sidewalk near the parking lot, a few small groups still linger.

The platform is empty now, the lectern mic still curved and waiting. I lean against the stage and stare out at the white chairs, now holding only the memory of the event. In some ways, it's a relief. Never again will I see so many of Sophie's Ingleside classmates in one place, her absence stark. But the simple shift of a tassel also felt like shifting, ever so slightly, away from Sophie.

A shadow enters my view, a silhouette that settles on the grass beside mine.

"Well," Gabi says flatly. "That was fun."

She's got her robe unzipped, with a thin, silk tank and matching pants beneath. There's an inch between us, right at center stage. My mouth forms the slightest smile. "Soph would have liked it."

The pretty sky, the earnest pop song, the midair caps. All of it. She would have cried, already nostalgic. There would have been photos of us—me, with one side of my mouth pulled up to humor my mom, and Sophie, with watery eyes as she crowded into my personal space.

"Yeah. She would have." Gabi looks down at her hands. "So. Finished. Next stop, California?"

I haven't told her yet. I didn't know how, in the midst of everything. "Actually, I landed on Wythe for Communications, Rhetorical Writing track. And a minor in Environmental Studies."

In my peripheral vision, I see Gabi turn. "For real?"

"Yep." The director of the library debate camp put me in touch with an environmental lawyer, who shared her thoughts. "Might want to try my hand at litigating corporate polluters."

Gabi's smile spread slowly. "I wouldn't want to be across the table from you—I can tell you that."

"Back at you." It's an understatement, really. Standing shoulder-to-shoulder with someone you suspect will really, truly change the world? The potential pulls me in like a magnet and, in the next moment, makes me want to scramble away.

Christian roams back from wherever he's been and settles in a front-row chair. He's got sunglasses on and his tie tugged halfway off. I smile, and he holds up one hand before settling back with his phone. It's nice to be waited on, patiently, by the person driving you home. Summer's finally here. Sometimes I look at him and can almost see fireflies blinking and serene, blue pool water. Sometimes I see heat lightning, and deluge.

For just this moment, I lean my shoulder to Gabi's, and she presses back, counterweight. Our parallel shadows link on the grass.

She clears her throat. "Can we have a standing meet-up day? Once a month or something?"

"Of course. And I'm gonna call you every time I need to talk about Sophie."

"Same. You'll edit my campaign materials when I inevitably run for student government?"

"Obviously." Then, quietly, "C'mon. I'm not gonna let you do any of it alone."

"No?" We turn to each other, so I can see her tentative smile. "What happened to the cynic?"

"She's still in there," I say. "But turns out I'm willing to be wrong. Hoping to be, even."

Gabi nudges me with her elbow. "Good."

A few moments pass before I hear a camera click, then another—the sound of Catherine approaching.

When I remember this moment, I'll see it from behind, like the pictures taken in the moment. Leaning on each other, steadying ourselves at the place where everything drops off. A stage draped with red, white, and blue bunting. Before us, empty seats and a lot of unknowns. The two of us, steeling each other.

Maybe, many years from now, I'll ask Catherine to take a similar picture from a larger, national stage: Gabi going for the big dream, and me bolstering the mission. Maybe Christian will be waiting, ready to talk it out and drive me home.

Or maybe we'll all drift before the end of college, and I'll carry Sophie's torch in quieter ways. It could be enough to know that Gabi's out there, the keeper of so many memories, and never so far away from me. It could be enough to know that I let Christian in, that I finally heard Lincoln, that I am trying to see the world in its full, dizzying, beautiful color.

But we've already lost so much. And anything we manage to build together? It will always be because of Sophie.

In the end, it wasn't even a debate. I have been learning—I am still learning—that I don't have to go it alone.

ACKNOWLEDGMENTS

I want to say thank you, first, to the people who read my books. Life is short, attention spans are easily fractured, and it means a lot to me that you'd spend time with something I made.

Enormous thanks to my editor, Mary Kate Castellani, for everything from keeping at the first chapters to always hearing a quiet beat I'm attempting to hit. Thank you to Kei Nakatsuka for many things, not the least of which was a personalized software tutorial.

Team Bloomsbury, I feel so lucky to work with you. Erica Barmash, Phoebe Dyer, Beth Eller, Lex Higbee, Jeanette Levy, Donna Mark, Kathleen Morandini, Oona Patrick, Lily Yengle—thank you so much for all you do. Special thanks also to the sales team and the UK team.

Thank you, Taylor Martindale Kean, Full Circle Literary, and Taryn Fagerness for representing my books with care for the past decade. (Decade?! Decade.)

Thank you to Bethany Robison, whose curiosity and good-heartedness make her a wonderful writer, reader, and friend. Professor Whitney Sage, dear pal and one of my all-time favorite artists: thank you for gamely acting as my personal art connoisseur for this book. Thank you to my husband for 2020–2021 in general and for being my sounding board, an unflagging co-parent, and the best hang this side of the Mississippi.

Lastly, I have to thank Winston for six books and eleven years' worth of companionship, despite never knowing what the tap-taps on the light-up screen were about. Writing is a solitary pursuit. I was never alone. Good boy.